PENGUIN BOOKS

SORRELL AND SON

George Warwick Deeping was born in 1877 in South-
end, England. He was educated at Merchant Taylor's
School and Cambridge. He studied medicine and prac-
tised as a doctor for a year until his success with a
series of romantic historical novels, of which the most
popular was *Love Among the Ruins*, enabled him to
become a full-time writer. *Sorrell and Son* (1925),
which draws on his wartime experience in the R.A.M.C.,
is perhaps his best-known work. Warwick Deeping
continued to write many more novels until his death
in 1950.

SORRELL AND SON

by

WARWICK DEEPING

PENGUIN BOOKS

PENGUIN BOOKS

Viking Penguin Inc., 40 West 23rd Street,
New York, New York 10010, U.S.A.
Penguin Books Ltd, 27 Wrights Lane, London W8 5TZ
(Publishing & Editorial) and Harmondsworth,
Middlesex, England (Distribution & Warehouse)
Penguin Books Australia Ltd, Ringwood,
Victoria, Australia
Penguin Books Canada Limited, 2801 John Street,
Markham, Ontario, Canada L3R 1B4
Penguin Books (N.Z.) Ltd, 182–190 Wairau Road,
Auckland 10, New Zealand

First published in the United States of America by
Alfred A. Knopf Inc. 1926
Published in Penguin Books 1987

(CIP data available)

Printed in the United States of America by
R. R. Donnelley & Sons Company, Harrisonburg, Virginia
Set in Caslon

TO THE MEMORY OF MY FATHER

SORRELL AND SON

SORRELL was trying to fasten the straps of the little brown portmanteau, but since the portmanteau was old and also very full, he had to deal with it tenderly. "Come and sit on this thing, Kit."

The boy had been straddling a chair by the window, his interest divided between his father's operations upon the portmanteau and a game of football that was being played in Lavender Street by a number of very dirty and very noisy small boys.

Christopher went and sat. He was a brown child of eleven, with a grave face and a sudden pleasant smile. His bent knees showed the shininess of his trousers.

"Have to be careful, you know," said Sorrell.

The father's dark head was close to the boy's brown one. He too was shiny in a suit of blue serge. His long figure seemed to curve over the portmanteau with anxiously rounded shoulders and sallow and intent face. The child beside him made him look dusty and frail.

"Now, the other one, old chap. Can't afford to be rough. Gently does it."

He was a little out of breath, and he talked in short jerky sentences as he pulled carefully at the straps. A broken strap would be a disaster, for the clasp of the lock did not function, and this dread of a trivial disaster seemed to show in the carefulness of the man's long and intelligent hands. They were cautious yet flurried. His breathing was audible in the room.

"That's it."

The words expressed relief. He was kneeling, and as he looked up towards the window and saw the strip of sky and the grimy cornice and grey slates of the house across the way, his poise suggested the crouch of a creature escaping from under some huge upraised foot. For the last three

years, ever since his demobilization, life had been to Sorrell
like some huge trampling beast, and he—a furtive thing
down in the mud, panting, dodging, bewildered, resentful
and afraid. Now he had succeeded in strapping that portmanteau. They were slipping away from under the shadow
of the great beast. Something had turned up to help the
man to save his last made-to-measure suit, his boy, and the
remnant of his gentility.

Horrible word! He stroked his little black moustache,
and considered the portmanteau.

"Well,—that's that, son."

He smiled faintly, and Kit's more radiant smile broke out
in response. To the boy the leaving of this beastly room in
a beastly street was a glorious adventure, for they were going
into the country.

"It will want a label, pater."

"It will. 'Sorrell and son, passengers, Staunton'!"

"How's it going to the station?"

Sorrell rose, dusting the knees of his trousers. Each night
he folded them carefully and put them under the mattress.

"I've arranged with Mr. Sawkins. He'll take it early and
leave it in the cloak-room."

For Sorrell still kept his trousers creased, nor had he
reached that state of mind when a man can contemplate with
unaffected naturalness the handling of his own luggage.
There were still things he did and did not do. He was a
gentleman. True, society had come near to pushing him off
the shelf of his class-consciousness into the welter of the
casual and the unemployed, but, though hanging by his
hands, he had refused to drop. Hence Mr. Sawkins, and
Mr. Sawkins' coster's barrow, transport for the Sorrell baggage.

"What time is the train, pater?"

"Ten twenty."

"And what time do we get to Staunton?"

"About three."

"And where are we going to stay?"

"Oh,—I shall get a room before fixing up with Mr. Verity.
He may want us to live over—over the shop."

There were times when Sorrell felt very self-conscious in
the presence of the boy. The pose he had adopted before
Christopher dated from the war, and it had survived various

humiliations, hunger, shabbiness, and the melodramatic disappearance of Christopher's mother. Sorrell turned and looked at himself in the mirror on the dressing table. He patted his dark hair. "Over—the shop." Yes, the word had cost him an effort. "Captain Sorrell, M.C." To Christopher he wished to remain Captain Sorrell, M.C. He felt moved to explain to the boy that Mr. Verity's shop at Staunton was not an ordinary shop. Mr. Verity dealt in antiques; the business had flavour, perfume; it smelt of lavender and old rose-leaves and not of cheese or meat. Mr. Verity—too— appeared to be something of a character, an old bachelor, with a preference for a man of some breeding as a possible assistant. Also, Mr. Verity was a sentimentalist—a patriotic sentimentalist. He had been in correspondence with the Ex-Officers' Association, and Stephen Sorrell had been offered the job.

He was going down to Staunton to discover whether he and Mr. Verity would harmonize.

Sorrell adjusted the wings of his bow tie, and considered the problem of Christopher and Mr. Verity's shop. Should he be frank with the boy, or keep up the illusion of their separateness from the common world? He could say that he was going into business with Mr. Verity, and that in these days a shop—especially an antique shop—was quite *à la mode*.

Yells from the street broke in upon his meditations. Someone had scored a goal, and someone else had refused to accept the validity of the goal.

"Damn those kids!" said the man.

He looked at his own boy.

"Pater."

"Yes."

"Shall I go to school at Staunton?"

"Of course. I expect there will be a Grammar School at Staunton. I shall arrange it when I have settled things with Mr. Verity."

"Will it be a gentleman's school, pater?"

"O, yes; we must see to that."

There was a pause in the adventure, for on this last evening in London there was nothing left for them to do, and on warm evenings Lavender Street did not smell of herbs. Its smells were very various and unoriginal. It combined

the domestic perfumes of boiled cabbage and fried fish with
an aroma of horse-dung and rancid grease. It was a stuffy
street. The clothes and bodies of most of its inhabitants
exuded a perfume of stale sweat.

The boy had the imagined scent of the country in his
nostrils.

"Let's go out."

"Where to?"

"Let's go and look at the river."

They went, becoming involved for a moment in a mob of
small boys who were all yelling at once and trying to kick
a piece of sacking stuffed with paper. Kit was pushed
against his father, but reacting with sensitive sturdiness,
upset one of the vociferous crew into the gutter where he
forgot Kit's shove in the business of eluding other feet.

Sorrell noticed that the boy was flushed. He was conscious of himself as something other than those Lavender
Street children. He did not want to be touched by them.

"We'll be out of it, to-morrow, son."

"I'm glad," said the boy.

Sorrell was thinking of Christopher's schooling, and he
was still thinking of it when they paused halfway across
Hungerford Bridge and stood leaning on the iron rail. The
boy had had to go to a Council school. He had hated it,
and so had Sorrell, but for quite different reasons. With
the man it had been a matter of resentful pride, but for
the boy it had meant contact with common children, and
Kit was not a common child. He had all the fastidious
nauseas of a boy who has learnt to wash and to use a
handkerchief, and not to yell "cheat" at everybody in the
heat of a game.

Sorrell stood and dreamed, and yet remained aware of
the kindling face of the boy who was watching the life of
the river, a pleasure steamer going up-stream, a man strain-
ing at a sweep upon a barge, a police-boat heading for the
grey arches of Waterloo Bridge. To Sorrell the scene was
infinitely familiar yet bitterly strange. The soft grey atmosphere shot through with pale sunlight was the atmosphere
of other evenings, and yet how different! His inward eyes
looked through the eyes of the flesh. To him London had always seemed most beautiful here, a city of civic stateliness,
mellow, floating upon the curve of the river. He had loved

the blue black dusk and the lights, the dim dome of St. Paul's like the half of a magic bubble, the old "shot" towers, the battered redness of the Lion brewery, the opulence of the Cecil and the Savoy, the green of the trees in Charing Cross gardens.

He remembered that he had dined and danced at the Savoy.

Spacious days! Khaki, and women who had seemed more than women on those life-thirsty nights when he had been home on leave. Odalisques!

Women! How through he was with women!

He remembered a night when he had taken his wife to the Savoy. Two years ago his wife had left him, and her leaving him had labelled him a shabby failure. She had had no need to utter the words. And all that scramble after the war, the disillusionment of it, the drying up of the fine and foolish enthusiasms, the women going to the rich fellows who had stayed at home, the bewilderment, the sense of bitter wrong, of blood poured out to be sucked up by the lips of a money-mad materialism.

He looked at the face of his boy.

"Yes, it's just a scramble," he thought, "but an organized scramble. The thing is to keep on your feet and fight, and not to get trampled on in the crush. Thank God I have got only one kid."

Kit, head up, his cap in his hand, was smiling at something, the eager and vital boy with the clear eyes and fresh skin. To him life was beginning its adventure. He saw the river and the city in the splendour of their strength and their mystery. The Savoy and the Cecil were still palaces of the great and adventurous unknown, and Sorrell, full of the grim business of existence, felt a sudden deep tenderness towards the boy.

"I suppose it's egotism," he thought, "but I'll try to give him a better chance in the scramble than I have had. After all we are more honest in our egotism,—these days. The thing is not to love your neighbour, but to be able to make it unsafe for him to try and down you. Co-operation in bargaining, organized grab. But you have to bargain with some sort of weapon in your hand."

Standing there beside his boy and watching the light and the life upon the river, Sorrell felt himself to be weapon-

Sorrell and Son

less. What was he but a pair of hands, and a rather frail body in a shabby suit of clothes? He thought of his wounds, wounds of the flesh and of the spirit.

He met Kit's smile.

"I say, pater, is there a river at Staunton?"

"A small one."

He was realizing that the niche at Mr. Verity's might also be a very small one, but at least it was a niche in the social precipice.

2

Sorrell and son arrived at Staunton about three in the afternoon.

Amid the clatter of empty milk cans Sorrell addressed himself to the porter who was removing the brown portmanteau from the luggage van, but the porter either did not or would not trouble to hear him.

"Do you mind being careful with that? The straps——"

The porter swung the portmanteau out of the van and let it fall with a full flop upon the platform, and like Judas it burst asunder, and extruded a portion of its contents upon the asphalt.

Sorrell looked sad.

"You shouldn't have done that, you know."

It was a bad omen, and he bent down to recover a boot, a clothes brush and a tobacco tin, and to stuff the crumpled nakedness of an unwashed shirt back into the gaping interior. The porter, full of sudden compunction, bent down to help him.

"I'll find you a bit of cord. The stitching of the straps must have been rotten."

Christopher stood and looked on while Sorrell and the porter applied first aid to their piece of luggage. The incident had touched the boy; he had seen that look in his father's eyes, and he felt—somehow—that it was not the portmanteau but his father who had gaped and betrayed a whole clutter of painful and shabby problems. Poor old pater! But his boy's tenderness was touched with pride.

Sorrell was putting the porter's contrition to other uses.

Before reaching Staunton he had counted the ready money that remained to him, and it amounted to thirteen shillings and five-pence.

"Do you know of any lodgings; clean, but not too dear?"

The porter was knotting a length of cord round the body of the portmanteau.

"Staying here? What sort of lodgings?"

"I am taking up a post in the town. A bed-sitting-room for me and the boy. I don't mind how plain it is——"

"I've got an aunt," said the porter, "who lets lodgings. There's a room, up at the top. Fletcher's Lane. Not a hundred yards off."

"Would she board us?"

"Feed you?"

"Yes."

"She might. Look here,—I'm going off duty in ten minutes or so. I'll show you the way."

"I'm very much obliged to you."

Sorrell gave him the five pennies.

"Thank you, sir. I'll pop this round for you on my shoulder."

No. 7, Fletcher's Lane, accepted the Sorrells and packed them away in a big attic-like room under the roof. It had a dormer window with a view of the cathedral towers and the trees of the Close, and between the cathedral and the dormer window of No. 7 every sort of roof and chimney ran in broken reds and greys and browns. The room was clean, with a white coverlet on the bed, a square of linoleum in the centre of the floor, and a smaller piece in front of the yellow washstand. The chest of drawers had lost a leg and most of its paint, and when you opened a top drawer it was necessary to put a knee against one of the lower drawers to prevent the whole chest from toppling forward.

The landlady asked Sorrell if he would like tea, and he glanced at his wrist watch.

"I have to go out first. Would half-past five do?"

"Nicely. Will you take an egg to it?"

"Yes, an egg each, please. And could I have a little hot water?"

The hot water was forthcoming in a battered tin jug, and Sorrell washed himself, brushed his clothes and hair,

wiped the dust from his boots, and glanced at himself in the
little mirror. First impressions were important, and he
wanted to make a good impression upon Mr. Verity. His
blue suit was old and shiny, but it was well cut, and the
trousers were creased.

"I'm just going round to see Mr. Verity. You might
unpack, old chap."

Christopher was leaning out of the window and inhaling
the newness and the freshness of Staunton.

"Yes,—I will, pater."

"We'll have some tea when I come back, and a stroll
round. This is only a temporary roost."

"It's better than Lavender Street," said the boy.

Mr. Verity's shop was in the Market Square, and Sorrell,
on turning out of Fletcher's Lane found himself in Canon's
Row. A passing postman, questioned as to the whereabouts
of the Market Square, jerked a thumb and said "Straight
on." Sorrell did not hurry. He was pleasurably excited,
and as he strolled up Canon's Row he saw the short, broad
High Street opening out before him. It was all red and
white and grey. The Angel Inn thrust out a floating golden
figure. Higher up, a clock projected from the Market Hall
with its stone pillars and Dutch roof, and its statue of
William of Orange in a niche in the centre of the south
wall. The Market Square spread itself, a great sunny space
into which the more shadowy High Street flowed. It was
surrounded by old houses that had been built when Anne
and the Georges reigned. In the centre the market cross
carried time back to the Tudors. A vine covered one little
low house, and another was a smother of wistaria. There
were queer bay windows, white porches, leaded hoods, and
at the end the chequered Close threw a massive and
emphatic shadow. Above and beyond, the towers caught
the sunlight, rising from the green cushions of old limes
and elms, and backed by brilliant white clouds in a sky of
brilliant blue.

Sorrell paused outside the Angel Inn, for the old town
pleased him. Not a bad spot to settle in, to listen to the
bells, and to feel that life was less of a hectic scramble. And
dabbling in old things, handling old china and glass and
Sheffield plate, the creations of dead craftsmen who had not

hurried. No doubt old Verity had absorbed the atmosphere of oak and mahogany, maple and walnut. He might have a richly brocaded soul.

Sorrell strolled on into the Market Square. He looked about him, and then crossed the cobbles and questioned a policeman who was on traffic duty.

"Mr. Verity's shop?"

"Over there,—near the gate."

Sorrell was half-way across the Market Place when he realized that there was something queer about Mr. Verity's shop. He saw it as a red house with a white cornice and white window sashes, and painted in white letters on a black fascia-board "John Verity—Dealer in Antiques." But the shop was shut, the windows were screened by black shutters.

Sorrell glanced at the other shops. No, it was not early closing day; the other shops were open.

He crossed the rest of the space more quickly, and sighting a black door beside the shop, with a brass bell handle in the white door-jamb, he pulled the bell. He was puzzled, aware of a sudden suspense, and when the door opened he found himself staring at the face of a woman who had been weeping.

"Is Mr. Verity in?"

The woman's eyelids flickered.

"Mr. Verity died this morning."

Sorrell's mouth hung open.

"What——!"

"Yes—sudden——. It must have been his heart. He fell down the stairs.—O,—dear——"

She began to whimper, while Sorrell stood there with a blank face. He realized that the woman was closing the door.

He blurted something.

"I've just come down. I was to be—the assistant. It's very;—I'm sorry——"

"It was so sudden," said the woman. "Of course—without him—nothing—you know. I'm sorry. Have you come far?"

"From London."

"Dear, dear, and you will have to go all the way back—

for nothing. It's awkward,—but there it is. If you'll excuse me—now."

She closed the door, and Sorrell stood staring at it.

3

Sorrell's first feeling was one of bitter resentment against old Verity for dying in so sudden and inconvenient a fashion, but before he had recrossed the Market Square he had realized the absurdity of his anger. It died away, leaving him with a sense of emptiness at the pit of his stomach, and a chilly tremor quivering down his spine.

He was trembling. His knees were so weak under him that when he passed through the gateway of the Close, and saw a seat under a lime tree, he made towards it and sat down. He felt helpless, bewildered, for the disappointment,—coming as the last of many such disappointments, seemed to have fallen on him with the cumulative weight of the whole series. He put a hand into a pocket for his pipe and pouch. His fingers moved jerkily, and when he lit a match his hand was so unsteady that he had difficulty in lighting his pipe.

The nausea of an intense discouragement was upon him. He felt tired, so tired that his impulse was to lie down and to admit defeat, and to allow himself to be trampled into the mud of forgetfulness. His senses were dulled, and the whole atmosphere of this quiet old town had changed. Half an hour ago he had been vividly aware of the blueness of the sky and of the tranquil white domed clouds floating above tower and tree, but now the objective world seemed vague and grey. His feeling of despair cast a shadow.

He thought of Christopher waiting in that upper room for his tea.

He shrank from the idea of facing the boy, of going back there with a hang-dog illusion dead in his eyes.

All the sordid and trivial realities of the business buzzed round him like flies. He had thirteen shillings in his pocket; he would owe the woman for food and a night's lodging; there would be the cost of the tickets back to London; that damned portmanteau needed mending; and if they returned to London there was nowhere for them to go.

He realized the nearness of a panic mood.

He got up. "When you are in a blue funk, do something." That was one of the human tags brought back from France. He remembered that he had won his M.C. by "doing something" as a protest against the creeping paralysis of intense fear.

He walked back to Fletcher's Lane, and climbing the stairs, paused for a moment outside the door of the room. He was trembling. He heard the woman moving somewhere below, and leaning over the banisters he called to her.

"We are ready for tea, please."

His own voice surprised him. It was resonant, and it had a quality of cheerfulness, and it seemed to express the upsurging within him of some subconscious element that was stronger than his conscious self. He opened the door and went in.

The boy was standing by the window. He had unpacked their belongings; a nightshirt and a pair of pyjamas lay on the bed; brushes, a razor, a comb, and three old pipes were arranged upon the dressing-table.

Father and son looked at each other.

"Well, my son, what about tea?"

Kit continued to look at his father; his eyes were very solemn.

"Mr. Verity's dead," said the father; "he died this morning. So—Staunton's a wash-out. Well, what about tea?"

The boy's face seemed to flush slightly. His lips moved. It was as though he was aware of something in his father, something fine and piteous, a courage, something that made him want to burst into tears.

"Sorry, pater."

His lips quivered.

"We—we'll have to make the best of it."

And suddenly—and with a kind of fierceness, Sorrell caught his son and kissed him.

4

Afterwards, they went out and sat in the cathedral and wandered about the Close under the shade of the elms and limes. The evening was very still, and the sunlight sifted through the trees and lay gently upon the mown grass.

Swans cruised upon the moat surrounding the Bishop's palace. There was the sheen of water, and the mellowness of old red walls seen through the dappled foliage of trees. The canons' houses, sealed away in pleasant security, gave through their gateways glimpses of their gardens. Jackdaws circled about the towers, their cries dropping from above into the deeps of a green tranquillity.

A sunset filled the lacework of the leaves with red and gold, and the smooth and stately security of the Close caught moments of mystery. Sorrell and the boy were sitting on a seat above the water, with a slope of vivid grass going down to it, and a weeping willow trailing its branches in a stream of yellow light. It seemed to Sorrell that no one who lived near the shadowy splendour of these towers and trees could know what poverty was, or hunger, or the filthy dread that oozes like slime over a man's soul. Life seemed so secure here, so incredibly secure.

He sat there, a shabby man beside a shabby child, and yet the shabbiness had fallen from him, the shabbiness of little, suburban make-believes. He had discovered a sudden and helpful frankness. He had undressed his soul before his boy.

They sat and talked.

"I'm not going to bother about the crease in my trousers, my son. Keeping up appearances. I don't care what the job is, but I am going to get it."

The thing that astonished him was the way that the boy understood. How was it that he understood? It was almost womanish, a kind of tenderness, and yet manly, as he had known manliness at its best during the war.

"It was because of me,—pater."

"Captain Sorrell, M.C."

"But you will still be Captain Sorrell, M.C., to me, daddy. If you swept the streets——"

"Honour bright?"

"Honour bright."

Sorrell held Kit's head against his shoulder.

"Seems to me, kid, that you and I have got to know each other as we never did before. Thanks to poor old Verity. I was so damned afraid that you were going to be ashamed of me——"

The boy smiled.

"Dear old pater,—I'll help."

"Think of that poor old portmanteau! What its feeling must have been—when it burst open! But I have been burst open to-day, Kit. You have had a look at the inside of me. Yesterday—I was a sort of shabby gentleman. That's finished."

Christopher meditated some profound thought.

"I don't mind—just bread and butter."

"No jam?"

"No."

"Well, somehow—I think it was worth it," said Sorrell, "quite worth it. You and I know where we are."

The sunset was dying behind them, and the dusk and the shadows of the great trees seemed to meet upon the water. The Sorrells left the seat and wandered away together, united by a sudden understanding of each other and by a sympathy that was frank and tender.

"I am always going to tell you things, Kit; no more make-believe."

"And I'll tell you things too, pater," said the boy—"everything."

"No secrets?"

"No secrets."

It was the beginning of the great comradeship between them, and for the first time for many months Sorrell felt a happiness that surprised him. The shock of the day's disappointment had passed. The human relationship suddenly realized between his boy and himself swallowed up the sense of defeat. His courage returned. As they wandered in the dusk of the Close under the darkening trees he felt Kit's nearness, a nearness of spirit as well as of body.

"If I had not had the boy——" he thought.

Kit's hand touched his sleeve.

"Look——"

They had turned into a stone flagged path that ran at the backs of the old houses on one side of the Market Square. Gravestones and brick tombs showed between them and the houses. A high yew hedge screened many of the lower windows, but Kit's eyes were fixed upon a broad, arched window that was visible beyond the hedge. The window was brilliantly lit, and glowed with streaks of colour, orange, green, blue, cerise. A figure in black was moving amid the streaks of colour.

"What's that?" the boy asked.

Sorrell smiled. They were looking across the old graves into the window of a Staunton modiste's showroom, and it would seem that the modiste had received a consignment of silk "jumpers." She was unpacking them and hanging them up on the stands in her showroom where they glowed brilliantly like jewels in a case.

"Clothes,—Kit."

"They look like bunches of flowers," said the boy.

They passed on, and out by an iron gate into one of the Staunton streets, and so back to Fletcher's Lane, where Sorrell sat and smoked while Christopher undressed and went to bed.

Sorrell sat there for a long while after the boy had fallen asleep.

"Yes,—there's my job," he reflected.

Undressing very quietly so as not to wake his son, he slipped into the bed beside the boy and lay wondering how he would solve the problems of the morrow.

II

I

WHEN Sorrell placed two rashers of bacon on Christopher's plate he found himself reflecting that he and his son were eating this meal on credit, and that unless some sort of job was to be discovered in Staunton he might have to visit the sign of the three golden balls.

At the end of the meal he lit his pipe and glanced down the list of the advertisements in a copy of the *Staunton Argus*. Someone was advertising for a chauffeur; a farmer needed a cowman, and a number of ladies were asking for cooks and housemaids, but Sorrell had to recognize his own limitations. He could not drive a car, or milk a cow, or cook a dinner. Indeed, when he came to consider the question there were very few things that he could do. Before the war he had sat at a desk and helped to conduct a business, but the business had died in 1917, and deny a business man his office chair and he becomes that most helpless of mortals—a gentleman of enforced leisure.

At the top right hand corner of the page Sorrell noticed a paragraph that might have some bearing on his case. It appeared that there was a private Employment Agency in Staunton, conducted by a Miss Hargreaves at No. 13, the High Street. Sorrell tore off the corner of the paper, slipped the notice into his waistcoat pocket, and passed the rest of the paper across the table to Christopher.

"I am going out."

The boy understood.

"I'll be here when you come back."

No. 13 proved to be a stationer's shop, one half of its window brilliant with the wrappers of cheap novels. Its doorway looked across the road into the arched entry of the "Angel" yard, and Miss Hargreaves, from the moment when she pulled up her blind in the morning or pulled it down at night, lived in the gilded presence of the inn's

15

angelic figurehead. Sorrell entered the shop. It was long
and rambling and dark, and on dull days a light was needed
in the far corner where the circulating library lived in a tall
recess. There were no customers in the shop, and the
young woman behind the counter, turning a pair of myopic
eyes on Sorrell, moved instinctively towards where the daily
papers were kept.

"*Daily Mail?*"

That was the sound she expected Sorrell to make, but he
surprised her by uttering other words.

"I believe you run an employment agency."

"Yes," said the girl, "that's so."

She glanced in the direction of a kind of desk or cage
at the back of the shop where a woman's head was visible.

"You had better see Miss Hargreaves—there."

As Sorrell approached the desk Miss Hargreaves raised
her head, showing him the face of a woman of five and
forty. She was thin and wiry, with brown eyes of a hungry
hardness, and her nose marked out a little red triangle with
its congested lip and network of minute blood-vessels.

"Good morning."

He was a stranger, and to this woman all strange men
were interesting, yet as Sorrell looked into her brown eyes
he felt himself growing inarticulate.

"I want to consult you——"

"You are wanting a servant?"

"No,—that fact is——"

But at this moment they were interrupted by the rush
of a vital presence into the shop, something highly scented
and with a suggestion of the soft friction of silks. Its
movements were large and easy and swift, and bringing
with them a sense of disturbing and adventurous liveness.
It was at Sorrell's elbow, compelling him to glance over
his shoulder. He saw the mass of tawny hair, the broad
and handsome face, the red mouth, the blue of the eyes.
There was something brutal in the face, a vivacity, a sensual
energy. He felt as though a gust of wind had blown into
the dark shop, and that this large, blonde creature was
stifling his courage, overlaying it as though it were a feeble
infant. He turned to the cage, only to find that Miss
Hargreaves was all eyes for the newcomer. The thin woman
was smiling. Her face suggested some inward excitement.

"Morning,—Flo—dear——. How are you?"

"Do I look ill?"

There was some element of sympathy between these two women, contrasts though they were, but the lady of the tawny head was studying Sorrell. She stood aside, leaning easily against the wainscoting, her blue knitted coat vivid against the old brown wood.

"This gentleman—first. Mine's not business."

Sorrell wished her with the devil. He felt her eyes upon him, and had he followed the line of least resistance he would have bolted from the shop. To stand there and blurt out his shabby business while she embarrassed him and made him acutely self-conscious!

"Damn!" he thought, "haven't I decided to plunge?"

Miss Hargreaves was fingering the leaves of a ledger, and waiting upon his silence.

"You said you wished to engage——"

"I want a situation."

"Oh——? For yourself? I'm sorry,—but,—only domestic service—you know."

"Of course," said Sorrell, stiff as a frightened cat, "that's what I mean; a place as valet, or footman or something of that sort."

He felt that the two women despised him, especially that big, blonde creature with her blueness and her hard world-wise eyes. Why couldn't she clear out and leave him to the thin woman in the cage?

Miss Hargreaves pretended to glance through the entries in her ledger.

"I'm afraid I have nothing of that sort,—nothing at all."

"I see."

"Why not try the Labour Exchange?"

"I might. Thank you. Sorry to have troubled you. Good morning."

He turned abruptly, his back to the blonde woman and made for the doorway. He noticed how the worn boards of the floor squeaked under his feet, an uncomfortable sound caused by a discomfited man. He arrived at the doorway. A voice reached after him like a restraining hand.

"Hallo—one moment——"

Sorrell turned in the doorway, and saw the blonde woman sailing down the shop, and he stood aside to let her pass, thinking that his necessity was no concern of hers, but she paused by a revolving stand of picture postcards, and taking one at random, gave Sorrell the full stare of her blue eyes.

"Serious?" she asked.

He looked at her rather blankly.

"I beg your pardon?"

Her smile puzzled him.

"Well,—if you are—come across to the 'Angel' in a quarter of an hour. There's a job—vacant."

She passed out, almost brushing against him, and he watched her cross the road and enter the arched gateway of the Angel Inn. She turned to the left towards a doorway, but she did not look back, and he wondered why she had left him with a feeling of having been crushed against a wall. She had suggested immense strength, a brutal and laughing vitality.

Sorrell went back suddenly into the shop, and along its dark length to the woman in the cage.

"Excuse me—would you mind telling me——?"

She caught his meaning.

"That's Mrs. Palfrey; she runs the 'Angel.'"

"Oh. Have you any idea——?"

Miss Hargreaves looked at him queerly.

"They want an odd man—for the luggage and the boots and things——"

He stared at her thin face.

"Well,—why didn't you——?"

"Because I didn't know," she said tartly. "If it is any use to you—well—there it is."

2

Sorrell stood on the footway and looked across at the Angel Inn.

The exterior of the building pleased him. It had the creamy whiteness of last year's paint, and a well proportioned cornice that threw a definite shadow. The window sashes were painted maroon, and from the centre of the façade an old iron balcony projected like the poop of a ship. The gilded angel appeared to have floated from off this balcony, and there could be not doubt as to the rightness

of the angel's political opinions. She was a solid Tory
angel who had pointed the way heavenwards to generations
of Staunton crowds, carrying with her the eloquence of
many triumphant Tory orators.

Sorrell's glance travelled towards the arched entry by
which coaches and carriages had entered and left the inn
in the old days. Above this entry a fine semi-circular
window overhung the footwalk, two tall Ionic pillars,
painted white, supporting it. Sorrell noticed that the curtains were of green taffeta. The window was fitted with
window boxes, but the flowers in the boxes were dead.

He strolled up the street, across the Market Square and
into the Close. He was undecided. He had glanced for a
moment at the shuttered windows of Mr. Verity's shop, only
to realize how rapid had been the drop in his expectations.
Odd man at a provincial pub! Assuredly he was landing
with a bump at the very bottom of the social precipice.

He sat down on the seat and watched the swans, casual
and stately creatures gliding as they pleased.

"Well,—anyway," he reflected, "if one starts at the
bottom one has the satisfaction of feeling that one cannot
drop any farther."

He thought of Christopher.

"I said I would get a job. Any kind of job may be a
ladder—to push the boy up. Or if he can climb up off my
shoulders——?"

He rose and walked back to the Angel Inn, and turning
in at the arched entry, found a doorway on his left that
led into a broad passage. He was to learn to know that
passage very well, and to hate it and its slippery oil-cloth,
and the stairs that went up from it into the darkness. A
lounge enlarged itself on the right, the windows looking into
the courtyard; and opening from the other side of the lounge
were the office, the passage to the kitchen, the "Cubby
Hole," and the back entrance to the "bar"!

Sorrell paused in the passage, with his back to a map
of the surrounding country. Two or three visitors were
seated in the lounge, smoking and reading the daily papers.
A ruddy woman in a leather coat was turning over the pages
of a Michelin guide. Sorrell noticed that the tables in the
lounge had an uncared-for look. Tobacco ash and used
matches littered the trays. There were the marks of glasses.

The chair nearest him needed the hands of an upholsterer.
Moreover, the place had a distinctive and stuffy smell.

Sorrell approached the office window, and as he did so a
man appeared at the doorway of the "Cubby Hole." His
suffused and injected eyes sighted Sorrell.

"Good morning, sir."

"Good morning," said Sorrell.

The man was in his shirt sleeves, unshaven, and his
close-cropped head glistened white between his heavy
shoulders; in fact his head seemed attached directly to his
broad, short body without the interposition of a neck. His
shortness made his bulk more evident, and even the effort of
speaking appeared to render him short of breath, for Sorrell
saw the labouring of the ballooned waistcoat. The man was
not old, and yet he made Sorrell think of some poor, obese,
mangy old god with bleared eyes and panting flanks.

"What can I do for you, sir?"

His bluffness had a certain pathos. He appeared the
master, a hearty, loud voiced creature, and he was nothing
but an obedient sot.

"Mrs. Palfrey told me to call. It's about——."

"About what——?"

"She is needing a man."

"Oh,—ah,—that's it."

The brain behind the blotched face functioned very slowly,
nor did the suffused blue eyes express any emotion. They
did not change their look of solemn obfuscation.

The man moved to the door on which "The Cubby Hole"
was painted in black letters. He opened it.

"Flo."

"Hallo."

"Someone to see you, a fellow after Tom's place."

"Show him in."

As Sorrell responded to the gesture of a fat hand he
divined the fact that this poor, rotten shell of a man—the
bruised and swollen fruit—was Florence Palfrey's husband.

3

He closed the door and stood by it, holding his hat in
his hand. It was a darkish room, with one window looking
out upon a yard, and beneath the window ran a long sofa

full of crimson coloured cushions. The woman was sitting
on the sofa fiddling with some piece of needlework.

She did not tell Sorrell to sit down.

"Well, what's your trouble been?" she asked abruptly.

He answered her with equal abruptness.

"Is that any business of yours?"

Her eyes seemed to take in his thinness, the black and
whiteness of his rather solemn face with its little moustache
and neatly brushed black hair. His quick reaction to her
insolence did not displease her.

"Do you want this job?" she asked.

"That depends——."

"On your pride, my lad. Gentleman and ex-officer and
all that!"

She pretended to fiddle with her needlework, and he
looked down at her and met her occasional and baffling
glances. He could not make her out. Her immense vitality, the brutal glow of her handsome strength made him
feel like an inexperienced and shy boy. Why had she told
him to come to her? Was it pity, good nature?

"I want work," he said.

"Married?"

"No. But I have got a boy."

She gave him a comprehending stare.

"What made you come to Staunton?"

"I had a berth offered me. At Verity's. I came down
yesterday. He was dead."

She reflected for a moment, her head bent over her
work.

"Rather a comedown for you."

"That's my affair."

He had a feeling that she was amused at finding a man-
creature in the corner of her cage.

"What about references, a character?"

"I could get you references from the Ex-Officers' Association. My name is Sorrell, Captain Sorrell."

"You will have to drop the 'captain.' Temporary, I
suppose?"

"Yes. And what is the job?"

She dallied over revealing the details of the post he was
to fill, as though it piqued her to discover at her leisure how
much mauling the man-thing could bear.

"Of course—you are pretty raw.   The thing is—you won't be able to put on side.   A man who cleans the boots in my house doesn't put on side."

"Point No. 1," he said, "I clean the boots."

"And carry up luggage."

"Yes."

"And keep an eye on the yard and the garage.   By the way,—know anything of billiards?"

"I play."

"Then you know how to mark.   Then—there is the 'Bar.'   You will have to scrub that out every morning, and give a hand sometimes with the drinks."

"Right."

She felt him growing stiffer with the swallowing of each detail.   His pale face confronted her with an air of defiance.   With each scratch of the claw he forced himself to a grimmer rigidity.   He refused to wince.

"Anything else?"

"Oh,—any odd job I may want done."

"Yes."

"And you will call me 'madam.' "

She gave him a stare, and in it was a brutal curiosity. He was like a slave in the arena, down in the sand, and she was wondering whether he would cry for mercy.

"Very well, madam.   And may I ask—what I get out of the job?"

"Thirty bob a week—and your keep."

"Is that all?"

"Tips.   Don't forget the tips.   If a man's obliging——"

She gave an indescribable twitch of the shoulders.

"It's a posh job—in the right place.   You'll live in—of course."

Sorrell stood fingering his hat.

"And what about my boy?"

"I'm not engaging a boy.   We don't have children here. You can board him out somewhere, and he can go to school. How old?"

"Eleven."

"Very well; it's up to you, Sorrell.   I can fill this place ten times over in half an hour."

She saw the white teeth under the little black moustache, and she understood how he was feeling.   He hated her.

He could have struck her in the face, and his suppressed passion gave her the sort of emotion that she found pleasurable. She liked using her claws on men, driving them to various exasperations, and not for a long time had she had such a victim.

"I'll take it," he said. "When shall I start?"

She had turned on the sofa to place a finger on the push of an electric bell. Sorrell heard the distant "burr" of it. She sat as though waiting for someone in order to keep him waiting.

"What did you say?"

Her manner was offhand.

"I asked you—madam—when I should start?"

"Right away. I'll give you an hour to fix up that kid of yours."

"Thank you," he said, and opened the door to go.

But she called him back as her husband entered the room.

"I've taken this man on. He is going to fetch his things."

Mr. Palfrey, stertorous and staring, was nothing but a fat figure of consent.

"Right, my dear."

"That's all, Sorrell. Be back in an hour."

It took Sorrell five minutes to reach the upper room of the house in Fletcher's Lane, and he found Christopher at the window looking out upon the world of Staunton's roofs.

"I have got a job, Kit."

The boy gave him that happy, radiant smile.

"I am glad, pater. What is it?"

Sorrell took one of the first steps towards the greater courage.

"I'm porter at the Angel Hotel."

III

I

IT took Stephen Sorrell the best part of a week to understand the "atmosphere" of the Angel Inn at Staunton.

It was a little world in itself, a world dominated by that woman of blood and of brass, Florence Palfrey. The other humans were little, furtive figures, scuttling up and down passages and in and out of rooms. There were the two waitresses, the cook, the two chambermaids, and the apathetic young lady who helped in the bar. Poor, besotted John Palfrey, waddling about like a pathetic yet repulsive old dog, a creature of wind and of nothingness, was a voice and nothing more. He was perpetually fuddled. His hands trembled; his swollen waistcoat was never properly buttoned; even his gossipings in the "Cubby Hole" were like the blunderings of a brainless animal. Sometimes Sorrell found him in tears.

"What is it, sir?"

"I've lost—my slippers——. It's that damned pup—again."

He gulped.

"Who cares——? I'm—I'm asking you? Not a blessed —soul——"

Sorrell would find his slippers for him, or his pipe, though he could not dry the poor creature's silly tears. There were times when he himself was on the edge of tears, tears of rage or of exhaustion. He went to bed each night, worn out in mind and in body, so tired that he would lie awake and listen to the cathedral clock, or to the noises of his own body. The work was new to him; he was on the go from morning to night; the luggage pulled him to pieces. Moreover, the food was execrable, and those slovenly meals snatched anyhow and at any time in the slimy kitchen, turned sour in his tired stomach. Very often he was in pain.

But the thing that astonished him was the dirtiness of the place. From the street the Angel suggested cleanliness and comfort; the paint was fresh, the door-step white, but an observant eye might have noticed the dead flowers in the window boxes. Within, a cynical slovenliness prevailed. It was not safe to look under the carpets, or to reflect upon the blankets hidden by the treacherously clean sheets. There were places that smelt. As for the kitchen, and that awful dark and greasy hole where the dishes were washed, they made Sorrell wonder at the innocence of the people who ran their cars into the Angel yard and ate the Angel dinner, and slept in the Angel beds.

The place had a sly filthiness. It was like a wench in silk stockings and lace whose ablutions were of the scantiest. Yet there was money in the "house." Trade was good; Florence Palfrey never gave you the impression that she had to deny herself anything. She was brazen, voracious, insatiable, an animal with bowels full of fire. It was she who made out the bills, and in most of them there was some flagrant item against which the easy English visitor should have protested. In nine cases out of ten they remained mute, and paid. Florence Palfrey knew her world. She bluffed. She chanced the protest, knowing that people would pay and go away and grumble and forget. She knew the world's moral cowardice, its inertia.

Sorrell soon realized that the Angel as an hotel did not matter. The coffee-room, the commercial-room, the bedrooms were of no importance; what mattered was the bar.

Men came to booze.

In fact the "Cubby Hole" of the Angel Inn was a pivot, a fly-trap, a cave into which all sorts of male things crowded, and drank, and made silly noises and sillier laughter, and looked with lustful eyes at Florence Palfrey. At night the room would be full of them, and even in the daytime it was rare for the room beside the bar to be empty. This cavity had a secret, conspiratorial air. The men who sneaked into it dreamed of catching old Palfrey's wife in a mood of consent, and of exciting moments among the red cushions.

The "Cubby Hole" filled Sorrell with nausea.

He began to know the names and the faces and the callings of the men who drifted into it. There was Romer—the managing clerk of Spens and Waterlove, a polite person with restless brown eyes and an unpleasant tongue. He had an amazing collection of stories. Biles, who owned the big butcher's shop in High Street, would slip in with his red, greasy and furtive face, and would spill silly compliments from his coarse lips. Sadler the "vet" went away each night stiffly drunk, moving like a figure on wires, his eyes fierce in his thin and debauched face. But there were dozens of them, farmers, tradesmen, commercial travellers, young bloods, all slinking in like dogs, drinking, and lounging and lusting.

"The fools——!"

Sorrell called them fools, and his scorn of them was part of his own pain. He had to mark for some of them in the billiard room, to listen to their dirty stories, to fetch them drinks. It was their amusement, and his torture, for often he was drooping with fatigue and boredom, and yearning for the fools to go to bed. And he would hear the laughter in the "Cubby Hole," and the splurgings of these tradesmen who made love like bullocks.

"Floe—on thou shining river."

That was Medlum's jest, Medlum who kept the bookshop and sold prayer-books and Bibles and pretty-pretty art tourist guides, and who had a wife and seven children. He was a sandy man who looked as though he had been dipped in a bleaching vat, all save his mouth which was thin and red and lascivious.

They spent much money.

They would send poor old Palfrey up to bed, bemused, shuffling in his slippers, grabbing at the handrail. Often Sorrell would have to help John Palfrey up the stairs, listening to his pantings and to his fuddled confidences.

"She don't care—not a damn. I've got water in me——. I'm like a grape, Steve. What did the doctor call it? Ass-i-tis——. Wish I were dead."

He would pause at the top of the stairs, panting, and staring solemnly at Sorrell.

"You mark my words——. A coffin—in six months. I'm asking you——. Who cares——?"

He would weep.

"You're a good chap,—Steve. Don't know why. God,
—I feel sick."

There were other things that Sorrell began to understand.
Women came to the "Cubby Hole"; Miss Hargreaves from
across the way, red nosed, excited, ready with thin, hard
giggles; the lady who kept the fruit shop and who looked
like an over-ripe plum, and who was always protesting
that she could not bear to be tickled. "I'll scream."

These earthly souls soon ceased to puzzle him, but the
woman of brass remained an enigma. She bullied these
people, even when she treated them with brutal good-
humour. She knew exactly how to handle each fool-man,
and how to repulse some flushed face that was breathing
too near to hers. There were times when Sorrell felt that
she despised the whole crowd as much as he did.

And since a man must wonder, he went in pursuit of her
motives. Did her huge vitality suck something from her
herd of swine? Was it money? Did it cause poor Palfrey
to disobey his doctor's orders and to shuffle nearer to the
inevitable coffin?

She was shrewd, like a strong and cunning animal. She
never lost her dignity, or allowed the amorous clowns to take
liberties.

"I have seen something like her before," he thought.
"Where——?"

One wet night he remembered. The den was full of her
Circe troop, and Sorrell, going in with a tray of glasses,
saw her sitting on the sofa and looking over the heads of
her adorers. Yes, he remembered. He had seen a lioness
at the London Zoo, couched, and looking just like that,
savagely and superbly indifferent. He could remember the
way the tawny beast's eyes had looked over the heads of
the humans fidgeting and chattering outside the railings,
those tame people, those monkeys. The lioness, couched up
above, eyes fixed upon some distance of her own, had ignored
them.

But she met Sorrell's eyes, and a sudden glitter came
into them.

He was closing and locking the hotel door when he heard
her calling him.

"Stephen."

He went to the door of the den. She was sitting on the

sofa, yawning, and with the naturalness of a fine animal.

"What damned fools!"

She looked at him, and picked up a cigarette from the table.

"I want a match."

He produced a box, and striking a match, held it for her to light her cigarette. She blew smoke. Her eyes lifted suddenly, and he saw the big black pupils and the vivid blue of each iris.

"You looked fagged."

"It's the end of the day."

"You ought to get off more. You work too hard."

Sorrell's eye dropped.

"If I could get out for an hour—after tea. There's my boy; I don't see much of him——"

Instantly he was aware of the fact that he had offended her.

"O—your boy! What's he doing?"

"Going to school."

"The Council school?"

"Well, it's that—or——"

"A summons. All right,—clear out for an hour each day. Have you locked up?"

"Yes, madam."

He had a glimpse of her profile as he passed the door on his way to the stairs. She was smoking and looking at and through the wall opposite her. The corner of her mouth was drawn down and she was frowning.

2

Sorrell had particular moments in the day when life was worth living. One of the moments was when he got to his attic at night, and counted up the day's tips and entered the amount in a little black note-book; the other moment of happiness came to him with a daily glimpse of the clean, frank face of his boy.

Kit would come to the arched entry, and Sorrell would meet him there, and Kit would see his father in the old, familiar blue serge suit grown more shiny and less neatly creased about the trousers. There were times when Sorrell wore an apron, but he contrived to appear before Christopher minus the apron. His pride allowed itself this little satisfaction.

They would stand together for five minutes beside one of the white Ionic pillars supporting the bow window of the dining-room, the boy looking up into his father's face. He was an observant child, and his love for Sorrell had undergone a transfiguration. Christopher noticed changes in his father's face; it looked more waxy; there were little wrinkles as of a troublesome knot of effort lying between the eyebrows. Sorrell was thinner; he stooped more.

But Sorrell's eyes smiled.

"How's she feeding you, son?"

Christopher had no complaint to make of the food that Mrs. Barter gave him at No. 13 Fletcher's Lane. She was a good woman.

"She's been mending my shirts, pater."

"Ha," said Sorrell, "has she!"—and glanced at the boy's suit. Yes, that fresh face contrasted with the shabby clothes.

"Time I took you to the tailor, my lad. I think I can manage it next week."

Christopher could not analyse all that lay behind his father's eyes, but he felt the warmth of the love in them. He noticed that his father's eyes had a filminess, a veiled and secret delight, a moment of deep dreaming. They were the eyes of a man who was thirsty, and to whom the boy brought pure, clean water. Christopher refreshed him. His candid eyes and the brown warmth of his clear skin were unblemished fruit after the rottenness of those squashed and purple souls, those men who made Sorrell think of faces trodden on by an ever-passing crowd of sordid and unclean thoughts. His boy had youth, a future, possibilities; he was the sun in the east.

And poor Palfrey!

"My God!" Sorrell thought; "one must hold on to something, even if it is nothing but a clean shirt and a piece of soap."

Christopher never asked questions, awkward and embarrassing questions. He accepted his father's job, and he understood the significance of it far more subtly than Sorrell knew. It reacted on the boy, and deepened his sensitive seriousness.

At school he was very careful of his clothes. He did not say much about the school. It was all right. Better than London. What did he do in the evenings? O,—went for walks, mostly. There were woods outside the town, and the river.

Those few minutes were very precious to Sorrell, but they tantalized him. His boy was so apart from him all through the day, and whenever they met he would look eagerly at that frankly radiant face for the shadow of any possible blemish.

He felt so responsible, greedily responsible. The boy's clean eyes made the life at the Angel possible.

On one occasion when he had walked a little way along the footpath with Christopher he became aware of a face at a window. The woman was watching them. He caught her bold, considering eyes fixed on the boy.

He went back rather hurriedly into the passage, and met her there.

"That your kid, Stephen?"

"Yes, madam."

"He's not a bit like you. The mother's dead, I suppose?"

"I divorced her," said Sorrell, pale and stiff about the lips.

Usually, it was about eleven at night when he went slowly up the narrow staircase to the top landing where the staff slept. He carried a candle. Sometimes he would hear giggling and chattering in one of the girls' rooms, but he always went straight to his own, shut the door, put the candlestick on the chair, sat down on the bed and turned out his pockets. At this hour he did his precious calculations. His little black note-book was a model of neatness, with credit and debit entries.

July	7.	Wages £1	10	0	Christopher—Board £1	0	0
"	7.	Tips	4	6	Tobacco	2	0
"	8.	"	3	0	Tooth brush ..	1	0
"	9.	"		0	Christopher—Boots 1	0	0
"	10.	"	7	0			
"	11.	"	5	6			
"	12.	"	1	0			
"	13.	"	9	0			

He found that his tips averaged about twenty-five shillings a week. He paid Mrs. Barter a pound a week for Christopher's keep. He spent a few odd shillings on himself. He was contriving to save about a pound a week. £52 a year? If his health held out?

Already he had a plan for his boy, an objective that showed like a distant light through the fog of the day's confusion.

"It's my business to do my job thoroughly," he thought, "in order to get Kit a better one. I'll save every damned penny."

Life, the life that should have appealed to the cruder of his own appetites, had ceased to attract him, and all his energy appeared to concentrate itself and to flow in one particular channel. He developed a peculiar passion for thoroughness, even though he might curse the inanimate things upon which he had to exercise this thoroughness. Queerly enough, much of his thinking and his philosophizing were done while he was cleaning the various pairs of boots and shoes left outside the bedroom doors. He did not mind this job,—though scrubbing the bar floor made his gorge rise. It was like cleaning out a pen where unclean animals had left their ordure. But boots——! Boots had character. He got into the way of estimating the owners of the boots by their footgear. He had a preference for neat brown shoes, gentlemen's shoes, and his favourites came in for more polish. Young women's shoes—were they ever so chic—gave him no thrills. The boots he detested were the boots worn by a particular type of middle-aged commercial traveller, men who trod heavily and whose waistcoats bulged. He never put a hand inside one of these "swine's trotters" as he called them.

But with a free hour each day snatched from the Lioness's rather jealous paws, Sorrell began to see more of Christopher. He took his hour off from eight till nine, for he had found that too many motorists arrived after tea and he was not there to handle the luggage and to carry it up from the garage. He wished to be in evidence because of the subsequent tips. But in these long summer evenings he and Christopher wandered together; sometimes they chose the Close, on other evenings they wandered out a little way into the country; if it was wet Mrs. Barter let

them sit in her parlour. She was kind to Sorrell; she
offered to do his mending for him.

Christopher loved trees. There was a particular elm in
the Close, a green giant with a ring seat round its bole,
under which the boy liked to sit. Nor was Sorrell sorry to
sit. It conserved boot leather, and rested his tired feet.
Kit had noticed on their short country rambles that his
father walked as though his feet hurt him. He had noticed
—too—that one of the boots was patched.

"Your turn next—pater?"

"What for, son?"

"Boots," said the boy.

He had fatherly moments towards Sorrell. He too had
his plans, vague ambitions, and impulse that pushed him
towards some magnificent job in the doing of which he would
earn much money. He had sensed the effort in his father's
life; he dreamed of taking his share of the effort.

"I can start work at fifteen, pater."

Sorrell was astonished.

"I hope not," he said, and glancing from the boy's face
to the spreading branches of the elm he saw life and its
effort symbolized.

"Most people grow like cabbages. Look at this tree.
How many years—eh? O,—it was not in a hurry. We—
are not going to be in a hurry."

The boy's eyes were questioning.

"Not as long as that—— With you—sweating—and doing everything——"

"It's my job, Kit."

He looked mysterious.

"I've got plans. The thing is——Well, you don't know
yet,—what you will want to do—I mean. No blind alleys,
or office stools."

"You mean—dad—what I would like to be?"

"That's it."

"Seems—one's got to earn money."

"Wait a bit. There's something better: how you earn it.
The real job matters more than the money."

"Yes," said Christopher very solemnly, "the sort of thing
you love doing. Well,—I suppose I shall find out."

IV

I

AN incident that occurred about five weeks after Sorrell's arrival at the Angel startled him into a sudden aliveness towards the drift of other people's temperamental whimsies.

It was early in the morning, before the paying part of the hotel had descended to his breakfast, and Sorrell was down on his knees in the lounge cleaning up the spilt contents of one of the ash trays. Someone had knocked it off the table the previous night. The two waitresses were busy in the coffee-room, and one of them, a little sallow girl, with a shock of black, bobbed hair, running out towards the kitchen with a serviette over her arm, saw Sorrell kneeling. He had had glances from the girl; she was always passing him in the passage, but Sorrell was too tired for life's little thrills. He had forgotten the fact that he might be attractive to women. Anyhow, the girl slipped the napkin over Sorrell's eyes,—and drawing it tight, bent down till her mop of black hair touched his head.

"Guess who it is——?"

She giggled, but before Sorrell had made any effort to free himself, the napkin was whisked away, and he had a glimpse of Millie's slim legs disappearing urgently down the passage leading to the kitchen. Some one had come down the stairs, and was passing behind him, and glancing round, he saw Florence Palfrey going towards the office.

It was the most trivial of incidents, a mere piece of hoydenish mischief, but when the staff of the Angel sat down to its midday meal Sorrell realized that the little dark girl was not present.

"What's become of Millie?"

The other waitress gave him a sour look.

"You—ought to know."

"But I don't know."

33

"She—sacked her."

"What for?"

"Romping."

Not much was said, though it was obvious that the other
girls felt themselves injured by the peremptory ejection of a
comrade, but they were afraid of the Lioness, and they mis-
trusted Sorrell—the man. He became aware of the mis-
trust; it made him uncomfortable; moreover he had felt a
sudden, sordid tremor of fear.

That which had happened to Millie might happen to him,
and he knew that for the boy's sake such a thing must not
happen.

The keenness of his own anxiety was a humiliation, and
he accepted the humiliation, explaining it to himself quite
frankly as though he were explaining the wearing of a
shabby suit of clothes. He was alarmed at the possibility
of his being pushed out into the street, of losing his thirty
shillings, his keep, and his tips. Yet this fear shocked him.
That a man should be afraid of being evicted from such a
caravanserie! He had not realized how much the Angel
Inn had become his "straw," and that he was ready to cling
to it with the instinctive terror of a man who feared the
unknown.

That afternoon he spent himself in a passion of activity.
He went about eagerly looking for work. He made work.
He attacked the various slovenliness of the place.

He was aware of the constant nearness of the woman.
She—too—appeared to be in a restless and active mood.
She kept coming out of the office of the "Cubby Hole," going
out or up the stairs and returning. She saw Sorrell in all
sorts of postures and places, on his knees polishing the "sur-
round" of the lounge, cleaning the glass panels of the doors,
carrying out the aspidistras and washing them in the yard.
She had one particular glimpse of him doubled up under the
big walnut table in the passage, but what he was doing
there she did not pretend to know.

Though she passed him a dozen times that afternoon she
neither spoke to him nor appeared to look in his direction,
but each of them was conscious of the other. The feline intuition of the woman divined Sorrell's fear. He was like
some busy thing in a cage, propitiatory, eagerly turning a

wheel. Also, she knew that he was cursing her, himself, and his activities.

Captain Sorrell, M.C.!

She was moved to brutal laughter, but her laughter was silent. There were thoughts in her too that purred. She had Sorrell on his knees, and she could tell him to get up or remain there, to come or go. And there were inclinations in her that were whetted by her sense of power.

"Damn the woman! Is she going to——?"

He had a queer feeling that her passings and repassings were not haphazard. They concerned him. She took notice of him by ignoring him; her seeming indifference had an intimate and veiled significance.

He had carried in a pair of steps and was polishing one of the big mirrors in the lounge. He saw himself in it, his anxious, sallow face, the sweep of the hand carrying the wash-leather. He threw silent abuse at his own reflection, that sedulously active and worried creature.

"You wretched failure,—you grovelling idiot! Rushing about to create a good impression——"

Suddenly, he saw her figure drift into the mirror. She was standing behind him, looking at him. He fancied that he detected amusement in her eyes, the kind of amusement a lioness might be expected to enjoy if a lioness had a sense of humour.

"Very busy to-day,—Stephen."

"Yes, madam."

He went on with his polishing, believing that he was going to hear about the silly incident of the morning. He waited. She stood and watched him for fully a minute, and he felt the back of his neck and his ears all flushed. Confound her! What did she want? Why didn't she go away, or stick her claws into him and have done with it?

He reached up to a far corner of the glass, and when next he searched for her reflection, he found that she had .gone. He was conscious of relief, but the sense of relief was only partial. He felt her somewhere. Where?

The door of the "Cubby Hole" was wide open, and he could see a part of the interior reflected in the mirror, a strip of green carpet, a red cushion, part of the frame and glass of the window. She was in there, sitting on the sofa, watching him. He saw the gleam of her hair, and two eyes, very dark, like the eyes of a creature watching him from the gloom of a wood. He fancied that she smiled.

He tried to concentrate his senses upon the mere glassy surface of the mirror, and to keep his vision and its accompanying thoughts from passing through to the deeps of it where the woman was, but he could not help focusing her. She remained there, watching him, enigmatic, motionless, like a great tawny cat. Sorrell decided to leave the mirror. He came down the steps, and was folding them up when he heard her voice.

"Stephen——"

"Yes, madam."

"There is a glass in here. It hasn't been touched since —since——"

She laughed as he stood in the doorway with the steps and bucket.

"Since Adam and Eve."

Sorrell obeyed her with an air of great briskness. The mirror was over the mantelpiece, a gilt-framed thing of the "Regency" period, and when he got on the steps he found that the top of the frame was black with dust. Florence Palfrey had picked up a paper that had been lying on the sofa, but instead of reading it she fanned herself with it, for the day was hot.

"Anyone in the lounge?"

"No."

Sorrell came down the steps to dip his leather in the bucket.

"Very warm to-day."

She did not reply, but watched him get to work, and his movements told her that he was nervous. She was satisfied in a part of herself. And then she began to talk to him with an air of casual intimacy, and in a way that she had never talked before. He was both Captain Sorrell, and M.C., and her "boots" and porter.

"Rather different from the war, Stephen."

He agreed. He felt strangely alert.

"How did you get your M.C.?"

"I didn't know——"

"Oh,—I know most things. Well? How?"

"Oh, in a trench raid."

"Were you raiding the others?"

"No, madam, the others were raiding us."

He was working hard at the mirror, with his back to her, and somehow he felt that he had to keep a distance, though he could not analyse the feeling.

"Well,—what happened? Don't be so dashed modest."

"The Germans came into our trench."

"Yes."

"And they stuck some of our chaps. It's a nasty tool, the bayonet. And there was a bit of a panic. I was in a deuce of a funk."

"That's funny!"

"It wasn't at all funny. But something seemed to go off inside me—and I saw red."

She nodded her head. She was considering him, eyes half closed and fiercely languid.

"So you can see red. Well,—I shouldn't have thought it. It's rather—interesting. You must have been stronger then."

"I was. But it's not mere beef——"

"No. Not bullock's strength. Wounded—I suppose?"

"Twice."

"Badly?"

"A bit of H. E. in the chest—the second time. I had to come home—after that."

He both felt and heard the rustling of the paper as she fanned herself, a disturbing sound, like the rustling of leaves or lace. He had finished cleaning the mirror, and he came down the steps rather hurriedly, folded them up, and grabbed the bucket.

"Anything else, madam?"

She observed him steadily above the rustling paper.

"No. You are an odd fish, Stephen."

He stared, and she laughed.

"Odd as odd. Go and see if you can find anything else to polish."

2

From that day Sorrell began to perceive Florence Palfrey more and more vividly as the tawny creature, the lioness who had him shut up in her cage. She did not say much, but she managed to convey to him the impression that he was dependent on her, and that she had but to raise a paw——. Her way of dealing with him was both subtle and simple; it mingled moments of provocation and of caressing cruelty with sudden flashes of naked intimacy. Her badness was so unclothed at times that it frightened him.

For Sorrell was thinking of the boy, and his thoughts turned to escape from any entanglement, a shabby affair with a woman who was both elemental and cynical. He did not want it. He was tired of life as a merely personal adventure, and when this thing loomed over him he realized that he was living vicariously, and that the very roots of the will to live drew their sustenance from the youth of his boy.

He was frightened.

For he had a most absurd feeling that he was being kept and fed and played with in order to be devoured. He divined her ruthlessness, her ferocity, her stealthy, amused strength. For some reason he had piqued her, and he wondered why. Was she intrigued by the fact that he was a gentleman handling luggage and cleaning boots? Or had the obvious man, the blatant, butcherly people who stormed into her den ceased to pique her? He could imagine a lioness being bored and looking about her for some new sort of victim.

Moreover, Sorrell was helping poor old Palfrey up to bed, and though Florence Palfrey's husband might be no thing of loveliness, the very act of helping a man begets a sense of comradeship. John Palfrey was derelict; no one bothered about him now; he might shout feebly down the stairs with that husky voice of his, and no one would take any notice.

"Hallo,—hot water,—shaving water——"

On more than one occasion Sorrell found him standing on the landing in his old blue dressing-gown, weeping.

"I—want—my breakfast."

He had it in his bedroom, and it was Sorrell who took upon himself the duty of carrying up poor Palfrey's shaving water and his breakfast tray, for in Palfrey he saw the husk of a man, a man who had been devoured.

"You're a good chap, Steve. I'm of no account now. Who cares?"

"I do, sir."

Palfrey made a sudden clutch at his arm.

"Don't you ever marry, Steve; don't you ever let a woman get you. She'll eat you up."

And Sorrell understood.

It happened one evening when he had helped the dying man to bed that Sorrell found Florence on the landing outside the door. The landing was badly lit, and she was standing by the stairs with one hand on the rail as though in the act of pausing. She was in low-necked dress of black, with her arms bare to the shoulders.

Sorrell still had his hand on the handle of John Palfrey's door. Her sudden presence there agitated him; he felt that he had to get by her quickly and go downstairs. He could smell the particular scent she used.

He walked towards her,—and remaining where she was she closed the stairs to him unless he should push rudely past close to the wall.

"Put him to bed, have you?"

She looked Sorrell full in the eyes as though her stare could beat down any independence that was in him.

"He won't last long now."

Her tone was callously significant. It was as though she was trying to convey to him her appreciation of his soft-heartedness, to humour something childish in him, even while she conspired with him as to the future. O, well, she could lie sleekly in her cage and wait for this odd fish who boasted a sort of absurd integrity of his own.

Sorrell felt shocked. Something flamed in him; he could have struck her, thrown her down the stairs, with furious abuse, but behind her he seemed to see the face of his boy.

"It is pretty rotten for a man——" he said.

He felt ashamed before her. His eyes looked over into the well of the stairs, and then—with an abrupt and awkward "Excuse me," he pushed past her and went below.

He felt that he needed air, to be alone somewhere under the stars, and daring the desertion of his post he went out into the High Street, and along it into the Market Square. The place was deserted. He saw a great yellow moon hanging in the tops of the elms, and beside it the blackness of

the cathedral towers. He walked up and down, hatless,
and in his shirt sleeves. He felt that he wanted to rush
round to Fletcher's Lane, and catch up Christopher and
hold him.

"The one clean thing left to me," he thought.

His lips made a movement as of spitting.

"Good God! That a man should be left to die like that,
—like a piece of rotting meat in a corner! If I should·have
to die like that? Damn her——!"

He was in a fever to escape,—but how? Necessity held
him chained. If he broke the chain and plunged? He was
saving money, just a little money, and if he could win a
breathing space he might have time to look about him. It
was the boy who mattered. If he the man—surrendered—
and allowed himself to be cajoled and to be devoured——?

But why this niceness? How easy it would be for
him——. She had hinted so broadly. But his soul's ex-
clamation was a "Pah!" To step into that poor sot's
shoes, and to be pushed eventually over the edge of all
decencies when the feline creature was tired of him.

No. He struggled. The nature of the struggle was
vague and elemental, and he did not visualize it as one of
those primitive crises in a man's life when something that
is stronger than his mere appetites pushes him a step higheı
up the precipice. He clung to a prejudice, and to the one
human thing that mattered. He was not going down into
the dubious muck, and to feel himself smeared with it when
he met the eyes of his boy.

"Damn her," he said, "I'll fight through," and he went
back to the hotel with his eyes staring as they had stared
at horrible moments during the war.

3

Sorrell's frenzy of activity continued. It seemed as
though he were trying to lose himself in a desperate combat
with the multifarious slovenliness of the Angel Inn, to hide
himself in the dust cloud of his own energy. He was never
still. He ran round and round in his cage, sweeping,
polishing, tidying, carrying things. His indefatigable activity
impressed itself even upon the loungers in the "Cubby
Hole."

"That chap of yours seems full of juice, Flo."

"Well,—why not? He doesn't belong to a Trade Union."

"Queer sort of beggar. Looks as though he thought your pub. wanted a wash."

"That's not unlikely."

"Oh,—I say! That's a bit thick. Hallo, Bob, old bean. Crush in here. What's yours?"

In this vulgar world Sorrell's nausea became too chronic and too real. He began to be afraid of his meals, and to wake at night with a knotted pain under his ribs. He thought of going to see a doctor, but it was not a doctor that he needed, and he knew it, but he did arrive at the more economical expedient of slipping into a chemist's shop. There were no other customers, and Sorrell made his confession across trays of soap and washing gloves and toothbrushes.

"I've got indigestion. Can you give me something?"

The chemist was a colourless little man with thin and peculiarly compressed lips.

"Pain after meals?"

"Yes."

"How long?"

"Oh, it varies."

He met the man's scrutinizing eyes.

"Looks as though you wanted a tonic. Run down. I'll give you something."

Sorrell sacrificed a precious three and ninepence for a bottle of tonic and some tablets.

"Help you to get rid of the wind, you know."

The stuff did him no good, for he was worried, and overworking himself, and eating bad food and rushing about after he had eaten it. The constant pain and the discomfort began to depress him; he felt less and less of a man, and more and more of a sick animal in a cage. He had moods of melancholic apathy when a voice within him played tempter, saying—"What's the use? You are a failure. Even your wretched body is a failure. Why not give in, slide, go down the shoot? After all, what is the fuss about? A woman and a boy and an adventure that most men would laugh at? You're a fool."

Kit saw a change in his father. Sorrell's eyes looked strained, and the whites of them were muddy; he stooped more, and appeared uneasy when he was sitting on the seat under the elm. A discouraged figure. And yet Christopher did not like to ask questions.

"The work makes you rather tired, pater."

"Oh,—a bit. I shall get used to it."

"Couldn't there be—something else?"

"I've got a plan," said Sorrell.

He was always talking about that plan. The more difficult it seemed of attainment the more obsessed was he by the contemplation of it. His plan was like a hypothetical sun invisible during the greater part of an English summer, but there, and liable to shine some day next year. He forced himself to appear confident before the boy, for he realized that Christopher was the only living person who believed in him, and he wanted Christopher to go on believing in him, especially when he was in danger of ceasing to believe in himself. It was suggestion, the dear—trusting stimulus of youth.

One day he was sick, and he went about with a face all pinched and the colour of cream, making himself do things. He was tidying up a disorder of papers in the commercial room when the woman glided in.

"You don't look well, Stephen."

There was a seductive kindness in her voice, and he mumbled something about his dinner not having agreed with him.

"You fuss too much," she said.

He went on tidying the papers, feeling that her presence radiated a false sunlight.

"You—might—do much less—if you cared, you odd fish."

He understood her.

"It's my job," he said.

"As you please."

When she left him he sat down in one of the chairs, and held his head in his hands.

V

I

SORRELL was leaning against one of the white Ionic pillars that supported the bow window when the claret-coloured car drew up outside the Angel Hotel. The car was a two-seater, and in it sat a man wearing a grey suit and a soft grey hat. He was very brown. He beckoned to Sorrell.

"Any rooms here?"

"Yes, sir."

The quality of Sorrell's voice surprised the man, and he showed his surprise by looking at Sorrell for half a second longer than was necessary.

"Right. The car won't be in the way here?"

"No, sir. Would you care to go straight into the garage?"

"Presently," said the man.

He climbed out and stood on the pavement, glancing up at the windows of the hotel. He appeared to be about Sorrell's age, one of those square men, but not too square, with a fresh brown skin, blue eyes, and a firm but human mouth. He moved easily, and you gathered from his steady eyes and his rather measured movements that he was a deliberate person, no great talker, a man with courage, but one who never rushed at life haphazard. There was something about the man that attracted Sorrell, his freshness, his obvious strength, the calm way his eyes looked at you and then gave you a sudden and pleasant smile. Sorrell had known one or two such men in the war. They had made good soldiers.

The man entered the hotel, and Sorrell remained by the car. He liked the colour of it, and the compact brightness of the dash-board, and the neatly covered leather hood. He himself would have liked to possess such a car, but he did not grudge the man in grey the possession of it.

43

Sorrell heard the pleasant and deliberate voice at his elbow.

"All right. I'll drive in."

From the way the newcomer looked about him in the Angel yard, Sorrell divined his disapproval. Nor did Sorrell approve of the yard.

"No lock ups?"

"No, sir."

"I want an inner tube mending."

"I'll take it round to a garage for you, sir. Luggage in the dicky?"

"Yes."

Sorrell extracted the luggage, a massive leather kit-bag, a suitcase, and an attaché case.

"Do you know the number of your room, sir?"

"Fifteen."

The visitor paused at the office window to sign his name in the registration book, while Sorrell carried the luggage upstairs. No. 15 was no better and no worse than the average bedroom at the Angel, and though Sorrell had grown accustomed to the rooms, there were moments when he appreciated their depressing casualness. He unfastened the straps of the kit-bag, and went downstairs, to find the visitor talking to Mrs. Palfrey, and Sorrell came by the impression that it was the woman who had begun the conversation.

He turned to Sorrell.

"Which way?"

"This way, sir. First floor, second room on the left."

The man disappeared up the stairs, and Sorrell glanced at the visitors' book.

"Thomas Roland. London."

The handwriting was like the man, broad and deliberate and without affectation.

Five minutes later Sorrell, who was rearranging the magazines and papers in the lounge, fancied that he heard a bell ringing with aggressive persistency. It was an up-stairs bell, and on going to investigate he found Mr. Roland standing outside the door of No. 15.

"Isn't there a maid on duty?"

"There should be, sir."

"I have no towels and no soap, and no one has brought me any hot water."

"Sorry, sir."

"And look here—at this."

Sorrell looked, and gave a little lift of the shoulders.

"These confounded wenches——. I'll see to it myself, sir."

He went out on to the landing calling "Maggie—Maggie," but no Maggie materialized, for she was somewhere below at one of the many back doors, and busy with the other sex, so Sorrell went to the chambermaid's closet, and collected towels and hot water, and purloined a new cake of soap from another bedroom.

Mr. Roland was unpacking his kit-bag, and had thrown a pair of orange·and blue striped pyjamas on the bed.

"Thanks."

That was all he said, but he smiled at Sorrell and gave him one of those quietly observant glances, and Sorrell went below feeling warmed by something pleasant and human and wholesome in the man. He wondered who Thomas Roland was, and what he did.

Meanwhile, Roland had paused in his unpacking, and was sitting on the bed and examining the room as though it interested him. Its deficiencies, its perfunctory slipshodness interested him. He happened to be interested in rooms, and he was a man of detail.

His mental comments followed immediately upon his visual perceptions.

"No wardrobe. Now—where the devil——? Faded green paint,—dirty paper—strings of pink roses between black and white lines. One hook off door. Carpet—h'm—, I wonder what a vacuum cleaner would fetch out of it. Brass bed, one knob missing. Yellow chest of drawers, one handle missing."

He got up.

"I bet the drawers stick, and that the paper inside them is last year's *Daily Mail*."

He was right.

His observations ran on.

"Swing mirror plugged into place with a wad of paper. Blind torn. Japanese mats on floor need burning. Slop pail minus a handle. Marble top of wash-hand stand stained. Tooth glass smeary. Over washing-stand advertisement of Jeyes' Fluid. Over mantelpiece—tariff and advertisement of local tradesmen. Sheets need mending. Blankets,—yes,— just so!"

He resumed his unpacking and his meditations.

"How many of these places have I stayed in during the last month? A dozen—I suppose. And only one decently run place in the dozen. Slovenly holes, especially in these cathedral places. Here's a great opportunity under the noses of our inn-keepers, and all they seem to think of is the booze and the 'bar'!"

He put out his boots.

"The cheek of them—too. Give you every sort of slovenliness and inattention, and bad food, and then charge you top prices. Now take this place. Nobody seems to care a damn, except that porter chap. No supervision, no discipline, no conscience."

His sponge-bag was extracted from a brightly polished cavalry mess tin, the two halves of which found receptacles for his sponge, washing gloves, nail-brush and tooth-brush. He glanced at the cracked sponge-basin belonging to the inn.

"No thanks! Obviously—no. Now—if that tow-headed female downstairs did her job properly instead of——. O, well, that's the curse of these places; a lot of soaking fools, and yellow-headed women. But what I never can understand is—why—if people take on a job—they can't do it properly. And yet—not three in ten can. Socialism! What rot!"

He lit a cigarette and looked out of the window into a back yard that contained the rotting relics of an old brougham, a pile of bottles, and a derelict dog-kennel.

"Cheerful prospect! I wonder what that porter fellow is doing here? Queer chap. Takes trouble, but looks ill. A gentleman's voice—and eyes. Does his job."

It was five o'clock, and Mr. Roland went downstairs into the lounge, and rang for the waitress, for he desired tea. He had to ring twice before a girl appeared as though the last thing in the world she was expected to do was to answer a bell.

"Tea, please."

"For one?"

"For one."

She went away, and Mr. Roland waited twenty minutes, and when the tea tray did arrive he noticed that the girl had forgotten to fill the milk jug.

"I take milk with my tea."

She whisked the jug away. Sorrell was tucking letters under the tapes on the green letter-board, and he happened to turn and catch Mr. Roland's eye. A faint, sympathetic and understanding smile seemed to pass between them.

"You haven't forgotten that tube?"

"No, sir. It has been done. I put it in the dicky."

"Did you pay?"

"Yes, sir. Two shillings."

"Thanks."

A two-shilling piece passed from Roland's hand to Sorrell's, and again their eyes met and smiled.

Sorrell felt cheered, though he had no great reason for feeling cheered. He went upstairs to No. 15, possessed himself of Mr. Roland's brown shoes, two pairs of them, and cleaned them as they had not been cleaned for a month.

2

Dinner was late.

Roland was chatting in the lounge with a big and genial person who had grown suddenly testy with hunger. The genial man was asking his casual acquaintance to explain to him how it was that a certain stereotyped piece of work that was done day by day could not be made to keep pace with the clock.

"We abuse machines,—but hang it all—they have rhythm."

Roland laughed softly.

"Well,—I don't suppose it will be anything great when it does come. And I think I could give you the menu."

"Guessing?"

"No, the law of averages. We shall begin with tomato soup, go on to tough chops—boiled potatoes and cabbage, pass thence to fruit salad, tinned apricots and stewed prunes. And we shall finish with rather bad cheese."

"I don't care what it is," said the testy man. "I feel inclined to go and hammer that gong."

The gong sounded at ten minutes to eight, and Roland, strolling into the dining-room, saw the usual number of small tables arranged under the window and along the wall. Each table had a cruet stand from which most of the plating had long ago been worn away, and a vase of perfunctory flowers. A long table occupied the centre of the room.

Roland waited for the waitress, his pose that of the interested observer.

"One, sir?"

"Please."

The waitress indicated the long table, and Roland smiled.

"I prefer a table to myself."

"We have only tables for two or four, sir."

"Are all these tables reserved?"

"No."

He smiled again.

"If I can get a bedroom for one—I suppose I can get a table. You don't put me in a dormitory—thank you."

He was one of those unusual men who not only thought of things to say, but actually said them, and said them with a smile.

He was given his table.

"Have you a menu card?"

"No, sir."

"What are we going to have?"

"Tomato soup. Roast beef and veg. Fruit salad."

Roland caught the eye of the testy man who was unfolding his napkin at the next table.

"I gave you the menu. There is only one alteration."

"What's that?"

"Roast beef instead of chops."

"Ah——!"

"And 'veg.' A vague and comprehensive word that—veg."

Wandering out afterwards in the cool of the summer evening under a tumultuous yet quiet sky Roland saw the great trees of the Close all edged with gold. He passed in, and stood looking at the cathedral's western façade, the magnificent window recessed between two towers, the arcades and niches, and all that grey and delicate silence in stone. The lawns, like rich old velvet, sheltered by the trees, and

refreshed by the mists from the moat of the palace, were
vividly green in spite of the heat of the past week. Roland
could see the gilded cupola and the clock above the Tudor
gateway of the palace. He strolled upwards along the
canons' gardens, pausing to look in through the old gateways, and his chance strollings brought him to the great
elm where a man and a boy were sitting.

Sorrell had been talking to Christopher of Thomas Roland,
though he himself was puzzled by the impulse that moved
him to speak to the boy of a man who was a mere passing
stranger. But he let the impulse have its way, and the
spread of it had surprised him. "So I cleaned his shoes,
my son, put such a polish on them." Kit had noticed a
sort of shine in his father's eyes. "Strange—how your
heart and your hand go out to some people. He made me
suddenly feel good, and smooth. I knew that I could do
anything for him, and that he would never ask me to do
anything dirty. Instinct. He looks as though he had
come straight out from swimming in the sea, when it's all
blue and the sun makes a glare on the yellow sand."

Roland recognized Sorrell before Sorrell was aware of his
nearness, for Sorrell was leaning forward with his hands
clasped between his knees, and his eyes on the ground.
Roland went towards them, and Sorrell, sensing a presence,
looked up, startled but smiling.

"Your boy?"

"Yes, sir. This is Mr. Roland, Christopher."

Kit stood up and lifted his cap, and he and Mr. Roland
took a steady look at each other.

"Are you at the Angel?"

"No,—I have him boarded out," said Sorrell; "we get
an hour together—when I'm off duty."

"So you get an hour?"

"Yes."

Sorrell was looking at Roland's shoes. He was wondering whether the other man had noticed the polish that had
been put on their comrades in No. 15. Roland sat down on
the seat, and laid a big brown hand on Kit's shoulder.

"Sit down, old chap."

He filled a pipe.

"Pretty peaceful here. Do you ever go to any of the
services down there?"

"Not often."

"I've been," said Kit. "If you want to be alone—when the organ is playing."

Roland made a slow movement of the head.

"I know. Service; a full choir, half a dozen priests, three lonely women, a verger and a forest of empty chairs. And the organ notes quaking, and a boy's voice soaring up to the grey roof like a bird. Perhaps a few spectators standing at the west end of the nave. It always makes me feel queer."

Kit was watching him with solemn eyes.

"Queer? How?"

"Oh,—as though I had fallen suddenly through a trap-door into another world. Not our world. Men saw the sunset through trees in those days. I suppose they looked at the stars. Do you ever look at the stars?"

His eyes were on Sorrell.

"No,—hardly ever. Never thought about it."

"Quite so."

"Too busy or too tired, and under a roof. I used to look at them a lot in the trenches."

"Ah,—you were there too," said Roland, lighting his pipe.

And when he had lit it he got up, stood a moment, smiled at the Sorrells, and tilted his head slightly in the direction of the moat where the water was dappled with gold.

"Think I'll wander down there. They still keep the swans —I suppose?"

"And there are two peacocks, sir."

"In the bishop's garden. I remember. So—like us— they survived the war. Good night."

The Sorrells watched him go down the path to the water, holding himself very square and straight, and yet moving with an air of lightness.

"I like that man," said the boy, "he's—he's——"

Kit searched for some particular word.

"How do you call it, pater, when you feel right up close against someone you've never met before?"

"Sympathy?"

"No, not quite that. I can't get it."

"I think I know what you mean," said his father.

3

On the first floor of the Angel Inn, and at the end of a dark passage there was a little, dim drawing-room, musty and sad, with engravings of Landseer's pictures on the walls, and a Kidderminster carpet on the floor. On the hearth, behind the brass fender, stood a cheap Japanese screen in black and gold, the centre piece between a mock-mahogany coal purdonium on the one hand, and an occasional table on the other. The wallpaper displayed faded pink roses blooming a strangely detached way on a dull grey background. There were a few books on an octagonal table, a Dunlop guide, bound copies of the *Illustrated London News* twenty years old, Tennyson's poems and a Latin grammar. How the Latin grammar had got there—heaven alone knows, but it remained there because no one troubled to remove it. A gilt clock that had not ticked since Queen Victoria died, escaped the dust by standing on the white marble mantelpiece under a glass case. Two bronze gentlemen on horseback, mailed and armed, menaced each other from opposite ends of the mantelpiece. The armchairs were of that bastard breed in which each wooden arm bears an excrescence of padding covered tightly with a material that is reminiscent of a footman's breeches sixty years ago.

People rarely entered this room. The windows remained closed, and it lived shut up in its own dark mustiness. Occasionally some lone woman sat in it, and knitted, and looked at the books and put them back again, but the women who sat in this room had no men attached to them. Any man chancing to open the door, looked in, stared, and, feeling the room's unwedded deadness, fled. No one ever left the door of this room open. They closed it carefully, as though the room's emptiness were best sealed up.

Sorrell was coming down the stairs when he heard strange sounds drifting from the dark passage. There was a piano in the drawing-room and someone was playing it, and playing it extraordinarily well, feelingly, and with a strong, rich touch. Sorrell paused. Music, such music was so unknown in this haphazard house that he felt like a man

in a factory yard who suddenly hears a blackbird singing.
It gave him a moment of exquisite pain. He stood with
quivering throat, .and a sense of strange and deep emotion
stirring in him.

The pianist was playing Chopin. He or she was in the
midst of the First Prelude when Sorrell first paused to listen.
Then came the Berceuse, and after the Étude in A Flat.
Sorrell, leaning against the wall, felt his memories going
back to the days of his youth when he had sat and dreamed
in Queen's Hall. Romance. Those days when he had
imagined——

But who was the pianist? A car with two or three
women in it had arrived an hour ago, and Sorrell had carried
up their luggage, but these ladies had suggested rag-time
rather than Chopin. He felt curious. He approached the
drawing-room door, telling himself that it would be easy
for him to enter the room as though in search of some
visitor. He could wait for an interlude.

Leaning against the wall opposite the door, he let the
surge of those sweet sounds go through him. A pause
came. He was about to slip across the passage when the
door opened.

It was Mr. Roland who opened the door. His face had
a kind of radiance, a happy rapture.

"Hallo!"

Sorrell had straightened up.

"Sorry, sir. I was listening. Was it you?"

"Yes."

The two men looked at each other, and the light on
Thomas Roland's face seemed to have spread to Sorrell's.
They were together for a moment in a transcendental world
of mystic sounds and symbols. And life was drawing them
nearer.

VI

I

THOMAS ROLAND was a man of observation, and yet he was more than a mere observer, and he saw much more than he seemed to see. He registered atmospheres. That was the musical part of him. The practical part of him would sit comfortably in a chair behind a book, and watch without appearing to watch, and his tranquil solidity was so deceptive that his neighbours saw nothing but a man and a book.

His interest in life might be catholic, but it was also fastidious and very quick to seize upon an arrestive figure or an intriguing situation. He had intended staying two days in Staunton, but his two days enlarged themselves into a week.

He was interested in Stephen Sorrell, both as a practical man and as a psychologist, and he became interested in Sorrell's entanglement. When he sat in a corner of the lounge and watched, he could not help being struck by the porter's fanatical activity, his thoroughness, his air of contending with the Augean slovenliness of the Angel Inn. Sorrell was never still. His thin and slightly stooping figure went to and fro, with its dark head, pale face, and intent and rather sorrowful eyes. He appeared to be always looking for things to do; he was for ever clearing out the ash trays on the tables or dusting the tops of the tables, or collecting the scattered papers and magazines and putting them in order. Nor was it mere fussing, or a parade after effect. The man was driven by some urgent spirit within him; also he was reacting against some painful pressure. That was how Thomas Roland understood it.

Then there was the brass-headed woman, the lioness, the creature couched in that den. Roland was puzzled by her attitude towards Sorrell. She was for ever harrying the man, finding some petty excuse for hounding him off on an

53

errand. She spoke to him with a queer, intimate brutality.
She was like a woman with a whip who found an elemental
pleasure in flicking the man with it, tormenting him, as
though just to see how much of it he would stand.

"Stephen, run around to Pavits. The fools have forgotten the fish. You'd better bring it back."

"Get down on your knees, man, and scrub that hall.
It's a disgrace."

"Hallo,—Stephen. No. 7 has been complaining that one
of the mudguards on his car has been buckled. What!
You don't know anything about it? What do you think
you are here for?"

She showed a sly unfairness in her persecution. She
appeared to watch Sorrell's activities, and would then
descend upon him and heckle him for not doing the very
thing that he was always doing. She would sweep out of
her den and discover a match and a cigarette end in one
of the ash-trays.

"Stephen!"

"Yes, madam."

There would be something very like fear in the man's eyes.

"Why don't you empty these ash-trays? I've told you
a dozen times."

"I emptied them ten minutes ago, madam."

"O, don't tell me! Look at that."

Roland wondered why Sorrell stood it. Also, it seemed
to him that the woman's attitude was illogical. If she
pretended to such a passion for detail why did she find
fault with the one member of her staff who did this job
thoroughly? Was it because he was a man, and a man
obviously out of his station? Why didn't she go upstairs
and stimulate the casual energies of the young wenches who
swept the dust under the beds and crammed rubbish behind
the grates? Or why didn't she supervise the cleaning of
the table silver, and discover that one fork out of three had
the remains of some previous meal between its prongs?

For five days Thomas Roland watched this piece of interplay without appearing to watch it. A tacit sympathy had
sprung up between him and the Angel porter; the one
man gave service and gave it with open hands; the other
accepted that service and accepted it as it was given.

Some time after tea on the sixth day when the lounge

happened to be empty, and the lioness had deserted her den, Roland sat and watched Sorrell over the top of a book. Sorrell was on one of his usual rounds, going from table to table, and Roland's eyes studied his long-fingered and intelligent hands. They were very quick and deft, but a little hurried.

He came to Mr. Roland's table, and Roland, putting down his book, looked up at Sorrell.

"What are you doing here?"

"Tidying up, sir."

"No,—I don't mean that."

There was no resentment in Sorrell's questioning stare. He emptied Mr. Roland's ash-tray into the old metal flower-pot he used as a receptacle.

"I have got a boy. You saw him."

"The father for the son instead of the son for the father! I needn't ask you whether you loathe this job."

"It isn't the job, sir. The job's necessary."

"But the place. And yet you stick it. There's a reason."

"Necessity."

Roland moved easily in his chair.

"Look here, Stephen——. What's your other name?"

"Sorrell, sir."

"Rank?"

"Does that matter?"

"I'm a deliberate person. Well, as one man to another——"

"Captain."

"War service,—only?"

"Yes."

"Any decorations?"

"M.C."

"I got nothing but a mention in dispatches. Are you going out to-night?"

"I expect so, sir."

"Well,—let's meet at that elm tree and have a talk. If you could leave your boy at home—for once."

Sorrell stood there looking at the ash-tray that he had emptied. His face was intensely serious. His right hand gripped the lapel of his coat.

"This talk of yours, sir, is it personal?"

"As personal as you please."

"What I mean is—anything—is so—infernally serious to
me—— When one is just hanging on, and out of breath.
Like bad weather.—You are afraid to expect—any sunlight."

The expression of Tom Roland's eyes altered.

"I might depend on what would seem to you to be sunlight. Relatively. Suppose you had to do the same sort
of job, but in different surroundings? Would that be sunlight?"

"Absolutely."

"All right. We meet about half-past eight. This place is
impossible."

                                    2

The astonishing thing was that Mr. Roland kept an
hotel—or rather that he was about to keep an hotel. He
sat under the great elm and explained.

"What did you think I did, man?"

"I hadn't the faintest idea," said Sorrell.

"Nothing—perhaps! I am rather music-mad, and after
the war I could not settle,—just drifted about. But I have
a practical part to my soul, and it began to cry out."

He rested his head against the trunk of the tree. He
looked amused; he was smiling at himself, and to Sorrell,
who had been living in a world that could not smile happily
at itself, this smile was like Tom Roland's music. It took
you into the big, wise heart of the man.

"Knocking about, a dilettante, scribbling songs, with
some sort of idea that I could write an opera. And so I
can. But, my dear chap, the queer way things happen.
The way we react. One day I met a man I most cordially
detest, a fellow who is a financial light—or something.
'Hallo, Roland, still scribbling music?' Well, it set me
off. 'Damn these commercial people,' I thought, 'I'd like
to prove their game is easier than mine.' But—you know
—there was a rightness in what that fellow said. He had
knocked a chip off me. You can get many a good hint from
a man who dislikes you if you are not too pot-bound to
soak it up. I had been getting a little—Londonish—shall
we call it. I took my car out—and went touring, and then
the idea was thrown at me. I had it in my soup; I found

it in my bedroom. These hotel places! I went about wondering if there were half a dozen men in England who
could run a country inn as it might be run. Well, there
seemed to be precious few. And so the idea hit me. 'Why
not run an hotel, just to show yourself that you can do it?
An Etude Pratique instead of too much Chopin.' Well,
that's what I'm doing."

Again, that pleasant, roguish smile, and a match held
meditatively to the bowl of a pipe. A man of few words
as a rule, when the rhythm or verve of a movement took him
Roland would break away into a series of short, sharp
sentences, pithy and vigorous. He described to Sorrell
how, when the idea of managing a country hotel had come
to him, he had set about visualizing the scheme with complete thoroughness.

"That is where we people with any imagination ought to
score over the commercialists. If we have any vision—
surely it should be broader and more far seeing than the
wall-eyed stare of a mere money-maker?"

He told Sorrell how he had spent a whole day studying
maps and distances, for he had realized that the motorist
was the man to be caught and catered for.

"It seemed to me that I ought to fix upon a place on one
of the main roads going south-west, half-way between London and Exeter. I drew a circle round a certain area, and
dotted in the most likely centre for my spider's web. Then
I got in my car and went exploring."

Another match was needed for his pipe, and as he threw it
down he smiled at Sorrell.

"I'm not boring you?"

"Is it likely?"

Roland went on to describe how he had gone in search of
the ideally situated inn, and how he had found it, an old
coaching-house called the Pelican on the main road on the
outskirts of Winstonbury.

"The name took me at once. Pelican! Unusual. And it
was sited just as I wished. A big old red and white place,
part Queen Anne, part Georgian. It stood by itself. It
had an atmosphere. Plenty of room for expansion. Other
advantages too, a good garden and old trees. Our pub-
keepers rarely visualize the atmosphere of a garden. Stuffy
people. Also—the Pelican catches the eye; three or four

hundred yards of straight road on either side of it. Also
—it is within two miles of Hadley school,—parents—you
know. Also, Bargrave House—where all the Americans
go to do homage to the memory of one of their great men,
—two miles off. Then take the road-web for the ordinary
tourist. London some hundred miles; Salisbury thirty or
so, Bath about thirty-two; Cheltenham, the Cotswolds not
so very far away, and Amesbury and Stonehenge. Exeter
right down the road south-west. Gloucester too—and the
Wye valley. Well,—there you are. The Pelican had a
reputation of sorts, clean and rather old-fashioned. I offered
to buy."

He paused as though passing to another line of thought,
and his face grew more serious.

"I am putting nearly all my capital into the show. It is
sink or swim. But—after all—one ought to be ready to
back one's theories. There has to be courage in commerce.
It's an adventure. I am taking the place over in a month.
The end of the season you'll say. Queer time! Well—
no. There are alterations to make, a lot of building.
Meanwhile I'm going to carry on and get things organized
and ready. Then—there is the question of the staff."

Roland had realized the importance of a good "staff."
In fact it was as important as the setting in which it was
to function.

"Difficult these days. But I am being extraordinarily
careful in picking my people. I want character, conscience,
and above all—smiles. I want people who'll take a pride in
their work—and stay with me. I am going to pay good
wages, and house and feed my people well. Besides—if
the thing goes—and we tap the stream on the road—it is
going to be a comfortable and paying proposition for the
staff. Perhaps—sixty bedrooms—the place full each night,
a constant flux, and tips—mind you—from people who are
always coming and going, people who have been well fed
and well looked after. I have got my housekeeper and
cook. Also—the head waitress,—a rattling fine woman.
There are the maids, one of the chief problems. I want
two porters, and I have got one—a head porter. He can't
join me till February."

Again, Roland paused, and his pause was explanatory.

"My one piece of sentiment, this Buck. My first porter.

An ex-sergeant-major. He saved my life out there. I owe him—his chance. He'll get it. The rest depends on—himself."

His mouth and eyes hardened.

"I'm not a fool, Sorrell. You know what the war was, managing men. It is no use being soft. I am not sure of Buck, but he shall have his chance. Now, what about it? I've watched you. I don't know anything about you,—but I do know something of men. If you think my job is better than the one—there."

Sorrell sat very still, with his clasped hands between his knees.

"Wait. I'll tell you my history. I have nothing much to be ashamed of."

He told it.

"That's that. My job—is my job for the boy. It's my centre-board—my sheet-anchor. If you offer me this chance I'll do my best to see that you don't regret it."

"Second porter——?"

"I realize that. I have learnt a lot—there."

Roland smiled.

"At least you have learnt how—not—to do it. But—remember—it's an adventure. I may go under. I want people——"

Sorrell nodded a grave head.

"I understand. You want helpers—not merely employees. I shall be a helper. You have given me—a chance —a chance to get out of hell. I'm grateful."

They gripped hands.

"Gratitude! They say that gratitude is a slave virtue."

"Call it good will, Mr. Roland."

"Ah, that's it,—every time."

3

Sorrell was crossing the Market Square, and he paused by the market cross to look back at the cathedral and its trees. He felt happy, most extraordinarily happy. It was not only the sudden, pleasant human relationship that had opened before him that had cheered him, but the feeling of self-congratulation. The fact that Roland should have

offered him work had given a flick to his self-respect. What
did the nature of the work matter? He was a hotel porter
and he was a success as a hotel porter. He had put a plain
and human back into the job, stuck to it in spite of pain and
weariness and persecution, and someone had come and said
—"You are the man."

He glanced at old Verity's shop and walked on. He
was going to tell the boy, and to say to him—"I have been
offered a better job," and he was immensely and absurdly
proud of it. The afterglow—all yellow above the deep
shadows of the old streets—was the colour of his mood of
exultation. Second porter at the Pelican at Winstonbury!
The Palfrey menage done with. To work for a man for
whom he felt respect and liking, and more than that!

Fletcher's Lane was all shadow, with the pale primrose
and blue of the sky above. He saw a small figure on the
footwalk under the overhang of an old Tudor house, an
attentive and expectant figure. The boy had been waiting
for him as though he knew, or had divined a change in their
fortunes.

"Hallo, son!"

Christopher looked at his father, and it seemed to him
that his father's shoulders were straighter, and the flesh
of his face more firm and clear.

"I have got a better job, Kit. Mr. Roland is opening
a new hotel. We are going there."

The boy's face lit up.

"He asked you to go, pater?"

"Yes."

Christopher snuggled up beside his father.

"He—knows," he said.

And Sorrell smiled.

"Another step nearer—the plan."

VII

I

THE Sorrells marched out of Staunton with drums beating and colours flying, and the little old portmanteau newly bestrapped trundling to the station in a handbarrow.

The Angel had cast them out, for Sorrell had walked into the lion's cage, and given notice.

"I have obtained another situation, madam."

She had stared at him fixedly.

"O, have you! Very well."

"I shall be able to carry on for you until——"

"There is a gap, is there? No,—I don't do things that way. Out you go,—to-night."

She had called him a fool, and he had left her without asking for his money, a piece of fastidiousness which he did not regret. He had packed his belongings, and gone out by the back way, and so to Fletcher's Lane where Mrs. Barter had given him some supper, and he had slept in Kit's bed. In the morning Mr. Roland appeared at the door of No. 13 Fletcher's Lane.

"You left rather suddenly——"

"Well,—I thought it only fair, sir, to tell Mrs. Palfrey. She turned me out."

"What are you going to do?"

"I thought of going to Winstonbury, sir,—and of putting up there till you take over."

"Can you manage?"

"Yes."

Roland did not offer help, and Sorrell did not hint at the fact that he needed it. Yet both men were satisfied, for neither of them desired to cadge or to be cadged from. The relationship between them began on a plane that was above the baser level of employer and employed. The relationship had elements of sensitiveness, delicacy.

Roland produced a card.

"You'll want a bedroom. There is a very decent old soul whom I happen to know. Garland's the name. No. 6 Vine Court, off Baileygate. Wait; I'll write it down. And by the way, go to Bloxom's the tailor in Lombard Street and get measured, and tell him to fit you with the Pelican uniform. He knows about it. I'd better write him a note. Sure you can manage?"

"Quite sure, sir."

"Good. I am going on to-day to Bath. I expect to be in Winstonbury in a week or so."

Sorrell had exactly three pounds, two shillings and four-pence in his pocket, for only three days ago he had bought Christopher a new suit and himself a pair of boots and two new shirts. But his motto for the moment was "I'll manage." He was not going to spoil this new friendship by cadging, for he regarded the relationship as a friendship; he might be at the bottom of the ladder, but the first few rungs of it were made of human stuff. He cherished the human sympathy.

Roland went away satisfied. He was a generous man, and like most generous men he appreciated an independence that did not attempt to exploit his generosity. The world was so full of cadgers, of people who levied blackmail upon those more capable few whom the blackmailers described as "Them as 'ave 'ad all the luck." Roland's interest in Sorrell felt itself justified. Being of a cheerful nature he hated snivellers.

So Christopher and his father got aboard a train, and after two changes, made Winstonbury, that city of new strivings and adventure. They saw the square, grey Norman tower of the Abbey, the clump of beeches on Castle Hill, the soaring spire of St. Faith's Church. The old portmanteau was deposited in the cloak-room, and the Sorrells went in search of Vine Court.

Mrs. Garland opened a green door to them in the narrow face of a queer, beetle-browed red cottage. Sorrell showed her Roland's card. She had to fetch her spectacles to read it. They were round like her face, which was of a high-cheeked rotundity, and with a spry little nose cocked in the middle of it. Her head was as neat as the head of a Dutch doll.

"Step inside."

Yes, she could lodge and feed them, and Mr. Roland's recommendation was good enough. Sorrell sent Kit outside, while he spoke frankly and honestly to Mrs. Garland.

"The fact is I don't take up my new job for three weeks or so, and I have about two pounds in hand. It is only fair to tell you this, but I promise you you will be paid. I will hand over the two pounds to you and just keep the odd shillings."

Mrs. Garland looked at him round-eyed. She had not seen a great deal of the world, but it seemed to her that Sorrell was an unusual sort of hotel-porter. He spoke like a gentleman, a real gentleman; the distinction was important.

"I dare say I could manage your food on that. The room will be five shillings a week, and two shillings for attendance. So, at the end of three weeks——"

"I should owe you twenty-one shillings."

"That's so."

"And by the way,—I shall have to board my boy out. He has no mother; he's not a noisy youngster, or selfish. Do you think you might be able to manage him? I shall be able to pay you well when I get settled at the Pelican."

"I might," said the old lady, "there is only me and my daughter in the house. She's a waitress at the Pelican, but she sleeps at home. Mr. Roland has engaged her. She's to be head waitress."

"I have heard about her," said Sorrell.

"Have you now?"

"Mr. Roland seems to think a good deal of her."

"Fanny's a good girl. Well, would you like to look at the room?"

"I should. I'm sure we shan't give you much trouble."

They called Kit in and went up a narrow pair of stairs into a little, low, pleasant room, the casement window of which opened on a garden. The floor undulated, and a beam divided the ceiling into two equal parts. The furniture was genuine cottage furniture, rarely seen outside a curio shop; it was all old, save the bed, which was a plain, black iron concern. The window had white curtains, and the white quilt on the bed was the colour of swansdown.

The little room had an atmosphere of its own, a quaint

and simple spirituality that was so different from the casual
"take it or leave it" air of the rooms of the Angel Hotel
that Sorrell felt touched, though why a cottage bedroom
should have touched him he was not able to say. Christopher had gone at once to the window and was looking down
into the garden.

"There's an apple tree, pater."

"So there is."

Mrs. Garland gave a tweak to one of the white curtains. The apple tree was a Blenheim, and full of pale gold
fruit, each with a blush of redness on the side towards the
sun.

"My man planted that tree. It's a Blenheim Orange.
Well,—young gentleman, you didn't take long to find it."

Christopher turned and looked at her. Mrs. Garland's
tone had accused him of a desire to get up that tree, whereas
Kit had been struck by the beauty of it, and had been guilt-
less of elemental greed.

"They are quite safe with me, Mrs. Garland."

"Oh,—are they,—my dear! Well,—I don't mind one or
two, so long as you don't break the branches."

"But I mean what I say, Mrs. Garland."

"Bless us,—I believe you do."

Sorrell agreed to rent the room. He said that he was
pleased with it, and taking out his wallet he handed Mrs.
Garland his two pound notes. She made as though to give
them back to him, but Sorrell asked her to keep them.

"Well,—just as you please. You can take your meals
in my kitchen, if that will suit you. It will save me trouble."

"Thank you very much," said Sorrell.

Thereupon he and Christopher went back to the station
to fetch the portmanteau, which Sorrell prepared to hoist
upon his shoulder. Their possessions did not weigh much,
and as Sorrell put it to his son—"I'm getting used to
luggage." Christopher, however, was himself as a partner
in the adventure, and insisted on helping his father with
the portmaneau, and they returned to Vine Court carrying
it between them.

Mrs. Garland gave them eggs and bacon for tea; in
fact the three of them sat down together, amalgamating
very happily in the kitchen, the window of which showed
the apple tree lit up by the afternoon sunlight.

2

After tea came the event towards which all the other events of the day had been tending, an exploration of their new world, of this Darien with the Pacific of the unknown beyond it, and floating upon the edge of the unknown Mr. Roland's "Treasure Island"—the Pelican Inn.

It was Christopher who thought of it as "Treasure Island," and the symbolized nature of the conception was very evident to his father. In the train from Staunton they had had a carriage to themselves, and Sorrell, as though inspired by the hum of the wheels, had talked much of the future. He had been very frank with the boy. He had told him that he regarded the future as Christopher's, and that the Pelican was a place in which he meant to dig for treasure, and to gather money for Kit's education.

"You must have your weapon, Kit. It is no use being able to do nothing but sit on a stool and scribble figures. The thing is to have some sort of knowledge, and a craft which other people can't get on without. Then you are a master. The world has to come and ask you to do something for it. You must be a necessity, not a mere fellow who opens and shuts doors."

Christopher understood much of this but vaguely, but he did understand the nature of his father's sacrifice.

"I am carrying other people's luggage up and down stairs, Kit, in order that your job may be a better one. That's my ambition,—my goal."

And Kit, in the quiet sturdiness of his young and growing consciousness, had begun to realize what manner of man his father was.

The Pelican first showed itself to the Sorrells some three hundred yards beyond the red brick Unitarian church at the end of Lombard Street as something that glittered beside a great mound of trees. The something that glittered proved to be an immense, old-fashioned sign suspended across the road on an overhead beam that was supported by two huge oak posts. Here was the Pelican—that Bird of piety—glittering for all the world that passed along the road to see, men who went west, and men who went east. Yes, assuredly, Mr. Roland was no fool. The very road itself here had a spaciousness, and the inn—all red and

white—with a group of magnificent trees behind it,—looked
south over meadowland to the hills beyond. Winstonbury
had not splurged in that direction; there were no prawn-
coloured villas or post-war bungalows to spoil the English
landscape. Moreover, Tom Roland had bought the land on
the other side of the road.

Sorrell and his son stood under an immense chestnut
tree and absorbed the scene. The leaves of the chestnut
were crisped with gold. A clipped holly hedge met the red
angle of the building, giving place later to white posts and
chains. The building itself was in the shape of an L, and
the space between the links of the letter formed a species
of court or space, partly flagged and partly gravelled. A
white cornice topped the rise of the red walls, and there
were dormers in the roof above it, also a copper cupola
with a bell. A part of the building draped itself with
wistaria and clematis. The main entry had a hooded porch
with tall, white pillars. A clipped yew, surrounded by a
bright border of flowers and a small, well-mown lawn, broke
the open space between the road and the building.

Sorrell saw the beauty of it, for the old inn had a
presence, tranquillity. It was like a stately and gracious
old lady who could smile on the new age and understand
it, and impose upon the new age's restlessness a measure
of her own tranquillity. Several cars stood on the broad
space behind the posts and chains. Voices came from beyond the holly hedge, but they were not unpleasant voices.
Green and white curtains fluttered at the windows, and the
crisping leaves of the chestnut dappled the road.

"Mr. Roland's no fool," said Sorrell.

Strolling on, he saw the further possibilities of the place,
and he pointed them out to Christopher. The Pelican had
immense old stables, solidly built, and easily to be absorbed
into the inn. They were being used as a garage, but Sorrell
imagined that Mr. Roland would lay a jealous hand on all
that Georgian brickwork. There was plenty of room for
the erection of an up-to-date garage beyond the stables
where the noise of the cars would be less troublesome.
Sorrell and Christopher strolled into the yard, and beyond
it they had a glimpse of a kitchen garden and an orchard,
and of a couple of old walnut trees growing in the centre
of a little paddock.

Christopher—the boy—had no doubts as to the future of the Pelican. The place had romance. You could imagine yourself leaning out of one of those little dormer windows, and watching people coming and going. The broad road suggested adventure. There were fields and woods, and the hills in the distance. And wild life, rabbits, birds,—perhaps a river where you could fish!

He glowed.

"It's a lovely place, pater."

"I think it is. The old Pelican will cast a persuasive eye on people. And Roland? Some people seem to change one's luck."

Returning they had a view of Winstonbury against the sunset, the beeches and the castle mound looking like a huge plumed sable helmet. The spire of the church had a trailing crimson oriflamme attached to it, and all about the town the country lay a bluish green.

"I like this place," said Kit, "and I like Mrs. Garland and our bedroom. Weren't the bacon and eggs good, pater?"

"Very, my son," but Sorrell was thinking of other things.

3

During the next seven days Sorrell and Christopher began to know Winstonbury very thoroughly. They had a feeling that it belonged to them, that it was theirs, with the wise old Pelican keeping watch upon it. They explored every corner of the town. It was a place of pleasant sounding old names, richly English, and romantic. It smelt of history, and of the old life before commercialism invented galvanized iron and gas-works. The names of the streets fascinated Christopher: Green End; Lombard Street; Baileygate; Golden Hill; the Tything; Market Row; Vine Court; Barbican; Angel Alley.

On the second day Sorrell walked into Mr. Bloxom's shop in Lombard Street, and was measured for his Pelican uniform, a neat dark blue jacket with light blue lapels and brass buttons, and dark blue trousers. Mr. Bloxom was polite to Sorrell. A porter at a prosperous hotel was a person to be considered.

"Your Mr. Roland is going to make the Pelican hum, I hear?"

Sorrell did not know the exact noise that a pelican made, but he did not think that it was a humming bird.

"Mr. Roland's a man of ideas."

"Ha!" said Mr Bloxom, "we are rather conservative down this way. How will that feel under the arms? Don't want it too tight, do you, for handling luggage and things."

"I think this coat of mine is about right."

He found Mr. Bloxom examining the tailor's mark inside the collar of his blue serge coat. That suit had been a post-war extravagance.

"Ponds. H'm, good people. I suppose——"

Mr. Bloxom did not complete the sentence—but Sorrell read what was in his mind. He supposed that Sorrell had been a valet or porter at some flats, and that the suit had been passed on to him by some member of the aristocracy, moneyed or otherwise.

The castle mound became a favourite haunt of the Sorrells. There were seats under the beech trees, but Kit and his father preferred the turf. Winstonbury lay below them in crowded picturesqueness, and Kit played a game of his own with the town, treating it as a sort of jig-saw puzzle. He began to know all the more prominent buildings, and he could tell exactly where Vine Court lay beyond the little grey bell-turret of the Grammar School.

Castle Hill was more than a view point. It formed a height from which the two Sorrells looked out and down upon the immediate future, Kit's future. There was the problem of his schooling. Was it to be the old Grammar School of Henry the Eight's founding, planted in an old house of the Carmelites, or the town school, visible from Castle Hill, and lying near the gas-works, an ugly barrack of a place built of yellow brick, surrounded by an asphalted playground and iron railings?

"No humbug, Kit," said his father; "there is going to be no humbug between us. Firstly, it's a question of money. I dare say I shall be able to afford the fees later on. At the Grammar School you would find yourself with the sons of local tradesmen, clerks and farmers. You would learn a little Latin, some mathematics, less history, and perhaps a smattering of science. Not much real use in life. You would get games. Now, at the town school,—a lot of cheap rubbish——. It's a bit of a problem."

Christopher betrayed a preference for the Grammar School. It was a question of æsthetics, of boyish fastidiousness, for at the Grammar School you had a beautiful old building, the boys looked clean and wore a neat apple-green school cap. Kit did not want to go to school near the gas-works, and play hobbledehoy games in an asphalted yard.

"I'd get cricket, pater, and footer."

"You would. But there is one thing that we must face. You would be the son of a porter at the Pelican. They might refuse to take you. That's my fault, not yours."

Kit was silent.

"And boys can be terrible snobs. I shouldn't like to think——"

"It seems rather silly, pater, that a chap should be obliged to go to school."

"Compulsory stuffing."

"Most chaps don't want to be stuffed. A fellow is ready enough for his grub,—but when it comes to lessons——. Seems to me there is something wrong, pater."

"How?"

"Well,—if the stuff they taught you at school was like your dinner——. So that you wanted to swallow it—Hungry for it. There are all sorts of things to interest a fellow,—but you don't get them at school. It's such tosh, pater."

"I suppose it is. I was six years at a public school, and I don't think I learnt anything that was of much use to me afterwards. They call it 'forming your mind'—character building."

"But couldn't one's mind grow, pater, of itself? Scrambling about among interesting things?"

"What interests you, Kit?"

"O,—birds, and the country, and cricket, and all that."

"Not books? Be honest."

"Not school books, pater."

Sorrell felt challenged. He knew that he had loathed school books just as Kit loathed them, but then the conventions of civilization demanded that a boy should be stuffed with facts that bored him.

"Well, if you are not keen, what is the use?—still, you have got to learn to hold your own with other chaps. And some day, my son, you will have to make up your mind what you want to be. And most things that are worth doing mean education—of a kind."

"I shall work, pater."

"But why——?"

"Because—you will be paying."

Sorrell clasped him across the shoulders.

"A sense of duty? Is that it?"

"No,—something more, pater. Because I know you are keen for me to learn——. O, you know why."

"I think I do, my son."

They had many more talks on the same subject, and Sorrell confessed that his own particular ambition was to send Kit to a good preparatory school, and after that to a public one. At least—that was his plan for the moment. He might change it. All academic education had its disadvantages. He explained them to Kit.

Also, there would have to be an element of concealment. It could not be known that Sorrell was the son of an hotel porter.

"You would have to apologize for your father, Kit. Or —if it were found out they might ask me to remove you. Well, we'll see. I'll ask Mr. Roland about it."

But the decision was taken by Christopher himself. He announced it after three days of solemn heart searchings.

"I'll go to the town school, pater."

"Why?"

"Must I tell you?"

"Not if you don't want to."

"I'm not going to a place—where——."

He flushed and grew suddenly inarticulate, and Sorrell understood. It was not that Kit was ashamed of his father, —but he was not going to apologize for him to other boys, or to join in a concealment. That would be humbug.

"I shouldn't have to stay there—very long. I'm nearly twelve, pater. And then—after that—I should be free to learn what I wanted to learn."

"I'm not sure that you haven't got it," said his father.

4

Mr. Roland turned up one day without any warning. The Sorrells, returning frome one of their councils of state upon Castle Hill, found the red car standing outside the entrance to Vine Court. Roland himself was sitting in Mrs. Garland's parlour, and Mrs. Garland was telling him about the Sorrells and how she had agreed to board the boy.

"Oh, he has arranged that, has he?"

"Yes, sir."

Roland felt relieved. He had made up his mind to show no favouritism, and he had half expected Sorrell to ask him to allow Christopher to live with him at the Pelican. Sorrell's decision had saved him the effort of a refusal, for Roland knew that his own particular weakness was a too sensitive good-nature.

"Well, my lad, getting ready to go to school?"

He held Kit by the arm.

"I am going to the council school, sir."

"You are? And I hear you have been up Mrs. Garland's apple tree."

"Only once, sir. And she knew about it."

Kit's three elders laughed, and he wondered why.

Mr. Roland was staying at the Pelican, and he took Sorrell back with him to show him over the hotel, and in the hotel garden as they were passing through an archway in one of the yew hedges Roland paused with a question.

"That boy of yours? What's your idea?"

"In what way, sir?"

"About the school?"

"The town school. He decided it himself. I had thought of trying the Grammar School,—but I think the boy realized——."

"Did he?"

"We agreed on our motto: no humbug. He won't have to apologize for me—at the town school."

"I don't look at it in that way, but the boy's right. I rather envy you, Sorrell."

"He is the only thing I have got, sir."

They walked on, and Roland stopped to look at an old

mulberry tree the trunk of which had had to be trussed up
with a chain.

"Don't push him too much."

"I know what you mean."

"Education; damned rot—most of it. The healthy young
idlers often do best in the end. They don't get all their
individuality compressed into a mould. If I had a boy——"

He smiled at Sorrell.

"We bachelors and spinsters——! Well, we do see something of the game. I'd let my boy play hard; I'd have him
taught to box; I wouldn't have him crammed. Natural
growth. Later I should give him the best tutor who was
to be had."

"And what about his career?"

"Leave it to his natural appetite. In a clean, straight
boy who has been treated healthily the appetite is bound to
develop. Surely? And then let him go ahead. Tell him
to go ahead like blazes."

So, the autumn came and Christopher went to school, and
Sorrell, in his blue coat with the brass buttons, began to
carry luggage up and down the stairs of the Pelican. He
carried it more easily than he had carried it up the stairs
of the Angel Inn at Staunton, for his heart was lighter.
The new world was a beneficent world because of the man
who ruled it. And Sorrell, piling logs and coal upon the fire
in the hall, felt the glow and the cheerfulness of it. In the
garden the old trees were magnificently coloured, and the
vivid grass was flaked with gold.

One of Sorrell's most pleasant memories was of walking
in the garden just as the sun was setting at the end of a
still October day. Robins were singing, and from the window of a sitting-room came the sound of music. Roland
was playing Chopin's First Prelude. The slanting sun
poured through the trees. The robins sang.

VIII

I

THERE followed a winter of strenuous preparation. The tourist traffic upon the road had dwindled to a very casual stream, and the Pelican,—during the process of putting on a new plumage, was glad of the respite. As Sorrell had foreseen, Mr. Roland was laying jealous hands upon the Georgian stables and joining them to the main building, and the transformation gave him ten more bedrooms and accommodation for the staff. A new garage was being built, and two tennis courts and a croquet lawn were to be laid out in the little paddock.

Roland had his own particular ideas. One of his first measures was to eliminate the public bar, and to add the space thus gained to the lounge. He decreed that commercial travellers—as such—were not to be accommodated, and the old commercial room became the card and smoking room. The whole place was to be redecorated, and much of it refurnished and recarpeted, and the various colour schemes were of Roland's own planning. He believed in any number of comfortable chairs, and in atmosphere of rich and pleasant simplicity. The china was to be of a plain white biscuit with a dark blue and gold border. The bedrooms were black, white and orange, or white and cerise. He used soft blues and greens with touches of purple and old rose in the living-rooms. All ugly and wasteful furniture was got rid of. Two new bathrooms were installed, and a small library arranged on one side of the hotel office.

One of Roland's most practical innovations was his attitude towards the "staff." He treated the principal members as fellow workers; he challenged their co-operation, and stimulated their keenness. There were queer, patriarchal little meetings in his sitting-room—"My Soviet" he called it laughingly. The committee consisted of Mrs. Marks the housekeeper, Fanny Garland the head waitress, Mrs. Lovibond the cook, Sorrell, and Bowden the gardener. To them Mr. Roland was a figure of encouraging and deliberate frankness. "This is our show. I take it that we are all keen on making a success of our show. We are all going to benefit by it. Suggestions. That's what I want from you. Anything to improve the efficiency or the comfort, or to wash out unnecessary work. My idea is to make the Pelican the most famous roadside inn on the south of the Thames. 'Where to stay?' 'Why,—the Pelican at Winstonbury. No other place to touch it.' "

Within a month he had the whole staff in his pocket. He had extraordinary powers of persuasion; it was the pull of his personality,—his air of calm and deliberate kindness, his assuming the other person to be as interested and as efficient as he was. He never fussed. He had one of those peculiarly pleasant and consoling voices.

The women ran about for him like happy slaves. He treated them all as though they were gentlewomen, and if they did not say it to each other they thought him a very great gentleman.

Mrs. Marks, that little dark woman, silently gliding everywhere, would look at him with the eyes of an intelligent little dog.

Fanny Garland, cheery and big and blonde, spread an atmosphere of smiling efficiency, using a brisk and philosophical tongue.

"A dirty fork's no use to anybody. Doesn't it make you feel all nice inside to see twenty white and glittering tables all laid and to know that there isn't a spot to be ashamed of anywhere? If the job's worth doing——! Yes, and think of the tips, my dears!"

Bowden the gardener, rather a surly person, thawed gradually like the soil on a sunny morning after a frost. He found that Roland was providing him with a strong lad upon whom he could exercise a tongue and a passion for dour thoroughness.

"The idea is, Bowden, that we should be self-supporting as to vegetables."

"We ain't got the ground, sir."

"Well,—you shall have it. I am going to have the market value of all the vegetables sent in—checked. And you will get a percentage on results."

And Bowden's broad and rather Simian back was bent urgently over his spade.

To Sorrell those winter months were full of a steady encouragement. He had good food and a clean bed; he was not overworked; and Kit was happy with Mrs. Garland, and not too unhappy at the town school. Moreover, his job interested him; he was working for a man who was keen on detail and who appreciated thoroughness. Also, the human relationship seemed to matter more and more, and Thomas Roland and his second porter reached a pleasant and solid understanding. Roland talked to Sorrell more than he talked to any of the others, and always it seemed to Sorrell that their words went below the surface into the human realities beneath.

"After all," as Roland said, "a man must have a job, and it is the job that matters. Not so much what it is,— but how a man does it. That's how it strikes me."

He made Sorrell feel that he respected him and the work he did.

"An objective, sir."

"Of course. The nice people who want to flatten out all the social hills and bring us all down to a sort of board-school playground! No good."

The work went on, the internal economy of the Pelican being so arranged that the casual few upon the road could be accommodated while the alterations were being carried out.

Roland was spending a great deal of money, and Sorrell appreciated the effect that was being produced. Those sumptuously pleasant rooms, the great chairs and richly coloured rugs, the clean paint and paper, those rows of pleasant bedrooms all so fresh and cosy, the sleekness of the garden, the beautiful cleanness of the freshly appointed kitchen, the bathrooms and pantries—white tiled and white enamelled, the linen, the table silver, the hundred and one nice details!

But was the Pelican going to pay? Had not Roland the musician and artist overwhelmed Roland the hotel keeper?

The problem worried Sorrell not a little. He had begun to identify himself so thoroughly with the Pelican and all that the Pelican stood for——.

He was surprised when Thomas Roland showed him that he had divined his anxiety.

"You think I am overdoing it?"

"I don't know, sir."

For Roland had found Sorrell economizing coal and electric current. He would go about switching off unnecessary lights.

"I am all in on this adventure. Either we touch port—or we founder. I am going to give people the best—the best I have in me. I wouldn't give them shoddy music——. The pride of the craftsman."

Sorrell stood looking at the fire upon which he had been carefully banking a scoopful of "ovoids." His small but intelligent head was bent, and its darkness caught the firelight. His seriousness was a friend's tribute.

"One always likes to believe, sir, that if we give the best that is in us——."

"I do believe it——. After all—it should matter to us most. If the best doesn't pay, it is not our fault."

"All people are not as generous, sir."

"I'm not generous, man. The fact is I can't bring myself to do a thing meanly. Even the fitting up and the running of an hotel——. Still, I appreciate it——."

Their eyes met.

"Scientific fire building, Stephen!"

He smiled.

"Do you do it because you have a conscience?"

"Partly. There's another reason."

"I think I know it. You and I are mixed up together—somehow, heart and pocket. Well,—I would not have it otherwise."

2

The other problem that worried Sorrell was the inevitable advent of George Buck.

The ex-sergeant-major seemed to project a menacing adumbration, and to Sorrell he suggested the blond beast dominant, something hectoring and elephantine.

Buck!

He did not like the name; it was both too male and too American. He agreed that it was absurd of him to worry

about the fellow, and yet he would catch himself at all sorts
of moments creating a shadowy image of the prospective
head-porter. What was the man like? Would Buck be a
big, muscular creature, all belly, voice, and blond moustache? Would he order him about?

Sorrell began to dislike the man weeks before he had
ever seen him, and his dislike was instinctive and natural.
George Buck was a possible menace to his security; he
might prove a destroyer of the pleasant and calm activity
that Sorrell had begun to associate with the Pelican Inn.
He might interfere with the nice little efficiencies that the
second porter was evolving. Moreover, he might pocket a
sergeant-majorly share of the tips.

Sorrell was doing quite well in tips, in spite of enforced
quietness of these months of transfiguration. He was saving
money fast; he had a Post Office savings book.

But his prophetic hostility to George Buck was not only
the hostility of a dog with a bone towards the bigger dog
who was to share it. It was as though Sorrell had a pre-
monition, a sensitive fore-feeling of what the man's presence
would mean in the lounge and the luggage-room, and on
the stairs and in the staff's quarters. Buck cast a shadow,
a shadow as of something huge and menacing and hairy.
Even the flicker of a fire at twilight throwing shadows about
the lounge brought on this mood of depression and restlessness. Or a blustering wind at night. Sorrell fought against
it. The thing was becoming an obsession, a clawing monkey
at the back of his mind.

About a week before the head-porter's arrival Sorrell
compelled himself to speak to Roland.

"I suppose, sir, that when Buck comes—I shall have to
take orders——?"

Roland was at the piano, and Sorrell had come in with a
fresh supply of coal.

"Yes,—just a word. I told you——. Buck will be responsible. That's only fair, Stephen."

"Quite fair, sir."

"He's not a bad sort of chap. Though, of course, I
only knew him as a sergeant-major. I want him to have
his chance."

Sorrell had a feeling that Tom Roland was maintaining
certain mental reservations with regard to Buck. He did

not quite know his man. There was an obligation, or what Roland conceived to be an obligation, and Sorrell found wisdom in reticence.

"I will do all I can to help him, sir."

"I'm sure you will. So far as I am concerned, Stephen, a man makes good or cuts his own throat. I observe things."

He began to play a piece of Debussy's, and Sorrell, after putting coal on the fire with careful noiselessness, went softly out of the room.

"Do your job and hang on," he thought. "Whatever that other man is he is not going to make me cut my own throat."

3

Ex-Sergeant-Major Buck arrived at the Pelican in the station bus. He wore a bowler hat and a blue overcoat with a velvet collar, and he travelled with a solid leather suitcase and a steamer trunk.

Sorrell had gone out to meet the bus, and he stood momentarily staring, watching an immense blue back emerging from the bus doorway. The figure separated itself, and turning showed a face that was like an uncooked round of beef, with two blue pebbles for eyes.

"Catch hold, my lad."

The man was holding out his suit case, and Sorrell, coming suddenly out of his trance, took the suit case.

"Are you Mr. Buck?"

"I am. Suppose you're the chap—under me."

Sorrell nodded. He was conscious of a sort of nausea. "Under me!" Yes, it seemed to him that those two words exactly expressed the situation. The man was all that his fears had pictured him to be, the big, raw-faced creature, all belly, voice, and blond moustache.

"You might fetch that trunk down."

"All right."

Buck's eyes rested on him consideringly for a moment, for he had divined in Sorrell something of that sulkiness that the private soldier's hatred had struggled to express without daring actual utterance. For Buck was less heavy in the uptake than he looked. "Dumb saucy! You are that sort, are you? We'll see about it!" And then Thomas Roland appeared, and Buck clicked the heels of his brown boots and gave a guardsman's salute, his big hand quivering.

"Come to report, sir."

Roland was smiling. He held out a hand.

"I'm glad to see you. Quite like old times, Buck. We have another ex-service man here in Sorrell."

Sorrell was struggling with the ex-sergeant-major's trunk, and loathing it as he had never loathed any other piece of luggage. He was aware of Buck watching him.

"Can you manage it?"

"Yes, thanks."

"You don't look as though you could," said the blue eyes. "Weedy sort of chap."

He went in with Mr. Roland.

4

During the winter months Sorrell had had time to make the acquaintance of a number of books, for Roland's sitting-room was full of them and he had allowed Sorrell to borrow. Sorrell's reading was various. It included Shaw, Edward Carpenter, Maurice Hewlett, the local history of Winstonbury and its surroundings, and the Michelin Guide. He kept a note-book. In it he had jotted down the distances between Winstonbury and all the places of note within a hundred miles of the town. He knew all the inns. He would go to the garage daily and extract from the chauffeurs any information as to the state of the different roads.

For, if a touring owner-driver appealed to him for information Sorrell felt a pleasing sense of efficiency when he was able to reel off the necessary facts.

"Quendon, sir? Forty-three miles. Forty-seven if you go by Langton. The Langton road is in better condition. On the other road they are laying a new water-main at Foxley."

Or——

"Holmdale House, sir? Open every Thursday from ten till twelve. You present a card at the lodge. The Italian gardens and the Vandyks are worth seeing. But—of course you know that, sir."

Somewhere in one of Mr. Roland's books he had read
that with the subtilizing of consciousness the field of man's
eternal struggle had changed. The contest had ceased to
be physical and had become mental, psychical. Man no
longer contended with external forces and with other men;
the struggle was with himself.

He agreed, and he disagreed.

It seemed to him that in his own case the struggle was
a double one. He had to fight himself, that more primitive
part of himself that wanted to break out into rages, to
despair, to grow moody or cynical, or to run for comfort to
some woman. On the other hand his battle with the
physical and natural forces was only too real. There was
luggage, and there was ex-Sergeant-Major Buck.

There was tacit war between them from the beginning.

It was most natural.

Each saw in the other a complete representation of all
that was disliked, a collection of characteristics that caused
the opposing prejudices to bristle. Sorrell was a brain,
Buck a voice. One man's objective lay twenty years ahead;
the other's was immediate and physical, the satisfying of
the grosser appetites. Their contrasts did not attract; they
repelled.

The struggle began at once, though there was no apparent struggle, for Buck, like many men of his type, had
a good deal of cunning. He could truckle. He went about
with an air of bluff cheeriness.

"Now then—my lad——."

He took control on the very first day. There was to be
no doubt as to who was head-porter and who was second.
His bulk rolled briskly about the place. In the army he
had learned how to convey an impression of immense activity, while in reality he did nothing. He used his voice on
the others.

He began by being genial to Sorrell, but his geniality
was contemptuous, and intended to be contemptuous.
There was shrewd malice in the blue eyes.

For to Buck, Sorrell was a type, the type of the over-
educated, sly, argumentative, sullen, weedy, mutinous re-
cruit. A clever, circuitous, insolent devil. Uncomfortably
quick too, a fellow who needed watching.

If Sorrell found Buck's self-confident bluster offensive,

his own quietness and his reticences were equally offensive
to the other man.

Buck had his own justifications.

"Nasty,—weedy,—supercilious chap. Ex-officer. I'll
teach him a thing or two. Jealous of me. Of course. He'll
need watching. He's not the sort of man I want under me,
no, not by a long chalk. Some big, good-natured chap,
quick with the luggage, and not too quick with anything
else. Well,—I think I know a thing or two."

At the back of his mind was the wish to get rid of Sorrell.
He realized that in spite of the other man's weediness he
was a competitor who was to be respected.

5

In the little room where Sorrell used to clean the boots
and brush the clothes there was a window overlooking the
garden, and here Sorrell had been in the habit of reading
when there was nothing else that needed doing. He had an
old Windsor armchair by the window, and Mrs. Marks had
given him an old red cushion. She liked Sorrell better than
he knew. And through the window he could glance from
his book to the old trees, or at the yew hedges beyond the
lane, or at the bulbs spearing up in the borders, or at clumps
of purple and yellow crocuses.

He was looking out of this window one afternoon, with
his book, one of Galsworthy's plays, lying folded over his
knee, when he was surprised by a voice.

"You—seem—pretty active—Sorr'l."

That was one of the many petty details that annoyed
Sorrell. Buck pronounced his name—abbreviating it—so
that it sounded like "saul." He had not heard Buck come
to the door. The big man could be very soft on his feet.

"Quite" was all that Sorrell said.

Buck came into the little room, his bulk seeming to fill
it. He had the air of a righteous overseer. Seeing the book
he reached for it deliberately, and picked it off Sorrell's
knee.

"Doing a bit of reading. Well,—this sort of stuff is no
use to a man. Don't you think, my lad, that you might find
something better to do?"

Sorrell sat still,—but he was quivering.

"Perhaps you'll suggest a job."

Buck threw the book on the window-sill.

"Look here, don't let there be any doubt about it. I'm responsible here. And I'm going to do my job, see. I've got the 'Skipper's' interests in my mind. He's a sport——"

The implication was obvious, but Sorrell kept his temper. He was not going to uncover himself to this big creature.

"I agree. But this is one of Mr. Roland's books."

"Did he lend it you?"

"Yes."

Buck nodded a sage head.

"He's one of the easy sort. That makes it a bit more obvious, don't it? You look about and get busy. I don't blab,—but I use my eyes. You get busy."

IX

I

SORRELL realized that he had changed his animal, that was all. At Staunton he had had to contend with a lioness; at Winstonbury his enemy was a bull.

The lioness had been hated, but the bull was popular. He was a playful and genial beast. He took the head of the table in the staff's room; he teased the women and made eyes at them; he was always in evidence when being in evidence was worth while.

He went about with the air of carrying the whole establishment on his shoulders. He was excessively polite to all visitors, especially to the women. He delighted in the sound of his own voice.

By the female members of the staff he was spoken of always as "Mr. Buck." No doubt he was a very fine figure of a man, and it astonished Sorrell to find how popular he was. The average wench asks for so much and so little.

Yet Buck seemed to fill his position, and to be a convincing figure in the picture. He looked well in his uniform; he had a presence; he could be impressive. He met people coming in from their cars as though they were royal persons and he a Lord Mayor.

"Allow me, madam. Rooms, yes. Will you speak to the lady in the office. I'll have the luggage brought in. Saul, —luggage."

Buck would wait for the number of the room to be announced.

"Number seven, madam. First floor. Turn to the right at the top of the stairs. The luggage shall be sent up at once."

His voice would change.

"Saul,—luggage number seven. At once."

That was just it. He was efficient and polite and impressive, but he used Sorrell's narrower shoulders and frailer

83

back. If he got hold of anything it was a woman's hand-
bag, or her camera, or an armful of rugs and umbrellas.
He left the heavy luggage to Sorrell, and with complete
complacency, as though it was the under-porter's business
to act as baggage animal. Which, no doubt, it was, but
not to the extent of breaking the poor devil's heart and back.
Sorrell struggled and said nothing. Vaguely at first, but
more definitely later, he realized that this was part of the
struggle. Buck was playing a sergeant-major's game well
known to all Tommies, he was putting upon a man though
with every appearance of proper authority; either the man
would break and become humble, or fly out and betray
himself. In the latter case—"Sorry to have to report, sir,"
an orderly-room manner, and the Skipper persuaded it was
necessary to enforce discipline.

"Damn him," thought Sorrell; "I'll play his game—and
make it mine."

He changed none of his ways. He was as indefatigable
as ever, or as much as Buck would allow him to be.

"Don't go fussing about so much, man. People don't
always want you stepping over their feet."

And Mr. Roland? Sorrell wondered whether Thomas
Roland had noticed anything, whether he was ever dimly
aware of this obscure scuffle between two unimportant
porters. Why should he notice anything? Most men, so
full of their own affairs, are apt to regard with impatience
the silly disharmonies that seem no more than unnecessary
grit in the machine.

Sorrell was seeing less of Thomas Roland. Buck had
managed to insinuate himself into Mr. Roland's sitting-
room, for he was the responsible man. And his extrusion of
Sorrell was done with a bluff and genial neatness. For such
a big thing he was remarkably smooth and agile.

Moreover there was the matter of largesse. Most of the
departures took place after breakfast and while Sorrell was
labouring on the stairs with the luggage, Buck, like the
senior partner in the firm, would be attending to the social
amenities, helping ladies into their cars, arranging hand
baggage, spreading rugs. Sorrell would arrive with the
heavy luggage for a particular car, but Buck would not
allow him to remain there.

"Number thirteen—Saul. Look sharp. I'll see to this."

So, Sorrell would be sent for more luggage, while Buck gracefully loaded that which had arrived, and took the tip or tips.

"What about the chap who carried the luggage down?"

If that question were asked Buck would have his answer ready.

"You can give it to me, sir. We pool our tips."

Needless to say Sorrell never saw that shilling or florin, and since Buck so contrived it that Sorrell was always fetching and carrying while he remained at the receipt of custom, Sorrell's pocket suffered very considerably. He had been making a pound or so a week in tips even in the slack season, and the drop in his revenue was serious.

He took the matter up with Buck.

"We ought to have some arrangement."

"What d'you mean?"

"Well,—I seem to miss most of the tips."

"That's not my fault, my lad. If people don't pass it over to you—there must be a reason."

"I expect there is," said Sorrell grimly.

"I'll tell it you. A sulky face doesn't fetch out the silver——."

"They pool their tips in the dining-room, and upstairs."

Buck trampled with loud dignity upon such a suggestion.

"Think—I—pool—with the chap under me? Not likely. I've worked for my position. I don't share out,—with the boot-boy."

And Sorrell left it at that, though he felt bitter.

For he had arrived at one of those periods of loneliness when he felt that the other humans about him had ceased to regard him as a distinct personality, though the impression was due to the fall in the level of his self-respect. He was eclipsed, and by the sort of man whom he hated and despised. His sense of failure returned. He was repressing himself, going about with a frown, and an air of melancholy self-absorption. There were no smiles in life—or at least it seemed to him that there was no smile, for he did not smile at other people, and a smile is a flash of vitality. He thought that he was being ignored, when it was he who hid himself behind a gloomy reserve.

Mr. Roland still played Chopin. He went about as usual,

deliberate, fresh faced, ready with a pleasant word, observ-ing without appearing to observe.

One morning he spoke to Sorrell.

"Feeling all right, Stephen?"

"Quite, sir."

"I thought you looked tired."

"No,—I'm quite all right, sir."

Roland did not push his inquiries further.

"Take an extra hour off.   Get out with your boy."

"Thank you, sir."

Sorrell was shocked by the sudden rush of mean thoughts. This was part of Buck's slyness; he had been hinting to Mr. Roland that Sorrell was not up to his work, and not capable of handling the heavy luggage. And Roland believed him. He was unaware of what was going on under his very eyes.

Sorrell tried to rid himself of this meanness, but he was human, and when the opportunity fell to him, he seized it, for when a man has an enemy he is justified in making reconnaissances. He happened to see Buck going into Mr. Roland's room, and he found something to polish outside the door of that room.

He could hear what was said.

"What about Sorrell?   It struck me this morning that he looked ill."

"I don't know about that, sir.   But the fact is—well, I don't like to have to——"

"I prefer frankness, Buck."

"I don't think he's fit for the work, sir.   Clerking is his job."

"Not strong enough?"

"That's it.   Of course—I take my share——"

"I'm sure you do,—Buck.   I have told Sorrell to take an extra hour off——"

Sorrell slipped away, raging against the liar, and almost despising Roland for accepting his lies. His great Mr. Roland was not so shrewd and world-wise as he had imagined!

But he caught himself up.

"Don't be a cad.   Stick it.   The fellow will have you beaten unless you stick it.   Think of the boy."

2

Christopher was his refuge, his secret inspiration. Sorrell was off duty from eight till nine, and he had the half of each alternate Sunday. Kit would come along the road to meet his father, and as the evenings lengthened they would wander a short way into the fields, or climb the Castle Hill and sit and talk for twenty minutes. Christopher was rather silent about the school, and when his father's voice grew intimate the boy would leap two or three years and carry their gossip into the future.

"I think I'd like to be an engineer, pater."

"What sort of engineer?"

"Oh,—design things. I went over the electric light works the other day. Bert Lumley took me. His father runs the dynamos."

"Wonderful thing—electricity."

"It seems alive. It's there—and yet you can't see it. Like the blood going round in your body, pater."

"You'd like to work on live things?"

"Yes,—I think so."

But one evening Christopher did not appear upon the road, and when Sorrell arrived at the cottage in Vine Court he came upon a little scene that shocked him. Kit and Mrs. Garland were in the scullery, and Kit's head was over the sink, and there was a redness, and Mrs. Garland was using a sponge.

"Hallo! What's happened?"

Kit gurgled something, but it was Mrs. Garland who explained the affair. She was angry.

"That young beast of a Blycroft. Always tormenting something. He'd got hold of a cat, and of course our Kit——. Well,—young Blycroft's two years older, and a strong young savage."

"I got one in," said Kit, eluding the sponge for a moment.

And then he burst into tears. He did not explain his tears, but Sorrell understood them, and his angry heart yearned over the boy. It was the shame of being licked by a boy whom he despised, sensitiveness writhing under the bulk of the savage. Did he not understand it? Had he not had to bear it? For he knew that had their quarrel come

to a vulgar scuffle Buck would overwhelm him as the Vine
Court bully had smothered Kit.

"We must do something about this," he said,—stroking
his moustache.

And all the way home he was thinking over the problem,
the age-old problem of how the brain can outwit the brute.

3

Easter came, with six days of sunshine, and a brisk life
upon the road. The buds of the chestnuts were bursting,
and in the garden daffodils swung yellow in the wind amid
a spreading glimmer of greenness. Bowden's pugnacious
and swarthy head began to go to and fro behind his lawn-
mower.

There were hyacinths, rose, white and blue in the border
close to the window where Sorrell used to sit and read, and
the scent of them drifted in, but Sorrell and his books saw
little of each other. For the city people were pushing the
noses of their cars westwards in search of the spring, and
the glittering Pelican saw them swirl and hesitate and pause.

Life became strenuous, and for Sorrell in particular more
than strenuous. He laboured, groaning inwardly, jaw set,
his eyes taking on a tired and blank stare. He cursed the
people who travelled with solid trunks; heavy suit cases and
kit-bags were not so bad, but a trunk was an uncompromising brute of a thing.

One evening he had paused on the second landing to get
his breath when he heard a voice behind him.

"Why do you do all the work?"

He turned and looked into the pale face of the housekeeper, Mary Marks. She was a plain little woman,
reserved, thin lipped, but with clear dark eyes. They were
very intelligent eyes, and they had suffered, for somewhere
a Percy Marks led a brisk and lascivious life. As a rule she
was not a woman who offered sympathy, for she would have
resented sympathy.

Sorrell, surprised, stood there panting.

"Pride," he said.

"Oh,—that's very well. But it's a shame. A great beast
like that letting you——."

He was astonished at her bitterness. He had thought that all the women were on Buck's side, and he felt cheered.

"Then—you have noticed it?"

"Of course. Why do you do it?"

"Do you think I would ask him——? He thinks I'll break. I shan't."

With an effort he picked up the trunk, and getting it on his shoulder, went swaying along the corridor. Mary Marks stood and watched him, and had Sorrell been able to read her mind its fierce goodwill would have surprised him. She knew something of men; she was full of scorn for the fine, breezy fellows, the gentlemen with the "Hallo, my dear" eyes.

"He won't stand it," she thought. "Mr. Roland ought to have the sense to see. That boy of his keeps him going."

Nor was Mrs. Marks the only woman in the place whose sympathies were with Sorrell. It happened one wet Sunday afternoon that Sorrell had spent his half-day at the Vine Court, and Fanny Garland—also free—was one of the party. They had tea together, Sorrell and Kit, Fanny and her mother. Sorrell ate very little; they noticed it; he looked in pain.

Sorrell and Fanny Garland walked back together to the Pelican. It was raining, and Fanny had an umbrella; she offered half to Sorrell, frankly, as a comrade; her cheerfulness was a straightforward virtue, and though Sorrell refused the umbrella she was not offended. Most men would have shared it so readily, thinking it to be an invitation towards other intimacies. Buck, for instance.

One of them, probably it was Sorrell, happened to mention the ex-sergeant-major.

"Him! You put up with too much. I know the sort he is."

And then she added—"I know the length of his rope. You wait."

Her meaning was an enigma to Sorrell.

"I don't quite take you."

"No? That fellow will hang himself. You wait. If he gets caught—I don't think Mr. Roland's the sort of man to mince matters——"

Sorrell went to bed wondering how George Buck could be expected to hang himself. Also, it was in his mind that

Christopher should have boxing lessons. A man needed a weapon, and it was a good thing to be able to use one's fists.

For—he—Sorrell had no weapon, nothing but his dogged patience. It seemed to him that he would have to let life pull pieces of flesh from him until life got tired of it. All that he could do was to out-live life.

X

1

SORRELL'S second persecution had lasted for two months.

The year gave an unusually beautiful spring, the spring that a gardener prepares for and so rarely enjoys, but to Sorrell the green budding of the year was a season of strife and of humiliation. George Buck, flourishing like an elm tree, sucked all the sustenance and the moisture from his weaker rival.

"Saul,—luggage for number twenty-seven."

Sorrell was enduring blindly, but not so blindly as he believed. The work was now incessant, for the majority of the visitors stayed only one night, and their baggage had to be carried up one day and brought down the next. A strong lad would have thought nothing of the work, but to Sorrell it was travail and anguish and bitter sweat. There were times when his heart and lungs laboured so heavily that he imagined his old wounds to be bursting, and the healed tissues tearing themselves apart. At night he would look ghastly, and crawl up to his bed with shadows under his eyes. The old pain was coming back; he was afraid of food; he would lie awake with his heart labouring under his ribs.

But he would not surrender. Buck's trumpeting voice was an eternal challenge, and Sorrell felt that the struggle between them was physical, though their bodies never came into contact. The man meant to wear him out, to drive him to some outburst, to so vex and madden Sorrell that he would fly at him like a tormented animal. The rest would be so easy. One punch of the big fist on that sallow face, and a solemn report made to Mr. Roland. "Saul's assaulted me, sir. I had to hit him——. I think he is a bit touched in the head. Queer. He won't do the place any good, sir."

Certainly, Sorrell was growing quick-tempered. There

were times when he was so intensely irritable that he had to
hold himself in, grip something. It was the irritability of
over-tiredness and dyspepsia. His impulses could be murderous. He would find himself looking at the back of Buck's
head and neck; Buck had one of those round flat heads with
the pink skin showing at the crown, and a great broad neck
that bulged slightly over his collar. An axe, a hammer,—
and one smashing blow on that pink, bald patch——!

Sorrell had to suppress these murderous rages. He rea-
soned with himself.

"Hang on. Violence won't help you. The only way to
balk the beast is to refuse to be broken."

But these rages tired him, for intense self-suppression is
exhausting. He had an air of bored calmness. But he was
beginning to feel bitter against Thomas Roland. He had
imagined a possible friendship only to discover that he was
of so little importance that Roland remained blind to his
martyrdom. Self-absorbed, like most other humans!

Well,—why not complain?

There was a morning when Sorrell paused with his hand
on the handle of Roland's door. Buck had been teasing him
before the women, making a mock of him, and Sorrell was
raging.

"I'll give notice."

He stood there for nearly half a minute, fighting his
anger, and trying to convince himself that this anger was a
wound that should be hidden. He was about to do the very
thing that George Buck intended him to do.

He overcame the impulse. He was moving away when
the door opened, and Roland came out. He looked inquir-
ingly at Sorrell.

"Oh,—Stephen,—you might get that grey suit of mine
pressed."

"Yes, sir."

"How's the boy?"

"Very well, sir."

Sorrell's answers were tense and abrupt, like sentences
snapped out by an automaton. His face had a pale rigidity.

"You haven't borrowed any books lately."

"Not much time, sir."

He was aloof, haughty, but Roland did not appear to
notice Sorrell's attitude, or if he noticed it he hid his aware-

ness. Sorrell's melancholy eyes reproached him, for Roland looked so strong and fresh and unhurried, a man who had time to play and read, but who did not trouble to observe.

"No,—I suppose not" was all he said; "but things change, Stephen."

"And people" Sorrell added to himself.

2

The rush of visitors quickened, and the crowd was increased by a number of Americans who came to visit the birthplace of one of their great men.

To Sorrell it seemed that he had reached the crisis of his struggle. He toiled like Sisyphus, but unlike the man of myth, he pushed and heaved his rock to its objective. He panted and sweated; sometimes his shirt was so wet that he had to go and change it. And the luggage became alive; malignantly alive; it played tricks with him, it resisted, it hurt him, jammed his fingers or bruised his shoulder. Once or twice he fell, and lay clutching some gloating burden, rolling with it on the floor, or in some dark corner on the stairs. He tried dragging the things up by the handles, till Buck caught him at it, and hectored him.

"Here, nice for the new carpets. That ain't the way to handle baggage, my lad. Hump it."

Sorrell flared.

"Why don't you give me a hand,—you——"

"Now,—no sauce. If you can't do the job, my lad,— you say so."

And he stood and watched Sorrell shoulder a trunk and stagger with it up the stairs.

It happened that a gentlewoman arrived one day in a car like a "Cunarder." It had a super-trunk strapped behind it. The lady came into the lounge and was met by the head-porter.

The lady wanted a "suite."

But she took the room, and ordered her luggage to be sent up at once.

Sorrell was unstrapping the super-trunk, a vast black thing, bound with iron and plastered with labels, when Buck came out.

"What number?"

"Thirty-five."

"Third floor——!"

The two men looked at each other. Sorrell knew that it
would be absurd for him to try and handle that trunk alone,
but he was not going to ask his enemy to help him.

"All right."

There was a smirk on Buck's face. He took one end of
the trunk and helped Sorrell to carry it as far as the foot
of the stairs, but here he dropped his end.

"Looks heavier than it is. Get it up quick; she's one of
the puss-in-boots sort."

Sorrell said nothing. He felt that he was on the eve of
his Waterloo.

He tried to get the thing on his back, and as though to
make certain of Sorrell's overwhelming, Buck helped to load
him. "That's it; up you go."

Sorrell managed the first flight, though by the time he
reached the first landing his heart was racing. He felt that
he would burst asunder. He tried to let the trunk down
gently, but it swayed down, twisting his wrist and striking
his ankle with one of its metal capped corners.

And suddenly, Sorrell saw red. This beastly bit of
opulent inertia seemed to typify life, George Buck and all
the damnable and cruel cussedness of the tormenting forces
that seemed eager to break him. He fell upon the trunk.
He fought it half-way up the second flight, tearing and
pushing the thing up with a mad fury, heaving it over and
over. Half-way up it jammed, and in trying to force it
farther he slipped and struck his head against it.

"Damn you——!"

He held his head, and burst into sudden, wild sobbing.
He did not see a face looking down over the railing of the
second landing, a shocked and compassionate face. A moment later someone was on the stairs.

"Anyone would think some of the people travelled with
their coffins."

Sorrell glanced up furiously. He choked.

"What's that? Coffins——. I slipped——. I'll get the
damned thing——"

"Wait. I'll help——"

"You shan't. By God,—get out of the way,—Mrs. Marks."

He tore at the trunk, heaved it up, leaving a great scar upon the wall, and the woman, retreating, watched his wildness with scared eyes. For he looked like a man storming a breach, mouth awry, eyes protruding; panting, cursing. But he did not curse; he had no breath for it. He banged the thing over and over, and thrust it up on to the landing, and there his knees gave way and he had to sit down hurriedly on the vanquished trunk.

"Oh,—my God——!"

"Put your head down, Steve," said she.

Sorrell put his head between his knees, and the housekeeper, running into one of the bedrooms, returned with a glass of water. She stood over Sorrell, her hand resting lightly on his shoulder.

"Drink this, Stephen. This has got to stop, you know. I am going down to tell that mountain of laziness——"

Sorrell's face, still ghastly but slightly smiling, appeared from between his knees.

"No,—please don't. I lost my temper, that's all. I am going to get this thing up. I shall be all right in a minute."

"Drink some water. If you must try and kill yourself——"

His hand shook as he held the glass.

"It's better to be killed—than to give in—to him."

"Oh, is it! I'm going to help you with that trunk, Stephen. What's the number of the room?"

"Thirty-five."

And help him she did, for she was a little woman of great determination, and between them they manœuvred the "black coffin"—as she called it—up the last flight and along the passage to No. 35. Sorrell knocked. The lady told him to enter; she had been waiting.

"I thought you had gone to sleep with it," she said.

Sorrell hauled the thing into the room.

"It is rather heavy, madam."

She presented him with a sixpence, an ironical sixpence so it seemed to Sorrell, and he went forth with the coin shut up in his fist to show it to Mrs. Marks, but the housekeeper had disappeared. On his way downstairs he paused to look

at the scar on the wall where a corner of the trunk had bitten
into the plaster. The wallpaper was a dull red, and Sorrell,
pondering the problem, bethought him of a little plaster of
Paris and some red ink. The rent in the wall was a wound,
but an honourable wound.

Returning to the lounge hall he came upon George Buck
leaning through the office window, talking to Miss Murdoch
the hotel clerk. The pink, baldish patch on the crown of his
head showed between his two red and prominent ears.

Sorrell began tidying up the papers and magazines. He
was waiting for Buck to discover him and to ask the obvious
question, and Sorrell was ready with the answer.

Presently, Buck withdrew his blue bulk from the narrow
window. His eyes saw Sorrell indefatigably busy, and the
gallant glimmer melted out of them. They seemed to stare.

"Get that up to number thirty-five, Saul?"

"I did."

Sorrell gave him a queer and twisted smile, glancing
round over his shoulder, and he saw that his enemy was
puzzled.

                                    3

Mary Marks knocked at the door of Mr. Roland's
sitting-room.

"Come in."

Roland was sitting on the music-stool, his hands resting
on the keyboard. They were very brown hands. Beyond
him was the open window between curtains of old gold; the
window framed a stretch of grass, two beds full of purple
Darwin tulips, and the trunks of two old trees. The
atmosphere of room and garden seemed to merge, save that
the old gold of the room was of a deeper quality than the
yellow downpour of the spring sunlight.

"May I speak to you, sir?"

"Why certainly; come in."

The Chinese carpet made Mary Marks think of a bed of
flowers. A shame to tread on it! She was sensitive to all
beautiful things, and her hard exterior was a wall that had
been built to protect and to hide what was left to her of
her love of beauty. She closed the door. Her eyes looked
across the room at Thomas Roland, and in them was a

vague and questioning censure, unwilling censure. There were times when she wished to believe that certain people were better than the common crowd; she asked to be convinced, to be allowed moments of secret romanticism. She had thought Roland a romantic figure, one of those men upon whom women lavish an instinctive devotion. She had thought him strong, just, wise, deliberate, generous.

"Well,—Mrs. Marks?"

His eyes interrogated hers. His glance, falling upon the severity of her face, questioned it. She stood there with her back to the door, and it seemed to her that he was being reproached.

"It's not my business, sir; not like that other affair."

Roland turned on the music-stool.

"Yet it must be, or you would not have come."

"Perhaps——"

"Tell me. You have something to tell me."

"It's about Sorrell."

She saw at once that he was not indifferent.

"You don't mean——?"

"O, nothing of that kind, sir. But that other man——"

"Buck?"

"Yes. It's unfair,—a shame, all the heavy luggage; the man's not strong,—physically I mean."

It seemed to her that Roland smiled and yet did not smile.

"I know," he said.

She gave a quick lift of the head, an intelligent and bird-like movement.

"About—his being delicate?"

"No. Buck's share of the work. I do see things, Mrs. Marks; I'm not asleep."

"I wondered."

Her eyes were still questioning. Since he knew what was happening her impulse was to ask him why he had not interfered, for his partiality seemed to her a very foolish blindness. Not to be able to see which was the better man! But, perhaps he did see? She looked across at him eagerly, tempted to venture farther, yet half afraid of what he might infer.

"It has made me angry," she said.

Roland stood up, and half turning towards the window, he spoke to her as though he were speaking to himself.

"No, it is not favouritism. I'm a deliberate person, Mrs. Marks. I like to test people, to be sure. And now— I think—I'm very nearly sure."

Her face softened.

"He's killing himself. He won't give in."

"As bad as that?"

"It's pride."

"I am glad you have told me. I like to trust people. Do you think that unwise?"

She met his steady eyes, and began to wonder why she had doubted.

"No, not in his case. You see, he has got an object, sir, something outside himself that matters."

"The boy. Exactly. I loathe distrusting people. I wanted to be sure. Now,—listen."

He came and stood near to her, his hands in his pockets, and with an intimate, wise air.

"I wanted that other man to have his chance. I had my reasons. Naturally—I want very good reasons for taking his chance away. The very strongest reason——"

"You mean—that other affair, sir?"

"I do."

She knew that he was asking her to help him, not ungenerously, but rather to take sides against his own too human kindness. It meant a kicking into the street of a memory, an obligation, and the man to whom he owed it. He had always confessed to a fondness for "the old blackguard." But not for a mean and bullying blackguard.

"So you see—I want my reason, my justification. I suppose it is weak of me."

She stood with a hand along one cheek, looking down at the pattern of the carpet, but her eyes did not see the carpet.

"I'm sitting up to-night, Mr. Roland."

"You think it—necessary?"

"Oh,—I heard something. The girl——. Besides, in a way—I feel myself responsible."

"To whom?"

"To my job. I'm not a prude, sir——. Oh,—I know they have every right—if a man and a girl are made that way——. But there—there is what I am here for. It's not fair——"

"To whom?"

"To me,—to you."

"And the girl?"

"I'm not thinking of her. She is only trying to get what she wants,—but she shall not get it—here. That's where my job would suffer."

Roland nodded his strong, square head.

"All right. I'll sit up too."

XI

I

THOMAS ROLAND'S enthusiasm for detail had extended to the dresses worn by the chambermaids of the Pelican Inn. Someone in Chelsea had designed for him this feminine uniform, a simple creation in blue linen, short in the sleeve and open at the neck. The white cap suggested a butterfly's wings, with a knot of black velvet for the body.

The housekeeper had admired the æsthetics of the costume, —but when it came to practical politics she regretted the provocation of such clothes. For clothes do provoke, both the wearer of them and the person who has an eye for the way they are worn. And Mary Marks felt responsible. Clare and Kate were steady girls and not too good-looking, but the very flick of Nelly Barrett's neat black ankles promised her anxieties.

Even Sorrell, who was too tired to be piqued by adventure, and who had a prejudice against all baby faces, had understood the nature of Nelly's provocation. A little, sallow thing with a bobbed head of jet-black hair, and a yellowish tinge in the skin of her forearms and her throat, she moved quickly on slim legs and with a slightly undulating movement of the hips. She had a way of swinging her thin forearms as though she were balancing herself like a dancer on a rope. She caught the eye with her liveness, and the mischievous "Come and catch me" of her pert, pale face. Sorrell had seen other men looking at her as men look at certain women. And she, alive to it all, moving with little flicks of the head, would glance back, self-consciously arch, smiling, showing her white teeth.

Sorrell was very tired. A party of motorists who had booked rooms at the Pelican had wired to say that they would not arrive till midnight, and Sorrell was sitting up for them. Everyone had gone to bed, and he had taken one

of the big leather armchairs in the lounge, and had lit a
pipe. A pile of illustrated papers lay on the copper-topped
smoking table beside his chair, and he had been looking
through them idly and with the inattention of a man who
was weary. He wanted to go to sleep. The very silence
and gloom of the big lounge invited him sleep. A clock
ticked somewhere, and its ticking was the only sound to be
heard as the minutes slipped away. The window of the
office was closed, though the visitors' book lay open on the
ledge.

Everybody was asleep, and Sorrell lay relaxed, thinking
of all those comfortable sleepers up above, and of how good
a thing bed was, and of how long it might be before he
would be able to lock the door and go across the yard to his
room in what had been a part of the old stables. Buck had
a room over there, next to Ponds the garage attendant. The
female members of the staff slept on the top floor in a little
wing that jutted out from the main building.

Sorrell contemplated the image of George Buck. The
fellow would be snoring; he could snore most aggressively,
so much so that Ponds had spoken facetiously of fitting a
silencer to the big man's proboscis. But Sorrell's thoughts
revolted from the contemplation of the persecutor. Surely
he had enough of Buck during the daytime without sitting
there and brooding over him at night?

He closed his eyes; his head sank forward; he fell into
a doze, but it was only for a minute. Something startled
him into wakefulness; he sat up, listening; he fancied that
he could hear a shuffling sound upon the stairs, but the
sound was so indefinite that he could not be sure that he
was not imagining it. He listened, head cocked. Then,
something more definite reached him, the creaking sound
made by a stair-tread under a cautious foot.

Sorrell got up. There were half a dozen possible explanations of the sound, legitimate explanations. He
walked to the main door and tried the handle to make sure
that it was locked. There was another door opening from
the yard into the corridor leading to the kitchen and the
service quarters, and Sorrell walked down the corridor.
Both he and Buck had keys for this side-door, so that they
could come in and out at any hour without calling on any
of the rest of the staff. Sorrell paused half-way down the

corridor; he had noticed something, a movement of cold night air. He found the door half open.

He remembered closing it less than an hour ago.

The possibilities grew more serious. He asked himself whether the open door had any connexion with that creaking stair-tread?

He turned and walked back towards the lounge, opening the swing-door cautiously, and closing it with a carefully restraining hand. He remembered that there would be a considerable amount of spare cash in the office safe. But if a prowler had entered the hotel why had he gone upstairs? To pilfer in the bedrooms?

Obviously he ought to investigate, and perhaps rouse Mr. Roland. Mr. Roland slept on the ground floor in a room that opened from his sitting-room, and Sorrell was moving towards the broad passage leading past the public rooms when he heard something more decisive. Screams, a woman's screams, faint and far away,—and coming from above!

His first thought was that he was weaponless. He ran back into the lounge, grabbed a poker from the fireplace, and made a dash for the stairs. He had reached the first landing and was switching on the lights when he heard a whole choir of voices coming from above. There was a man's voice, and an hysterical voice that belonged to the screamer, and the voices of other women. Obviously, something dramatic was happening up there. A burglar perhaps, caught and cornered by three or four frightened but eager women?

Sorrell dashed up, switching on lights. The voices seemed to come from the staffs' quarters, and he turned up the flight of stairs leading to the outjutting wing. He fancied that he recognized the voices. Lights were on up above. And then he came suddenly upon the scene, staged for him above the tread of the top step.

He paused, astonished.

He saw one of the chambermaids in her nightdress, with hair streaming, and he guessed that it was she who had been screaming. Her mouth was still voluble, but none of the others were paying any attention to what she said. He saw Mrs. Marks fully dressed; Mr. Roland in his blue and orange dressing-gown. George Buck in shirt and trousers.

Two other doors were open, and girls' heads were protruding.

Then—Sorrell understood.

2

The fool lover had blundered into the wrong bedroom.

Also, he had been ambuscaded. Mrs. Marks' black dress had been keeping vigil, and Roland's dressing-gown was a mere piece of camouflage.

Sorrell remained where he was, watching his enemy standing there, a mass of foolishness, and of cringing plausibility.

"I've apologized to her, sir. I can't do more than that, can I? Besides——"

Buck kept glancing at a closed door, the door of Nelly Barrett's room. He knew the right door now, because it had remained discreetly shut.

Sorrell could see nothing of Mr. Roland save his back. It seemed to him to be an uncompromising and disgusted back.

"Come downstairs."

He wanted Buck away from the women where his presence was an offence and a confusion. He turned to the stairs, and saw Sorrell and his poker, and a smile came into his eyes.

"We've startled you, Stephen."

"I wondered what it was, sir."

"Come with us. I shall want you."

Sorrell stood aside to let Roland and the egregious lover pass, and Buck, evil-eyed, went by him with a stiffening of the neck. Sorrell followed them down, and when they were away from the paralysing presence of the women Buck began to blurt more boldly.

"Between men, sir——"

"Well?"

"She asked me to go——"

Roland's voice was abrupt and contemptuous. What a scene! The sex adventure at its worst, caught in a corner, meanly ashamed.

"Shut up, man. I don't want such explanations."

"I've been spied upon. Jealousy, sir——"

Roland paused for a moment on the stairs.

"Look here, Buck, you can wait till we are in my room. There has been quite enough noise. People want to sleep."

The lights were on in Mr. Roland's sitting-room, and on seeing the glass bulbs all aglow Buck's blue eyes became illuminated from within. Behind him Sorrell had closed the door, and was leaning against it, still holding his poker. Roland was rummaging for a cigarette.

"So it was you—you—who gave me away."

Roland turned sharply.

"Buck, I don't want a scene. Don't be a fool."

"I was just telling a rat, sir——"

"Sorrell had nothing to do with it. You have no one to thank but yourself. You will go to-morrow, after breakfast."

The big man seemed to hang there like a red sun, hesitating between a glare of rage and a fog of servility. He could not bring himself to look at Sorrell. His neck, with its roll of fat, had a purplish tinge. He glowed. Like most common men he took refuge in sentimentality. "Do the gentleman behind his back,—but slobber him up in the public."

"And I saved your life, sir."

Roland was looking at him through a little cloud of cigarette smoke.

"You did. That's why I offered you this place. I never expect gratitude. Sportsmanship's better——"

"Gratitoode!"

He extended a fat hand.

"Chucking me out—because I'm made like a man, not like that parsnip there. I'm no angel; don't pretend to it."

"Nor am I,—Buck. But then——"

"Because a girl—a hot little bit——. Why, it's human nature——. To hell with——"

"Buck," said Roland, interrupting him with that deliberate voice of his, "I'm not quarrelling with your morals. Sex is nature. It's no more immoral to go with a woman than to eat your dinner—provided——"

Buck tried to speak, but Roland had not finished.

"Provided—you don't hurt anybody. There's the woman

to be considered. And—me, the job, the hotel. You are not a sportsman. That's my point."

"I beg to differ, sir."

"Oh, of course. But you are not a sportsman. I've known that for some time now. You're a greedy animal. That's that."

He nodded at Sorrell, and Sorrell opened the door.

"You shall have your money in the morning, before you go. Now, clear out to your room."

"Well, sir, I never thought you would treat me like this."

"Buck, I'm not a fool."

The big man went out with a kind of pitying swagger, and Roland, smiling faintly, made a sign to Sorrell that he was to remain.

"I want to speak to you, Stephen. By the way, have those people arrived yet?"

"No, sir."

"Wait, isn't that a car?"

"I think it is——"

"Well, go and get them fixed up, and then come back here, unless you are too tired."

"I'm not too tired, sir."

"Good. I have a few things to say."

3

Sorrell dealt with the late arrivals and their luggage, and never had luggage seemed so light. He was beyond tiredness; he felt that he had climbed above things physical, and that he was on the peak of months of moiling and of effort, looking down and back and upwards in an air that was clear and stimulating. The bull had gone the way of the lioness, and he was left in happy relationship with a man.

Roland's door was ajar, and Sorrell knocked.

"Come in, Stephen."

He saw a decanter of whisky, a siphon, and two glasses on the table; also a box of cigarettes. Sorrell closed the door, for he felt that Mr. Roland wished him to close it upon the sealing of a new and more intimate comradeship.

"How do you like yours, Stephen?"

"Not too strong, sir."

"Well, help yourself. That's a good thing over. My one mistake, and yet—it had to be."

His voice expressed relief. The dirty business was over, the make-believe done with.

"I suppose you thought I didn't know——?"

He was filling his glass, and he looked up and across the table at Sorrell.

"But I did know. You will have to forgive me my one blind eye. That blackguard was giving you hell. But—I wanted him to hang himself; I wanted to be sure."

He raised his glass.

"There's forgiveness in good drink. Your health, Stephen."

"The same to you, sir."

"Then you do forgive me?"

"I had began to wonder——"

"Yes,—I felt that. Besides—I didn't quite know how bad it was. Well,—that's all over."

He pushed the cigarettes towards Sorrell.

"Sit down, man. You don't know what a relief this is. How I loathe that class—in the mass. We are outside the pale to them. Their sense of honour—such as it is—does not include us. It wasn't always so."

He went and sat on his music-stool, while Sorrell took one of the chairs.

"We are fair game to most of them, we who have anything, or can do anything a little better than the crowd. We are to be robbed, lied to, blackmailed, slandered. Isn't that so?"

"I suppose it is. But—not all——."

"Oh,—I know. Some of us have the remnants of souls. I have good people here; I know it. They don't look on me as their natural enemy. To me it is the individual that matters. Breed. O, well, what is it? A fastidiousness, a sense of humour and a sense of proportion, the knowledge that hitting a better man than yourself with a pick-handle doesn't make for progress. Beauty. Wisdom. Disdain and pity instead of scorn. You know."

Suddenly, he laughed, and his laughter was quiet and self-amused.

"Declamation! But, hang it, character does count. You and I understand each other; or—at least—I think we do. You are out for your boy."

Sorrell nodded.

"That—kept me going. That—and the hope——."

"That someone realized——?"

"Yes."

"Oh,—I realized——. So it comes to this—I offer you Buck's place,—and I shall think myself lucky to get you. Well,—what about it?"

"There is only one answer to that. But I ought to tell you,—I'm not much good with heavy luggage——."

"My dear chap——."

He raised his glass.

"You have more in you than a cart-horse. I have my eye on a big good-natured cart-horse. It's your head I want, Stephen, and your heart,—and your grit—my dear chap."

4

Sorrell woke to see white clouds moving in a blue sky, for he slept with blind up and his window wide open, but on this particular morning he lay for five minutes looking at the sky.

"I'm first porter at the Pelican."

He smiled. What a very humble pride was this, and how modest a triumph, and yet he had had to work and struggle for it and to suffer.

Fragments of Thomas Roland's philosophy drifted through his head.

"It is not so much the job, but the way you do the job, that matters."

Yes, wasn't that true. That much misused and obscured phrase—"The dignity of labour!" But the dignity was in the soul of the labourer, not in the matter he worked upon, and a man who cleaned boots with love and care was worthy of the respect of kings. To be respected for the way you did your job, to be respected by a man like Thomas Roland.

This little room of his had a new atmosphere, a suggestion of homeliness and of security. He foresaw it be-

coming more intimately part of himself and his schemes, a
little corner where he would collect his books and his trifles,
and sit at a table and enter his takings in his ledger.

He got up, and washed with a sense of exhilaration.
No more—"Saul,—luggage number So and So," no one
to mess him about, no more bovine interference. He was
lord of his own job.

"News for the boy," he thought, as he sluiced water
over his head. "I ought to be able to make five pounds
a week,—two hundred and fifty a year. The odd fifty will
do for me. Why,—there's his education. He will be
thirteen next November. Say—twelve years, and at
twenty-five he ought to be armed and ready."

While he was shaving he heard voices below. Mr.
Roland was up early. He had come to hasten the departure
of the adventurous lover.

"Here's a month's money, Buck. Is your luggage ready?
I have told Ponds to drive you to the station."

"You seem in a hell of a hurry, sir, to get rid of me."

"Buck,—if I had made such a fool of myself before a lot
of women——"

Sorrell saw the ex-sergeant-major off with his leather
trunk and his suit-case, his blue overcoat over his arm, a
sulky animal, trying to look aggrieved. "Damned lot of
humbugs!" The car whirled him out and away under the
glittering symbol of the Pelican, and Sorrell, going to his
work, felt the blessedness of the day's labour.

"My job. I'm responsible."

Mr. Roland, strolling into the lounge, found him with
his coat off, whistling softly, and polishing everything that
it was possible to polish.

"You sound very cheerful, Stephen."

"I am, sir."

They exchanged a look of liking and respect.

"I am going over to Bath to see the fellow I have in
mind. His name is Hulks. A good lad—I think. He will
take all his orders from you. The understanding is that
he will be luggage-porter."

Sorrell gave him a smile of gratitude.

"I can manage some of the luggage, sir. There is one
point——. I should like your advice——"

"Well?"

"About tips——. They pool theirs in the dining-room, between the three. Fanny Garland takes two-fifths, and the other two girls halve the rest."

"They agreed to that?"

"Yes, and between Hulks and myself,—what sort of proportion would you think fair?"

"Three-fifths to you, and two-fifths to him."

"Will you put it to him, sir, or shall I?"

"I'll do it. It will be more official, Stephen."

"Thank you, sir."

At eight o'clock that evening Sorrell met his son on the road where Winstonbury's old water-mill still took the river upon the paddles of its great black, dripping wheel. A stone wall separated the mill-pool from the road, and Sorrell and Kit stood by the wall, looking at the still water and the green willows.

"Buck's gone, Kit. I'm head porter now."

He had his arm across the boy's shoulders.

"It will make a difference. I shall be able to give you something better than that school,—that's to say—if the old Pelican pays."

Kit looked up at his father. More and more was he coming to realize what manner of man his father was, and the knowledge was giving that radiant smile of his a sacred seriousness.

"You don't seem to think of yourself, pater."

"Oh,—I'm a means to an end, my lad. I've got an object in life. I'm to be envied."

Kit pondered a moment.

"And I'm the object.—I mean—my——"

"That's it."

"I'll try and not waste your money, pater. I know how hard you have to work."

XII

I

THERE followed some weeks of peace, and once more Sorrell became a "person." The stoop went out of his shoulders; his eyes were clear; he sat at the head of the staff table and was addressed as "Mr. Sorrell." He had not realized his own incipient dignity, or that he was developing a certain "presence," and that the women respected him. They forgave him his rather silent attitude, his air of gentlemanly reserve, for after all he was a gentleman, born and in action, and his long thin figure and dark and intelligent head were topped by a halo of mystery. For Sorrell was something of a mystery, and women love a mystery, especially when their intuition divines a kind and staunch reality at the back of it.

He was much discussed on the back stairs and in the kitchen.

"He's devoted to that boy of his."

"And a nice kid he is too. He's got such eyes, and a big laughing mouth. When he gets a bit older the women will want to kiss him."

It was not evident that the women wished to kiss Sorrell. He was more than a sex-man, and even the working women of to-day are more practically romantic than were their mothers. It seemed that Sorrell was not a marrying man; like Mr. Roland he was married to his job; but there were one or two women who were interested in his attitude towards marriage. Fanny Garland for one, fresh faced, cheerful, wholesomely ambitious. She had reasons for asserting to her secret self that she and Sorrell would make very good partners, that Sorrell's boy liked her and that she liked the boy. Both of them were saving money——. Even Miss Murdoch—"the girl in the cage,"—who lived in rooms in Winstonbury and walked out each morning to immure her pale primrose gentility in the Pelican office, had a secret partiality for Sorrell. In fact—she did not hide it. From her cage her tired eyes watched life, the life that

could come and go as it pleased. She envied it its freedom,
but without bitterness, for she had not the vitality to be
bitter. And she would watch Sorrell, and her pale face
would light up whenever something brought him to the
window of her cage.

She thought him "distinguished," yes, even in the Pelican's blue uniform.

But the chief contributor to Sorrell's peace of mind was
Mr. Roland's "stout lad," Albert Hulks. The breadth and
strength of him were comforting, as was his infinite good
nature, and from the first glimpse of his great rosy face
Sorrell had every cause to bless him. Albert was a modest
creature. He hadn't much head, and he said so, but his
good temper and his strength were of more value to the man
who had the head. Albert dealt with the luggage; it was
nothing to him; he enjoyed man-handling it; he had the
vigour of a young steam-engine. His attitude towards life
too—was so easy.

He had two or three characteristic phrases.

"I'm not worrying. You leave it to me,—I'll tackle it
Keep smiling."

Bert was proud of his strength, and was ready to spend
it with healthy enthusiasm, for no one had persuaded him
that he ought to bottle it up, and dole it out in careful drops.
He admired Sorrell, and they got on famously.

"O, yes,—I've got a back, but he's got a head, some
head."

They were straight with each other over the tips, agree-
ing to keep a box in the office into which each slipped his
takings, and the box was opened each night and the money
shared out, three-fifths to Sorrell, and two-fifths to Hulks.

Had any interfering "Friend of the people" challenged
Bert's attitude towards Sorrell and their work, he might
have looked puzzled.

"Being exploited—am I? Don't see it, chum. I've got
the back and he's got the head. Besides—he got a bit
smashed up in the war. Dicky inside, see. Carrying
luggage upstairs don't hurt me. He's got the head piece.
We get on champion. What's wrong with that?"

The plain fellow's good nature had solved the problem.

Sorrell now found himself with more leisure, for Mr.
Roland had not objected to his porters so arranging the

work that one of them should be off duty twice a day.

"I leave it to you, Stephen. I know you'll not let me down."

Sorrell's free hours were from twelve till half-past one, and from eight till half-past nine. The evenings were sacred to Kit, but that midday hour he spent reading in his room, or in wandering about the garden. He knew very little about gardens, and on one occasion he had drawn a rare and hoarse chuckle from the churlish Bowden.

"What are those things,—sunflowers?"

"Sunflowers! Don't 'ee know an artichoke?"

But Sorrell enjoyed the garden. He used to wander up and down a broad grass walk in the vegetable garden, where vegetables and fruit and flowers were intermixed. Sweet peas grew here, and Fanny Garland, coming out to cut flowers for her table vases, would see Sorrell walking up and down, and usually he had a little black note-book in his hand.

She wondered whether he wrote poetry.

But Sorrell found his poetry in figures. He was enjoying the romance of hard cash. These little glittering sixpences, shillings, florins, and half-crowns, they were the stars above his immediate world, and of far more significance and import than the stars. His means to an end, his material plunder for immaterial needs. For with his savings he was going to arm his son against a world that babbled of socialism and still clutched a knife or a club.

Skill and knowledge were to be Kit's "arms," some craft in which he should use hand and brain, and could say to the miner "Bring coal, or my skill is not for you," or to the baker "Bread, or you die." For Sorrell's sufferings and struggles had not led him towards the illusion of socialism. He had seen too much of human nature. Labour, becoming sectionalized, would split into groups, and group would grab from group, massing for the struggle instead of fighting a lone fight. Only the indispensable and individual few would be able to rise above this scramble of the industrial masses. It is the few who matter and who will always matter. So Sorrell thought.

Social service? O, yes, ten thousand years hence—perhaps. But for the moment—arms—and not too much trust in your neighbour.

So, he wandered in the garden and carried his little book, and discovered the delight of scientific hoarding for the benefit of his pride and for the future of his son.

"Week ending June 23:

Wages £2 10 0
Share of Tips .. .. £5 3 6"

Sacred symbols! He was not unconscious of the flowers and of the fruit, or of old Bowden putting in an extra hour each day,—not for love—but because of his percentages. His figures set him dreaming dreams. Tips averaging £5 a week in summer! With good health he might count on an income of £250 to £300 a year, and with his keep and his uniform thrown in. Kit was costing him about twenty-five shillings a week; his own personal expenses were very small. That should leave him at least £5 a week to play with.

"Save half,—and use the other half on education."

He began to think that he might launch out on his first adventure.

He wanted to take the boy away from the town school.

2

Sorrell spoke to Thomas Roland on the subject, and each man found that the other had very definite views on education, and that on some points they differed.

"What is your idea, Stephen?"

"A private tutor for a year or two."

"Can you afford it?"

"I might—if I can find a good local man."

"And what about games?"

Yes, that was a difficulty. Neither man believed in mass production as applied to education, but Roland did believe in games.

"Getting kicked on the shins, you know, and learning to keep your temper, and not to squeal 'off-side' on every possible occasion. A boy wants it."

"All boys?"

"I think all boys ought to know how to take punishment."

"I want my boy to be something more than a healthy young animal with nice manners."

"Health and good manners are not a bad foundation, Stephen."

"Better than being a half-educated young prig with no manners. I grant it. But I want my boy to be a free man. I want him to be in a position to be able to say 'Go to hell' to both capital and labour."

"Do you want to send me to hell, Stephen?"

"You are a free man, sir; that's different. But it has always seemed to me that half one's youth is wasted; fooled away, rotted with boredom. A boy just drifts, or is pushed along by his parents. You stuff him with things in which he has no interest——. Why, at eighteen, after seven years at a public school——"

"Exactly.—But my sympathies are with the boy who refuses to be stuffed——. He comes in fresh and big at the finish."

"Yes,—I don't want to stuff the boy. If he had two or three hours coaching a day,—and could then run free——. He's keen on country things,—birds—and the river. I can have him taught to box and to swim, and perhaps to manage a horse. My idea is to give him plenty of fresh air—and enough book stuff, until he shows some inclination. Or— I might send him to a good school for a year or two— after he has had a year or two's coaching."

He smiled.

"The business would be—to get him in, the son of a hotel porter."

"I think you could camouflage that," said Mr. Roland.

Sorrell began to make inquiries in Winstonbury. Neither he nor Mr. Roland knew anything of the inner life of the place, for to the people who lived in the Queen Anne and Georgian houses of the Minster Close the Pelican was nothing more than a glorified "pub." Sorrell knew a few of the tradesmen, and one of the doctors. It occurred to him that Mr. Towner who kept the book-shop in Angel Row might be considered some sort of a guide to the intellectual possibilities of Winstonbury.

Mr. Towner was able to offer a suggestion. It arose from the fact that he was one of the few Victorians left in Winstonbury who put on a top hat and went to church on Sundays, and his church was St. Peter's. St. Peter's had a curate.

"There's Mr. Porteous. I believe he takes pupils."

Sorrell jotted down the Rev. Robert Porteous's address, and that same evening, having changed into mufti, he hunted out the curate's house in Gold Hill Lane. It was an old stone cottage with a leaded porch, sad and austere, and overshadowed by a great elm that seemed to bend over it menacingly.

A young woman of thirty or so answered the door.

"Is Mr. Porteous in?"

"Yes."

"Can I see him?"

She appeared flustered, and upon her pinched face was visible the vague fear of a woman whom poverty and conventional pride had turned into a social coward. The Porteouses kept no servant; they could not afford one. This shabby girl with the red, yet refined hands strove to be both a servant and a lady; her sensitiveness had been banked up in a narrow channel; she was ashamed of things that were not shameful; she had let herself be overawed by other people's cake-stands and carpets.

"I'm not quite sure. What name—please?"

"Sorrell—Captain Sorrell."

"Will you come in——"

All her movements were self-conscious and secretive. She could do nothing naturally, and even when she showed Sorrell into a stuffy little drawing-room she seemed to be drawing curtains, preparing pathetic and futile excuses.

"Mr. Porteous's sermon, you know."

"I don't want to disturb him."

"I'll go and see."

She closed the door with care, and departed to find her father, who was engaged upon something far more practical than the writing of sermons. For Mr. Porteous, in his shirt sleeves, and wearing the oldest trousers he possessed, was attacking a choked flue in the kitchen range. Somewhat sooty about the face, he was enjoying himself like a child, for Mr. Porteous—robust and stout and bald—with a little fringe of butter-coloured curls waving over his occiput, cared not a damn for social niceties. His lack of pretence was a great trouble to his daughter. "Father's so unconventional." He was. Hence—his poverty, his obscure, fumbling life in a back street in Winstonbury.

"A Captain Sorrell to see you."

Mr. Porteous withdrew a flue-brush. He looked hot and cheerful.

"Sorrell? Don't know the name. What's he want?"

"I didn't ask him."

"All right. I'll go and see."

He would have gone as he was had not his daughter insisted that a sooty face and hands were sacrilegious, and that he must put on a collar and slip a pair of detachable cuffs over the sleeves of his grey flannel shirt.

"You can't go in like that."

Mr. Porteous showed a very neat set of false teeth.

"I'm a bounder, my dear; I know it. Who was it said that Peter and Paul were bounders? Anyhow—I take off my hat to him."

Miss Porteous sighed.

In the interview that followed Sorrell and Mr. Robert Porteous discovered in each other a mutual surprise, and also an element of delight in their surprise.

"You'll excuse me—but our kitchen flue was stopped up. A rather sooty undertaking. What can I do for you, Captain Sorrell?"

Sorrell was absorbing Mr. Porteous, the squareness and the muscularity of him, his short, slightly bowed and stalwart legs, his round face and vast bald head with its butter-coloured halo. An uncouth, clumsy, powerful, yet intelligent figure, with boyish and bright blue eyes.

"I hear you take pupils, sir."

"I do when I can get 'em, day pupils."

"I have a boy. I'm head porter at the Pelican Inn."

"Head porter. Splendid!"

Mr. Porteous made a movement as of bouncing in his chair. His false teeth gleamed. For years Winstonbury had been trying to suppress him, to squash him into a decent dullness, but Mr. Porteous's joy in life was of such a resiliency that the natural and eager swell of it returned. To him it was really splendid that a captain should be a hotel porter.

"How old's the boy?"

"Nearly thirteen. At present he is at the town school. It was a question of funds."

Porteous nodded.

"I know all about that, sir. Or I shouldn't be using a flue-brush, hey—what! What's your idea?"

Sorrell explained his ideas to this round and sympathetic and vigorous man whose head was bigger than any other head in Winstonbury. Mr. Porteous was a learned failure, as the world understands failure. His unconventionality and the uncouth vigour of his exterior had rendered him unacceptable to the gods behind his God.

"In brief—you want your boy coaching for a good school?"

"That's it."

"Any special subject?"

"He has not developed any special inclination—yet."

"So much the better. I can give him anything from Sanscrit to the Differential Calculus. But you said something about boxing——."

"Yes,—but——"

"I can teach him to box."

"You can, sir?"

"Well,—I was the middle-weight man of my years at Cambridge. Knocked out the Dark Blue in the first round —two years running. He's a Cabinet Minister—to-day."

They smiled at each other.

"I think you are the very man I want, sir. I don't wish my boy to be pushed into a groove——."

"Quite so. I shan't bore him, my dear chap. I'm never bored. Light a pipe."

Then came the question of fees. Sorrell began a little tentatively, only to find that there was no need for him to be tentative with Mr. Porteous.

"I like teaching, my dear chap. I get paid for it. Fees? Well,—what can you afford?"

"Would two guineas a week——?"

"That would satisfy me. Two and a half hours in the morning and two in the afternoon. I may have to go out sometimes, but the boy can carry on. Method's the thing. Now, what about you?"

"How,—sir?"

"I shan't be bleeding you——?"

"No. I can manage two guineas quite well."

"Well,—that's that," said Mr. Porteous; "come and watch me finish my flue."

XIII

I

SO Christopher left the town school, and went daily to
Mr. Porteous's stone house in Gold Hill Lane, and there
he began to learn that which no schoolmaster had ever
taught him before,—method. For this unconventional
clergyman was not only a great scholar, but a born teacher.
He was full of enthusiasms, and his enthusiasms communi-
cated themselves to Kit.

They sat in a big, bare room on the first floor. The room
had no carpet; it was lined with books; it had two windows,
one of which looked into a dark and damp garden, and the
other into a yard. The windows had no curtains. A long
plain deal table, clothless, stretched from the fire-place to
one of the windows.

Kit and Mr. Porteous sat opposite each other, for when
Kit was at work on Latin prose and algebra, Mr. Porteous
would be amusing himself with Einstein's theory or a book
of MacDougal's on psychology.

"Psycho-physical parallelism. What's that, Sorrell?"

"Don't know, sir."

"As a matter of fact it's rot. To be able to realize that
a theory is rot saves one a lot of trouble. Now, what about
ten minutes' boxing? You haven't hit me yet."

The table would be pushed back, and Christopher—wearing gloves that looked half as big as his head, would be
given the most practical of demonstrations. In spite of
his fifty-five years Mr. Porteous was very quick on his
feet.

"Better than quadratic equations, Sorrell?"

"A bit, sir."

"Even when I tap you on the nose—like that! You ought
to have blocked that blow."

So far as Christopher was able to discover there was
only one living creature that could annoy Mr. Porteous and

118

make him lose his smiling poise, and that creature was the common house-fly. In his attitude to the house-fly Mr. Porteous was a thorough pragmatist. The pink sheen of his bald head seemed to attract the unclean insects, and with words of wrath he would rise to vigorous attack. The windows would be closed, and yesterday's paper folded into a swatting stick, and Mr. Porteous would bound about the room, flapping and slamming and declaiming.

"Filthy things, Sorrell. They wipe their feet on your food, and are sick on your sugar. Take that, Beelzebub. Ha, you carrier of germs!"

He kept it up until no single fly was left alive in the school-room, and then he would sit down with a beaming smile and the air of having accomplished something, and peace would return. It was a peaceful room, a happy room, in spite of its austerity.

For Christopher was very sensitive to atmospheres, even more so than was his father. He had inherited his mother's strong physique and his father's temperament, and in after years he often looked back to that bare room with its un-carpeted floor and its kitchen chairs and deal table. He would remember the ink marks on the table, and the cracked pane of glass in the window overlooking the yard—the result of some devastating blow with yesterday's *Daily Mail,* —the green mould on the bricks of the yard, the greenish light that seemed to filter down through the great elm. Mr. Porteous's room—and the life therein—coincided with the last months of Kit's rather impersonal outlook on life. The atmosphere was clear and happy, but a little colourless and cold, for as yet sex was but vaguely present, no more than a faint glow rising above the boy's horizon.

Mr. Porteous had attained to mental and physical celibacy. He lived in his work and his books and his rotund enthusi-asms, in the Boys' Club which he ran, and to which Christopher was introduced. As a social force in the polite sense Mr. Porteous was a failure, for he was not pleasing to women, but in his setting of Kit's feet upon the path of true knowledge, and in his influence upon many of the Winstonbury boys, the curate did great work.

He made Christopher play football with the Club boys, and encouraged him to box with them, and with the gloves Mr. Porteous taught him a lesson. Sorrell's son was apt

to flinch, not from the blows, but from physical contact with
a less sensitive human. He was fastidious, proud, a creature of vivid impressions and strong feelings.

Porteous noticed it. There was one particular boy whom
Kit seemed quite unable to tackle—a little, loutish youngster with a face like a frog.

"Sorrell,—what's the matter with you—when you box with
Bugson?"

Kit flushed.

"I don't quite know. I think it's his face, sir."

"Ugly. I tell you what it is—you don't like the idea of
being hit on the nose by a boy—well—what shall we say—
a boy whom you despise."

Kit's colour deepened.

"That's true, sir. It's silly,—but directly you put me up
to box Bugson I feel helpless——."

"You flinch, or rather—the pride in you flinches. You
must get over that, Sorrell. Personally I don't like young
Bugson; I don't like his name or his face or his nature.
But we have to put up with the Bugsons. They are here—
there—everywhere. You'll meet cohorts of them—later.
But don't you see, Sorrell—that it is foolish to let oneself
be upset by the Bugsons? Go in—and hit. Don't flinch
from a thing because it's ugly—and makes you feel squeamish. We oughtn't to give way to the Bugsons."

Christopher took these words of wisdom to heart. He
boxed the frog-faced boy two nights later, and though
smiling, he let his natural hatred overcome his sensitive
impulse towards recoil. Kit was a strong boy, and capable
of explosive and emotional bursts of vigour. After that
evening he had no fear of Bugson. He had punched the
frog face, and punched it hard.

To his father he drew even closer during these months.
Sorrell had each alternate Sunday free, and he and Christopher would start off on some expedition into the country
or to some neighbouring town. They did a great deal of
talking. Mr. Porteous had brought no overclouding of the
happy candour with which they could look into each other's
eyes.

"No secrets, Kit."

"No, pater."

"Porteous tells me you are getting on very well."

"He makes things look different,—interesting. He'll tell you a funny tale in the middle of the 5th Prop."

"Jam on the bread."

"Besides—he seems so keen, pater, that he makes one keen."

As to the future Sorrell was very frank with the boy. He discussed it with him,—not as a father—but as a fellow of Kit's own age who had had the benefit of a man's experience.

"It is no use being a smug. When you have found out what you want to do—then go at it like blazes."

"It will come,—I suppose," said Kit. "Mr. Porteous says I'm not to trouble my head—beyond letting him fill it. But —then—you see, pater,—I know you want me to be good at something."

"I want you to be good at the thing which will pull you. Lots of chaps don't get the chance to do the thing they want to do. Just bread-and-butter jobs."

There were occasions when Sorrell went to smoke a pipe with Robert Porteous, and the more he saw of the man the more he liked and respected him. As yet the tutor had not discovered any special aptitude in Christopher, or as he put it "No monkey tricks," but he had discovered virtues that were much more important.

"The boy can't help doing well, my dear chap. He's got grit. He doesn't slink. He is one of those boys who develop—an early sense of responsibility. It's quite quaint in him,—no—not a bit priggish. He realizes what you are doing,—and I believe the ruling thought at the back of his mind,—no—don't let's say 'thought'—let's say feeling—is that he is not going to let you down. You are a great man to him."

"I'm an hotel porter——!"

"The time will come when he will think even more of the hotel porter."

"I hope he will."

"Sorrell," said Mr. Porteous with emphasis, "surely—you don't doubt it?"

Sorrell was looking out of the window into the dusky little garden.

"Women," he said, "one has to remember—that some day —there may be a woman."

For he had been fore-feeling these possibilities very strongly during the last few months. Lying with Kit on some hillside or under a tree, he would become aware of the boy as a vigorous and separate personality. He was on the edge—too—of the great adventurous sea of sex.

"I suppose that some day," Sorrell thought, "a woman will take him away from me. That's life. Have I any right to complain? Isn't it my job to make life as full and as rich for him as I can? But what sort of woman will it be? That's his affair. I'm not going to be the fool father, throaty and pompous. But I hope it will be a woman who won't want to leave the hotel porter at the bottom of the back stairs."

Needless to say he did not speak of this to Christopher, for when sex dawns certain reticences are born with it. The fig leaf is symbolical.

2

Late in the autumn the most unexpected of coincidences emphasized Sorrell's sense of the imminence of woman.

About four o'clock on a Saturday afternoon a big silver-coloured car with red wheels turned into the space behind the posts and chains. It had been raining and the hood of the car was up. A man in a leather coat emerged, a man with a ginger-coloured moustache, blurs of redness on each cheek, and the angry eyes of the heavy drinker. Sorrell, who was standing by one of the lounge windows, went out to meet him.

"Got a room here?"

"Double or single, sir?"

"Double."

"Yes,—on the first floor, sir."

"Right. Where's the garage?"

"Round to the left, sir. Shall I bring in the luggage?"

"Yes,—I'll go and have a look at the room."

"There is the office, sir. I expect it will be No. 7."

Sorrell went out towards the car. A woman was seated in it, but it was dark under the hood, and he had begun to speak to her before he realized who she was.

"The gentleman has decided to stay, madam. The luggage——"

The woman in the car was Christopher's mother.

She was the least embarrassed of the two. In fact she had recognized Sorrell and had adjusted herself to meet the situation while he was approaching the car. She appeared amused.

"Well—fancy meeting—you—here! Are you the porter?"

"I am."

She had changed very little, save that she looked more highly coloured, and more expensively dressed. Fatter, too, but Dora Sorrell had always been a solid creature. He remembered in a flash that it was her fine solidity, her glow, the fineness of skin and flesh that had first attracted him. She was beautifully built. In the old days he had often thought of her as a ship cleaving life with her bosom. And now her blue eyes looked at him ironically, yet with just a trace of compassion.

"Do you want to be introduced to my second?"

He retorted with a question.

"How long are you staying?"

"O,—just the night. Don't get windy, Stephen. Arthur does not know you from Adam. We can leave it at that. He's coming."

Sorrell got hold of the two leather suit-cases, and carried them into the hotel. His successor, in passing him, had spoken of a trunk on the luggage grid, and Sorrell sent Hulks out for the trunk. The incident had disturbed him, perhaps because of the surprise of it, though emotionally this chance meeting with Christopher's mother had been negative.

But the rampant sex of her! Those bold, clear eyes, the nose broadening slightly at the nostrils, the luscious yet shrewd mouth! She was the very essence of sex, and in the mother Sorrell had seen the physical prototype of the son, and it was this impression of her sex, forced upon him after all these years, that had disturbed him. Would Kit

inherit those impulses from his mother, that mixture of
passion and shrewd, worldwise contriving?

The second husband had entered his name in the visitors'
book.

"Mr. and Mrs. Arthur Sampits—London."

Some time after tea Sorrell strolled across to the garage
and looked at the silver-coloured car with the red wheels.
It was a Heartwell, one of the *de luxe* machines, and most
sumptuously fitted. Ponds,—the garage man, came and
stood at Sorrell's elbow.

"Some 'bus?"

Sorrell nodded a meditative head.

"How much would that cost?"

"Round about twelve hundred. Don't she glisten?"

It was evident that Dora had not mismanaged the business side of her second romance. She had obtained material
self-expression, and it had been the lack of it that had
caused the inevitable rift in her first marriage. She was
not a bad woman, only a highly sexed one, and Sorrell had
never satisfied her sex and its various desires; he had realized that there had been much that had seemed lovable
in Dora. For the first four years they had been very happy
together.

Yet her second husband was obviously a hard liver; a
full-fleshed, damn-your-eyes sort of man. Generous, no
doubt, ostentatiously generous. They suited each other.

It occurred to Sorrell to wonder whether they had any
children?

Also, did the mother ever think of the boy?

He hoped not.

Sorrell saw nothing more of the pair until half an hour
before dinner. He was putting coal on the lounge fire when
he heard a woman's voice behind him.

"Can you sell me some stamps?"

He turned quickly.

"Certainly, madam."

She was in evening dress, a black and gold affair, and
her fine throat and shoulders showed soft and white. The
big lounge was nearly empty. Her sang-froid was perfect.
She watched Sorrell take out his pocket-book. No one was
very near to them. She threw one sweeping and easy glance
around her.

"Thank you. A nice place you have got here. Is he—here?"

Sorrell's eyes met hers.

"No, madam——."

"At school—perhaps?"

"Yes."

She smiled faintly, instantly divining his antagonism and the cause of it.

"Of course—it is no use my asking you——."

"None at all——."

Sampits came into the lounge to find the porter putting away his pocket-book, and his wife placing stamps on two or three letters. Sampits' shirt front bulged. The sides of his trousers were widely braided.

"I say—can you get us a couple of drinks?"

"Certainly, sir."

"What's it to be, Do? An orange cocktail?"

"Yes, that will do me."

"Very good, sir."

Sorrell had no further speech with Kit's mother, and the silver car carried them off next day, yet when Sorrell placed the two suit-cases in the back seat and Sampits was paying Ponds for petrol, Dora beckoned to her first husband. She slipped a five-pound note into his hand, and nodded meaningly. Her nod meant "The boy."

Sorrell went in thoughtfully, with the note crumpled in his hand. He met Hulks' rosy face clapped against the side of a trunk that was balanced on his shoulder. Hulks had just taken unto himself a girl, one of the waitresses.

When Hulks returned from strapping the trunk on to a car Sorrell gave him the five-pound note.

"A swanker gave me this. You can have the lot, Bert."

"Me? Why?"

"My contribution to the ring, you know. And the best of luck, old lad."

Hulks stared at him.

"Was it the bloke with the silver car?"

"Yes."

"Why, he gave me five bob. He starts getting squiffy pretty early. But—I say——"

"You keep it, Bert. It's a little return for the way you have backed me up."

3

Some time in November news that was more disturbing
than the meteoric passing of his divorced wife brought back
the little intent frown to Sorrell's forehead. Mr. Roland
called him in one evening into his sitting-room. There was
whisky, a siphon, and glasses on the table, and two arm-
chairs were drawn up before the fire.

"I want to talk about things, Stephen. Help yourself
and sit down."

Roland's room was full of bachelor comforts, but Sorrell,
as he helped himself to whisky and soda, had a feeling that
Mr. Roland was about to speak of uncomfortable things.
For there were certain doubts that of late had grown to a
distant shadowiness in his mind. Sorrell was a man of
detail. He kept in his little note-book a daily record of the
number of people who passed through the hotel.

"We are not paying our way, Stephen."

"I wondered, sir."

The soda from the siphon hissed into Mr. Roland's glass.
He was as deliberate as usual, but his quiet blue eyes had
a calculating look. Sorrell, in front of the fire, felt a
chilly sensation trickling down his spine.

"You are a man with a head——. Besides, one wants
to talk sometimes. Have you any idea——?"

"We have never been quite full up, sir."

"No."

"And the figures have been dropping."

"I expected that. Look here,—I have been working out
a table of averages. A statistician could draw a nice series
of curves from them. Anyhow—it shows our position pretty
clearly."

He picked up a paper, and crossing to the fire, sat down,
his glass in his hand.

"I find that with forty out of our sixty rooms occupied we
cover expenses. Our summer average was 47, our autumn
36, our present 29. Take three four-monthly periods. That
gives an average of 37, which means that we are losing
roughly at the rate of three rooms a day."

"Do you count double and single rooms, sir?"

"I have allowed for that."

"Well, is that so bad, sir, for the first year?"

"No,—but is our winter average going to stand at 29? I look at it like this. We ought to be full for six months, and half full for the other six months. That would give an average of 45. Five—daily—on the right side."

"I see that. But—next—season——?"

"That's the problem."

"What about cutting expenses?"

"I don't want to do that. Cheese-paring. All wrong. One ought to go out for the generous success. I hate doing things meanly."

Sorrell sat staring at the fire, as though to pluck inspiration from the glow of it. He heard Mr. Roland say that he had contemplated the possibility of running the Pelican at a loss for two years, but if at the end of two years the balance was still against him he would have to consider ending the adventure.

Sorrell seemed to see the old gulf opening again, and swallowing himself and all those dearly conceived schemes. Kit's education sacrificed. Yes, and after all the desperate fights that he had fought upon the stairs, and his hard-won victories over the lioness and the bull.

"What about more advertising, sir?"

"I shall try it."

"The slack time in the winter is the trouble. Couldn't you run the place for hunting people?"

Roland's blue eyes seemed to focus the idea.

"Sorrell,—that's worth thinking about. But—what we want is something original,—even though it is something quite silly."

"Yes,—something original, sir,—something to get the place known."

Sorrell went to his room in a gloomy mood, worried by the thought of slipping back from the foothold he had established.

A startling advertisement! If only it were possible to erect a huge stentophone somewhere, and set it shouting "Stop at the Pelican, Winstonbury."

But would the public listen? Were people such sheep as they seemed? Was not the Englishman still somewhat of a person who resented being shouted at?

There might be subtler ways,—but what were they?

XIV

I

THE number of the Pelican bedrooms occupied during the winter months averaged twenty-three. Mr. Roland was losing money steadily, and Sorrell saw the old black gulf reopening under his feet. Moreover, his income from tips had fallen by half, and after paying Mr. Porteous and Mrs. Garland he had little to boast of in the way of savings.

Yet his dread of disaster made him work the harder. His thoroughness was fanatical, nor was he the only member of the Pelican's staff who had no desire to seek work elsewhere. An enlightened self interest reinforced the popularity of Thomas Roland, and Mrs. Marks and Fanny Garland were every whit as keen as Sorrell to make the Pelican a place of comfort and of efficiency. As a matter of fact Tom Roland had received but one solitary complaint during the course of six months, and this was from an American who thought that he had bought the earth.

The responsible members of the staff knew nearly as much as Sorrell did, and Fanny Garland, in her abrupt and cheerful way, put her philosophy into words.

"It must pay if Roland holds on long enough. I've been in a dozen places—on and off—and not one of them was a patch on the Pelican. Charged their people much the same prices too. You should have seen some of the kitchens and the bedrooms! All I can say is if people don't know the difference between a place like this—and the ordinary take it or leave it pub——"

"People are such easy fools," said Mrs. Marks. "They go on taking the same second-rate stuff,—and grumbling. Honesty doesn't always pay."

"It depends on who you are dealing with," Sorrell put in. "Mr. Roland's idea is to run a place properly for the people who can appreciate it."

"Ah,—there you are! But the wrong people have got the money, my lad. Why,—look at some of the lot I had last night. Didn't know how to feed themselves properly. You have only got to shove an underdone steak and some chipped potatoes and a glass of beer under their noses. They're not educated up to our standard."

Sorrell laughed. There was a lot of wisdom in Fanny's words, for the Englishman can be such a creature of good-natured inertia that he will accept what is second-rate and not trouble to encourage the enterprising person who offers him something better. It is a mistake to offer first-class material to second-class minds.

Fanny would have her say.

"We have to cater for the swank crowd, and the grocers and the butchers who can afford to chuck money about and mean to do it. If a place is too gentlemanly it makes 'em feel uncomfortable. There aren't any gentlefolk these days."

"A few, my dear," said Sorrell.

"Precious few. Not enough for us to live on. Our job is to get the fat people in the big cars, the people with plenty of money and no manners. What's the matter? We might be able to teach 'em manners. Besides, you can always put your tongue in your cheek."

Sorrell wondered if Fanny Garland was right. He went so far as to put her points before Mr. Roland, but Mr. Roland would not alter his atmosphere, or attempt to adapt it to a post-war society.

"She says we are too gentlemanly, sir. I understand what she means. Too much like a good old club in Pall Mall."

"Quite. But I am not going to adjust—downwards—Stephen. I won't do it. The other people can adjust upwards—or stay away. Besides, hang it all, we give them the best——"

"Well, sir, a man who has left the sty rather late—may feel a bit uneasy in a drawing-room."

"I know what you mean. If we are all 'bar' and I had two or three fluffy-haired fascinators and a 'loud speaker,' and went about in my shirt sleeves with a grinning alcoholic face? Quite so. Making the new aristocracy feel at home. Not for me, Stephen."

"I feel the same, sir,—but then——"

"I know. You have got that boy of yours. We'll hang on as we are. I don't believe—yet—that giving people the best—means bankruptcy."

The spring came and the Pelican's average rose gradually to 33. The Easter holidays took it to 57, and Sorrell's forehead began to clear, but a week later the average had fallen to 39. Yet Sorrell happened to know that the George and the Black Bear, two very indifferent inns in Winstonbury itself, were doing good trade. Gossip reached him. The tobacconist from whom he bought his tobacco, a rosy and garrulously cheerful person, asked him bluntly whether "Roland hadn't bitten off more than he could chew?"

Sorrell said something sarcastic.

"That depends on what the public wants."

"The public knows what it wants," said the fat man arrogantly.

"The trouble is that it doesn't."

"Well,—I'm not worrying. It's not my funeral."

He beamed. He appeared to regard anyone else's failure as a tribute to his own self-complacency.

"Too swanky, you know,—too refined. Hardly trouble to serve a caller with a drink. A regular snob-hole I call it."

Sorrell guessed that certain unwelcomed commercial travellers had been talking. Roland had offended a large and mobile class of customers in closing the commercial room.

A snob-hole!

Yes,—but wasn't snobbery of a sort universal? Refine it slightly and it became a useful aspiration. Carry it still higher and it shows itself as man's love of mystery, beauty, queerness, something a little different from himself. Snobbery is the foot-stool at the feet of reverence.

To put it in the language of the journalist—"What the Pelican needed was to become the Motorists' 'Mecca,' the goal of the sentimental, sensation-loving public, a place where some astoundingly romantic or astoundingly sordid thing had happened. If you could put up a notice across the road 'The notorious Nemo murdered his French mistress here,' or 'It was here that the Bishop stayed when he spent the night with a lady from London.'"

Sorrell's mood was growing cynical. Failure, undeserved failure, would be both bitter and absurd.

2

Yet the Pelican was to have her picture on the illustrated pages of the daily papers, and Sorrell, when he looked back in after days on the ironical splurge of life's coincidences, was moved to a little, mischievous laughter.

It happened in May. A light blue two-seater car drew up tentatively outside the hotel, and a neat, sallow-faced man with a smudge of black hair on his upper lip, got out and approached the porch. Behind him, in the car, he had left one of the most pleasantly pretty creatures Sorrell had ever seen, a soft, short-nosed, merry, insouciant, child-eyed little lady who looked out on life wisely from under the brim of her black "cloche" hat. She had an air of extraordinary unaffectedness, as though she had come straight out of a convent, and found life wonderful, and innocent and good.

The neat and sprightly man with the minute black moustache addressed himself to Sorrell. "Is the manager in?"

"I think so, sir."

Thomas Roland was at the piano, and since the owner of the blue car had asked to see him privately, Sorrell took the stranger to Roland's room. The man's face was vaguely familiar to Sorrell, but he could not remember where he had seen him before. During the war—perhaps? He returned to the lounge so as to be ready to deal with the two light trunks strapped to the luggage grid of the blue car, should he of the little moustache and the quick and restless eyes decide to put up at the Pelican.

Five minutes later Sorrell saw Roland and the stranger mounting the stairs together, and when they reappeared Roland was laughing, and offering his cigarette-case to the visitor.

"That's quite all right. I'll have everything arranged. Stephen, will you take this gentleman's luggage up to No. 1."

The blue car was put away in the garage, and the two

young things vanished into the garden, where Fanny Garland
was told to take tea out to them under one of the chestnut
trees. Sorrell was redescending the stairs after carrying up
the luggage when he saw Roland beckoning to him from
the end of the passage.

"Stephen——"

"Sir?"

"One moment; come to my room."

Roland was smiling.

"Guess who our new visitors are."

"Honeymooners."

"Well, yes,—but rather important honeymooners. They
are here incognito. Guess."

"I seem to have seen the man's face."

"I expect you have. Ever heard of Ethel and Duck?"

"Not Ethel Frobisher and Duncan Scott? Why—that's
the man of course."

"Just so. The wedding has been a world event. But
you wouldn't expect a couple of cinema super-stars to be
running away from publicity."

"I could understand it,—personally."

"That's the position, Stephen. Scott put it to me—
straight up. 'We want to get away from the confounded
reporters and their cameras. We're just fed up with it. We
want to be our two selves for a week. See?'"

Sorrell nodded.

"Don't tell any of the others, Stephen. I am fixing them
up in a little private suite. I have promised Scott that he
shall have peace here."

Sorrell understood Mr. Roland's laughter, for it was kind
laughter, even though these two immensely rich young people
could have bought the unprofitable Pelican Hotel and
thought no more of it than of buying a box of chocolates.
Bedrooms No. 1 and 2 were turned into a little private suite.
All meals were sent up to the two lovers, the World's Pet
Lovers, for that was what they were.

Sorrell confessed to human curiosity. He was interested
in these two young things who were so bored by the world's
frenzied favours that they had fled away together into the
green deeps of an English countryside. He watched them
in the garden. They appeared to him quite ordinary young
people, and very much in love with each other and that,—

in spite of the fact that Duck had been making public love to Ethel for the last three years, playing the gallant rescuer in all sorts of situations, and posing in a sentimental embrace at the end of some hundreds of reels. To Sorrell it all seemed incredible—and rather absurd. That it should have been necessary for special police to be detailed to control the crowds when these two arrived at a London railway terminus or departed from one! Thousands of people scuffling, and pushing and cheering, men with cameras climbing on other men's shoulders; girls throwing flowers! There was but one other person in the world who inspired the same furore. The World's Pet Lovers! Little Ethel Frobisher making the romance seem "his" to the milk-boy, the clerk, and the collier. Duck, filling factory girls with the delight of being loved just like that.

As Mr. Roland had put it—"The wedding had been a world event." And then—the two had disappeared, slipped into that little blue car and fled, yearning wisely to be themselves, to be able to sit under a tree and feel natural—or to feel nothing at all. No cameras, no crowds.

The suggestive temptation struck Sorrell with mischievous abruptness. Obviously, the human heart of the world would not be content to be left in the steps of the church. It would be crying to the purveyors of news—"The honeymoon! We want to hear about the honeymoon. Where—are—Ethel and Duck? Where? We want to know."

Sorrell stood leaning against his porter's desk, scribbling nothings on an odd piece of paper.

If it were known that Ethel Frobisher and Duncan Scott were staying—or hiding in the Pelican at Winstonbury? What a coup for the press-man or the photographer! What an advertisement for the Pelican!

3

Sorrell was tempted, and so much was he tempted that he knocked that evening at Mr. Roland's door. He had a smile on his face, a mischievous and surreptitious smile.

"Has it occurred to you, sir——? The two upstairs?"

"In what way, Stephen?"

Sorrell had closed the door, and was holding the handle.

"Suppose it were known——? I know it is a silly world, —but the news would be all over the country in two days. And look at this——?"

With one hand he unfurled the chief page of a popular morning daily, and Mr. Roland was able to read the headlines at a distance of five yards:

THE WORLD'S LOVERS MARRIED.

GREAT SCENES.

WHERE HAVE ETHEL AND DUCK GONE FOR THEIR HONEYMOON?

Roland rubbed his deliberate chin.

"Yes, quite so, Stephen," he said; "I see the idea. I suppose a million or two people are interested in this honeymoon. The mysterious and romantic disappearance of the World's Lovers! But it can't be done."

"But what a chance——!"

"I know. I suppose we shall never have such another chance of getting the old Pelican up in the sky like a *Daily Mail* smoke advertisement,—but it can't be done."

"Not if—I did it?"

"Stephen, you Jesuitical rogue! No, I promised Scott to keep quiet. He's a very decent little chap. I had dinner with them."

"I see——"

"They asked me. They have a sense of fun. I enjoyed my dinner. And Mrs. Scott has a nice taste in music. We had our coffee down here, and she played Debussy to us. You see?"

Sorrell folded up his sheet of paper.

"It's a pity,—but you are quite right, sir. How long are they staying?"

"A week."

"Well,—towards the end of the week there wouldn't be any harm in getting a local photographer to take a few snapshots. Besides,—I happen to know the reporter who sends up any local news to the *Daily Sun*——. It would be a magnificent coup for him, and for us——"

Roland looked up at him with droll and ironical gravity.

"The man of ideas! You ought to be a publicity agent, Stephen. But it is worth considering. I can't see how it can hurt anybody. Wait,—I'll go up and ask them."

He did, and Sorrell, following him half way up the first flight of stairs, heard amused voices and a girl's laughter. It seemed that the World's Lovers had a sense of fun. Moreover, the man who was hiding them deserved his reward.

Roland caught Sorrell on the stairs, and behind Sorrell Mr. Roland saw the face of Sorrell's son.

"Nothing like frankness, Stephen."

"They are willing——?"

"Yes,—I have permission to introduce a tame photographer on the sixth day. They are rather amused at the idea of our getting some reflected glory. When they leave here—no one will know where they are going."

Sorrell stood rubbing his right cheek. He was visualizing other possibilities.

"It will be all over the world. Their 'first hiding-place on the great honeymoon.' We could have one or two of the plates enlarged and hung up——"

"Stephen," said Mr. Roland, "I believe you would like me to hang a banner across the road. 'This is the place where Duck and Ethel stayed on their honeymoon.'"

Sorrell looked at him solemnly.

"So few good chances——. It is pretty beastly to have been down in the mud. Is there anything to be ashamed of in seizing one's chances?"

"I know," said Tom Roland,—"I know."

XV

I

ETHEL FROBISHER and Duncan Scott were peculiarly wise young people, and not in the least like the "Duck and Ethel" of the shop-boy's world, wonderful creatures who lived in an atmosphere of champagne and motor-cars, yachts and fur coats, Monte Carlo and mystery. The common man dreams of a heaven paved with gold; the wise man would be well content with a heaven of flowers. Nor is it unnatural that the poor, envious industrial crowd should clutch at material things. And, no doubt, the shop-girl viewed Ethel Frobisher as a sort of super-courtezan, loaded with sensual love and diamonds, a gorgeous butterfly, the symbol of all the garish and sensational life that exists only in the mind of the poor little materialist.

Scott was a Balliol man; and had been a schoolmaster, and Ethel Frobisher had come from a Somersetshire parsonage. Both had a sense of humour, and an ironical appreciation of "fame" as it had befallen themselves. They laughed over it. There was nothing American in their mental make-up.

To "Ethel and Duck" Mr. Roland brought other refreshments than the Pelican could offer, and they accepted him with delight and a sense of happy relief. Escaping from a world of cads and of bounders it was pleasant to meet this placid and humorous person to whom it was not necessary to explain the fact that a bowl of roses, or a piece of music, or a rolling puppy might be utterly satisfying things.

They spent the evenings in Roland's den, talking and making music, and laughing at life and each other.

"Guess my wife's ambition, Roland?"

It was to have a garden and a paddock and a small car and two dogs, and to grow Darwin tulips and Hybrid Teas and Phlox, and to go up to town three days in every month, and never to enter a picture-house.

"That dream ought to be realized—rather easily."

"We are giving ourselves another three years,—and then we shall retire."

"And break the great public's heart!"

"Before it breaks ours," said the wife.

Duncan was going to grow fruit. In some ways they were most amazingly unsophisticated. Fame had disagreed with them, as too many sweets disagree with a healthy child, or too much wine with a work-loving man. Both were the happy victims of an incurable simplicity. They had had a surfeit of sensation, of notoriety, of cheap splendour; they had come to resent being regarded as the spoilt darlings of Demos. It was their very simplicity, their vital sense of fun that made them beloved.

Roland pointed this out, when their child-like intimacies included him in their philosophy of life.

"But—ought you to retire?"

They gave him to understand that it was not "the job" that bored them, but the whole atmosphere in which they were expected to work and play and breathe. It was too horribly artificial, and tainted, and commercialized. They had made up their minds to leave it before the taint spread to their souls.

"For—it does—you know," said the wife; "you may say to yourself, 'It shan't'—but it does. Imperceptibly. Like autumn in a garden——. Before you know where you are everything is rotten."

Scott had his own peculiarities. He hated what he called "Being messed about." He had a passion for doing the small things of life for himself, tinkering at his car, making his own early cup of tea. To him a "valeted world" was his idea of Hades. He hated crowds, he—the crowd's film-hero. He liked old clothes and old books, and an old pipe.

"And they expect me to smoke a pipe studded with diamonds—and to dress like their idea of a Bond Street lord! A sort of bastard creature, a mixture of a duke—an actor and a jockey."

They made Roland feel very fatherly towards them, as towards two fortunate but unspoilt children. He bequeathed to the wife his piano and all the flowers in his garden, and to the husband his own little lock-up garage where Duncan could play about in private with the works of the blue two-seater. He provided them with a luncheon basket when they went picnicking. The vases in room No. 1 were full of his flowers.

Bowden complained.

"That there young woman's bin at my toolips."

"I gave her permission."

"Why can't she let 'em grow where they was meant to grow?"

"Because she wants to paint them, Bowden."

"Paint 'em? Paint Clara Butt and William Pitt? Ain't they good enough?"

"Portraits, Bowden."

"Yar,—why can't she let 'em alone. Treadin' on the beds —too."

Roland, laughing, told the little lady that she was in disgrace.

"My gardener doesn't approve of your painting the lily."

"I'm so sorry. I only took a flower here and there. The next time—I'll ask him. What's his name?"

"He goes by the name of Bowden."

She did dare to ask "His Surliness" for tulips.

"Please, Mr. Bowden,—Mr. Roland says that I may have three or four tulips. Would you cut them for me? I don't want to spoil your beds."

Bowden cut her a dozen, which was rank treachery to all the grumpy ideals of his gardener's soul. For when Ethel smiled, the whole world smiled with her, and her smile went all over the world.

Such was their honeymoon, the simplest of affairs, a kind of rustic reaction from the glare of the studio and the searchlights of the Press. They had played pathos to the public, and it so happened that they were to play pathos to each other, and to touch the great heart of the world—in reality, as well as in romance.

Sorrell saw them start out on that sunny May morning, with a luncheon basket in the dicky. A dilapidated looking lorry was rumbling Londonwards, and the blue car overtook it, just where the broad straight road began to curve, and a row of Lombardy poplars raised their spires against the blue of the distant hills. In fact, Sorrell saw the thing happen not two hundred yards from the hotel. He heard the note of Scott's horn and saw the grey bulk of the lorry swerve suddenly across the road. It caught the blue car amid-ships, and drove it against one of the poplars.

Scott was slightly cut about the face with broken glass, but with his little wife things were different. The lorry had smashed the side of the car, and the radiator had struck her.

Sorrell ran.

But before he reached the place Scott had got his wife out of the wrecked car and was carrying her towards the hotel. He looked as he had never looked on the films, with his partner lying like a wounded bird in his arms.

"Man,—get a doctor, 'phone,—hurry."

And the driver of the lorry, a man with a face like "Old Bill's," was standing in the middle of the road, staring at the wreckage, and repeating the same words over and over again, though there was no one there to hear them.

"The bloomin' link-rod dropped. I can't think 'ow it came to 'appen. Just when they was passin' me—too. The bloomin' link-rod——"

2

This accident on the London road within half a mile of Winstonbury was to give the Pelican an advertisement such as Sorrell had never dreamed of.

He had mounted a bicycle and ridden into the town for a doctor,—two doctors. The whole place was in a flurry, and when the Winstonbury doctors had seen the little lady and taken counsel with her husband there were 'phone messages and telegrams to London. For half an hour Sorrell was standing by the telephone with Duncan Scott fidgeting and smoking cigarettes beside him.

"Through yet?"

"No, sir."

"O,—damn it——! Offer the girl a five-pound note, anything——."

"Through now, sir."

Scott grabbed the receiver from him.

"Hallo,—hallo, is that Sir Magnus?—It is? Thank God——. We have had a smash. The doctors—here, —pretty gloomy. Could you come down at once? Me?

No, my wife—Ethel.—What? You will come? O,—that's great——. At once. They're afraid——"

With all these comings and goings, these alarms and anguishes, the inevitable truth filtered out. No one thought of concealing it, and two hours after the accident had happened Sorrell was caught by a local reporter.

"I say—it is a fact?"

"What?"

"The injured lady is Ethel Frobisher?"

"It is a fact. They were here on their honeymoon."

"Great Scott——! If I'd known——. Here's a scoop!"

The reporter dashed out to examine the site of the accident, and to interview the lorry driver who was still moping at the side of the road, and Sorrell thought no more of him for the moment. His self and its affairs were obscured by his human involvement in the morning's tragedy. He had seen the little lady carried in and up the stairs by a man with a face whose whiteness was streaked with red.

Sir Magnus Ord came down by car. It seemed that the case was as serious as it could be, and Ord wished to move the little lady to the quietest room in the hotel, away from the road and overlooking the garden. It was arranged. People moved out to give place to her. Two nurses arrived from Winstonbury. A little crowd of interested humans began to move out from Winstonbury, to gather round the wrecked car and to stare at the Pelican windows. Hulks came to tell Sorrell that he had found three men taking photographs in the garden, and what was he to do about it?

By eight o'clock, when the Winstonbury shops had closed, a considerable crowd stippled the white road and the broad grass verges. Sorrell found his son sitting on one of the black chains, a little figure by itself, youthfully interested.

"Is she going to die, pater?"

"How did you hear about it, Kit?"

"Oh, everybody's talking about it. I saw her in *The Great Love*—you know. Only two weeks ago, pater. Fanny Garland took me."

"I suppose it depends on the doctors."

"I think—it must be rather fine to be a doctor," said the boy, reflectively.

The Winstonbury *Evening Argus* began the great game of "headlines."

"DUCK AND ETHEL IN GRAVE MOTOR SMASH AT
WINSTONBURY."

But the *Evening Argus'* hoot was a mere rustic bleat when
the London press took up the cry; Sorrell became a student
of "headlines":

TERRIBLE ACCIDENT TO ETHEL FROBISHER.
TRAGIC ENDING TO THE GREAT HONEYMOON.
THE WHOLE WORLD GRIEVES WITH THE WORLD'S LOVER.

By mid-day Sorrell was able to count some forty cars
strung along the side of the road between the Lombardy
poplars and the Pelican. The number steadily increased,
and so did the noise they made when the later arrivals had
to find room somewhere and began to use the space beside
the inn as a field of manœuvre. People crowded into the
hotel,—and asked to be given lunch. Knots of them stood
staring at the piece of grass where the accident had happened, and from which the crumpled car had been removed.
The bark of one of the poplars had been torn, and from
the gash curious people pulled fragments of splintered wood.
Even the hotel garden was invaded. Roland found a lot
of women staring up at the bedroom windows and talking
in loud voices.

"That's it,—that's her window. I saw the nurse——."
They walked over the flower beds.
Roland lost his temper. He went out to them.
"Haven't you ladies any sense of decency?"
He cleared them out, and had the garden doors locked
and the gate chained,—but when the garden had achieved
silence the lounge became like Babel. People were standing
there as though it were the deck of a channel steamer, and
the passage leading to the dining-room the gangway to the
quay.
Roland stood on the stairs.
"Ladies and gentlemen——"
No one paid the least attention, and he had to shout.
"Ladies and gentlemen—may I be permitted to remind
you that a woman is—dying. A little silence, please——.
If you will go out by that door——."
With Sorrell and Hulks to help him he got the lounge
cleared, and he ordered the hotel doors to be locked.

"Hulks, get a chair and sit down by that door. The only people you will allow in or out are the people staying here."

The noise and the hustle then concentrated themselves outside the hotel. Cars were drawn up two deep, with a central passage between them through which the passing traffic sorted itself out slowly. Roland rang up the Police Inspector at Winstonbury.

"Will you come out and clear this road. We have a mob of cars and people here. And what we want is—silence."

The Inspector came out in person, with a couple of constables, and the road was cleared—and the traffic kept on the move. And yet though persuasion was used, human and reasonable persuasion, people stood backed at a little distance like cattle turning stupidly to stare, and passing cars would slow up and attempt to stop outside the hotel.

Roland stood inside the locked front door with his hands in his pockets.

"Here's your nice—sensational—civilization," he said to Sorrell. "Cattle——!"

"Cattle can read, sir."

"Damn it,—let us give them something to read."

During the afternoon a ladder was reared against the great cross-beam supporting the sign of the Pelican, and Albert Hulks ascended the ladder and hung up two boards so that travellers from west and east could read what was printed upon them.

"SILENCE—PLEASE.
ILLNESS—HERE.
THIS HOTEL IS CLOSED.
PLEASE PASS—QUIETLY."

The appeal had considerable effect.

3

The Press of the country had resumed control of the lives of "Ethel and Duck," and the autocrat of the *Daily Sun,* having heard of the crowds and of Mr. Roland's notice-boards, dared to admonish his readers.

"GIVE ETHEL A CHANCE."

The illustrated pages of the various papers reproduced photographs of the wrecked car, and of the poplar tree with the wound on its trunk indicated by a black cross. There were pictures of the Pelican Inn, and of the crowded road, and of Sir Magnus Ord leaving his car. Sorrell read what the driver of the motor lorry had to say about the accident, and what a local garage proprietor thought about it, and what he himself was supposed to have said about it. One paper produced a photograph of Thomas Roland—"The Man who asked for Silence." Gentlemen of the press were discovered entering the hotel by back doors, and even by a passage window, and one adventurer was found outside the door of Ethel's room, waiting to question one of the nurses.

Scott, slipping out noiselessly with that tense, stiff, patched face of his, walked into the gatherer of news.

"Excuse me, sir, but how——?"

"What do you want——?"

"I'm a journalist, sir."

"O,—hell!" said the husband softly, "can't you people let us alone?"

For there was just a little flicker of hope fluttering like a bird in that silent room. The flame still lived, and poor Scott seemed to stand watching the flame, and holding his breath. If his wife rallied sufficiently there was to be an operation, and to Scott every noise or sound of movement of the hotel was like a gust of wind troubling that feeble flame. When he was not sitting in his wife's room he had a chair in the corridor, and he spent the whole of the first night in that chair.

It is almost impossible to silence an hotel, however considerate people may be, and Sir Magnus Ord's pet fad was a professional detestation of all noise. Discords impinging upon the brain, and helping to exhaust it. His prejudice against all noise added itself to Scott's suppressed anguish of restlessness. He appealed to Roland.

"I say, how many people have you in the hotel?"

"About twenty. I have turned away all new-comers."

"Look here, my dear chap,—I'll rent the whole of your hotel for three weeks—if you can persuade everyone to clear out. It's not a question of money."

"It isn't. I'll do it."

"I say—, Roland, you——."

"That's all right. There is only one thing that matters. I'll go and interview all the people staying here and get them to move."

"And you'll charge me——."

"For your two rooms, and your board, and for the two nurses——."

"No, no,—that's nonsense."

"Well, it's my nonsense. I like to do a thing thoroughly."

"But—my dear man—I'm rolling——"

"That doesn't make any difference."

"But I can't let you shut up the whole place for three weeks——"

"That is what I am going to do."

Scott's face twitched. He gave in, but he gave in with a passionate reservation. He was not going to quarrel with a *beau geste,*—but some day he would reply to it.

"I shan't forget this——, old chap."

"My dear lad,—I want her to have every chance. I'm not going to sell you her chance. That's all. I'll turn the staff out into the annexe."

And that was what he did, and that evening the little lady rallied. The flame grew bigger, and Scott, walking up and down the carpeted corridor on his bare feet, or sitting in his chair, blessed the silence and felt that there was some healing virtue in it. No gusts of noise causing that little flame to waver. Old Ord had smiled at him. "To-morrow, —if she goes on rallying through the night."

About dusk, Sorrell, moving quietly across the empty lounge, saw a dim white face behind the glass of the hotel door. He moved to wave the intruder away, and recognized his son. Softly he unlocked and opened the door.

"What do you want, Kit?"

They spoke in whispers.

"How is—she?"

"Better. There is to be an operation."

Kit looked immensely solemn.

"An operation——."

"Yes,—if she can bear it. And if—she can——."

Christopher's eyes had a far away look.

"I think I'd like to be a doctor, pater."

"Would you?"

"And mend things,—save people."

They gazed steadily into each other's eyes.

"It's good business, Kit,—an idea. Now, run along, old chap. Perhaps there will be good news to-morrow."

4

There was good news. The little lady had rallied remarkably during the night and the very eminent surgeon who had been waiting on the threshold of her room for Nature's beckoning finger, went in and laid his succouring hands upon her. Scott, unable to keep still while the operation was in progress, wandered about the garden and in and out of Roland's room. When in the garden he was for ever looking up at the window of his wife's room, for one of the nurses had promised to wave a handkerchief if things seemed to be going well.

Roland, who was writing letters at his desk, found Scott leaning in at his window.

"She's waved——!"

"I'm glad."

"Isn't it great?"

He resumed his pacings up and down the grass, and round the flower beds and under the vivid green fringes of the beeches and the chestnuts. He had a peculiar, gliding walk of his own, the movement of a dancer, gay and debonair, and Roland noticed that his characteristic movements had come back to him. He had trailed; now he went like a winged Mercury. This was the vivid Duncan of romance, the world's happy hero.

Roland watched and smiled.

"Sorrell ought to be satisfied," he thought. "Fortune has sent us her favourite children."

Moreover, Fortuna appeared to have taken her place beside the Pious Pelican poised on the oak beam. The eminent surgeon was returning to town; he had the satisfied air of a man who had dined well, and Duncan walked at his elbow as though he wished to embrace him.

"So—you think—sir—really——?"

"We are not out of the wood yet, but everything has gone off most satisfactorily."

"Then—you really do think?"

"I think your wife will recover."

Duncan saw the great man into his car and at this happy moment a small, spry man waylaid him just as the car was moving off.

"Excuse me, sir——."

Scott turned on him with an excited laugh.

"What are you, the *Mail*, or the *Express*, or the *Gracers' Journal?*"

"The *Daily Sun*, sir."

"Right. Well,—they think she is going to live."

"I am very glad to hear it, sir."

"Good chap. Everybody's been most amazingly good. I wish I could thank everybody——."

The pressman was being given a priceless interview, and he knew it. He had arrived at a happy moment.

"We could do that for you, sir."

"Of course you can," and Duck looked at him with big eyes as though for the first time in his life he had discovered the virtues of the Press.

"Heard about Mr. Roland,—I suppose?"

"The proprietor. No,—but——."

"Shut up the whole hotel, turned everybody out, to give Ethel the best chance. I offered to hire the whole hotel for three weeks."

"Indeed, sir——!"

"But Mr. Roland wouldn't hear of it. Made us a present of three weeks silence. What do you think of that? I could tell you what I think—. He's a great man."

That Duck was over-excited, and exultant, and on the edge of laughter or tears was as obvious to the little pressman as was the unique personal atmosphere of the interview. He had got the real sob stuff. He could give the great public a picture of "Duck—the Live Man."

He did so, and he did more.

The *Daily Sun* came out with pictures of the Pelican and of Mr. Roland.

> "THE MAN WHO HAS GIVEN HIS HOTEL
> TO DUCK AND ETHEL
> FOR THREE WHOLE WEEKS."

When Sorrell saw the *Daily Sun* he realized that—somehow—without thinking about it—Mr. Roland had done a great thing. And he had done it thoroughly and without meanness. A little journalist had sent the magic bread back across the waters.

Sorrell took the paper to Roland, and if anything Roland appeared annoyed.

"I suppose you are pleased, Stephen."

"I can't afford to grumble, sir. If this does not make us —nothing will."

XVI

I

EACH morning a neat little bulletin in Thomas
Roland's writing was pinned on a board outside the
hotel, and the eighth of these bulletins declared Mrs.
Duncan Scott to be out of danger.

The surly Bowden sent her up armfuls of flowers. She
had asked to see Thomas Roland, and with Duncan sitting
at the head of her bed she gave the owner of the Pelican
Inn that world-wide smile of hers.

"What a horrible nuisance I have made of myself. You
have been so good——"

"Not a bit of it."

"Duncan has been telling me——. You must let us make
a fair return——. Mustn't he, dear?"

Roland held one of her hands.

"My dear little lady—I am getting my return. Don't you
realize that you have made the Pelican the most talked
of hotel in the British Isles. See what it is to be Ethel
Frobisher."

At the end of three weeks they were able to carry her
out into the garden, where she lay in a long chair padded
with cushions under the shade of one of the old trees. And
it was she who insisted upon Roland opening the doors of
the Pelican to the public.

"I shan't be able to prevent people coming into the garden
to stare at you," he said.

She laughed. Life seemed so good that she was ready
to be tolerant.

"I don't think I shall mind. After all——"

"It is not unpleasant to be——?"

"Oh,—within reason. One's human, you know. I really
did create a sensation?"

"An enormous sensation. At one time I thought that we

148

should have to barricade the place and put up a machine-
gun."

He stood looking down at her, whimsical and fatherly.

"Curiosity. That's a good sign."

"How?"

"I do believe that you are just a little bit curious as to
whether people will come and stare."

"Perhaps I am."

"Yes,—one must have an audience. If we can't pose before other people, we have to pose before ourselves."

"That's rather horrid of you."

"Not in the least. I'm one of those persons who poses to
himself. I find it most important that I should look well in
my own mirror. While—you——"

"But do I pose? I've always tried——"

"My dear little lady, I did not say you posed. You are
one of those fortunate persons who cannot help doing the
natural thing. That's the secret."

"Of what?"

"Of your fame. You get half the world tumbling over
itself to see a little woman whose naturalness is not a pose.
Most of us are swathed up like mummies. But you must
have your audience. Why not?"

So the embargo was removed, and on the second day the
Pelican's nest was full, and some thirty people had to be
turned away. It would appear that the little lady had
slipped a magic nest-egg into the circle of Thomas Roland's
enterprise and that the fortune that was to be hatched from
it was to be neither transient nor illusive.

And yet, as Roland said to Sorrell, afterwards—"It wasn't
our thoroughness or our hard work, Stephen, that saved us,
but luck, and the noise made by a section of a sensation-
mongering press."

Sorrell thought it over, and was moved to disagree with
him.

"No,—I think it was the human touch. It is always the
human touch that matters."

"Yes,—my dear chap,—but that was our luck. That it
should have happened here to Ethel. Thousands of people
might have been smashed up—and have died here—and the
great public would not have cared a damn."

"But why should they?"

"That's one of my points. We don't care. Like the war. Life's got too crowded and confused. You have to make such a great noise in order to be heard,—and I loathe noise. Short of blowing Vesuvius into the middle of Naples! Well, —Ethel blew up the Sensational Press for us, made it explode."

"She has done something more than that," said Sorrell, "she has blown up my boy."

"Oh? How? He wants to be a film star?"

"No, he wants to be a doctor."

"And achieve dramatic cures?"

"I think there is more in it than that."

Christopher had taken unto himself an autograph book, which meant that he had taken to hero worship, yet at the back of his mind Kit's most convincing hero was his father. Convincing because his heroism was not too obvious; it had that quality of steadfastness; it was like the seaman's heroism, the practical and un-self-conscious heroism of the man doing his job in foul weather and in fair. Kit had his admirable enthusiasms. That Dicker the Hampshire fast bowler, and Blackett the "heavy-weight" who travelled with a circus, had put their fists to Kit's book, was the ripe joy of the moment. Sorrell had never had his photo in the papers. He did not appear in a roped space wearing a purple and orange dressing-gown, and yet, as Christopher matured his father became to him—not quite a great man— but something more human, a very lovable one. His own life was permeated by his father's patient and indomitable purpose.

But for the moment Kit desired a particular autograph, and when Sorrell was told, he offered his services.

"I dare say I could get it for you."

"But, if you don't mind, pater, I would rather try and get it myself."

"You'll have to be introduced, my son."

"Shall I?"

"I'll ask Mrs. Scott."

Sorrell was one of those men who became a "person," and in after years habitués who pulled up at the Pelican would greet him as "Stephen." It was a familiarity that assured liking and respect. Stephen was a character, a person of importance, a man who never forgot anything and who did not react to the size of a tip. The Little Lady was one of the first to discover and to recognize the "Stephen" in Sorrell. He carried out her chair cushions; Roland had told her his history; to her Stephen was very much a person.

"I wonder if you would grant me a favour, madam?"

She liked the dignity with which he managed to invest his job.

"What is it, Stephen?"

"My boy wants your autograph."

"Well,—if you will bring his book."

"The fact is—he wants to collect it in person."

"Tell him to come. Tea time. I invite him to tea with us."

"It is very good of you, madam."

So, Christopher came to tea with Ethel and Duncan, and sat on a green garden chair under one of the chestnuts, and was fed on raspberry jam and iced cakes, and gazed upon the Little Lady with the eyes of a boy's adoration. He was shy without being awkward. It was plain that he thought her to be the most wonderful creature in all the world, just as wonderful as she was in the "Pictures." He fell in love with her; she was of more significance than the cakes.

The Little Lady soon had him talking in his wise and rather deliberate way, for Christopher never chattered. He was a silent and watchful child.

"I hear you are going to be a doctor."

"Yes,—I've decided——"

"And what made you want——?"

Christopher coloured and looked at her with the full can-dour of his serious eyes.

"You."

"Me? But—how——?"

"Well,—you see, everybody wanted you to get well, and Sir Magnus Ord was the only man who could get you well. He can do things. It must be great to be able to do things like that—when everybody else is feeling—just—helpless."

"So you want to be a second Sir Magnus Ord?"

"Well,—I don't suppose I shall be such a great surgeon, —but I should like to mend people."

"People like me?" she asked, with a gleam of the eyes.

"Sometimes,"—and he added quietly, "that would make up for the others."

"That's a rather remarkable kid," she said to Roland later.
"The son of a rather remarkable father. An hotel porter!
But what a porter!" he answered.

2

When the Scotts left the Pelican Inn at the end of June
it was like the departure of the fairy Prince and Princess.
Every member of the staff received a five-pound note,—and
the whole staff collected outside the hotel to say good-bye
to the Little Lady and her man. They shook hands with
everybody. Bowden arrived with a great bunch of roses,
and wearing a clean collar. Kit had persuaded Mr. Porteous
to allow him to take leave of his equations and the Gallic
campaigns of Cæsar. He stood, devotedly gazing.

The new car carried them off, and the cook—who was a
sentimentalist—laid her emotion upon Mr. Bowden's bache-
lorhood.

"She's as good as she's pretty."

And Kit,—with his youth throbbing to the sad but sacred
moment, thought the cook a very wise woman.

Afterwards, the Pelican settled down to solid business,
and Christopher went back to Mr. Porteous with an even
stronger inclination towards the sign of the Rod and the
Serpent. The hotel had been full for the last three weeks,
and it continued in that happy state all through the summer
and autumn, and even in November its average was 45.
Sorrell had opened an account with the branch of the Midland Bank at Winstonbury. Mr. Roland was composing an
operetta and building stables with a dozen loose boxes and
quarters for grooms. For he had adopted Sorrell's suggestion, obtained an interview with the local M.F.H. and come
to an understanding with him. The Master had business
instincts, and the Hunt needed funds. An up-to-date hotel
in the district ready to cater for those people from among
who could be persuaded to hunt with the Winstonbury pack
would be an advantage to both parties. Roland agreed to
advertise the Pelican as a hunting-hotel, and the Master
promised to give it his official recommendation.

"But don't sink too much capital, Mr. Roland. In these
Bolshie days—we wasters who have the courage to try and
break our necks——"

"But your coats are the right colour, sir. And I shan't make it a bricklayers' job. Timber and asbestos sheeting. If possible—I should like you to give the Pelican two meets a season."

"I think we can manage that."

So Mr. Roland's brown and white stables went up with quite moderate dispatch, and in November the hounds met at the Pelican. Kit dragged Mr. Porteous away from the austere schoolroom where a paraffin oil stove made a stuffy heat and threw a pattern on the ceiling. They watched the waving tails of the hounds and the red coats of the whips move off to draw Bar Holt wood. Kit went with the foot-followers, and after scrambling over gates and plodding across muddy fields was lucky enough to see a fox with the pack in full cry. He returned some time in the dusk to find Mr. Porteous and to tell him about it, for Mr. Porteous' fat little legs had not carried him very far.

In December the Pelican was singled out again by Fortune, for Royalty came west for a gallop with the Winstonbury pack, and Royalty stabled two horses in the Pelican stables and slept in a Pelican bed. In fact it was the very bed which the Little Lady had made historic. And again, there were pictures of the Pelican in the daily papers, showing a coyly smiling young Prince in the act of raising his top-hat to the spectators.

Half of Stephen Sorrel's head and body appeared on one of these pictures, but his good fortune occupied the middle of the plate.

The Pelican's December average was 43. The winter proved an open one. A dozen or more hunting men and women came down regularly. Parents who arrived to visit their sons at Hadfield School began to develop the Pelican habit. Mr. Roland was planning a Christmas season, and Sorrell's tips were pouring regularly into the Winstonbury branch of the Midland Bank. The cashier was becoming conversational across the counter.

In January Sorrell had an interview with the manager. He was admitted into the manager's private room. The manager expressed himself as only too ready to arrange the purchase of War Loan for him.

"A hundred pounds of 4½, 1925–45, Mr. Sorrell. The order shall go up at once to our brokers."

In February Albert Hulks married his waitress, and Mr. Roland's operetta was performed by the Winstonbury Musical and Dramatic Society. Mr. Porteous took the part of "Fra Domenico"; he wore a black beard and had a voice like Big Ben. Christopher and his father sat in the five-shilling seats, and Christopher's only disappointment was the Little Lady who was not playing the part of "Francesca." The lady who took the part of Francesca smiled all the time, but her smile was not the smile of Ethel Frobisher.

3

Christopher had been with Mr. Porteous for a year and a half when Sorrell decided to send him for two years to one of the best of the private schools. Christopher was fourteen. In eighteen months Mr. Porteous had given him so solid a grounding that he could have held his own with any boy of sixteen.

Sorrell had taken a long time to make up his mind, and Kit's mind had been included in the process. It was not merely a question of the wisdom of the step, but of how the boy felt about it. Feelings matter. There were the advantages and the disadvantages to be considered, and Mr. Porteous was co-opted to serve on the Sorrell Committee.

Nor was it a mere question of education, but a problem of class prejudices and of social "atmosphere."

As Sorrell put it to Porteous—"Envy—not love—is becoming more and more the driving force. That's how I view it. One has to weigh up hatreds and prejudices."

Porteous was not wholly in favour of the school.

"What's it going to give him?"

"Experience—of a sort. Confidence. He will mix with boys of the class that is going to be his,—and yet I don't want him to belong to any particular class."

"Can you help it?"

"I know what you mean. Our voices, our faces, our very way of wearing our clothes put us in a certain category. Because I have set out to give my boy advantages—I shall expose him to hatred and envy."

"My dear chap!"

"Isn't it true? The world has entered on a period of envy and bitterness. Industrialism and education—of a sort —have bred it."

"So you think of sending him to school——"

"Where he will not be exposed to class hatred. My idea is to keep him there two years. Then he can come back to you for another year or so, before he tackles the real adventure."

"Doctoring?"

"That seems to hold."

"A University first?"

"I don't know—yet."

"That will expose him to the sneers of the new young working-class intellectuals.—'A college man.'"

"I think that he will be exposed to that—in any event. As I see it—the social war is going to grow more and more bitter. You will be damned by the crowd class—even for having a certain sort of voice and face."

"Rather a gloomy view——!"

"No,—not gloomy,—but a little grim. Life is bound to sort people out, and the envious fools will always end up as the under-dogs. I don't mean my boy to be an under-dog."

Yet, the incident that finally decided both father and son in the choice of the path that Christopher was to follow, was a trivial one, and yet to Sorrell convincingly significant.

The incident occurred at a boys' football match in which Mr. Porteous's boys' club was playing the Winstonbury council school. Kit was playing for the boys' club, and Sorrell was watching the game. He had a knot of noisy youngsters near him who began to jeer at one particular player.

They called him "Collars and Cuffs." They mocked him every time he came near them or when he had the ball.

"Now then—Nosy."

"Haw—Mr. Fellah."

What was more Sorrell saw that the boys of the council school team had Christopher marked. They made a dead set at him; he was something alien; he did not belong to their class pack. He was different.

Sorrell saw his son "fouled," on more than one occasion, and the boys near him gloated and laughed, but when Kit

showed legitimate spirit in a charge or a tackle they snarled
at him.

"Foul——!"

"Dirty!"

"Play the game—'Collars.'"

"His father's only a por-tah."

Sorrell walked back with his son after the game, and a
few pregnant confidences passed between them.

"Do you like playing with those boys, Kit?"

"No—I don't, pater."

"All right. We'll alter that."

For Sorrell had seen that these sons of working men
hated the son of the ex-officer. They hated his face, his
voice, his pride, his very good temper. They hated him
for his differences, his innocent superiorities.

Hatred, a cheaply educated hatred was loose in the world.

The obvious thing was to educate the boy above it,—
and if possible to make him triumphant over it. Sorrell
and Kit arrived at their decision.

4

Mr. Launcelot Lowndes, M.A., the "head" of St. Benedict's at Westbourne received a letter from a Captain
Sorrell who appeared to be staying at the Pelican Hotel—
Winstonbury. The letter had been written on the hotel
notepaper, and by the hand of an educated man.

Mr. Lowndes promptly replied to it. He sent Captain
Sorrell a booklet on St. Benedict's, with photos of the school
playing-field, the gymnasium, the chapel, the type of dormitory that was used, and the infirmary. He gave Captain
Sorrell all the necessary information as to fees, and they
were heavy. The extras connected with the school games
amounted to a considerable figure. St. Benedict's engaged
the services of a games master who was an old Oxford
"blue."

Mr. Lowndes informed Captain Sorrell that there would
be a few vacancies at the beginning of the summer term.

Sorrell and his son talked it over.

"There is no reason why anyone should know, Kit, that
I am an hotel porter."

Christopher was troubled. He was neither ashamed of his father, nor did he wish to conceal his father or to apologize for him. If St. Benedict's demanded the concealment of the elder Sorrell's means of earning a livelihood,—well,—he would rather not go there.

Sorrell argued it out with him.

"A school like this has certain advantages; I want you to enjoy them. My job here must not stand in the way. You can tell the other boys that your father is a retired officer who lives at hotels. There is no reason why we should put all our cards on the table."

"But, supposing, pater——?"

"They found out? Why should they? You see, if you go up to Cambridge later,—it won't hurt you to have been at this school. When you leave I want you to coach with Mr. Porteous for a scholarship."

There was a part of Christopher that was keen to go to St. Benedict's. He would be able to play games there without being singled out for mean little persecutions; he would be able to make friends; he would not have to perform on the footer field with a lot of young louts who were more keen to kick him than they were to kick the ball. The atmosphere would be different, the clothes, the cleanliness, the traditions. Certain things would be bad form. Sorrell had explained all this. He said that it was quite good that certain things should be considered to be bad form. "Like not cleaning your teeth or not using a handkerchief, you know."

The end of it was that Kit decided that he would like to go to St. Benedict's, and to St. Benedict's he went, rigged out with a school-kit, and wearing the orthodox bowler and black socks. He had his cap and blazer with the purple and green colours of the school. He had his "sports-box," and a pound in pocket-money.

Sorrell had spent two days in town with him, and he saw him off at Victoria for the Sussex sea-coast town.

"Good-bye,—old chap."

Kit's lips quivered a little. He kissed his father.

"I shan't forget you are Captain Sorrell, M.C. I'll work hard."

"And play hard,—the big game, you know. Our game, my son."

XVII

I

THERE followed for Stephen Sorrell a season of
happy accomplishment. He was able to pause and
to think, not as a man thinks in some hustling crisis,
but calmly and pleasantly. He strolled instead of walking.
The Pelican had become very prosperous; the bird's feathers
were turning to gold.

In one week in August Sorrell had taken nearly ten pounds
in tips.

That was a solid basis upon which to build reveries, and
at eight o'clock each evening Sorrell would change into a
blue serge suit and a soft hat and walk out along the great
black road that led Londonwards. These evening walks
became dear to him. The road was a spacious terrace along
which he paced, and looked out on life and the landscape.
When it rained and blew he still took that walk, but he
loved most those evenings when there was no wind, and a
half moon shone in a sky of horizontal greyness. There
were the distant chalk-hills, sometimes seen, sometimes obscured, and of the quality of tarnished silver. They seemed
to set a soft and impartial limit to the landscape, like death
closing in life.

The green world would turn to grey and from grey to
black. The further trees merged into one dim mass. Sometimes the nearer trees remained distinct and green. There
were the tall poplars, and an occasional old spruce or pine
striking an individual note. The wires hummed, and cattle
pulled softly at the grass. Dim flowers looked out of a
gently flowing dimness.

An occasional car would rush by, full of plethoric people
hurrying dinnerwards.

A star or two would appear, and lights, the lights in
cottage windows.

There were times when he was made to realize the in-

credible dreariness of the English country. Its beauty
vanished in slush and slime, and man would thank God for
man-made London, or some such place as the Pelican where
you could eat and drink and feel alive. These Northern
countries! And those horrible northern towns, full of people
who were becoming conscious of their own horrible ugliness,
and who were beginning to utter savage and resentful cries.
Winstonbury was still somewhat English, not Wellsian, or
a snarling, love your brother sort of town, but love him,
with reservations. Hate him if he happens to have five
shillings in his pocket, or is a little more clever and energetic
than his neighbours.

Sorrell philosophized. He thought of that other young
life away over yonder, of his boy whose face was not a
half-finished smudge. Kit was going to be a good-looking
fellow, with his large and expressive mouth, and his rather
silent but smiling frankness. Kit would be a complete
person, not a plaster-cast of a man whom Life had got bored
with and not troubled to finish.

When the grey chalk-hills showed, Sorrell would think
of boundaries and of the finality of a man's experiences.
Death, oblivion, extinction—perhaps, a melting into a soft
greyness. And all man's passionate little tricks to escape
it, his myths, his gods and his immortalities, his theosophies,
and spiritisms. A yearning, a chilliness—after life's full
meal. The soft dusk, the obliterating darkness, the unknown and the unknowable.

"Consciousness, is less," he thought, "than the planks of
a boat between you and the deep waters. Some day you
will sink, disappear, be forgotten. You will be less than
some tree that once grew here.

"Accept. Do your job. Then, be ready to close your
eyes and sleep."

He was a pragmatist. The satisfaction of life lay in
accomplishment. He was content to gaze at the unknown
as he looked at the distant chalk-hills, and he felt no urge
to climb them. The whole world of the senses might be
an illusion, but man's business was to behave as though
it were real. The job mattered, the thing you had set out
to accomplish, and not for yourself alone. Fighting mattered, striving, enduring, loving the few, disdaining the
many. When struggle ceases men cease to be men.

Besides, who could tell where life ended? Death might be the opening of a door, especially to those who climbed to it after a life of stubborn effort. And without effort there might be no door? Or was death like a sieve, letting the finer spirits through, and throwing the baser back upon the muck-heap?

He was conscious of a sense of maturity, of a feeling of mellowness within himself. He could look at women without desiring them too fiercely. The money he made was a spiritual essence stored up for his son; opportunities, wings, arms, a buckler to ward off humiliation. His whole life orientated itself towards this other rising, younger life.

He found Kit's letters vastly interesting. They were not the letters of a boy who could think of nothing but footer and cricket. Kit observed, and asked questions.

There were some questions which Sorrell could not answer, and he said so. There were others, human appeals which he had to answer.

For when Christopher came back to Winstonbury on his first holiday it seemed to Sorrell that the boy was troubled. Roland had allowed him to live at the Pelican, and he occupied a little bedroom next to his father.

It was sex that was troubling Christopher, and all that sex implied,—his mother, other fellows' mothers.

Sorrell had dipped into Freud, and his inclination was to laugh at Freud, but he took Christopher much more seriously.

He told him everything, cleanly and frankly. He tried to make the boy feel the dignity of sex, and Christopher did feel it.

There were things at the school that had disgusted him. He appeared to be one of those boys who pass straight through the half-way house of sex, and come almost at once to a feeling of the mystery of woman.

He asked to be told about his mother.

And Sorrell told him. He tried to be utterly impartial. He gave his view of marriage as a great comradeship.

"Your mother and I were not comrades. It wasn't our fault, or rather—it was both our faults."

As for the so-called "Œdipus complex," it did not appear to exist in Kit. Nor had it existed in Sorrell. And yet it did not seem to him that either he or his son was abnormal.

He rather thought that the abnormality could be looked for on the Continent, and in the mental make-up of a certain sort of Continental youth who grew up to be a professor.

Desire was desire, and it could be clean, if you did not shut it up in a box till it turned musty.

He asked Christopher if he would like to leave St. Benedict's and come back to Mr. Porteous.

"No,—I'm all right there now, pater. Now—that I've had these talks. It is not being sure about things——"

"Work is the cleanest of all things, the game you are playing or the job you are going to do."

"I see that in a sort of way. But I suppose one has feelings——"

"Get your feelings to back up your job."

"You—and mother, pater——?"

"We didn't back each other. We were after different jobs; we played the game differently. Some day—you will have to think of the job and the woman——. If you can get them both—happily—into the same boat——"

"Pulling together,—pater? But—then—there are things, —you know——."

"All sorts of things," said Sorrell; "you will have to go through with them, Kit. We all have to. But because a girl has baby eyes—and pretty curly hair——. No, that's not everything; it may be no more than your dinner or your early morning tub. It is better to be keener on your job—than on girls. It's so difficult for me to explain. But get the job before you get the girl,—the real girl—I mean."

They left it at that, but each knew that there was a shadow-land before them, and the consoling thought in the heart of each was that if they kept shoulder to shoulder —the shadow-land would pass.

2

Once or twice a year Sorrell packed a prosperous-looking suit-case, put on a lounge suit made for him by Toole's, and a bowler hat, and white spats, and a pair of wash-leather gloves, and took three days' holiday. He travelled first-class to Westbourne; in fact, on these occasions he made himself appear as a gentleman of leisure and of means. He put up at the Salisbury Hotel on the sea-front, so that Kit should be able to say "My pater's staying at the Salisbury," for the Salisbury was the proper place for parents to stay at. Kit dined with his father, and Sorrell put on a dinner jacket, and in the lounge—afterwards—smoked a cigar, looking amused at life.

If it happened to be "school-day," Sorrell would take a taxi to St. Benedict's, and stroll on to the school playing-field with the air of being something of an old hand. He looked and was the gentleman; in fact, much more so than many other fathers.

He watched Christopher win the school quarter-mile for boys under sixteen.

He talked to Mr. Lowndes.

"Yes, Sorrell is doing very well."

Sorrell was not drawn to Mr. Lowndes. Nor did the "Head" appear to be the sort of man who wished to draw people. He took you by the collar—so to speak, and held you at arm's length, and talked at you. He had very blue and rather prominent eyes, and a high and baldish forehead, and a fine chin. He was rather young for a headmaster, sure of himself to the point of arrogance, confident in attack. Mr. Lowndes always attacked. He set out to impress people. He appeared to have views and opinions ready upon every question that you might raise, and he gave you his opinions with an air of saying—"Now—you can go home—and be reassured on that point for the rest of your life."

He had his inquisitorial side. His blue eyes searched people out. His class-consciousness was so narrow and yet so complete, that it made him careful and suspicious.

"The tradition of the 'school,' my dear sir."

His "tone" was unimpeachable. Looking down at you, for he was very tall, he seemed to be demanding that you should ascend to his level. To the average parent he was tactfully condescending.

"Tact" was one of his favourite words—"Value" was another. Everything had to have "value," the Lowndes' value.

Sorrell suspected him of being the most agile snob.

In conversation he had a way of cross-examining a parent, while pretending to show ordinary social interest. He liked to know exactly what he had got, and Sorrell puzzled him not a little. Obviously, Sorrell was a gentleman, but queer, reserved, a fellow who lived at hotels, and who lacked a domestic centre of gravity.

"I suppose you get a good deal of hunting at Winstonbury?"

"O, not bad country. I'm not allowed to ride now. The war,—you know."

"Ah,—the war!"

That was a favourite trick of Mr. Lowndes, the repeating of the last three words or so of the other person's sentence.

Mr. Phelps, the games master, was a much more easy person. A little, wiry man with very thin legs, he looked like a boy. He was not very clever, but full of infinite good nature,—and he made most comic jokes. Mr. Lowndes never made jokes. He thought Phelps a good fellow, but rather a tame monkey.

Christopher and Mr. Phelps were excellent friends, for Mr. Phelps had discovered that Christopher could box, and fight even better than he could box.

"Your kid's a great little man, Mr. Sorrell. He's in my 'house'—you know. A fatherly sort of kid."

Sorrell liked Phelps, and not only because Phelps liked his boy. He was tempted to tell Phelps his secret,—and he did tell him, and the games master thought the better of him for it. He had been in the war.

"Well,—I think you are doing a fine thing,—old chap. But—one word; I shouldn't let Lowndes know——"

"I think I know what you mean."

"He's the most filthy snob. Only took me on because was a rugger 'blue,' and my uncle's a baronet. You talk to him about me,—I bet you he'll drag in the baronet."

Christopher had one particular friend, a boy named Summervell, a sensitive and rather gentle creature, with long dark eyelashes and stag's eyes. Summervell was no good at games, though he had to play them; his passion was music. Christopher would bring Summervell with him to the Salisbury to sit at the table in the window and dine with them. It was obvious to the father that Christopher felt protective towards this fragile and sensitive boy, the only son of a widow who had to live on an inadequate pension.

"Poor old Peter's mater is not too well off."

He confided to his father the tragic story of a pair of torn trousers, the only decent pair of trousers that Summervell possessed that term.

"I passed him on one of my pairs, pater."

"All right. I'll write and tell Thompson's to send you another pair."

Christopher had every right to think of his father as the most understanding and generous of men.

3

Christopher had been a year and a half at St. Benedict's when his father received a letter from Mr. Phelps the games master. The envelope was marked "Confidential."

"MY DEAR MR. SORRELL,—It seems a beastly sort of thing to write about, but some of the boys here have found out that you are headporter at an hotel.

"Apparently half a dozen of them have been ragging your boy about it ever since the opening of the term. How I found out was through surprising a fight going on one night in my house-dormitory. As a matter of fact your boy got the best of it.

"There are times, my dear sir, when I loathe being a master,— and sometimes I loathe boys. Not all of them. Personally, I think Christopher had played St. George to the Dragon,—but the 'Head' has heard about it.

"I thought that the only decent thing I could do was to write and warn you. We have had a solemn conference, and a lot of palaver, —the 'Tradition of the School' you know, and all that. I tried to point out that the 'tone' of the school was not suffering,—but I got sat upon.

"I hope you will understand me——"

Mr. Lowndes' letter arrived a day later. It was ingenious and patronizing. It flowed from a higher level to what must be presumed to be a lower one.

"MY DEAR MR. SORRELL,—This is one of the most painful letters that I have ever had to write—etc.

"I think for the boy's sake you should remove him. Boys are sensitive creatures, my dear sir,—and when a sensitive boy is made to feel himself to be in a false position——"

Sorrell wrote off at once both to Christopher and to Mr. Lowndes. Nor was there any anger in his letter to the "Head." He was wondering how deeply Christopher had been hurt, and he felt that the fault was his.

Sorrell met his son at Winstonbury station. Kit was smiling. His hands came out quickly to meet his father's.

"I'm sorry, old chap, it was all my fault."

Kit held his father's arm.

"How did it happen——?"

"O, Barrington Smith—primus, was motoring with his people,—and they put up at the Pelican."

"I see. Did they make it rather beastly—for you?"

"O, not so bad, pater. I rather enjoyed some of it, especially when I got Barrington Smith hiding under his bed. Mr. Phelps came in. He saw me off at the station."

"Did he? Good chap."

"And he gave me his boxing-gloves. He asked to be remembered to you, pater. He said some rather——"

"I ought to have forseen this," said Sorrell.

"Dear old pater,—why—I enjoyed it."

"What?"

"Telling one or two of the swine that you were worth ten of their gov'nors. Besides—I had a whole lot of the fellows on my side. We have nothing to be ashamed of."

"Sure?"

"Well,—you should let me tell you what Mr. Phelps said about——"

So Kit returned to Mr. Porteous, and Mr. Porteous and Sorrell began to talk of scholarships and sizarships.

"My dear sir, it's a certainty," said the tutor, "if the boy makes up his mind to go through with it. Trinity or Caius or Pembroke. I'll get hold of all the necessary information. Nearly two clear years. If he doesn't get a scholarship I'll eat my hat."

XVIII

I

SORRELL had a few grizzled hairs on his temples, and his eyebrows had grown bushy.

He sat at a desk in the little room where in the early days he had spent so many hours with Thomas Roland's books, and he looked out upon the same garden and the same trees. Everything was the same—and yet different. He saw the sunlight caught in the purple cups of the tulips, the shadows of the trees lying placidly upon the grass, the wallflowers all crimson and gold. Someone was mowing the grass, a figure in a white sweater and grey flannel trousers that went to and fro with an air of lightness as though the twelve-inch mower were a child's toy.

Sorrell had been making entries in a ledger. He was wearing a blue serge suit. A box of cigarettes lay on the desk, and he put down his pen, and lighting a cigarette, leaned back in his chair.

It was Christopher who was pushing that mower to and fro, just for the satisfaction of spending his youth on the job, and with the idea of keeping fit. He had grown and grown amazingly, and this towering up and spreading of the little fellow had never ceased to astonish Sorrell. He had watched the boy changing into the man.

"Strong," he thought,—"I was never as strong as that."

The transfiguration had had its subjective reactions upon the father, for in watching the growth of the boy, Sorrell had seen in him an increasing likeness to the mother. Christopher had inherited Dora Sorrell's fineness of body. She had given him her physical glow, the nice co-ordination of movement, the texture of skin and hair. This likeness worried Sorrell not a little, for though Kit was more his father's son in his mental make-up, the physical resemblance was there, with all its implications.

The entering of a maid with a tea-tray interrupted Sorrell's thoughts. The girl was pretty and new to the Pelican, and to her Sorrell was very much Mr. Sorrell, a person who was head porter, and yet something more than head porter. He had authority, how much authority no one quite knew, —but when Mr. Roland was away, and he was away fairly frequently, Sorrell ceased to wear the Pelican uniform, and was seen in a blue serge suit.

"Shall I tell Mr. Christopher?"

Sorrell pushed his chair back.

"I'll call him, Minnie,—thanks."

He leaned forward over the desk, knowing that his wish was to place himself between Christopher and the figure of the eternal woman, even as he had denied this girl the chance of running out into the garden to get a smile from his son. But was it wise? He knew that he was jealous for the boy who was becoming the man, and that his life's work and purpose were built into Christopher's career. Kit was his job, his business, his ambition, something schemed for and greatly loved, and yet the father looked at him with a man's eyes. "I can save him—so much," was the thought at the back of his mind,—but it was chastened by that very necessary touch of scepticism. "Was it wise—or possible— to save people from themselves?" Sorrell was for ever warning himself against playing the hen with the duckling.

"Kit.—Tea."

Christopher swung the mower round in the direction of the window. He smiled,—and waved a hand,—and after a satisfied glance at the stretch of smooth turf, he came towards his father, collecting a coat from a garden seat. He had his mother's walk, that easy, gliding walk that had made Sorrell think of a ship in full sail in calm weather. The direct route to the tea-tray lay through the window, and Kit climbed in through the window.

"I'm twenty minutes up on old Bowden, pater."

Sorrell had taken the armchair beside the tea-table.

"You are more than twenty years younger."

Kit smiled. He was at the age when youth tries its strength on every imaginable labour. It was exuberant,— full of an emulous curiosity, but quite without arrogance. His mother had been arrogant.

Sorrell poured out the tea, beholding himself as both mother and father to Christopher who, as yet, had shown no signs of wishing to put up the badge of the Red Heart.

"Mr. Roland's not back yet?"

"No."

Kit, eating buttered toast with the air of a young man considering some very serious problem, came out of his silence to suppose that Mr. Roland must be making a great deal of money.

"Here?"

Sorrell was refilling the teapot.

"I was thinking of *Cherry of Chelsea*. It has been running nine months. Almost as big a hit as *Chu Chin Chow*."

"He was made to make hits. Some men are. But Roland's not in town."

"That's a jolly nice car of his," said Kit rather irrelevantly, reaching for more toast.

A thrush was singing in one of the trees, and Kit turned a quick head with the swiftness of a young thing whose consciousness is sensitive to colour and to music.

"Hear that,—pater! Cherry,—Cherry, Cherry. That's where Mr. Roland got that song."

He refrained from the buttered toast for half a minute in order to whistle a few bars of the song that was being whistled all over the earth.

> "Cherry,—Cherry of Chelsea,
> How do your red shoes go?"

Sorrell was thinking of that first night at the "Pelargonium" when he and Kit had sat in the stalls, and watched Roland's comic opera unfold its coloured music. The piece had been an amazing success. It flowed, and laughed, and made love. It was full of a thrush's song on a May morning, and of cherry-coloured bodices, and green petticoats and red shoes. Cherry of Chelsea! And Cherry herself like a piece of exquisite old china. The play had been running for nearly a year, and Cherry's lips were as red as ever. Extraordinary man—Roland!

"The new thing of his ought to hit them,"—and Kit began to whistle a melody—"Blackbird this time. Suppose he's gone off for an inspiration."

"No," said his father gravely, "he has gone to buy an hotel."

Kit fell into another of his reflective moods, consuming

cake instead of toast, knees drawn up and elbows resting on them, his inward eyes desiring to know why Mr. Roland bothered about hotels when he could write music that set half the world tapping with its feet and swaying a bewitched body. Sorrell was looking out of the window. He and Kit were such good friends that they were able to keep their silences intact, or to let their eyes meet with a sudden understanding smile. Kit's hand, reaching out for more cake, had a healthy grasp on the pleasant realities of life. The boy had a dignity of his own, a happy seriousness. He could run like a swift dog, or lie down and curl himself up like a tired one. Things did not seem to worry him.

"Just like some of the fellows in the war," thought his father; "the fellows without imagination. I used to be on wires, and biting my moustache. But he has imagination. In three weeks time he goes into action. It does not seem to worry him."

In fact Sorrell was much more concerned over Christopher's first serious adventure than was Kit himself. Success or failure? Mr. Porteous too was very excited over Christopher's chances of carrying off a scholarship at Trinity, for Kit was his Benjamin of pupils.

"Anyway—he won't get panic, and sit there staring at the clock."

Kit himself was rather silent about the immediate future. He had allowed it to be known that "Maths" worried him just a little, but he was neither over-confident nor fearful. He had worked hard and he had kept fit, and he had great faith in Mr. Porteous,—and what more could a fellow do? The thing was to keep calm, and not to get rattled.

Porteous was impressed by Christopher's calmness, and he and Sorrell had analysed it over their pipes.

"It's not bovine, my dear chap,—otherwise I should have been worried. You know as well as I do,—and better——. He's highly strung. All the people who are worth while —are."

To Mr. Porteous Christopher appeared as a healthy young athlete, trained to the last ounce, ready to stroll on to the track and wait for the starting pistol. He would not be free from quiverings of excitement, but he would not let himself be flustered.

"You see,—Sorrell, he has an unusual sense of responsi-

bility. He knows that it is your race as well as his. I have
watched him for two years. That gravity—of his—even
when he smiles."

Sorrell's face had had one of its luminous moments.

"What do you think yourself, Porteous? Frankly?"

Mr. Porteous had rubbed his bald head.

"One doesn't like to talk about certainties. He may be
up against one or two smug little prodigies who will fizzle
out when they are ten years older,—just when he is beginning——. But I look on it as a five to one chance."

A fanatical look had come into Sorrell's eyes.

"Scholarship or no scholarship—he shall get there. I can
manage it."

So, Christopher returned to his lawn-mower, and Sorrell
lit a pipe and sat down again at his desk. He had come to
love his desk, its orderliness, its solidity, its neat files and
ledgers and docketed bills. It was a rock upon which he
was building a new reputation.

"I wonder if you would take over the accounts, Stephen?"

Roland had made that suggestion more than a year ago,
and Sorrell had not hesitated to seize this new opportunity.
During the last few months he had become more and more
responsible for the interior economy of the hotel; he had
taken over the catering; he checked and paid the bills.
He was becoming a master of detail. He had begun to
know when electric light was being wasted, or the consump-
tion of coal suggested extravagance. He had the market
prices of food-stuffs at his fingers' ends, and none of the
Winstonbury tradesmen dared to play tricks with him. He
was too wide awake and too thorough.

He loved detail. His fingers, long and straight and sensitive, the ungual phalanges bent slightly back, were the
fingers of a man with a passion for exactness. His ledgers
and note-books were as neat as his finger nails. While
Christopher went to and fro across the grass, Sorrell smoked
his pipe and examined a sheaf of bills, turning them over
with a deft and deliberate first finger.

He made frequent notes.

"Tea. Up four pounds in the week.

"Laundry. Charged for fifty-three more towels.

"Seven table-napkins missing.

"Butcher. Pushing on that inevitable halfpenny. See him about it."

Sorrell had fallen to the fascination of figures and of "curves." He had plotted a series of curves, a grocery curve, a linen curve, a coal curve, a gas curve. The amount of meat consumed each week could be discovered at a glance. Sorrell's room was like a "staff" orderly room, the walls covered with typed notes and diagrams.

His day was not unlike an "orderly officer's" day in the army. He inspected everything, the kitchen, the meat, the vegetables sent in by Bowden, the store-room, the public rooms, the bathrooms and lavatories, the garage, the oil and petrol store. His knowledge of the Pelican's anatomy and physiology was becoming so complete and intimate that he was on the way to being an expert.

Ever and again he paused and watched his son. A well-mown lawn was as satisfying as a well-kept ledger, and Sorrell had come to know that it was the inward thoroughness that mattered, doing the job thoroughly, even though no one saw the objective results of it. A queer thing that inward pride, that scorn of all slackness and of all shuffling, that daily struggle with man's fatal inertia. Your job was like a ship; you had to sail it in all weathers, when you felt sick, and when your moods were like baffling and uncertain winds.

It seemed to Sorrell that Christopher had this passion for thoroughness. He had never been childish. Sorrell hated childishness, especially that most exasperating form of it, the childishness of grown-up children. The dreamy, drowsy, inconsequential imbeciles!

Neither was Christopher a prig.

"Anything's better than priggishness."

Kit had finished his mowing, and Sorrell saw him wiping the blades and knife of the machine with an oily rag.

2

Sorrell had asked for a week's holiday.

"I should like to go up with the boy"—and Thomas Roland said "Of course."

Mr. Porteous saw them off from Winstonbury station, exuding optimism, and taking great care not to suggest to Christopher that there was any likelihood of his being nervous. Sorrell had written to reserve rooms at the Bull, —and when they had dined, Kit took his first stroll along King's Parade, and past Caius to the great gate of Trinity.

They stood under the archway and looked across the Great Court, its greyness and its green lawns very tranquil under the evening sky. Wallflowers were in bloom about the fountain. The roof of the hall and of the Master's house were dark against a sheet of pale gold.

Christopher looked solemn. One of the moments to be remembered was his first glimpse of the Great Court of Trinity, though the significance of that stately quadrangle was to grow less and less in after years. A time would come when Christopher's memory of the college would grow strangely cold, as though only the shadow of himself had ever dwelt there. Later, he would wonder why the picture of the great college lacked glamour. Proud of it as he always was,—but not with the pride of a lover.

And on that first evening the spacious dignity of the place frightened him, nor did he ever succeed in arriving at a feeling of intimacy, though he spent a year in rooms in the Great Court. The college presented itself as a very large and stately old lady, a super-grandmother, to be respected as one respects a formidable social figure.

It is possible that Christopher was not a social creature, or not the true child of this prodigious old lady. In after years a Bloomsbury Square, or the Charing Cross Road left him with a sense of glamour that his college had lacked. For Kit's blood was not grey, nor was he quite like the mass of young men who wore the dark blue gown. He belonged to no particular class, nor would he ever belong to any particular class, for he had absorbed from his father a little of the aloofness of the man who has had to fight for his own hand. To Kit his three years were to be mere ante-rooms to the larger outlook; he worked better than he played, though he was utterly without smugness.

Sorrell and Kit made their way through Nevil's Court and across the river to the "backs." The grass and the foliage were approaching the greyness of the winter, and

a few idle punts and canoes went to and fro. Here—too—
were Tennyson's immemorial elms, and Tennyson's black
bat night descending. Clare Bridge with its stone balls
was a ghost bridge upon the pale silver of the water.
King's Chapel made its presence felt, like an obtruding
cliff.

"Are those chaps in the boats undergraduates, pater?"

"I suppose so," said Sorrell.

He felt himself to be very raw, but his feeling of raw-
ness was soothed by the thought that Christopher was coming here, and that there was nothing that Christopher need
be ashamed of.

"Taking it easy—those fellows."

"And why not?" asked his father.

"I thought one read in the evening."

Sorrell pinched Kit's arm.

"All work and no play——"

"Supposing your work's your play, pater?"

"Some day. I want you to row or play footer. And
box."

Sorrell smiled to himself. He had talked a good deal
to Porteous, and Porteous, never having been an academic
person,—had kept alive the memory of his vivid youth.
Disgraceful "rags," and most unparsonic adventures! Your
tailor might be of more importance than your tutor. And
to be a first-boat man, cycling along the towing-path and
shouting at the Lent crew you had been training. "Keep
it long,—keep—it—long. Damn you,—five,—you're late."
It was necessary to be neither a funk nor a sugarer, and
to be able to wear the particular sort of suit and tie and
waistcoat that gave you the proper atmosphere. Kit should
have the proper atmosphere, a good tailor, good digs, the
privilege of giving an occasional dinner, enough pocket-
money to make life easy in the company of idle young men.
Not that they were idlers in the conventional sense.

"Playing hard is just as good as working hard. I'd like
you to box against Oxford, like Porteous did."

"All right, pater; I'll have a shot at it. You see, I think I
know what I want to do."

They strolled back by way of Queen's, Kit's arm linked
in his father's.

"Did you know,—pater——? I mean——"

"I was blind as a bat. Pushed into a job by my people."

"You have never pushed me."

"God forbid. Send you up like a carrier-pigeon, Kit. Let you get your sense of direction. Fly straight and fast——"

Kit pressed his father's arm.

"Dear old pater——. I'm not much good at saying things,—but you are a brick to me."

"O,—that's all right," said Sorrell, swallowing something in his throat.

During the days that followed he sat on the edge of his suspense, and admired the morale of his son. Kit ate excellent dinners. It was he who behaved like the reassuring parent. He reported on each day's ordeal with tranquil frankness.

"I have done better than I thought I should, pater. If Mr. Porteous had seen the papers, they couldn't have suited me better."

"Many other fellows in?"

"O, quite a lot. I've a chap next me who sniffs all the time. Regular as clockwork."

They spent the evenings on the river, or in wandering about the colleges, and Kit's eyes had ceased to be troubled. It was as though he were getting the feel of the place, measuring the size of all these ancient buildings. He looked at the blazers and scarves in the outfitters' windows, at the books and the pipes and the marmalade pots. He had heard that he would smoke a pipe and eat a great deal of squish. He measured the other fellows whom he saw strolling about. They seemed to him to have become less stupendous,—more human. Would he be a middle or heavyweight? And would he wear one of those light blue blazers?

On the Sunday they went to King's chapel.

"The music gets there," Kit said afterwards to his father.

"Where, my son?"

"O,—somewhere. Where it was meant to. It's like a fellow climbing up."

Sorrell had felt the music to be like the desire of his heart; ascending, spreading, exulting.

3

Thomas Roland was breakfasting when Sorrell brought him the news.

"Kit has won his scholarship."

Roland lingered a moment in his chair, before pushing it back and rising from the table. He saw Sorrell as a man intensely pale, an inarticulate yet exultant figure, holding an official letter with a hand that trembled.

"By Jove, old man,—I'm glad."

Roland's hand went out. They did not look at each other, but stood close together, Roland very conscious of the other man's restrained emotion.

"I thought he would, you know."

"I hoped so," said Sorrell, staring out of the window; "we owe a good deal to you. I have always felt——"

"My dear chap——"

"It's true."

For the sake of doing something Roland turned to the breakfast-table and emptied his coffee-cup.

"Look here,—we must have a little dinner to-night. Ask Porteous.—Where's the boy?"

"Gone to tell Porteous. Do you mind if I take an hour off? I want to see Porteous."

There was a smile at the back of Roland's eyes.

"Take the whole day.—By the way—Stephen——. O, we'll talk about that later. I expect Porteous will be floating about like a cherub."

"He's a great little man," said Sorrell.

The broad road into Winstonbury was Sorrell's *Via Sacra* on that summer morning. The Roman celebrated his son's first triumph. "Seven years," he thought; "and this! Tears in the boy's eyes when I told him. Oh,—I'm happy, —happy——"

At the little stone house he found Kit sitting on one end of a long deal table in the study, and Bob Porteous in his shirt sleeves, flourishing a baton made out of yesterday's paper, his honey-coloured head shining like a planet. He was exuberant in his elation. He had got very hot; he had taken off his coat; he had kept smacking the table, the walls, and the windows with his paper truncheon. The little man could not keep still.

"I told you so,—my dear fellow. What,—what! Look at him——. Scholar of Trinity! Much cooler than we are. Get up, you young rascal, and dance on the table."

He punched Sorrell's chest.

"Licked all the little smug fellows! One of 'em sniffled all day—I hear. What are we going to do about it?"

"Roland is giving a dinner."

"By Jove,—that's it. Kit,—I'll box you three rounds after dinner. Scholar of Trinity!"

Triumphantly he flattened a fly on the page of a Hebrew dictionary that was lying open on the table.

XIX

I

FANNY GARLAND opened Sorrell's door.
"Bowden has sent these in," she said.
Sorrell turned in his chair. He was sitting at his
desk, and Fanny had surprised him in a moment of medita-
tion. She had her arms full of flowers, purple and white
iris, wallflowers, rose-red pyrethrum. Her round and
pleasant face smiled at him over them. Fanny was growing plump and mature; she had little wrinkles under her
eyes, but even her wrinkles had kindness.

"Flowers.—Bowden sent them in——"

"Yes,—for the table,—Kit's dinner."

"Good of Bowden.—You are all being very good to us."

He rose, and stood looking at the flowers, but with an
air of inattention, for the coming of Fanny Garland had not
broken the current of his thought. Indeed, a double stream
was running through his mind, each with its separate emotion, and as a result his eyes were happily yet gravely vague.

"They are being very good to us."

But the other current was the stronger. He had been
sitting there alone, seeing Kit in mortar-board and gown
crossing the Great Court of Trinity, Kit the son of an hotel
porter, and Sorrell's wish had been that the hotel porter
might be blotted out. Was it snobbery? He did not think
so. The world of men—of young men—values accomplishment. Half our democratic posing is fulsome humbug.
The captain matters more than the deck steward.

He became aware of Fanny's smiling eyes.

"What are you laughing at?"

Her smile became kind laughter.

"I don't wonder," she said,—"I don't wonder. I bet
—you are up in the clouds a bit. And quite right too. But
I want to decorate the table."

Sorrell stared.

"Well,—why not do it?" said his stare.

She pressed her round, fresh face against the flowers.

"I don't like to go in. Fact is—he's singing one of those songs of his, the songs in the new piece he is writing. If there is one thing that riles him——"

Sorrell pulled out his watch.

"Half-past six. I don't think he'll mind. Not to-night."

"Well,—you come and open the door for me."

"All right. I will."

They paused in the passage to listen to Thomas Roland's singing. He was in a gaillard mood, and his deep voice seemed to carry more than the mere burden of the song, for it was the voice of a man who was happy. A generous voice, it swept Sorrell back in a flash to the day when Roland had arrived in that claret-coloured car, and to his own struggles with Florence Palfrey and the confusion of the Angel Inn. Thomas Roland sang as though he had no regrets, and with the voice of a sea-rover.

Sorrell raised a hand,—but Fanny Garland held up a finger. She wanted to hear the whole of the song.

> "There was an old man who lived in a box
> On a hill—on a hill.
> Its walls were white and its windows blue,
> And round about it orange trees grew,
> Above the sea—so still—so still."

The great posy of flowers breathed on Fanny Garland's bosom. She looked at Sorrell, and moved a hand in time to the music, but Sorrell's eyes were not seeing her. The memories of the past were winding upwards to the triumphant peak of the day's good hope, and through all these memories of uplift and endeavour Thomas Roland's voice sounded like the voice of a romantic rover. Some men brought good luck, a happy concatenation of circumstances. They willed good things.

Fanny was nodding at him.

"Now—you dreamer—now," said her smile.

There was a pause in the singing, and Sorrell knocked.

"Come in."

Roland sang the words, and the opening door showed him sitting at the piano, with the old gold curtains framing the green of the garden. He seemed to glow, and as he looked at Sorrell his eyes had a mischievous tenderness.

"What's this?"

"Flowers, sir."

"It is twenty to seven, sir,—and I want to lay the table—for our Mr. Christopher's dinner."

Roland stood up, gaillard and sly.

"Did you pick all that, Fanny? My word, there will be a storm!"

"Bowden picked them himself, sir."

"Marvellous! Well,—I had better go and pick the champagne. And,—Stephen——"

He paused with a hand on Sorrell's shoulder.

"Will you warn everybody that I want them all to come in here after dinner and drink Kit's health."

He was looking into Sorrell's eyes as though he had other news for him, but was holding it back until the end of the feast.

"A real 'bump' supper, Stephen. Yo-ho!"

The drinking of Kit's health was only a part of the Pelican parade. Kit made a speech of five words. "Thanks—awfully—all of you." He blushed, and all the women wanted to kiss him. They drank Sorrell's health, and Mr. Porteous's health, and Mr. Porteous made a speech and flourished his serviette like a victorious flag. They drank Mr. Roland's health, with musical honours, Mr. Porteous crashing at the piano. They drank the staff's health, and good luck to the Pelican. Bells rang and were ignored.

It was the happiest of evenings, but for Sorrell the crowning happiness was yet to come.

2

Christopher had gone to bed, and Roland and Sorrell had seen Mr. Porteous fifty yards along the Winstonbury road, and were strolling back under the stars. The night was full of the smell of new-mown hay, and about the Pelican the great trees were asleep.

Roland,—breathing deeply because of the night's fragrance, paused, and in pausing looked up at the shadowy shape of the Pelican hanging from the cross-beam.

"Good bird, excellent bird."

His voice seemed to vibrate with concealed laughter.

"The wise people won't allow us to believe in luck,

Stephen. I should like to drown some of the wise people in champagne."

The paying portion of the Pelican had gone to bed, and the windows were dark. Roland, slipping a hand under Sorrell's arm, walked with him so that they entered the door together, like partners and equals.

"We had better lock up. And then a pow-wow and a last pipe."

He locked the door, while Sorrell shot the bolts, and though the evening had passed Sorrell had a feeling that it would revive and rise to a second climax. He had divined in Thomas Roland the almost roguish reticence of a man who was hiding a dramatic finale. Yes,—and enjoying it, gloating over it.

Roland's room showed deserted chairs, and empty glasses, old Porteous's table-napkin trailing across a dish of fruit, and Bowden's flowers a splash of colour in the centre of the whiteness. Roland closed the door. He edged towards the sideboard with an attentive glance at Sorrell.

"Have a whisky,—Stephen."

His teeth showed white in his brown face.

"I'm going to. All right. Fill your pipe. It has been a great evening."

He filled the glasses, and transferring himself and his to the hearthrug, watched Sorrell packing tobacco into the bowl of a pipe. Yes, the fellow's fingers were just a little jerky and excited. Had he any idea——?

"Sit down, old chap."

Sorrell sat down on the edge of one of the big arm-chairs.

"I haven't thanked you——"

"Leave it at that."

There was silence between them, and Sorrell, glancing up, found Roland looking down at him over the edge of his glass.

"I suppose you have saved a little money, Stephen?"

Sorrell struck a match.

"An odd thousand. It's for the boy."

"Just so. Well,—let's talk business. That New Forest place is going to boom. I told you that I have had my eye on an hotel in Salisbury,—and on another at Bath."

"I think you did."

"I'm simply spilling with money. Obviously, the thing

is to turn the whole show into a company, with the shares held by three or four interested people. 'The Roland Hotels.' How's that strike you?"

Sorrell sat very still, staring at the bowl of his pipe.

"It should be a sound idea."

"So—I think. And as you will be running the Pelican— I shall want you on the board. I have another man in mind. The three of us should do."

Sorrell's eyes rose slowly to Roland's face. He was very pale.

"You mean—me, to manage here?"

"Exactly. You know the business inside out by now. You are the very man for it. Obviously."

Again, there was silence between them, and the silence was understandable. It said more than words. They had worked together for six years.

Sorrell was smiling, but his smile had a glimmer as of tears.

"It's just like you——. To tell me—on an evening like this——. My dear chap—I——"

Roland pretended to drink.

"Rather a good stroke of business for me, Stephen, getting you as manager, and co-director. I think so."

"Roland," said Sorrell, getting up suddenly out of his chair,—"I think I'm a little—drunk. If you had known——"

He went and stood at the open window.

"It is what——. Well,—the boy——. I'm not a snob, —but perhaps you can understand—when he goes up to Trinity—this autumn——. To be able to say——"

He paused,—and half turning, looked at Roland with shining eyes.

"You are trusting me. You are giving me my chance. You shan't regret it——"

"My dear chap——!"

"Oh,—I know——"

"Good God, man,—I'm getting something out of it,— too, a friend and a partner. We are white men, Stephen. What's money but a means to an end. You can put just as much or as little as you please into our show. The Roland Hotels, Limited.—What!"

He laughed, and raised his glass.

"Here's to the old Pelican."

3

It pleased Thomas Roland to speak of their enterprise as an Elizabethan gentleman adventurer spoke of his ships, lovingly, and with a feeling for the roll of the sea and the names of the ships that sailed it. The Pelican, whose master was Captain Sorrell, the Royal Oak, the White Hart, the Lion. The Royal Oak had been launched at Brockenhurst in the Forest, and Roland was sailing with her for a season to see that all was shipshape. The Lion was to be launched at Salisbury in the spring. The White Hart was still upon the stocks. Meanwhile, Roland had taken a little house at Chelsea, engaged an ex-service man and his wife, proposing to make the Chelsea house his headquarters.

"In memory of 'Cherry,' my dear Steve. The young lady is still earning me a great deal of money."

Whether Cherry existed in the flesh was a question that did not trouble Stephen, though he could imagine her existence, the insouciant, red-lipped love of a man who did not choose to marry. Perhaps Cherry was sharing in the building and staging of the next colour fantasia, *The Blue Box*, which was to be produced at the "Pelargonium" in the autumn. Certainly, Thomas Roland had his head and his hands well filled,—and between bursts of song, was to play the rover in his car, visiting his ships and surveying their cargoes.

Christopher had gone up to Trinity, and was in rooms in Jesus Lane. Sorrell had seen him lodged there, had bought him two immense armchairs, and had had a long talk with Kit's tutor. Christopher's immediate objectives were the Science Tripos, and the first two parts of the M.B. Mr. Porteous, who could have taught a dog with no hind legs to walk, had grounded Kit in physics and chemistry. Also, Kit had elected to box and to row, and could be seen strolling down to the First Trinity boat-house in striped trousers and dark-blue blazer, to be tubbed and lectured by eloquent and serious young men. He weighed twelve stone three, and he received his notice to row in one of the scratch eights at the end of a fortnight's tubbing.

Sorrell, captain in a double sense, and in occupation of Roland's little suite at the Pelican, felt that life had enlarged itself. His salary as manager was £500 a year, with a bonus of ten per cent. on the Pelican's profits. He had sold out all his War Stock, and had taken a share in the capitalization of the Roland Hotels. How much the enterprise would bring him he did not know. The Pelican was a little gold mine; the Royal Oak was finding fair weather, and Roland was talking buoyantly of twenty per cent.

Roland was a solid man now, very solid, and so ballasted with capital that nothing could blow him over. He was a proof of the old saying that—"Money breeds money," but Roland had used his imagination. He could meet any tooth-brush merchant and smile in his face.

"O, Roland, the chap who writes that musical stuff."

But Roland was proof against the commercialists' envious patronage, for there were the Roland Hotels. The tooth-brush merchant had to swallow them; they were not musical stuff; they stuck in the unimaginative man's gizzard.

Exactly!

Sorrell had picked up one or two of Roland's characteristic words. It was obvious that his son was up at Trinity, and could refer to his father as "Captain Sorrell. Interested in hotels, a director. In with Roland,—you know, —the Roland. Quite a big show."

Kit could speak with the voice of a sea-captain. There was no need for him to hand out basins.

At times a man's outlook on life is so narrowed by the press of circumstance that his consciousness peers through a slit at the immediate happenings that concern him. Like a gunner in a steel turret, a part of the machine, he lays his gun upon the obvious target. So it had been with Sorrell for many years, but now he had become aware of an enlarging of his consciousness. He had leisure. The sky had grown more spacious above his head. He could sit on his quarter-deck and look about him, and see his ship moving, swinging her prow against blue horizons. He issued orders, and the urge of every proud man is to issue orders.

A deep contentment took the place of the facile cheerfulness of the good-natured slave.

He was a person. Other people knew that he had to be considered. Moreover, he was popular, whatever that may mean. He had never bothered himself about popularity; he had bothered about his job.

Good food was brought him with great punctuality.

Fanny Garland, sonsy and smiling, saw to that. He had
flowers on his table. Albert Hulks treated the sitting-
room fire as though it were a sacred flame in a temple. He
had a green and gold quilt on his bed; and tea and thin
bread and butter were brought him in the morning.

Someone else cleaned his boots.

And he liked it. Years of sweat had made him so
honest about the realities that he was quite ready to desert
his philosopher's tub when something pleasanter and more
sweetly smelling offered itself.

He began to allow himself little relaxations, small human
luxuries, and he found that he could work harder when
the bearings of life were oiled. He bought an occasional
book, and began to collect china, and old prints. Winstonbury had its "antique" shop, run by a depressed little man
who suffered from chronic dyspepsia, and whose face suggested that he lived on sulphur tablets. His name was
Grapp. The antique trade offered chances that he was too
congealed to seize.

Sorrell was often in the shop, and it was not long before
he came to realize that it was a dead business. Grapp had
no enterprise.

But there were times when Sorrell pondered the problem
of Grapp, and the opportunities that Grapp was missing.

"A fellow with energy could turn that business inside
out within six months. Fill up the shop with good stuff,—
and swank a bit. If I had a share in it I should put up a
case of photographs in the Pelican lounge,—and push the
Yankees along."

It was an idea, and Sorrell let it simmer.

Also, he had other outlets. The stern purpose in him
had mellowed. He had friends in Winstonbury, houses in
which he felt himself at home. He spent one evening each
week with Robert Porteous. He kept up his friendship with
old Mrs. Garland in Vine Court, for she had had a share
in Kit's success, in that she had fed the boy well.

Sorrell found himself standing outside the red cottage in
Vine Court on one autumn afternoon. Mrs. Garland had
influenza, and Sorrell had come to inquire for her, and to
leave her a bunch of grapes.

Fanny opened the door.

"Oh,—it's you! I came here early—to spoil her a little."

She held the door open, looking at him with a soft glimmer of the eyes. "I brought these."

"Grapes. How good of you. She's asleep just now, and I have sent Aunt Eva home."

The little sitting-room was just as Sorrell had first known it, save that Fanny had bought her mother a comfortable new sofa upholstered in green and blue. It stood under the window. Fanny was putting Sorrell's grapes on a plate. She was wearing a soft green jumper, with the sleeves rolled up, and Sorrell could not help noticing the pleasant plumpness of her arms. She had a comely neck, and her fair, bobbed hair hung over it.

"You'll stay and have tea."

They had tea together, sitting on the sofa. Kit's apple tree, full of yellow fruit, caught the light of the sunset. The greenness of it was enriched by the ripe apples, even as a woman is enriched by desire.

They talked of Kit, and then fell to talking of each other, softly, while the dusk began to fall. Fanny's hair became a shadowy wreath, and her arms and throat grew whiter.

The dusk seemed to draw them towards a pleasant, human intimacy. They discussed life, sitting sideways on the sofa, and looking into each other's faces. The body of each seemed to relax. Fanny's fair head drooped gradually towards the padded back.

"Sleepy?"

She smiled at him. "Are you?"

He found a cushion and placed it under her head, and their voices grew softer.

"I'm not a marrying man."

He was explaining himself to her, and she listened, with the inward smile of a woman who has learnt to laugh at an old-fashioned man's dear pomposities.

"Does it matter,—Steve? I'm not a marrying woman. In these days——"

He saw her hand pull the curtains gently across the window.

XX

I

SORRELL was writing letters. He had finished his weekly report to Thomas Roland, and had begun a letter to his son, but when he had covered the first page his thoughts began to wander. Kit's last letter lay upon the desk, a grave yet gossipy chronicle of Christopher's moods and doings, for he was able to write to his father with a happy frankness.

"You understand things, pater."

Precious words from a son, and Sorrell had taken them to his heart with a smiling humility. So, he understood things. His sensitiveness responded to the sensitiveness of his son. Like all individuals,—lone fighters, he had hated interference, intolerance,—but unlike so many men of a proud temper, he hated imposing himself upon others. "Neither to rule, nor to be ruled" was his ideal, though life had taught him the necessity of imposing himself—his will—upon others. But with Kit it was different, and Sorrell had fought all impulses towards autocracy, and his wisdom had served him well. In refusing to possess his son like a tyrant he had come to possess him in the only way that mattered. Kit had no fear of his father; Sorrell had remained the one person on earth to whom he hurried to tell things. Their intimacy had grown deeper, as Kit's roots went deeper.

This last letter of Kit's was responsible for Sorrell's wandering thoughts. There was one most significant paragraph in it.

"They want me to row in the 3rd May boat. Of course—I have felt rather bucked about it, because our lot did rather badly in the Lents. But I have decided that it can't be done. It isn't that I don't feel sure of pulling through the first M.B. in June. I'm out for a place. Don't you agree with me?"

Sorrell was not quite sure whether he did agree, because he was not quite sure what Kit wanted. His son was a creature of intelligence, and capable of choosing.

Sorrell bit the end of the pen, with his eyes on the flower beds under his window. Yes, the choice was with Christopher.

He began to write.

"Do just what you wish to do. I know that it is not wise—at times—to split one's energy. The thing is to concentrate. You know that as well as I do, old chap. But sometimes one can compromise. I'm pulled both ways. I'd like to see you rowing in one of the May boats,—and I'd like you to get a place in the M.B. Greedy parent! But it is a question of how you feel. It is not my business to coach your feelings."

It made Sorrell happy to realize that he could write to his son with such easy frankness, and that the invisible tie between them seemed to be growing stronger. His whole wish was to play the man to the man in Christopher. He raised his head and let his eyes rest upon the garden, for with the mellowing of his middle age he was becoming more of a garden lover, for there is no more pleasant place than a garden for the ripening of a man's thoughts. To be able to see the massive old tree trunks rising from the sweep of well-cared for grass, and to watch the play and pattern of the shadows, and the ebb and flow of the light among the leaves,—such contemplation pleased him. It gave him the same smooth feeling as did the glaze on an exquisite piece of old china, or the silky warmth of the skin of a woman's arm. It was good to enjoy such beauty, not greedily, but with magnanimous insight.

The Pelican's visitors made use of the garden, and occasionally the soul of it was offended, but since a lover of flowers increases as Adam and Eve grow older, and the Pelican's visitors were mostly mature people, Sorrell had little cause to complain. It is the child who is a garden's natural enemy, and Sorrell did not encourage children. The Pelican was so proudly placed that she could refuse children. They were a nuisance. This serenely efficient rest-house had no use for childishness.

Blessed maturity!

And at this very moment maturity presented itself before Sorrell's eyes in the shape of a voluminous lady dressed in black who was trailing slowly across the lawn in the direction of a seat under one of the chestnut trees. He had a view of her broad back, and her robust curves defying the most cunning of corsages. A Rubenesque figure, sumptuous and solid, with masses of blonde grey hair swathed under a black flower-pot hat! A visitor, obviously, and a recent arrival.

She turned and seated herself, and Sorrell's eyes suddenly hardened. He realized that she was looking across the lawn in the direction of his window, and that she could see him sitting at his desk.

He lowered his head and pretended to go on writing, while he considered the significance of this unwelcome appearance, this abrupt recrudescence of an unfortunate past. He scribbled nothings on a sheet of paper, occasionally glancing under ominous eyebrows at the figure on the seat. She sat there, wholly at ease, her broad face turned towards him. He fancied that she smiled.

He got up with a "Damn the woman," and went out of the room. At the foot of the stairs he met Hulks with a big leather trunk on his shoulder, and he made inquiries as to the trunk and its owner.

"Lady just arrived in a big Murchester saloon, sir. Booked for a week. Miss Murdoch has put her in No. 3."

Sorrell was scanning the trunk. It was plastered with Riviera hotel labels, and on its lid was painted in big black letters "D. Duggan."

He walked out to the garage and looked at the car. Its chauffeur, dressed in black livery, was reversing the big, dark blue machine into one of the lock-ups.

Sorrell spoke to him. "Is that Mrs. Duggan's car?"

The chauffeur replied, without troubling to look at him. "It is."

Sorrell went back to his sitting-room, and sat down at his desk. The woman had not moved from the seat, but as he drew up his chair he saw her rise and advance diagonally across the grass. Her movements appeared very deliberate and unselfconscious, but Sorrell knew that however circuitous her movements might appear they were directed towards his window.

"I suppose it's inevitable," he thought; "but she won't get any change out of me."

He set himself to finish his letter to Kit, compelling himself to concentrate upon it, and he had arrived at the "Yours affectionately" when the figure in black appeared at the window. She had followed the path between the beds planted with standard roses, tulips, myosotis, and violas, and to a casual observer she would have appeared as a lover of flowers, strolling at her leisure. Her poise was one of interest; her back ignored the window.

Sorrell scribbled his signature, blotted it,—and began folding up the sheet ready for its envelope. He had decided that he would leave her the initiative. His wisest course was to sit tight and to allow her as few openings as possible.

She turned to look at the flower-bed under his window, and he could not but admire her deliberation and her poise. Her eyes rose with a natural inevitableness to his. He was pressing down the flap of the envelope.

She smiled. He noticed that her blonde hair was powdered with grey. Knowing her of old he would have expected her to have had those grey hairs treated. Her acceptance of this greyness seemed to make her more dangerous.

"Still here."

He gave her an almost imperceptible nod and a steady stare of the eyes, and she drew up like a fine ship ready to use her guns or to parley.

"You have changed."

He turned the envelope over, and proceeded to address it.

"One does. Both of us. Married again?"

The leisureliness of her reply balanced his casualness.

"Let us see,—I was Sampits. Now I am Duggan. Mr. Duggan died last December. I suppose I shall remain Mrs. Duggan."

Sorrell raised steady eyes, and seemed to observe her.

"Is it necessary?"

She smiled.

"Really—that is very gallant of you."

"Not at all."

In their historic quarrels of ten years ago Kit's mother had nearly always bested Sorrell, and had sailed out of action leaving him with his more sensitive temper shot to pieces. She had controlled her fire more coolly; she had cared less; she had carried heavier guns. Her serene and healthy selfishness had given her a notable advantage over a worried and highly strung man, a scrupulous idiot, and a failure. But the woman who stood there, scanning him with an air of amused slyness, had a kinder outlook upon life,

because life had given her much that she had desired. She
was the mature cat on the cushion. She had an air of comfortable softness. Almost, she could refer to herself playfully as an old woman.

"I am greyer than you are, Stephen."

"You are older than I am."

"That's not quite so gallant."

She was firing blank shot at him, and the battle between
them was now more restrained and less vivid, but Sorrell
was aware of it as a battle. He was waiting for her to ask
the inevitable question, and the fact that she did not ask
it left him to meditate upon her tactics. He felt pretty sure
of her objective.

"Have you been running this place for long?"

"About a year."

"You do it pretty well. I know something about hotels."

Judging by the labels on her trunk she did. Moreover,
she could afford to stay at *de luxe* hotels. Messrs. Sampits
and Duggan had behaved very generously.

"What time's dinner here, Stephen?"

Her voice was friendly. Her whole attitude suggested
that they should agree to regard life as a humorous and
ironical experience.

"Seven-thirty."

"Thanks."

Sorrell rose from his chair.

"Just a word,—do you mind addressing me as Mr. Sorrell."

"Not in the least. I am much more easy to get on with
than I used to be. And you——?"

He stood with his hands resting on the desk, and looking
at her with deliberate steadfastness.

"I'm the boy's father."

2

An hour later returning from a wander in the Abbey
beechwoods, Sorrell decided that he had acted wisely in
hoisting his flag.

"Just as well let her know that I'm an enemy. I suppose it is fairly obvious what she is after. That grey in her
hair. No,—I'm damned if I will let her meddle."

During dinner Sorrell went and stood in the passage, and reconnoitred the dining-room through the doorway. Mrs. Duggan had a little table by one of the windows. Her back was towards him. She was in evening dress, black velvet, with a rope of pearls round her throat, looking a very handsome person, carrying her years with graceful resignation. If it was a pose it was admirably conceived, and as admirably adopted. He saw her give one of the waitresses a pleasant upward smile. The girl smiled back at her.

Sorrell retired to his sitting-room. He had asked Fanny Garland to postpone the serving of his dinner, and he sat on the window-ledge and sorted out his impressions.

Yes, Dora Duggan had mellowed. She had become something of the smiling duchess, an opulent and handsomely self-assured person. She dressed well. She had some exquisite jewellery, and a sense of humour. Dangerous creatures,—women! He divined the dangerousness of Kit's mother, the subtle interference she might exert, the seductions she could employ.

Fanny came in with his soup. She noticed his narrowed, intent face, and the way he looked at her as though all women were under suspicion.

"Shut the door, Fanny, will you."

His eyes swept the garden. He stood a moment, smoothing his moustache.

"Noticed No. 3?"

Fanny had.

"What do you think of her? As a woman——"

She was puzzled,—defensive.

"Why do you want to know?"

"I'll tell you,—when you have told me——"

"She looks rather a good sort. But—of—course—— A bit of an old soldier—too."

"A good sort!"

He sat down with the briskness of impatience.

"You and I—understand each other. Not a word to anybody, old girl. That—is Kit's mother."

He glanced up at her, meaningly.

"Married twice—since she left me. Widow. Pots of money. Not bothering about her grey hair. Sails down here in her two thousand pound car. What do you make of that?"

Fanny's shrewd fresh face was solid with thought.

"Well—if you ask me——"

"I'm asking you—as a woman——"

"She's after the boy."

"Exactly," said Sorrell, picking up his soup spoon.

Life happens less crudely than our descriptions of it suggest, and the human diagrams that we draw lack the subtlety of colour and movement. It was easy for Sorrell to rush at a conclusion, and to make a sketch of Dora Duggan as he saw her, and to compare it with the Dora Sorrell of his married days. In his mental diary he wrote her down a vampire, a woman, who, having had all the satisfactions she desired from men and sex, was seeking other satisfactions. That red mouth of hers was ready to feed upon the young vitality of her son.

The thought enraged him. He was offended by the infernal audacity of her intriguing reappearance. To return, smiling, after a digression that had lasted ten years, sleekly and handsomely prosperous and self-assured, and ready to claim the inevitable flesh-bond.

He could hear her saying—"After all, Stephen, I am his mother." She would say it deliberately, flaunting her grey hairs and her glowing, maternal maturity, suggesting that both he and she had arrived at that autumnal season when life ripens to a bland magnanimity. "I'm growing an old woman, Stephen. I'm through with my adventure. Why not let bygones be bygones?"

Had she other children, young Sampits or young Duggans? Or, now that her wildness was passing, was Christopher to be the one creature to be desired, a young man to be debauched by the maternal passions of a woman who was growing old?

Well, he had hoisted his flag, and he would wait for her to attack. She had engaged her bedroom for a week. Obviously there would be developments in the course of those seven days.

Sorrell decided that he would neither seek nor avoid her. He would order his life as though she had not reappeared on the figure of it with her perilous, easy opulence.

On the first day of the seven they had no speech with each other. Sorrell passed Kit's mother in the lounge, wrapped up in a magnificent musquash coat, and waiting for her car. She was going out for the day.

He gave her a vague, stiff bow, and she smiled at him, pulling on her gloves.

"Good morning, Mr. Sorrell. What do you think of the weather?"

"The glass is high."

"I am driving over to Bath to lunch with some friends."

Sorrell received the information with the impersonal politeness of a hotel manager. He hoped that her drive would be a pleasant one; he was in motion while he expressed this formal wish; his courtesy was the Parthian politeness of a busy man in a hurry.

On the evening of the same day he had a glimpse of Kit's mother sitting in a corner of the lounge, and looking up over a book at Albert Hulks. She was talking to Hulks, who had taken to himself all the Sorrell traditions. Hulks had an ash-tray in one big hand, and with the other he was feeling for his wallet.

"Stamps!" thought Sorrell; "I remember that day when she bought stamps from me,—and tried to find out——. Of course—she can make Hulks talk."

It would be easy for Kit's mother to discover the facts about her son. All that she had to do was to involve Hulks or Bowden in a friendly gossip, and ask what had become of that nice boy—Mr. Sorrell's son. "I remember him when I was here before." And she would be told that Christopher had won a scholarship at Cambridge, and that he was up at Trinity.

Two more days passed, and Sorrell was compelled to discover in her an aloofness that equalled his own. They saw each other in the distance, and while appearing to ignore the presence of the other, were not deceived by this mutual disregard. They appeared to avoid all opportunities of meeting.

Her presence in the hotel made Sorrell restless. He felt her about him, watching without appearing to watch, insinuating even in her aloofness. She was like a cat who sat and stared and seemed to see nothing; while nothing was lost upon her. He was unpleasantly aware of her as a creature gliding about in the jungle, leaving him to guess at her movements and her motives. By sitting still he had presented her with the initiative, and the power of holding him in suspense.

He was considering the question of writing to Kit, or of making a sudden descent upon him at Cambridge.

"But what could he say?

"The woman—who was your mother—is staying here at the Pelican. I think she would like you to resume your sonship. Personally, I do not wish you to have anything to do with her."

But would such frankness be wise? His whole purpose had been to perfect a complete comradeship between himself and his son, and to eliminate the shadow of the paternal tyranny. He had chosen the part of friend and counsellor; he had renounced the self-sufficient privilege of issuing orders. Christopher was very dear to him, and he believed himself to be very dear to Christopher. Why not trust to this mutual confidence and affection? Play the new Adam, and let Eve try her wiles? All life is willing and choosing, and Christopher would have to will and to choose.

On the fourth day something happened. The woman came and sat on the seat under the chestnut tree when Sorrell was sitting at his desk. She had a book. She pretended to read, while he made a pretence of writing letters, but the space between them was crossed by their mutual consciousness of an inevitable and approaching skirmish.

Sorrell rose from his chair. She saw his figure disappear from the window, but when he came out by way of the garden door, and crossed the grass towards her, her head was bent over her book. She allowed him to believe that she was unaware of his approach.

He paused in front of her.

"How do you find this place? Comfortable?"

Her quick and upward smile assured him that she had been taken unawares.

"Oh, it's you! Yes,—I'm very comfortable. So far as my experience goes—it is the best-run country hotel in England."

Her smile continued. She moved to one end of the seat, —and the space left was an invitation.

"But a hotel is always a hotel."

Her book was closed and laid upon the seat, and the upward glance she gave him still had the edge of a smile.

"Do you ever suffer from curiosity——?"

She divined his guardedness towards her.

"Funny thing, life! Here—we are—like a couple of strangers——. You and I——. Do you remember those days at Shanklin?"

"Nearly twenty years ago." He sat down.

"O,—well, we were incompatibles. I'm afraid I gave you some bad times——. I was much more greedy for life."

He was looking towards his window, and not at her.

"So you are never curious——?"

"About what?"

"What sort of success or failure I made of things—afterwards. Never thought——?"

"Why should I?"

He felt that she was smiling.

"So you never forgave me. Poor old Stephen! You married an explosive person. But when one comes to a certain stage——"

His silence neither encouraged nor repulsed her. He was letting her make all the thrusts.

"One begins to look back—instead of forward."

"You think so?"

"Well, I do. Of course—it depends——. A woman grows rather lonely."

She observed his profile. She had dropped one little stone into the pool of his silence, but so far as she could judge it had stirred no ripples.

"Suppose you just drift about now?" he said.

"I? Not a bit of it. I'm the comfy cat, my dear man. A house in South Audley Street. Three months at Cannes —perhaps,—and a few days in my car. Friends,—yes——. A busy old bachelor like you—doesn't bother. I'm so well off."

He remained utterly irresponsive, a man with a blank yet alert face, and a judicial manner. She gave a little humorous sigh, observed him ironically with her fine eyes, and diverged to other topics. He had shown no sign of reacting either to sentiment or to the hint of her prosperity. It seemed to her that he took himself with the same old, desperate seriousness. And he was desperately serious in his desire to keep her and Christopher apart.

"Hopeless—as ever—with women," she decided. "No idea of compromise."

She began to talk about the late Mr. Sampits, and when
she had exhausted her second husband, she went on to
speak of the late Mr. Duggan. She told Sorrell the most
trivial and intimate details of her two subsequent marriages,
overwhelming him with the steady and self-interested lo-
quacity of the hotel-bore, and she did it so naturally that,
Sorrell, growing bored, began to wonder at himself for sitting there and listening to her. He heard how Sampits
had died of alcoholic nephritis, and how Duggan's chief
characteristic had appeared to be a prejudice in favour of
the old-fashioned night-shirt. He heard what sort of clothes
they wore, and what they ate, and what they would not eat,
and he found himself yawning with immense surprise at
her banal confidences.

Why—on earth—was she telling him all this? She began
to appear to him as little more than a stout and rather im-
modest person, just like dozens of other elderly women who
loved to hold some helpless listener blockaded in a gossip's
corner. She seemed to become less and less dangerous the
more she bored him with her crude outpourings. The world
was full of such women. He had seen them by the score
in the lounge of the Pelican, sitting down solidly to exhaust
the patience of some too good-natured listener.

After half an hour of it he glanced at his watch.

"I'm sorry—but I have to——"

She drew her breath and smiled upon him.

"Of course——. You must be such a busy man. We
have had quite a nice talk, haven't we? And, O, before I
forget, my friends at Bath have asked me to go on there
to-morrow. Will it inconvenience you—if I give up my
room——?"

"Not in the least. We are turning people away every
day."

It was not till he had smoked a pipe after tea that
Sorrell grasped the curious fact that she had never mentioned Christopher. She had talked of no one but herself
and her dead men-folk. Curious! Had he been an alarmist, and was she just a fat commonplace egoist who asked
for nothing but an audience? People grew fat in mind as
well as in body. It seemed to him that he had exaggerated
her significance.

XXI

I

CHRISTOPHER SORRELL came up from the river
with two other men in dark-blue blazers. The 3rd
May boat had been rowing a course; the crew had
done so fast a time that their coach had shown an unexpected enthusiasm, and had blessed them from the towing-
path.

"Well rowed, you men."

His smirk over the stop-watch had been inspired by the
discovery that his crew—the third crew—had rowed over in
three seconds less than the second crew. At the First
Trinity boat-house he had gathered his men together and
had allowed this piece of news to escape.

"Damned well rowed—all of you."

He had smiled particularly at Kit, the No. 5, who was
standing with his oar over his shoulder, and his shorts well
daubed with grease from his slide. Sorrell was the coach's
pet heavy-weight. He had guts and style. The coach—
great man that he was, had let it be known in high quarters
that Sorrell was one of the best of the "freshers," and ought
to have a chance in the Trials.

The three large and healthy young creatures turned into
Jesus Lane. Kit's digs overlooked Jesus College, but the
two second-year men who were with him kept in Nevil's
Court.

"Coming round after 'hall'?"

Kit diverged towards the houses.

"No,—I'm swatting."

"Good lord,—what for?"

"Because I like it. Just that."

His still radiant smile flew back at them as he crossed the
road, and his seniors accepted it. Sorrell was a good lad.
His seriousness was without offence. He could row himself out with the same seriousness with which he read, and

197

youth has no quarrel with a fellow whose blade can shift
a good wedge of water, and who is not too cocky about it.
You could rag Sorrell—and get that smile, and healthy
physical retaliation with it. No one had ever seen him
ruffled or malicious. He boxed as he rowed—with the same
smiling seriousness.

A fellow named Burgoyne had the rooms below Christopher, and when Kit noticed a big blue saloon waiting outside the house, he assigned it to Burgoyne or to Burgoyne's
people. The rich fellow below him had many friends.
Hypothetical mothers and aunts and sisters and sisters'
friends were always arriving in cars to look up Bertie and
have lunch with him. Many of them were rather flashy
ladies, ultra modern young gentlewomen with flat chests
and shingled hair, who sat on Burgoyne's window sill and
smoked cigarettes. They were a cause of offence to Kit.

"Confound the women."

Their clothes and their chatter and the faint yet disturbing feminine aroma of them interfered with his work.

Kit ran up the steps and opened the front door. Burgoyne's part of the house struck him as being unexpectedly
peaceful, and he could only suppose that the whole carload
of colour had gone on the river. Kit had arrived at the
foot of the stairs when Mrs. Jowett, his landlady, appeared
from below. She was a stout person, swarthy, with a broad
nose and an expansive mouth, perennially interested in all
"young gentlemen." She had cared for Hindus and gentlemen of colour, and she had survived. Her only quarrel
with Kit was that she could apply to him the word
"worthy."

"A lady to see you, sir."

"A lady!"

"She's upstairs. Been here an hour."

"What's her name?"

"Duggan."

Kit looked mystified.

"What sort of—person, Mrs. Jowett?"

The landlady gave him one of her large and much-creased
smiles.

"Well,—a lady, sir. That's her car."

Kit went slowly upstairs, wondering who the woman
could be, and wishing her elsewhere at the moment. He

wanted to change, and he wanted his tea, and he had his
chemistry lecturer's notes to look through.

He opened the sitting-room door and saw his mother.

She was sitting by the window in one of the big wicker-
work chairs his father had given him, and she seemed to
fill it, sumptuously and easily, her black dress contrasting
with the purple and orange cretonne. He noticed that her
hair was grey, and that she was smiling at him.

Kit stood very still in the open doorway. He seemed
to have nothing to say. He was astonished, conscious of
nine dead years, and of those other memories that had
puzzled and hurt him until Sorrell had somehow made him
understand.

"I'm a ghost,—my dear Christopher."

He closed the door, remembering that Mrs. Jowett had
ears and that she used them, and when he had closed the
door he stood with his back to it.

"I hadn't any idea——"

They looked at each other, but their points of view were
very different. Christopher was a vivid person; he stood
five feet eleven; he looked very big in his rowing togs; he
had the glow of youth and of extreme fitness. He was
more than a good-looking fellow. His mother had despised
the so-called handsome men, knowing how thin and poor
the shell is, and that a good getter of the world's gear may
have apelike features. Ugly men can hug hard. And she
saw in Kit the likeness of herself, a superficial likeness. He
had her glowing skin, the same blue of the eye.

"Heavens, how you've grown!"

She put up her gloved hands and laughed,—but Kit's face
maintained an embarrassed and stubborn seriousness. He
stood and stared. He was looking at his mother across
those nine years. There were many things that astonished
him, and held him in a state of inarticulate staring. She
looked quite old. He felt himself in the presence of a
stranger. There was no whimper of welcome in him. He
was embarrassed, suspicious, immobile, at a loss to meet her
sudden intrusion into his life. He had not needed her, and
did not need her. He found himself looking at her and
thinking—"So—this is the woman who let my father down.
What does she want? How did she know?"

His mother was drawing off her gloves, and her down-

ward glance was like the dropping of a veil. She had seen
many things, that serious and curiously stern young face,
the puzzled and candid eyes. She was full of swift and
impatient comments. "What, if he is like me outside,—and
like his father—inside? Serious? Too beastly serious."
She smoothed out her gloves and her temper. Had she
expected him to rush at her and to cry—"Mother"? Of
course not! She made herself look smooth. She was the
well-dressed, presentable woman of forty-nine, the sort of
woman he might see any day in Regent Street, plump and
pleasant, a woman who went to church on occasion, but
who was nicely up to date. She had a house in South
Audley Street. She went to the Riviera. She played
Bridge. She had two or three nice girls who came and
nested in her chairs, and called her Aunt Dora.

"I happened to be in Cambridge——."

He crossed the room, and stood resting his hands on
the back of the other arm-chair. There was the same
attentive, self-questioning stare in his eyes.

"Yes,—I'm up at Trinity."

"So I had heard."

She raised her eyes and gave him a tentative and slightly
droll smile.

"I have been staying at the Pelican."

"Oh?"

"Your father looks very well. We had one or two talks."

His silence held her poised. His lips moved,—and grew
still. Then, he asked her a question, one of those terribly
direct questions that are so disconcerting to the sophisticated.

"Did he ask you to come and see me?"

She met the question full faced, but he had noticed a
momentary flicker of hesitation.

"I think he understood."

She watched his face. He seemed to be making some
calculation.

"I had a letter from him this morning."

"So you know."

"No."

The faint creases about her eyes and mouth seemed to
deepen.

"Well,—I should have thought——. You men are queer. Secretive creatures——"

She laughed, and playing with her gloves, looked up at him as she had learned to look at men at certain moments. Her voice was humorously reproachful.

"My dear,—there are things that seem extraordinary. At my age—one ceases to be surprised,—yes, even at one's self. One grows kinder——. So you have been rowing?"

He was looking at his hands resting on the chair.

"Yes."

"In strict training—I suppose. I'm staying at the University Arms. Would your rowing prevent you having a little dinner with me?"

He raised his eyes till they met hers.

"I have to dine in hall."

"I see. Well,—come in afterwards."

She waited like a gambler on the throw of his next words, smiling, maturely debonaire.

"I have an exam. in June. I'm reading hard."

She flicked a playful glove at him.

"You horribly serious boy. As if I want to interfere? Why,—after all,—I used to stop your crying when you were cutting a bad tooth. Well, my dear, let's leave it at that. I have kept my poor man waiting nearly two hours."

She rose, and he crossed the room and opened the door for her, the youth in him rigid.

"I'm sorry——."

She gave him a quick, kind glance.

"My dear,—if life doesn't teach one sportsmanship, what's the use?"

When she had gone Kit stood in the doorway of his room staring at nothing. His eyes looked like the eyes of those northern men that grow blue and fierce when they dwell upon the sea of their own equivocal thoughts.

2

Christopher dined in hall with the crew of the third May boat, and he had so little to say for himself and was so absent, that little Peabright the cox, who sat opposite, twittered at him like a friendly and mischievous bird.

"Buck up, Sorrell; you're late."

Christopher gave the little man a solemn and tolerant smile.

"All right, Peaby; I'm a bit slow in the water to-night."

Stroke, on Christopher's right, a ruddy, dark lad with roving eyes, grinned affectionately.

"Sorrell's doing calculations. I can feel him doing 'em behind me before we reach Grassy. Like this. If we row thirty, and gain two inches each stroke on Emmanuel 2, and Emmanuel 2 are rowing thirty-three, whereabouts in the Long Reach do we bump them?"

"We'll bump them before Ditton," said Kit; "you give us ten good ones, Skinny, when we get round Grassy."

And he relapsed into mysterious obscurity.

Strolling alone across the Great Court Kit considered the problem of his mother. For nine years she had been less than a shadow, and suddenly she had appeared before him as a woman of strange yet mature liveness. Never in his life had he felt more rigid and less impulsive than during those few minutes when he had stood looking down at her, feeling himself most strangely full of his father. The logic of youth can be very merciless, and Kit was not a sentimentalist. He was too big and vital to be sentimental. And what were the facts as he saw them? His mother had deserted his father at a time of wounds and misfortune. She had gone away with another man. Nine years had passed, and Sorrell had been both mother and father to him.

And she had talked of sportsmanship. What right had she——? He had been utterly ill at ease with her, and through the haze of his astonishment he had felt himself groping in the presence of someone who had an illusive motive, a cleverness that was strange to him, something plump and persuasive. And yet, after all, she was his mother. She might be expected to feel some interest in him. But what sort of interest? After nine years? Rather late in the day,—surely? And he did not think that he needed her interest. It roused no response in him. The man that was Christopher took sides, and his nascent manhood was on the side of his father.

Christopher passed through the Great Court, and across Sydney Street into Jesus Lane. The long May evening

spread before him its clear, persuasive light, and he knew
that the water would be lying very still and black under
the willows and the bridges, but he went to his rooms. He
threw his cap and gown into one chair, and himself into the
other. Through the open window he watched clouds flush-
ing a sky of pale azure.

Presently, he reached for a note-book scribbled full of
chemical formulæ, for he had told his mother that he had
work to do, and when you had made such a statement it
behoved you to be consistent. But what an extraordinary
situation was this, that he should be sitting there, mugging
chemistry, while his mother waited less than a mile away,
the mother whom he had not seen for nine years! Those
nine years! Yet, it was those nine years that had inhibited
any impulse that might have pushed him towards her. As
it was, he shrank from the idea of seeing her again; he
felt stiff and self-conscious, awkwardly and obstinately shy
of her.

But he could not read. His youth had been too deeply
stirred, and his young self challenged, and the carbon and
hydrogen molecules were jostled by live thoughts.

Why had not his father mentioned his mother to him
in that last letter?

What was the meaning of Sorrell's silence?

Their compact had never yet miscarried. "No secrets."
Kit the man was the son of Kit the boy.

"Perhaps it never occurred to him that she would come
up here."

Kit's impulse was to sit down and write to his father,
and he threw his chemistry notes aside, and got out a
writing-pad and his fountain-pen. He sat curled up in the
chair with the pad on his knee, full of an immense and
questioning seriousness.

Sounds of wild life began in the room below. Three
or four live young men had returned with Burgoyne and
were letting loose their liveliness. A gramophone began to
play, and voices in chorus to ask the whole of the impend-
ing night that most vital question—"Why did I kiss that
girl?"

"Confound them!" said Kit, frowning in the dusk over
his writing-pad and biting the top of his pen.

"Why—O—why," sang the voices.

"Because—you are blithering idiots," replied a voice from above.

The eternal question blew itself out, and four irresponsible young men big with youth cast about for other methods of self-expression.

"Let's go up and rag old Solly."

They arrived, tumbling up the stairs, and stood bunched in Christopher's doorway, sighting him as a shadowy figure in a chair with a writing-pad on his knee.

"Pomes," said one of them, "pomes to Alice."

"Hallo,—old H$_2$O."

"O, get out," said Kit, "I'm busy. Go and put on another fox-trot."

They fell upon him and there was a minute's commotion during which Kit with perfect good temper gave as good as he got, and having extricated himself and pulled Burgoyne's coat over his head, thrust him vigorously between the legs of a Rugger "blue."

"Kiss her—now, old thing."

Someone switched on the light, and got hold of Kit's writing-pad, but Kit's voice became suddenly unplayful.

"Drop that."

"Dear old pater——"

"Drop it——"

The *farceur* dropped it, not merely because Sorrell was a marked man with the gloves, but also because he was a decent lad.

"Right O, Solly."

Kit smiled at him.

"Quits, you chaps. I'll come down presently when I have finished a letter."

Hot and satisfied, they left him with a wildly ruffled head and went below. The gramophone resumed its melody.

"Why did I kiss——?"

Kit wrote his letter, and the inward refrain of it was —"Why did—she—come here?"

3

Sorrell sat reading Christopher's letter.

"What puzzled me—pater—was why you had not talked about it in your letter.

"She asked me to dinner, but I said that I had to dine in hall, and when she asked me to go in after dinner, I said I had to read. It made me feel queer and churlish, but the fact is I was pretty well astonished. She seemed like a stranger.

"I asked her whether you knew about her coming here, and she did not give me a straight answer.

"It seems pretty beastly writing like this,—but I have always told you things. There is something in me that can't call her mother. I can't help it——."

Sorrell laid the letter on his desk, and he remained for a long while, deep in thought. Christopher had asked him a very definite question, and he neither wished nor was able to avoid replying to it. That his mood had its moments of exultation was neither here nor there. Almost, he was ready to forgive the woman her attempt to raid his life's store of treasure, for the sake of the significant ineptitude of the attempt. At first, Sorrell had been angry, but Kit's letter had dispersed his anger.

His son was loyal to him, and to explain this loyalty the father could produce a dozen reasons. And was not the chief reason to be found in his own attitude towards Christopher, an attitude of deep and unselfish affection? He had refused to treat the boy like personal property, jealously, with arbitrary patronage. He had fought the spirit of the old-man father. He had never talked down to Christopher, coerced him against his reason, or worked off upon the boy a facile pomposity.

They were friends. This letter was the most signal proof of it.

4

Kit read his father's letter while he was eating his breakfast. It was a strange and rare letter for a father to write to a son.

"Kit,—I am not only your father but your friend,—and my wish has been to put the friend before the father.

"Old chap,—you mean a very great deal to me, more perhaps than you will ever know, but you are not my cake to have and eat. Your life is your own, and my share in it is the love and pride that will come to me out of it. All the things that will make you happy are

what I desire—you and your job. It is a man's job that matters to
him most.

"I have no feeling against your mother—now. All that is dead.
The only feeling that I should have against her would be—if—she
took you away from your true self and your job. I don't say that she
would. But women have powers of persuasion.

"Do what you feel moved to do. If you wish to see her—see her.
After all—she is your mother, and was—my wife.

"I do not believe that she can come between us.

"Your letter to me was rather a precious document, Kit. Do you
remember the old brown portmanteau?"

Christopher's bacon and eggs grew cold while he read
his father's letter. His eyes had a faint mist before them.
His father was a great man. He loved him.

4

Mrs. Duggan's chauffeur was strapping a trunk to the
luggage grid, while she herself stood at a window, still
impatiently dallying after three days of waiting for the
son who never came. She had expected him, and when he
failed to come to her, her expectation had grown more
urgent and angry. For she, who never allowed sentiment
to interfere with her appetites, had wished to employ sentiment in the seduction of her son.

The stare of his blue eyes, his rigid seriousness had remained with her. She had seen in him both herself and
his father, and the old jealous clamour had revived.
"Mine" had been her cry. But she had understood Kit's
obstinate shyness, and in dealing with men she had discovered the efficacy of attacking by retreating. She had
held aloof during those three days, unable to believe that
the elemental stuff in Christopher would not bring him to
her. She would handle him gently. Let him but tolerate
the first, subtle caress, and she would soon put her shears
to his awkward shyness.

She was in love with youth now, and youth found her
pleasant and easy. She had money to spend and she knew
how to fill her car with young things, to carry a bouquet
of youth about town to the dancing-rooms or the theatre.
Aunt Dora was such a good sort.

And Christopher had not come to be caressed. The rigid

and serious Sorrell seemed to be holding him back behind
the barrier of those nine years. She had expected difficulties, a course of careful persuasion, and she had prepared
herself to be patient.

But to be snubbed by Sorrell's son!

A porter came into the room.

"The car is ready, madam."

She prepared to abandon her strong point and to begin
her retreat, and as she passed out through the hotel doorway she became aware of an abrupt and blind rage, the
impatience of the woman elemental in her passion to possess.
She approached the car. The chauffeur was holding open
the door. He touched the peak of his cap.

"Beautiful morning, madam."

"A perfect morning, Gunter."

He arranged a rug over her knees, and closed the door
of the saloon, and as he did so a lad in a dark blue gown
came round the back of the car and appeared at the window.
He raised his mortar-board, and looked unsmilingly at
his mother. His lips moved. She leaned forward and
lowered the window.

"I thought it was your car. I'm just off to a lecture."

She put out a gloved hand, and her face had a soft and
secret radiance.

"Be a good boy, my dear. I can see that you are."

He took her hand, but she was aware of the irresponsive-
ness of his strong young fingers.

"Hope you will have a good drive. London, is it?"

She was all smiles.

"Of course. Now, don't be late for your lecture. Good-
bye."

She nodded to the chauffeur, gave a playful pat to Kit's
hand and sat back smiling at him with easy benevolence.

"My address in town is South Audley Street, No. 107,
Good-bye."

XXII

I

SORRELL was lying in a punt on a luxurious super-
fluity of red and blue cushions, his grey hat placed
carefully beside him, a good cigar sending its perfume
and blue smoke upwards into the trailing foliage of a weeping willow. The punt, propelled by Kit who sat and dipped
a lazy paddle, had glided in under the willow and come to
rest there. The evening was very warm and still; the soft
sheen of the river between the bridges reflected many other
punts and splashes of colour, reminding Sorrell of those
brilliant and quaint little mosaics made of flower petals
pressed upon brown paper under a piece of glass which a
country girl had taught him to arrange with his childish
fingers. He had dined in hall with Christopher. Like
Calverley he felt that fate could not touch him. He looked
at his neat brown shoes, and his well-cut, well-pressed
grey trousers. He enjoyed the fretted gold and the greenness of the weeping willow. He looked at Kit sitting square
to the sunset with the glow of it upon his face.

"We have arrived," was Sorrell's thought; "every
damned piece of luggage that I struggled with in the old
days was worth it. Life is good."

A punt-load of parents and young things drifted past
them, and the dark eyes of one of the young things dwelt
interestedly upon Kit. He was worth a girl's glance. He
seemed both aware of the dark eyes and unaware of them.

"Going to make your bump to-morrow?" asked the voice
of Kit's father.

Christopher came out of a brown study, but his immediate awareness of life was not concerned with the May
races.

"We ought to. We are faster than our second boat.
They don't allow it—of course."

His glance raised itself to the glowing tops of the elms,

and came back to survey the river. There was laughter under Clare bridge, and someone was splashing water with a paddle.

"I have had a letter from South Audley Street, pater."

"O," said Sorrell beneath the calm drift of his cigar smoke.

"She wants me to spend a few days there when I go down. A dance or something."

He looked questioningly at his father.

"Do you want to go?"

"Not much. Do you think I ought to?"

Sorrell was silent for a few seconds.

"There is no ought about it. But there need be no reason why you shouldn't."

"I'm not particularly keen on dancing. Would you go, pater, if she asked you?"

His father took a little time to answer the question.

"No,—I don't think I should. Not prejudice, you know. I have no feeling against anybody, so long as they don't interfere. One of the things in life is to keep clear of incompatibles."

Kit stroked the water with his paddle.

"You have got to set yourself a course. Most chaps just drift. Girls and things. You know, pater. And then— there is hurting people's feelings."

"Quite. But if you have got feelings, don't make the mistake of imagining that everybody else has got just the same feelings."

"I suppose they haven't."

"No."

"Some of them play up."

"The takers always play up to the givers."

Kit pondered this saying.

"You are one of the givers, pater."

"O, not always. Don't throw yourself away on the crowd."

There was much more talk between them under the edge of the dusk, with the sentimental river dividing the conventional sentiment of the grey colleges and the green spaces. Kit paddled the punt slowly up stream. They passed other punts with cargoes of hard young she-things; and Sorrell found himself wondering what Kit thought of

women. What was his attitude? Had this sentimental
dusk on this sentimental piece of water the mystery of the
old illusions, and would it make very ordinary young women
appear divinities? But surely—love—modern love—refused to pose upon pedestals. Sorrell could hear the lean,
long-limbed girl of the day saying—"Come off it—you silly
ass."

"Drifting,—just drifting," said Kit suddenly, and swinging the punt round; "what do people want?"

Sorrell surveyed the first stars.

"That is youth's trouble. It does not know what it
wants."

"Didn't you, pater?"

"Vague flashes. No,—not clearly. When I look back
now I see that I was in a sort of enchanted fog. You would
rush about and see—sudden things when the fog lifted for
a moment. A bit of red sky, or a tree, or a silly full moon,
or a girl's face. And you thought you wanted the moon
or the girl's face. Perhaps, you got one of them,—and
then the fog came down again, and you went on groping.
But it's worse for two to be groping."

"It's sex," said Kit suddenly, leaning over his paddle,
"sex,—that's what it is."

Sorrell raised himself on one elbow.

"The fog of sex. You have found that out——! It took
me twenty years, my son. But—hush——!"

He laughed.

"We shall shock—the May Flies."

Kit surprised him.

"They take a lot more shocking than one thinks, pater.
We aren't easily shocked. Were you?"

"We pretended to be."

"Why——," he dug the paddle into the water and closed
his mouth on some impulsive confession. Sorrell wondered.
He told himself that a man got out of date. The young
things had different ways of arranging the world, and at
present they walked instead of dancing, and eschewed elemental curves. Obviously, Kit had met other young things
and had parleyed with them. Sorrell's feeling was that for
Kit woman was not upon a pedestal.

"You are aways saying, pater. that the job matters—
more than—other things."

"So it does."

"That's what I think. But sometimes—a chap—feels he must go head over heels into—life."

"Of course," said Sorrell. "The unknown, woman, all that. The thing is,—though one does not realize it when one's young, that one wants—the sensation—not the particular woman. One wants all women that ever were. The sensation is natural,—but marriage——"

He paused, looking beyond Kit at the grey arch of a bridge.

"Marriage is—artificial. That's the whole trouble.—So—you see——"

"You don't believe in marriage——?"

Sorrell would like to have shrugged his shoulders.

"No,—not till the job is launched. After that—a comrade——. But the other thing,—like one's morning tub. Not a sort of cement pool in a Zoo with two bored animals—swimming around. If you must take a plunge—be sure—you can get out again——. Some day you'll know whether you want to get out. A few of us do, or think we do. Not many."

2

Sorrell found himself on the towing path between Grassy and Ditton. He had suggested going down to watch the boats start, but Kit had warned him that he might have to run half a mile if he hoped to see 1st Trinity 3 bump Emmanuel 2.

"I should hang about between Grassy and Ditton, pater. Ask somebody on the towing path."

Sorrell felt most absurdly excited. He had watched the boats of the division paddle down, and he sat on the bank and listened to the gossip of other interested people. It was a still, green English day, with not a breath of wind in the willows, and the river like glass. He could see the crowd at Ditton Corner, packed in the meadow and in the boats along the bank, a gaily-coloured crowd.

The boom of the starting gun reached him. He stood up. He was trembling. Absurd parent!

Presently, he saw figures running, the flash of oars round-

ing the green curve of Grassy, the nose of an eight. Young
men were shouting. The leading boat cleared the corner,
but Sorrell was not interested in this particular boat. Emmanuel 2 came next, and it seemed to him that their oars
were moving with a scuffling haste. By George, yes! Kit's
boat was right on top of them.

Sorrell ran. He ran down to meet the boats, got himself hustled by an eager crowd of young men in cerise-
coloured blazers, in fact he was nearly pushed into the
river. He was shouting, and waving his hat. "First,—
First, well rowed, First." He ran again in the opposite
direction, seeing for a while nothing but Kit with a very
stern face swinging and plugging at No. 5. The boats
were overlapping. At Ditton Corner the 1st Trinity cox
made his bump, and the arm of the Emmanuel cox went up.
Both eights drifted close in to the line of boats, and Sorrell
stood on the towing path bank, waving to Kit bent over his
oar and drawing deep breaths.

Kit saw his father, straightened up, and waved a hand.
His face ceased to be stern, and began to smile.

Sorrell put on his hat.

"I'm a bit excited. Damn it,—why not?"

Sorrell walked back with his son from the First Trinity
boat-house. He was just a little anxious. A gruelling game
—this rowing, bad—so he had heard—for young men's
hearts.

"Feeling all right, Kit?"

Christopher's smile was reassuring.

"Quite. We ought to catch the leading boat to-morrow.
Emmanuel were up on them. Then we shall be sandwich
boat."

"What does that mean?"

"We have to row twice, at the head of the second division
and at the bottom of the first."

Sorrell's sympathies were divided. An exhausting business, two races in one day! But perhaps he was growing
old, and youth was youth.

Kit's boat made their second bump on the second day,
but failed to catch the last boat of the first division. And
there they stuck, having to row for their lives on the last
day in order to keep away from a fast boat that had made
three bumps behind them. Sorrell ran all the way up the

Long Reach, and he was nearly as "done" as his son when First Trinity got home with half a length to spare, and so finished head of the second division.

There was a bump supper that night,—but Kit came back early to his rooms where Sorrell was sitting in one of the big chairs, smoking the pipe of peace.

"You're early."

Kit was very sober.

"I have had my rag, a good one. Let's talk, pater. There are one or two things——"

"South Audley Street?"

"Yes,—that,—and others."

3

As for the first part of the examination for the Bachelorship of Medicine Kit did less well in Physics than he had hoped to do, but his Chemistry and Biology were satisfactory. That was his own opinion, and he conveyed it to his father in a letter written after the last paper. The results would be known in a few days, and Kit was staying up to see the lists.

Duly, they were posted on the Senate House door, and Kit walked from his digs, and crossed King's Parade with a feeling of suspense. He was not thinking of himself so much as of his father, for time was money, and lost months would mean money, his father's money. He saw a small crowd of undergrads on the steps of the Senate House, and as Kit passed through the iron gates a figure detached itself from the group. It belonged to a man named Gorringe who had worked next to Sorrell in the "stinks" lab, a cocky and opinionated little man with a profile like a sparrow's. Gorringe had a sick face. He did not see Sorrell; he did not want to see him.

"Pilled," thought Kit, and was not sorry, for Gorringe needed a course of pilling.

He leaned against the backs of two other men, and peered between and over their heads. "Sanger, Smith, Smith, Snaith, Snowden, Sorrell." He felt a quick thrill at the sight of his name. He went away quietly to the post office, and sent off a telegram to his father.

"Through."

Sorrell read that one word some two hours later, and he sent the under-porter on a bicycle to Winstonbury with an answering message.

"Splendid.   Congratulations.—PATER."

Christopher joined him next day at the Pelican, and Mr. Porteous came to dinner. Two telegrams had been waiting for Kit; one had come from Tom Roland who had had the news wired to him by Sorrell; the other had been sent by Christopher's mother.

Kit had showed it to his father.

"How did she know?"

"Arranged with someone to have the lists watched, I suppose."

"Rather decent of her, pater, after the way I——."

Kit had found no answering approval in his father's eyes, and he had understood. Women,—yes, women, even his own mother! Wanting their fingers in the pie.

He had torn up his mother's telegram.

But there was that invitation of hers still hanging unanswered in the air, for he had written to her to say that he had decided to make no plans until the result of the examination was known. He had promised to write later.

Well,—what was he going to do about it?

4

Tucked under his porridge plate Kit discovered an envelope addressed to him in his father's handwriting, and on opening it he found that it contained a ten-pound note.

"I say,—pater——!"

Sorrell had been pretending to read the morning paper, and he glanced up at his son's serious face.

"Well,—old man?"

"You know—you oughtn't—to be so jolly good to me——."

"Why not? Something to celebrate with. You have worked hard."

Kit got up and, going round the table, bent down and kissed his father on the forehead.

"You are a sport, pater."

"That's all right," said Sorrell, blushing slightly, and gripping Kit's shoulder for a moment; "why not go up and spend that week-end with your mother?"

He saw Kit's face take on an expression of surprised solemnity.

"I have been wanting to talk about that."

"Right. I'm ready. The porridge is on the sideboard."

Christopher helped himself to porridge, sugared it liberally, and disposed of half a dozen spoonfuls before he found his voice.

"I think it was rather fine of you, pater, to give me that opening."

"Not a bit. If you want to go——."

"I don't want to go. I mean—if I go—it won't be because I want to,—but I have a queer feeling that I ought to go —just once."

"Because she is your mother?"

Kit sat silent for a little while, staring hard at the bacon dish.

"No,—because of you——."

It was Sorrell's turn to pause.

"O,—how's that?"

"Well,—supposing she thinks that she could matter as much as you? I want her to know—what sort of friends you and I are. It's fair to her in a way, isn't it, pater? I don't look upon her as my mother; I never shall."

Sorrell stared hard at his son.

"Kit," he said presently, "I don't know what to say about it. You have got me rather hard—over the heart."

"That's all right," said his son hurriedly, falling fiercely upon his porridge; "that's all right. So long as you and I understand each other——."

XXIII

I

POUNDS, Mrs. Duggan's maid, had been with her mistress for three years. A little, dried-up slip of a woman with a tight mouth buttoned up under a Roman nose, she knew her mistress almost as well as she knew Mrs. Duggan's wardrobe. Pounds dressed her ladyship's moods much as she clothed her body, with matronly black velvet, or tissue of gold and of old rose, and when flesh-coloured stockings were in fashion Pounds supplied them and suffered my lady's ankles to assume the responsibility.

On a June morning, with the sun shining, Pounds carried in Mrs. Duggan's early tea. She had come to know her mistress's various voices, and being a facile cynic she reacted to them. She knew the winter voice and the spring voice, the "I'm an old woman" plaint, and the plump autumnal cry of the comfortable egoist. There was the Monte Carlo voice, and the Albert Hall voice, and the voice of "Aunt Dora." Pounds was an echo in Mrs. Duggan's world, but in her own world Pounds rent calico and smashed crockery.

"Two lumps of sugar this morning, Pounds."

"Yes, madam."

Pounds popped in the two lumps. She made the appropriate remark—"It's a beautiful day, madam," for the voice from the bed expressed Ascot and a successful frock and strawberries and cream and a punt on the river and a good appetite and youth and the desire to fool somebody.

"Tell Randal I shall want the car at eleven."

"Yes, madam."

"Mr. Sorrell may be here for lunch. And Miss Merrindin. Tell cook that. And we shall be dining at my club."

"Yes, madam."

Pounds was wondering whether the colour of the day

should be a matronly and sumptuous black or something a little more June-like? What age was Mr. Sorrell?

"What dress, madam?"

"O,—something quiet," said the voice from the bed.

Mrs. Duggan drank her tea and ate two thin slices of bread and butter. She was all smiles and rotund beneficence. She had a feeling that she had her hand on the thing she wanted, and that a few careful caresses would make it hers. Or nearly hers, as much as a young thing could be hers. She wanted Kit, and she wanted him for all sorts of reasons, because he was flesh of her flesh, because he was young, because he belonged to Sorrell, because Sorrell had quietly defied her. She was a woman of strong appetites; she knew how to be generous; she had some knowledge of men. Her appreciation of Christopher had been instantaneous. Here was something difficult; his shyness and his reluctance had inflamed that sort of physical tenderness that was her love. He was a comely lad; he resembled her in his body. She was forty-nine, and she looked more than forty-nine, for in choosing to chase money she had had to live with oldish men, and that had aged her. They had been men who had drunk too much, and who had gone about like snappy old dogs. But youth,—the youth of her own son, to possess it, handle it, feel herself the mistress of it! A devoted son! To be able to score off that absurdly serious father——!

At a quarter past eleven Mrs. Duggan entered her car. "O,—Pounds,—if Mr. Sorrell should arrive before I return,—show him his room. I should be back about half-past twelve."

"Where to, madam?" asked the chauffeur, before closing the door.

"The Halcyon Club."

Christopher's mother was a member of the Halcyon Club. It was domiciled in the house of a dead grandee, and inherited an atmosphere of spaciousness and dignity. It was a cock and hen affair, but more hen than cock. The club gave Saturday night dances, and Mrs. Duggan dropped in to make sure of her dinner table. She wanted the table for four in the corner where the statue of the Venus de Milo stood in a recess. She asked for the steward, and he assured her the table was hers.

"You are quite sure? Last time—you know—I found Lady Truget in possession. And I have a little party."

From the club she drove to Gaiter's in Regent Street and bought flowers, roses, luscious but conventional red and white roses with plenty of perfume. None of your too exotic flowers for a very serious minded boy. She called at Fuller's and purchased chocolates. She descended at her modiste's, not because she wanted a dress, but because she was feeling well, and it was a pleasant thing to do. "Melanie's" mirrors were kinder than most mirrors; they made you look less of a fright than you feared you might be.

Then, she told Randal to drive her round the park. She lay back comfortably to consider her preparations. She decided that it had been rather subtle of her to ask two charming girls to meet and amuse Christopher, and she included them in the furnishings and drapings of her temple of Venus. She thought that if she meant to get at the boy she would get at him most successfully through sex, not crudely, but by way of the pleasant emanations of sex, by suggesting to him what a good time she could give him.

As for the two girls,—O,—well—they were very modern. Lola Merrindin's vivacity might suffice for a week-end in somebody's bungalow on the river. Fluffy Tarrant was like a pot of marmalade, but she was as hard as the pot.

"I wonder if the boy has arrived? And what has Steve's attitude been? Not liking it much!"

Christopher had arrived. He was standing with his hands in his pockets in the middle of his mother's drawing-room, looking at the photo of the double-chinned captain of industry who had been Duggan. Kit's mother had thought it a nice touch,—this putting out of the family photographs.

2

Christopher did not like the face of the dead Duggan.

His impressions of this opulent room in an opulent house were peculiarly vivid, perhaps because this was the first occasion upon which he had experienced the gilding of the lily. His modernity had a clean temper, like the knife which he was to use so skilfully in after years. So this was where

his mother lived upon the fortunate proceeds of two marriages, after her adventurous discarding of Kit's father. The
room and its furniture were as modern as Kit's unsentimental outlook upon life. The walls were blue, the furniture
gold, the carpet apple green, the cushions and curtains black.
It seemed to be full of bolsters and tuffets in gaudy colours
Kit had never seen anything like it. The sofa was so
upholstered that it resembled the overblown and spreading
petals of a flower.

It was a suggestive sofa.

"Oh,—it is all right.—I suppose," he thought, "for a
rather exciting half-hour. Makes one think of a highly
stained microscopic slide."

He preferred things to look shabbier, less vocal with
colour. He thought of the shabby old blue trousers his
father had worn in the old days.

A car stopped outside the house, and Kit went to the
window. It was his mother's car, and something in him
grew rigid. He retreated to the other end of the room, as
far as it was possible for him to get from the blue door,
and he stood there with his hands in his pockets, his eyes
curiously hard.

She burst in upon him. She had put on tortoiseshell
spectacles, things Kit particularly detested. The mature
and intellectual touch!

"My dear, well—here you are. I've been so busy. Congratulations. Now—sit down and tell me all about it."

He had remained at the far end of the room, looking very
tall and stiff in his grey suit. It was a good suit. He looked
well in it.

"Afraid I'm early."

"Not a bit. I've two girls coming to lunch. We have
got half an hour. Now—sit down and tell me all about it."

She sat down on the voluptuous sofa.

"About—what?"

She was very animated.

"Why—about your wonderful exam. I hear you were
third on the list."

"That's unofficial. How did you know?"

"Your tutor told me."

"O," said Kit, and sat down on one of the flimsy gold
chairs.

This highly coloured room was all surface, and without depth, and his mother's enthusiastic animation reduced Christopher to a mere surface. He found himself quite unable to respond to her vivacity, and since he persisted in sitting there like a graven image of his own youth, she had to continue her attack.

"I'm sure you must be awfully tired after all that work. And rowing—too. I'm going to give you a real—lazy—jolly week-end. There will be a little dance to-night at my club, but it will be over at twelve."

He told her that he was not much of a dancer.

"Fudge, my dear boy, an athletic child—with your figure. My two flappers will—make—you dance."

She thought him monstrously shy, and his seeming shyness did not displease her. Her eyes were making an intimate examination of him while she talked, taking in all the clean texture of his youth and enjoying it, contrasting it unconsciously with her many impressions of the oldish men with whom she had lived. She looked at Kit's fresh, brown hands with their young skin and supple fingers. How different they were from the blue and branny hands of John Duggan, or the wrinkled skinniness and yellow blotched claws of Arthur Sampits. Yes, old age was detestable. She herself was on the edge of it, and her urgent vitality craved the young blood of her son.

"You take after me, Kit,—a little—I think.". .

She was ready to let herself go. She wanted him to come across and kiss her.

"In looks—I mean. Just turn your head a little. Yes, you have my ears—exactly."

She laughed.

"You shy thing!"

His self-conscious rigidity became painful. She was making him feel a fool, and his glance glazed itself upon those American goggles of hers. Why on earth did she wear them? And talking about his ears—too! What perfect rot!

He withdrew his eyes as though he were plucking his glance away from her. He surveyed the room.

"I'm going to Vienna for two months. Rather a sound idea. The pater's idea."

She smiled right through this digression.

"To study?"

"The language, and other things. I don't want to loaf all through the Long Vac."

"You mustn't work too hard."

"What a fool saying," he thought, and just stared at her.

"The pater had to work pretty hard. Besides, it's the best thing. He and I understand each other."

"That must be very nice for you."

There was a pause, and Christopher sat through this pause in the conversation with a seeming stolidity that neither helped nor thwarted her. His mother's animation reasserted itself. He listened, with the appearance of an attentive young foreigner who was unable to understand the language she was using. He was not sorry for her. She was no more than a stranger who was trying to produce an effect, and instinctively he resisted, though his resistance was passive. He was wise as to her intention; though he could not disentangle all her motives, but his feeling was that she had made up her mind to win him over, and he did not mean to be won over.

His mother was growing irritated, but was able to hide it, and when a young thing in an amber-coloured frock floated into the room, Mrs. Duggan arose with enthusiasm and kissed her.

"Kit; this is Lola,—Miss Lola Merrindin."

Kit stood up, and bent stiffly at the hips, and his smile was vague. He was aware of Lola Merrindin as a very attractive creature, one of those slim, black, highly mobile young women with a brilliant white skin and gazelle's eyes. Her hair had a slight kink in it. Her nose spread its eager nostrils with some breadth above a capacious red mouth. She smiled a great deal and showed very white teeth. She was intensely alive, and she was never still, flicking herself into varying postures and evanescent expressions, getting up and sitting down, laughing and then looking out under her brilliant forehead with elfish and half-sullen solemnity.

Mrs. Duggan left them together.

"Amuse him, darling. I must go and tidy up. Fluffy will be here any minute."

It was Kit's first experience of this particular type of young woman, and he sat there and surveyed her with an air of polite suspicion. He had a feeling that she was too

furiously attractive to be safe, for how attractive she was
the young male in him knew. Her little nervous movements, the quick and provoking tricks of her eager body,
her laughter, her mobile mouth and sidelong and expressive eyes made his male shyness afraid. For the young
male can be as timid as a hare.

Miss Merrindin chattered. She had the voice of a
Neapolitan singing-girl. Wasn't Aunt Dora a dear? And
wasn't her house perfectly sweet? She tried to push Kit
into a flow of soul, to make him talk about the May Races,
and dancing, and motor cars and Wimbledon, but Kit's
soul refused to flow. He sat there and agreed smilingly with
everything she said, and sensed her as a sort of sexual
Chinese cracker jumping around his shyness.

Did he know "Why do I feel wicked?"

No, he didn't. What was it?

She flung herself at Aunt Dora's piano, and crashed out
a Fox Trot, her whole body vibrating on the stool. She
began to sing, while Kit sat there like a dolorous and dull
dog on the point of howling.

Aunt Dora returned in the midst of all this brightness,
followed by a very thin young woman with a flat, pale
face, and a bobbed head of fiery hair.

Kit was introduced to Miss Tarrant.

They went down to lunch.

The remainder of the day was kaleidoscopic. At lunch
Kit was made to drink white wine and a liqueur, and he had
to confess that he liked the wine; it assisted his flow of
soul. Lola Merrindin became less alarming. After coffee
and cigarettes in the new art drawing-room, they put on
hats and packed into Mrs. Duggan's car. Pound handed
in cigarettes, chocolates, rugs. Kit had proposed taking
one of the swivel seats, but he was made to go to bed in
the deeply cushioned back seat of the saloon between his
mother and Lola Merrindin. It was a bit of a squeeze, but
everybody seemed to like it. Fluffy Tarrant occupied one
of the swivel seats, and ate chocolates, or smoked cigarettes.
The car whirled them down to Maidenhead, with Kit lying
comfortably wedged between two perfumed and exotic
creatures. He felt the pressure of Lola's body, of her thigh
and leg. She fidgeted a great deal, and her movements
pleasantly disturbed him. He pretended to quarrel with her

over the chocolate box. They had a playful struggle. The smell of her hair smote him. His mother smiled.

At Maidenhead they had tea in the garden of one of the hotels. Fluffy Tarrant took Christopher on the river in a punt with orange and purple cushions. It appeared to be her turn. She looked at Kit with the considering eyes of a young leopardess; her pose was one of extreme and cheeky frankness; she pretended to be as old as Eve.

She told Kit that he was a child.

"You don't know—anything."

She did not say what anything was. She splashed him with her paddle, and appeared ironical and sophisticated and superior. On the way home she and Lola exchanged seats, and to Kit Miss Tarrant appeared all thigh-bone. The pressure was constant; it did not flicker and jerk and quiver. It was more ardent or might have been, yet was less disturbing. Kit's fate promised that dark women were to trouble him, dark women with a certain languorous and appealing type of brown eye.

They dressed and drove to the Halcyon Club. A young elderly man with a high forehead, a neat smudge of black hair, and a very small mouth, was waiting for them in the lounge. His name was Luke Sykes. He was to make the fourth for the postprandial dance.

Kit took an immediate dislike to Mr. Sykes. He was the sort of man who looked bored and wearily superior, and who said—"O, really!" to everything. He talked about places and people that Kit had never heard of,—and his trousers were too well braided.

They dined, and emptied two bottles of champagne. Kit was facing Miss Tarrant, also the naked statue of Venus, and he would not acknowledge the presence of the statue, and Miss Tarrant seemed wickedly aware of his self-suppression. Lola grew somewhat excited; she talked a great deal, laughed, jerked that mobile body of hers, while Kit's mother behaved like an amiable dowager. Mr. Sykes seemed somehow shy of Kit, and trailed his bored experiences through a series of night-clubs, and since Kit knew nothing of night clubs his eloquence was limited.

Afterwards they went up to the ball-room and danced. Kit found Lola on his bosom. She seemed to have flung herself at him and arrived there with one of those rapid and disturbing movements. She kept smiling and looking at him in the eyes; he saw the shadowy curves of her nostrils, her red and wavy mouth.

She danced extraordinarily well, like a Latin girl, and she made Kit dance better than he knew. Mr. Sykes and Miss Tarrant were striding up and down and round-about at a great pace, looking like a couple of wooden dolls with their thin legs stuck on with pins. Kit's partner kept up a humming to the music. She smelt good. Her mouth——. And then Kit trod heavily on her right foot and apologized.

"I say—I'm awfully sorry. Did it hurt?"

He felt the warm pressure of her body suddenly increase. She smiled in his eyes.

"A bit.—But I don't—mind, Kiddy."

He inhaled the scent of her hair.

3

Christopher woke with a headache.

His memories of the previous night encouraged him to believe that he had taken part in a rapid-motion picture whose movements had been quickened by the drinking of too much champagne.

A maid brought him early tea, and made it known to him that Mrs. Duggan was taking breakfast in bed, and that Kit could have his breakfast brought up to him if he wished it. Kit did not wish it. He got up and had a cold bath, used his tooth-brush vigorously, put away his tumbled clothes of the previous night, and felt better. He breakfasted alone on porridge, a boiled egg, tea and toast, and at the end of the meal Pounds appeared and made an announcement.

"Mrs. Duggan will be down, sir, by twelve."

"I'm going out," said Kit.

"Lunch is at half-past one, sir."

The sun was shining and Kit went out and walked with a concentrated energy that poured up from below. He walked without heeding the outer world, and he seemed to see neither the trees nor the people nor the dogs nor the motor-cars. He just walked. He began to work up his full speed in Hyde Park, and he went through it, and across to the Green Park, and over the Mall into St. James's. He stood on the bridge spanning the water and watched the various water-birds. His headache had gone; his stridings of the morning had broken the rhythm of those other stridings to syncopated tunes with a girl pressing close against him.

No. 3, Cheltenham Terrace.

No. 3 was the house in which Lola lived, and he happened to know that he had been walking away from it, and that in spite of the fact that she had said it to music in the approved fox-trot manner. Obviously, she had expected him to keep in step, but Kit's mood was very much out of step with the rapid movements of the previous day.

It wasn't that the young male in him did not desire her. He had gone to bed lying upon roses and thorns, but the Kit of the morning was Sorrell's Kit, the young man who had trained for the May Races, and for that other and greater race, and with the morning his father's grip came back to him.

"I must get out of this," was his abrupt reflection.

He remembered that he had to spend the rest of the day with his mother. His impatience and his disinclination to go back to her were so very strong that they permeated his whole unsciousness, compelling him to recognize in her some natural enemy. He had more than a suspicion that his mother was offering him bribes, the enticements that might be expected to make an appeal to a very young man. She was trying to get at him through his body, and through his more disorderly emotions. Sorrell had never done that.

Kit walked back less rapidly to South Audley Street. It was one o'clock, and he found his mother in the drawing-room, looking far fresher than he felt, and dressed in a shimmery blue dress. She smiled at him, and her smile had a confident roguishness, for Kit's rigidity had disappeared during the last hour at the Halcyon Club.

"You naughty boy!"

She patted the sofa, and the gesture invited him to share it. Moreover, it was borne in upon him that she expected him to kiss her.

"Well, how's Lola this morning?"

She was accusing him of having slipped off to No. 3, Cheltenham Terrace.

"I haven't seen her."

"Lazy young thing. Wasn't she up?"

"I have been walking," said Kit; "in the Park."

"And she didn't turn up? Sly-boots! Well,—you belong
to me to-day, my dear, and Lola can wait till to-morrow."

"I have got to be back to-morrow," he said stubbornly,
refusing to explain that he had no arrangement with Miss
Merrindin, and quite determined not to be over-persuaded.

"My dear, there is no hurry."

"Work,—you know."

She patted the sofa, and half jokingly she began to hint
that Sorrell was exercising a fatherly restraint, but Kit did
not allow the innuendo to pass. It was necessary for him
to make a stand.

"No. The pater and I understand each other. I'm keen
on my work."

"But it's the vacation."

"Oh,—I have plenty of reading to do."

She readjusted her attitude. She had seen his young
reserve unfold itself on the previous night, but this morning
its petals were firmly closed. She realized that she would
have to vary the quality of her emotional sunlight, temper
it to Kit's peculiarities, play upon his absurd seriousness.
She remembered that he had not told her what his future
was to be.

"You mean to be so tremendously clever. I want to hear
all about it. We will have a nice long drive this afternoon.
Leith Hill or somewhere like that. We don't know each
other properly yet, Kit, do we?"

He did not tell her that their mutual ignorance was not
his fault.

They drove to Leith Hill by way of Leatherhead, Dork-
ing and Abinger, sharing the road with a crowd of flurrying
Sabbath cars. Kit kept well in his own corner. Shut up
there with this stranger who was his mother, a hopeless and
inarticulate self-consciousness possessed him; he resented
her attempts to draw him out; he resisted. Failing to make
him talk as she wished him to talk, she began to put a
touch of pathos into her appeal, nor was her pose the result
of mere self-suggestion. She had begun to feel more than
she had expected to feel. She wanted Kit, she wanted to
possess him and his secret self, all the youth shut up in

the hard young casket of his reserve. She was the mother Pandora. His almost sullen aloofness had began to hurt her.

They walked up to Leith Hill, and she tried to sentimentalize over the view. She did it badly. Her rising emotion was making her jerky and impulsive.

"It's horrible," she said suddenly, as they were driving back to the Hatch for tea, "we seem like strangers."

Her sudden fierce frankness frightened him. He sat, rigid, looking straight through the glass screen at the road winding between the pines.

"I'm sorry," he said; "but I don't see—how it could be helped."

"O,—Kit!"

She put out a hand and touched a rigid arm.

"I know—I must seem all wrong to you——"

Kit's face looked old.

"Well,—you see,—I belong to the pater. He has been such a great pal to me. We—we understand each other——"

For a while she said no more.

4

Christopher never spoke to anyone, not even to his father, of that last emotional scene with his mother. Whenever he thought of it in after years it brought him a sense of flushed discomfort. He would feel himself shut up in that gaudy room with a woman who gradually had lost all self-restraint.

He had felt both scorched and cold, so terribly cold.

He had been so cruelly conscious of the unfairness of it, of her immoderate protestations, her appeals, her attempted caresses. He would remember how she had walked about the room, weeping, pressing a handkerchief to her mouth, looking at him ever and again with a kind of passionate rage.

"You won't understand. I—always—wanted you. You are my boy."

She had flung herself at him suddenly and seized him, her face red and convulsed.

"He's poisoned you against me.   It wasn't my fault that
I couldn't love him——"

Kit had stood like a prisoner lashed to a tree, rigid,
making no response, while she had hung about him, and
wept and raged.   It had been his first experience of woman
as an emotional creature, and he was never to forget it, and
doubtless it coloured his experiences with other women.   He
remained shy of the woman who showed signs of trying to
submerge him in an emotional storm.

He had ended it by breaking away and locking himself
in his bedroom, and he had got out of the house at six
o'clock next morning, and carried his suit-case to Paddington
Station.

At Winstonbury he strolled casually into his father's
room, and stood by the window, looking out into the June
garden.   He was glad to be back in this male room, more
glad than Sorrell knew.

"Enjoyed yourself, old chap?"

"Not much."

Sorrell asked him no bothering questions, for which wise
restraint Christopher was supremely grateful.

"I think I'll go out for a good grind, pater."

"All right," said his father.

Later in the day, when Sorrell was lighting his after-tea
pipe, he had the wise man's reward.

"I'm not going up there again, pater."

"Just as you like," said Sorrell, drawing a breath of
silent and profound relief.

XXIV

I

SORRELL continued to be interested in figures; in fact
his interest in them grew as their significance increased.

It seemed to him incredible, but the Pelican was earning
a profit of something like £4,000 a year, and the Royal
Oak after a year at sea could sail in with a balance of
£700. The Lion was trying her spars, and the White
Hart had not left the stocks, but the Roland Hotels declared a dividend of fifteen per cent. and placed a solid sum
to their reserve.

Sorrell's own income, with his interest on his shares and
his percentage on the Pelican's profits had risen above a
thousand pounds. He gloated over it with the practical
exultation of the man who has had to kick and struggle,
but his soul continued to kick at everybody and everything
connected with the Inland Revenue. He loathed Schedule
D. He loathed the beastly buff envelope in which it arrived; he loathed the man who sent it; he almost loathed
himself for making a correct return. He paid, but he paid
with an inward snarl. If anyone appreciated the pretty and
nicely winged jibes in *Punch,* Sorrell appreciated them.

The apportioning of his income was fairly simple. He
wrote £350 down for Kit, £200 for himself. That left him
a very comfortable margin, and it was the margin that had
value. He had decided to play with it, but to play cun-
ningly, not to wrap it up in a gilt-edged napkin, but to
behave adventurously. He was gaining confidence, and he
had his margin.

During that winter he decided to buy Mr. Grapp's antique
business, put in an energetic manager, and refresh the
stock. Lacking the capital, he went up to Chelsea and saw
Thomas Roland whose Blue Box was as full of money
as were Cherry of Chelsea's pockets. Roland, laughing

roguishly over the money glut, proved a very persuadable
financier, and offered Sorrell what he pleased. He said that
Christopher was a sufficient security, and Sorrell could pay
him five per cent. and refund the capital at his conven-
ience.

"I know the Pelican won't suffer, Stephen."

"When you have learnt to sail a good ship you stick
to her."

Sorrell bought out Mr. Grapp, and put in as manager a
man named Williams, an auctioneer's clerk, who knew the
neighbourhood and had picked up a working knowledge of
furniture, old silver, china and glass. Williams was a little
dark, good-natured and shrewdly energetic man who had
been looking for his chance to climb and had not found it.
Sorrell arranged to have the curio shop refitted, redecorated
and restocked. He and Williams between them bought in
some really fine "pieces" in walnut and oak. The shop
became alive, with liquid capital circulating in its blood
vessels.

"Now—go ahead. I'll see that our American visitors
come along to you."

Williams went ahead. He knew where old furniture,
china, Sheffield plate and pewter were still to be found in
the country towns and villages, and he knew the ways of
the people. He could haggle with farmers' wives and crack
a joke, and insinuate the thin edge of a bargain. He was
to prove himself a most successful and discriminating buyer.

Sorrell had an inspiration in the matter of rechristening
the business. Some time in the thirteenth century a Bene-
dictine monk had compiled a chronicle, and it was known
as the chronicle of William of Winstonbury. Sorrell's ear
was caught by the rhythm of it; the thing sounded like a
successful title, and it was distinctive. So "William of
Winstonbury" was painted in white on the shop's fascia
board. Sorrell had the shop and certain of their show
pieces photographed, and these photographs were grouped
in a handsome oak frame and hung in the lounge of the
Pelican.

During the winter he made a change in his own habit
of life. He was coming to an age when he appreciated
privacy, silence, and those precious moments of serene aloofness when a man's self sits and speaks with its very self.

He craved to push out the increasing noise of the world and to shut an autocratic door against it. Moreover, by vacating his two rooms he would be able to let them and add to the Pelican's margin. Also, he wanted Kit to have a quiet corner where he could read, a corner of his own.

At the end of the garden stood the old red brick cottage that Bowden had occupied, but the Bowden family knew nothing of Malthus and required a more capacious hive. Sorrell took over the cottage, had it redecorated and furnished very simply, and transferred himself there, turning his old porter's room into a manager's office. He had two of the cottage rooms fitted up for Christopher, so that when Kit came down for the vacations he could spread himself and his books in an atmosphere of his own. The rooms had stained floors and Oriental rugs, white taffeta curtains edged with green, buff-coloured walls, bookshelves, but no pictures. The blank walls were for Kit to fill, if he chose to fill them, and his ultimate filling of them amused his father. On one wall Kit placed a solitary picture, something from some art magazine, a picture of a French peasant coming back from the fields in the blue-green twilight. The remaining walls were covered with anatomical diagrams, sections of creatures' interiors, formulæ, neatly typed lists. Kit had saved and bought himself a typewriter. During the vacations his microscope stood on a little deal table by the window.

But Kit was not what his father called a "stuff-jacket." He had given up rowing because it interfered with his dissecting, but he was boxing for the University and carrying on the Porteous tradition. He played a fair game of tennis, could handle a gun, and swim a mile. His interest in life did not shut itself up in books. He was a great lover of the country and its life, and a keen observer; he would surprise his father on some of their walks by discovering plants and birds and insects that Sorrell would never have noticed. He had enthusiasm, not of the spluttering order, but that quiet, virile ardour that searches and sees.

Kit would get up first and make early morning tea over an oil stove in the cottage kitchen, for he and his father liked the informality of it and the sense of being undisturbed. Often he would sit on the end of Sorrell's bed, and smoke a cigarette and talk. They discussed Kit's work,

his friends, Tom Roland's music, the hotels, William of
Winstonbury, books, labour, the tendencies of the day as
each saw them, trees, flowers, human eccentricities, women.
Kit was shy of women. He had not forgotten Lola Merrindin, and that emotional adventure with his mother.
They never mentioned Mrs. Duggan to each other; she had
not troubled them again after a final and unsuccessful attempt on her part to persuade Sorrell that she was a lonely,
reformed and misunderstood woman.

For all that Sorrell knew she might be all she claimed
to be, but he had no intention of helping her to experiment
upon Kit.

So far as his experience of life served him Sorrell had
gathered that people did not change. Their distinctive
characteristics became emphasized or softened. They grew
kinder or more greedy or more stupid, or more crassly self-
absorbed. During the days of his portership he had observed human nature as it displayed itself in an hotel, and
his conclusions had made him a tolerant cynic in his attitude,
save to the very few.

To Kit he emphasized the need for independence. It was
the one god-like quality that a man should strive for.

"Be free. No foot on your neck. Get money; go armed.
Get money and go armed for the sake of the job you love."

Kit understood all this, for he had been a spectator while
his father had fought in the arena.

"Didn't you feel pretty desperate, sometimes, pater?"

"Sick in the stomach, as the Americans say. But I
wanted to put you on your perch."

"It's a pretty good perch. I want a first in the Science
Trip. Then—there will be the second M.B. and the first
part of the Fellowship. And London——"

"Yes, London," said Sorrell thoughtfully. "Have you
ever heard of fellows being afraid of London?"

Kit nodded.

"Pentreath is,"—Pentreath was one of Kit's friends.

"What is he afraid of?"

"O,—things," said Kit very seriously; "women and all
that. Queer, isn't it? Yet, he is perfectly genuine about it.
He's got sisters. They take things rather seriously, the
Pentreaths. Good people, a bit too—too sensitive."

"Cover up your sensitiveness," said his father; "lock it up in a safe and bring it out only for the few."

2

That summer Kit met Pentreath's people at Henley, and Lady Pentreath liked him so well that Christopher was invited to spend a week at their place in Sussex.

Sorrell was pleased. He did not quarrel with his feeling of satisfaction over the fact that the son of an hotel porter should be a friend of the son of Sir Gordon Pentreath, and that Kit should be a guest at Charneys. The Pentreaths were good people, serious people. They had Quaker blood, and a Victorian tradition that had striven very hard to adapt itself to the new confusion.

Kit found the Pentreaths very serious but extraordinarily kind. They were people who felt responsible for other people's ignorances, not priggishly so, for they were too sensitive and too well matured to be priggish. The two elder girls were pale copies of their mother, fair, cultured, quiet-voiced young women who would never inspire any man to dare disaster. Lady Pentreath sat on innumerable committees, and managed with serene and cold seriousness to make the normal blatancies of the day appear even more triumphant. Sir Gordon was a man of many affairs, a tired and worried man, a sort of industrial King Arthur troubled by the inroads of the barbarians.

Charneys was a revelation to Kit, with its beauty, its repose, and its green other-worldliness. It was the home of the people who had dreamed and whose dream was dying, and Maurice—Kit's friend—seemed to know that it was dying.

He approached life very seriously. He had elected to take up medicine instead of joining his father, and the elder Pentreath had not opposed the digression. The barbarians were growing too strong for him.

Lying on his back in the punt on Charneys' pool, and watching the clouds sailing over the tops of the oaks and beeches, Maurice would confide in Kit.

"It's the venom in things, Sorrell. When you have tried

to be a friend to your people and they turn and spit in
your face. The governor feels it. I'm afraid it is breaking
him up."

"You mean—Labour," said Kit,—"Labour with a big L."

"Of course."

"Well,—why doesn't he lay up the ship, pay off the
whole mutinous crew, and retire."

"The Pentreaths don't retire."

"Anyhow—you wouldn't sign on, old chap."

Maurice flinched; he flinched too easily.

"Father and I talked it over. I offered to give up medicine. He was quite frank about it. He said that the modern
industrial atmosphere is too beastly—and too humiliating
for any man with a sense of fair play. Besides, I don't
think there is any future——"

"You mean?" said Kit.

"Yes—things are too difficult. We may have to sell this
place."

"Like the old Roman Empire."

"Yes,—breaking up."

The Pentreaths were too disinterested to survive. Sir
Gordon's disillusioned dignity, his son's imaginative scrupulousness, flinched before the spoilt and greedy children, and
looked towards the shades of some misty Avalon. But there
was one young Pentreath,—the baby——.

"O,—Molly!"

Maurice was bothered about Molly; he was afraid of
Molly. A little savage!

And Kit saw Molly Pentreath as a long-legged, fierce
young thing of thirteen, with a queer square head and
face, dark and audacious eyes, and wavy and rebellious
mouth. She was an extraordinary child,—a little devil.
She appeared to combine an unholy insight into her elders'
interiors, with a violent lack of respect for anybody or
anything. A wild young egoist, a spitfire, she was the one
live Pentreath with the spirit to fight and to survive.

She observed Kit in ominous silence for the first two
days, and then betrayed her partiality by ragging him, and
provoking him to quarrel. She put a live slow-worm in his
bed, filled his tennis shoes with flour, and mocked him
openly.

Kit laughed.

His laughter both attracted and annoyed her. She made him play tennis and golf croquet with her, and she was ready to cheat with fierce assurance.

She had a supreme contempt for Maurice. She more or less ignored her elder sisters. She scandalized her father.

She called Christopher "Kit-bag" or just "Boy." She was home from a very notable school, but the school appeared to have had no effect upon her. To Molly most of the world's opinions were tosh.

She inveigled Kit into wild scrambles about the place, up trees, anywhere. She went adrift with him in the punt, heaving paddle and pole into the water. She would sit with her bony knees tucked up under her chin, and declaim and argue and mock.

She said the most extraordinary things.

"O,—father! Poor old father has forgotten how to grind the faces of the poor."

She was startling in her shrewdness. She seemed to have a Puckish intuition.

"Maurice won't cut any ice. He'll just give sugared powders to old ladies."

Kit talked back at her.

"You want to play—all the game yourself. You can't do that."

"O, can't I!"

"You must see the other person's point of view."

"Don't talk tosh. Poor old pater has always been trying to see his beastly workmen's point of view. They are all over him now like a lot of dogs. I'd teach 'em."

"How?"

"With a whip, old Kit-bag, a whip."

She hated losing; she could not play a losing game, and this fierce self-regard of hers led to a half-humorous yet very human incident. Kit had beaten her twice at golf croquet, and at the end of the third game when he won on the post she hurled her mallet at him because he had laughed.

The mallet caught Kit on the head above the right eyebrow.

It hurt him.

She flew at him with sudden contrition, and threw fierce young arms about his neck.

"O,—Kit, I'm a little beast.   I'm sorry——"

No one witnessed the incident, but Kit had to appear before the family with a palpable bruise on his forehead. He told a white lie about it.

"Silly of me, but I knocked my head against one of the beams in the boat-house."

Molly waylaid him on the stairs that evening.

"You sport!"

She kissed him.

3

Before going back to Cambridge for the autumn term, Christopher spent a week-end with Thomas Roland in his doll's house at Chelsea.

It was a particularly charming little house, furnished in a style that Roland called "Twentieth Century Queen Anne." The music-room had been formed of two rooms thrown together, and between its two windows stretched a black and polished floor with a vermilion-coloured border. There were two pianos, one in a red lacquer case, the other in one of rosewood stained black.

Roland gave Christopher music, and a new window upon life, a very modern window through which "Cherry of Chelsea" might have stepped with a shingled head and a cretonne frock. That she did appear in that echoing room was another revealing of the world to Kit. She appeared in the person of Iris Gent, the mezzo-soprano who had made "Cherry" famous, and who was teaching the world to laugh to music in Roland's "Blue Box."

Roland caused Christopher to think, and to take a step upwards, one of those hardly perceptible steps that yet bring into view a broader horizon and leave the young man gazing under the impression that it is he who has made the discovery. A few crudities loosened themselves from Kit during that week-end. He was breathing an air of laughing tolerance and breezy humanity, for Roland had cast many skins; the main structure of him was the same, but he had kept his doors and windows open.

For Roland and "Cherry" were lovers. Kit saw and won-dered, and out of his wonder grew a new attitude towards work and woman. He caught the glimmer of a charming intimacy, Roland at the piano, Iris sitting in one of the window seats, singing, so that her voice seemed to go through the room like a river of human laughter and tears and joy. Her singing brought a thickness into Kit's throat, and made him shiver.

The thing that astonished him was that these two were not married. The complete and happy understanding between them was obvious, even to a young man fresh from the Pentreath atmosphere, and it caused Kit much searching of soul. Youth explores, and Kit's questing had a serious and high ardour.

But the music! It was like all the laughing wisdom of the ages translated into sweet sounds, flexible and sensitive, vibrating high above a cast-iron system. This music-room suggested the eternal flux, a vortex with its spirals part of the dim past, and rising into the future. Kit felt that Thomas Roland understood life and the art of living as no young man could understand it.

They sat up till midnight one night, talking, and one phrase of Roland's stuck in Kit's memory.

"Everything is allowable, provided you take care not to hurt people, the people who ought not to be hurt."

Kit had asked him a question.

"But suffering? Oughtn't it to come? What I mean is, —well—look at my father——. I always feel——."

"Your father has had his dose."

"And you, sir?"

"Oh,—I! Don't let Iris hear you call me sir, you young vagabond. I have had my share, but I have set my fruit in the sun. It is the green apple stage that is painful."

On the morning of his leaving Kit made a request.

"When I come up to hospital, may I drop in here—sometimes?"

He felt that there were things to be learnt, unacademic facts and fancies, in this house at Chelsea.

XXV

I

MAURICE PENTREATH took life far too seriously. Both he and Sorrell "kept" on the same staircase in the Great Court at Trinity and on the night before the Science Tripos opened, Kit, who had not touched a book for the last three days, and had spent his time playing tennis and loafing on the river, found Pentreath reading at eleven o'clock at night.

"I should chuck it, Maurice."

Pentreath's eyes looked blurred and sunken.

"It's so final, so very final. One's chances don't recur."

Kit took Pentreath's book away; it was Jukes Browne's Geology.

"Go to bed, old thing. You'll be all muzzy in the morning. Look here, after the papers to-morrow, I'm going to make you play tennis."

Pentreath walked about the room like a restless dog.

"It's my memory, Sorrell. I wish I had your memory. It's maddening. There are times when I can't fix facts. I never can be sure, oligocene or eocene, the right order, I mean. My memory plays tricks."

"Go to bed, old chap," said Kit.

Christopher enjoyed the Tripos, for he felt like a well-trained boxer, confident and strong, and he had no panic moods and no fear of the clock. He would walk in, sit down, calmly read the paper through, and then punch his answers out with deliberate steadiness. Pentreath sat opposite him and away on the right, and Pentreath's face made him think of a frightened swimmer who doubted whether he would reach the shore. Maurice was always looking fearfully at the clock.

Christopher carried off a first class, Pentreath a third. Kit saw the lists, went off to wire to his father, and walked back to Trinity to face his friend. Pentreath's breakfast had not been touched, and Kit found him in bed huddled up, his hair over his face.

"Congratulations. You're through."

He saw that someone had told Pentreath the news, and that Pentreath was sick with shame. A third!

"They'll feel so let down at home, Sorrell."

"My dear old chap, exams. aren't everything."

Christopher saw that his friend wished to be left alone, and he closed the door on Pentreath, and going out by way of the "backs" he took the field path to Grantchester. His elation was far less deep than poor Pentreath's shame, the nice, Arthurian Pentreath with the sensitive mouth and the finely cut features, the brother of that little devil of a Molly. Kit's mood was one of frank and solid self-satisfaction, and as he walked with the vigorous leisureliness of an athlete who has won his race and can go out of training, it seemed to him that his success had been absurdly easy. He had been conscious of no feeling of effort. He had worked hard and steadily.

But he did recognize the fact that his first-class in the Science Tripos was not an isolated result, but a little peak in a series of peaks. It represented continuity; it had been foreshadowed years ago when his father had cleaned boots at the Angel Inn; Mr. Porteous too had had a very great share in it. Kit stood on the bridge and watched the water froth into the mill pool, and all the world that was green.

"The old pater will be pleased."

He agreed that it was his father's victory as well as his own. Sorrell had served his years as a gladiator in the world's arena, and Kit had watched him, and had absorbed the unsentimental lesson of that eternal spectacle. Man was a jealous beast. Take away his sword, and he fights with his wits, with a pen, with a bank balance. In the future it was probable that he would fight group against group, the collier against the carpenter, or the massed fools against the superior few. Kit had had his successes, and had blundered unconsciously against the jealousy of other men. It had surprised him, but he had taken note of it, and drawn his own conclusions.

"The pater was right," he thought; "go straight for your mark—and don't stop to argue. But you must carry a punch in your fist. Poor old Pentreath has lost his punch."

His consciousness centred itself for a moment upon his right hand, and he held it out and examined it as though it were the hand of a stranger. Kit's hands were very like his father's, but the fingers were stronger, and not recurved at the tips. Sorrell's hands had had to clutch at his chances and hold on to them; his son's fingers were straighter and more creative. Kit's hands combined sensitiveness and strength; they were dexterous, capable of fine and precise movements, yet very steady. They were to be a surgeon's hands, and for the best part of two years Kit had had the training of them ever-present in his mind, and in the physiology lab. and the dissecting-room he had gained a nice skill with forceps and scalpel. Dissecting was an art, laying bare the delicate tissue until you had made a picture, and Kit had perfected this skill. The Demonstrators of Anatomy had used his dissections for the benefit of other students. Poor Pentreath, eager and too much in a hurry, and never quite able to overcome a loathing of the pickled carcases, was always floundering, or niggling away with an uncertain scalpel.

Kit smiled at his own right hand. You had to have something behind the hand, and he felt that he had.

He remembered an afternoon at Roland's house when Cherry had told his hand, turning it over and over, and prodding it with the soft tip of a beautifully manicured finger, while Roland had quizzed them both.

"You are going to do things with your hands," she had said to Kit.

He remembered his smiling—"I mean to."

No, he did not feel arrogant about it, or full of a facile cocksureness, but he knew what he wanted to do, and how to set about the doing of it, and he had won his first battles.

"The old pater will be pleased."

Appreciation matters, and his father's understanding keenness was no small part of Kit's inspiration.

And while the son was hanging over the mill-pool and looking at the green willows, the father was ringing up Mr. Porteous on the telephone.

"Hallo,—that you——? Kit's got a first. What? You were sure he would?—Well,—so was I—in a way, but then —there is nothing like a certainty. Proud? I am—not a little. These things matter, old chap. We owe a lot to you, you know. Rot? It isn't rot. Come up to dinner."

2

In the autumn of that year Kit became a student of St. Martha's Hospital, with rooms in Brunswick Square.

Sorrell had taken a share in the choice of the rooms, for provided with recommendations by the Dean of the hospital, they had explored all that region that lies between Regent's Park and Oxford Street. Kit's rooms were on the third floor, and his sitting-room overlooked the square, with the morning sun shining in, and Sorrell, remembering the days of his squalid contrivings, had liked the house and its atmosphere. It was kept by a Mrs. Gibbins, a straight up and down woman, who had been none too eager to lodge a medical student, and who had met Sorrell with an air of vague antagonism. Nor were they cheap rooms,—but rather above the level of the ordinary student's finances.

At breakfast Kit could look out at the plane trees turning gold, and the patterning of light upon the sooty trunks. His room had two windows and a mahogany door, a bookcase, and two or three odd chairs. Mrs. Gibbins provided him with breakfast, and a hot meal at night. For the first week or two she observed Kit's comings and goings, for her little sitting-room at the back of the house on the ground floor was situated like a porter's lodge, and when her door was left ajar she could command the foot of the stairs. Mr. Sorrell was very regular in his habits. He came in about six, read till dinner, continued his reading for an hour, and then went out and walked. He would be back in his room and ready for more work by half-past nine. Ada, the middle-aged maid who had been with Mrs. Gibbins for ten years, was able to report that Mr. Sorrell read at meals. "He's always got a book stuck up against the teapot or the cruet stand."

It would appear that Kit was an earnest and hard-working young man, and Mrs. Gibbins felt relieved. She knew her London, and the young male,—though—for that matter—some of the old ones could be worse than the youngsters.

A practical woman who has her living to earn and a house to consider, and two very responsible women as clients on the first and second floors, desires to avoid complications. Young men with latch-keys! Mrs. Gibbins relaxed some of her inevitable hostility.

Each morning at 8.45 Kit plunged into his London. He walked up Guildford Street, half circled Russell Square, and proceeding across Tottenham Court Road, made his way down one of the shaggy streets leading towards the hospital. It was in Russell Square that he struck the flurry of London, the haste of young women and girls and men of all ages and sizes whom the suburbs poured into offices and shops and restaurants. Kit's course lay mostly across the track of these hurrying clerks and shop-girls, but sometimes he went a little way with the crowd. The femininity of it poured round him, those little bobbing hats, the slim legs swinging under those provoking skirts, those London faces pretty or plain, soft or hard, like pale flowers drifting. Sometimes at the same corner he would pass the same girl, or the same group of girls, silent or chattering, always hurrying. Sometimes a girl looked at him, and the look was neither hostile nor friendly.

Kit made a habit of walking very fast, as though he were vaguely conscious of something soft and impeding brushing against the impetus of his youth, and as though the impetus itself had a necessary virtue. His purpose propelled him out of the house in Brunswick Square, and past those tripping feet and little bobbing hats, to the grey forecourt of St. Martha's Hospital. He hung up his hat and coat in the cloak-room, picked up one of the other Cambridge men who had come to St. Martha's, sat through a lecture, dissected, or squinted down a microscope, read a book or talked or ragged for five minutes, and went out to lunch at "Lyons" in Oxford Street. He would spend some of his afternoons in the out-patient departments; he carried a stethoscope; for he had so thorough a knowledge of his anatomy and physiology that he could spare the time for clinical work. The second part of the Cambridge M.B. was to be taken in December and beyond it the first part of the Fellowship challenged his ambition. At half-past four he allowed himself a round of buttered toast and a cup of tea, and after that he would walk, turning into

Hyde Park, and making his way home by Piccadilly and Shaftesbury Avenue. His walking was a straight forward affair, swift and strenuous, a casual avoidance of other people, a scorn of shops and faces. His impetus swung him along, and he cultivated this impetus. Speed seemed to matter; it carried him past and over those insidious interferences.

On Saturdays he played "soccer" for the hospital. He was inoffensively popular, or rather less unpopular than some of the other 'Varsity men who had to meet the young male jealousies of men who had been at neither. He boxed, but less than of old, for he had begun to question its effect on his hands. Once a month he spent a week-end with Sorrell at Winstonbury, and on Sundays he had supper with Thomas Roland at Chelsea. Music had begun to appeal to him very subtly, and colour and pictures. He found pictures in music, and music in pictures. Occasionally he met Pentreath who was at St. Thomas's, a Pentreath who seemed to grow more sensitively serious.

Pentreath had rooms in a quiet corner of Clapham. He gave Sorrell to understand that he found Clapham less distracting, and more safe.

"I need not go north of the river, you know. Down there it is very dowdy and dull."

Kit confessed that he passed through the centre of the spider's web once each day. He spoke of Piccadilly Circus, and Shaftesbury Avenue, and Pentreath looked at him anxiously. To Kit it seemed that his friend was both fascinated and afraid.

"I wonder you dare. I promised my mater——. All those beastly women——!"

Pentreath's fear of his own desire, the trembling of his niceness on the edge of the elemental, were not without their effect on Kit. Pentreath's inward excitements and repressions were disturbing.

"They can't run away with you, old chap."

"It is the lights—too. The glare,—and the faces that come on you suddenly. And the eyes, looking at you from under the shadow——. You must think me a silly fool, Sorrell,—but there is an unholy fascination, a beauty, a damnable beauty——"

"You take it too seriously."

Pentreath's face had a pinched look.

"I can't help it. It—is—serious. Cambridge was different,—rather like an old house in an old garden. You weren't provoked there."

Kit nodded a sagacious young head.

"Suggestion, Maurice."

"That's it. Everything in London pushes you over the edge, the colour, the women, the shops, the lights,—even the food and the drink. I'm working ten hours a day, and living on fruit and brown bread and water."

Most young men would have laughed, but Christopher did not laugh at Pentreath's fear of that which was in him. He had seen the Pentreath home and touched the Pentreath tradition, and he knew that his friend was passionately sincere. Maurice had ideals; he wanted to think of all women as he thought of his sisters, pale, sweet, Burne-Jonesian, and he was terrified when he saw the Rossetti woman.

"One ought not to feel tempted, Sorrell. When I think of my people——"

"Why don't you get engaged? One can't help these things, you know. Everybody feels like it. I have lots of talk with my pater."

He found Pentreath's eyes looking at him with astonishment.

"You have talked to your father——?"

"Yes——."

"About all this?"

"We understand each other."

"My dear chap—I couldn't. In our family—some things are not mentioned."

Kit left Pentreath thinking that he had not been affected by his friend's quivering confusion, but he was to find that in some subtle way his friend's problem was to become his own. Pentreath had spoken of the lights and the beauty and the shadows, and the eyes, and the dim faces, and the play of the colours. Seduction. The natural desire of the young male. The flick of a skirt, a face seen suddenly at a street corner, those shapely ankles with the soft curves of the muscles above them, the shadow of a fur about a white throat, little half moons of dark hair showing under a hat! Kit began to find that he had to walk harder and faster, and that he had to resist a desire to loiter and to look.

Moreover, he was lonely, and he was young. When he shut himself in at night with his books he would find himself thinking of the vivid lights and the faces.

There were times when he felt that he was missing things, life, adventure.

There were men at the hospital who had mischievous and debonair tales to tell.

"Old Landon's been having a time of it. A girl in a flat, some old chap's special——."

Kit would put his hands over his ears, and glue his eyes to his book. Anatomy! Arteries, the blood, the heart! A redness! Hair—and its structure. A girl's hair!

One night he turned up unexpectedly at Thomas Roland's, and there was something in his eyes and in the excited restraint of his young manhood that caused the older man to wonder.

"I wish you would play to me, sir."

Roland sat down and played Debussy, thinking that Kit's too personal cry might be smoothed by the more impersonal beauty of Debussy's music.

3

Like Prosper le Gai every young man must ride out in the spring of the year and meet his Isoult or his Malfry, symbolical figures in the tapestry of life's happenings, yet Sorrell himself passed through a period of unrest during his son's first weeks in London. It was as though he felt all that Kit might feel, and feeling it realized his own helplessness. The young man had mounted his horse, and all those years of proud planning and building were to be put to the test, like a bridge or a sea-wall in flood time. Sorrell could do nothing but stand and watch, while trying to reassure himself as to the soundness of the foundations. There were times when he would address himself with scornful severity.

"Don't be an ass. Every man has to face life for himself, and make his choices."

But it troubled him to remember how he himself had gone astray in making the supreme choice, and that in making it he had wronged both himself and Kit's mother. He had thrust his incompatibilities into Dora's life, and she had

had her legitimate grievance. What a pity that she was not other than she was, and able to take a share——! But that again was the trouble. She would emphasize in Kit all those qualities that make for dispersion and failure, and produce those half-lives, those wounded efforts and dreary bafflements.

"He has got to go through with it all," was all that Sorrell could say.

He imagined that his anxiety resembled the anxiety of a father whose one and beloved son had gone to the trenches. Nothing that he could do would alter the inevitable. But why the inevitable? Was not the whole problem unnatural, the product of conventions and repressions?

He was grateful to the woman who understood him, and whose understanding came as a surprise and an assuagement. In the winter darkness he would hear a soft tapping of fingers upon his window, and he would rise and let her in.

"You're worried about Kit."

Her supreme common sense was like a cool hand laid upon his forehead.

"London, you know, Fanny."

"Well,—what about it? Didn't you have your share of London?"

"I did."

"And here you are. You had to worry it out. So will Kit."

"I know. But one longs to give the boy the right solution."

"There isn't a right solution,—only one's own—my dear. We are not as young as we were. Interference doesn't work. What worked in our day,—see——? Kit's got ballast."

"I have tried to help him in every way."

"Yes,—and a boy like Kit will find out how to help himself. Don't you see——? We have to."

Moreover, she insisted upon the woman's point of view, and was at pains to remind Sorrell that there was a woman's point of view.

"You men talk, Stephen, as though it was all our fault. The old Eve idea. You men run after us, and then curse us for making you do it,—which we don't, not always. Be fair."

Sorrell agreed that it was dangerous to generalize, and

that each sex had to suffer because of the other, and that
neither cynicism nor idealism can be relied upon to control
the energy of life.   The problem was so to direct it that it
did not drive people over precipices and into quagmires.

"My whole point is that I don't believe in a man marrying until he is well up the ladder."

"You want him to think more of his job than of his wife?"

"Well,—doesn't a man——?"

"And meanwhile——?"

Sorrell gave a little shrug of the shoulders.

"Perhaps I am prejudiced, Fanny.   Life's so big, and for
the last ten years or so I have had my eyes on one little
figure.   Whatever happens he will always get the best from
me."

She bent down and kissed his forehead.

"You are a good man, Stephen.   I think yours is the sort
of goodness that helps other people to make good.   If I
were Kit's mother——"

"You would be worrying like anything."

"Perhaps.   Perhaps not.   People who have been brought
up cleanly don't like dirt.   And they don't like the sour taste
that comes after too much drink.   Start a lad with a clean
stomach—and it will want to keep itself clean.   Don't worry
too much."

4

None the less, when Kit came down to Winstonbury for
a week-end the whole of Sorrell's consciousness would be
exposed like a sensitive plate hidden behind a lens, ready to
register every secret impression.

One winter morning while Sorrell was tying his tie in
front of his cottage window, he had one of those moments
of illumination, for the world outside his window seemed
more real than reality.   Real because he saw it in a sudden
garment of mystery, and the dimness of the dawn, grey,
gradual, yet like the soul of itself, a moon still shining somewhere upon the leafless trees, the grass frosted between
night and dawn.   The illusion of the material reality departed from him while he stood there.   It was as though
everything were spirit.   He felt the beauty of feeling and
of seeing as he did, the illimitable significance of the human

interplay. All was gradualness and growth, and no measure of worrying could make a tree shoot its leaves in winter. The seasons came and went, but all that a man loved went on, like the sap, sleeping or rising.

He watched a streak of sky grow blue.

"Kit will be here to-day," he thought.

5

Kit came.

He seemed older, and yet to Sorrell his face was the face of Kit the child.

"Pater,—I want to ask you to do something."

"What is it, old chap?"

"It's about money."

Kit stood at the window and held the curtain aside to watch the sunset, much as his father had watched the dawn. The young outline of his face had a tender severity, and the tenderness was for sky and trees. Sorrell, bending over a kettle that was beginning to hiss over the sitting-room fire, looked up and sideways at his son.

"I say—it's jolly here.—That sky——. One sees so little sky in London."

Sorrell was wondering why Kit needed money.

"I have arranged for you to have a horse to-morrow if you care to ride."

"I'd rather walk, pater,—if you can spare the time."

"I think so."

Sorrell waited. Kit lingered at the window, but not with any air of avoiding his father, and Sorrell watched the kettle.

"How much do you want, Kit?"

"What,—pater?"

"Cash, old chap."

Kit turned suddenly, and leaned against the window casing.

"I don't want money. You are so jolly generous to me. I want you to pay Mrs. Gibbins's bills for me, if I have them sent down. Will you?"

The kettle was boiling, and Sorrell filled the teapot.

"Yes,—but why?"

"Reasons, pater. I can manage my lunches and teas and

tobacco and things on a pound a week. If you would send me up a postal order for a pound—every week."

Sorrell placed the teapot on the table. They drew chairs up to the fire and sat down.

"Just as you please, old chap. There's no need for economy——"

Kit reached for the black-currant jam.

"I don't think one wants too much money in London, pater. Just as well knock about without it, especially when you want to get on with your job. Do you mind?"

"I think you are wise," said his father.

CHRISTOPHER, having put the second part of the
Cambridge M.B. behind him, and sailed through
the Anatomy and Physiology of the Fellowship of
the Royal College of Surgeons, now moved in the thick of his
hospital training. There were the lectures on medicine and
surgery, pathology and bacteriology, and gynæcology, also
the clinical lectures on the same subjects. He rolled ban-
dages and applied splints. He served as out-patient clerk
and dresser, and later as clerk and dresser in the wards. In
the out-patient departments of St. Martha's he was brought
into touch with the realities of sickness and disease, and having more vision than the ordinary medical student he began
to understand what was at the back of these realities. He
saw what London did to people, and what people did to
themselves and to each other. He saw the blotched bodies,
the sores, the rottennesses, the stigmata stamped there by
poor festering souls. He saw men and young girls filthy
with venereal disease; and the blurred and shiny faces and
angry eyes of the drunkards. Often it seemed to him that
Fate herded these people like cattle into the white-tiled gal-
leries and the out-patient rooms, poor stupid cattle sinned
against, ignorantly sinning. It was the problem of the ig-
norant, of the unfit, of the people with uncontrolled lusts
and greeds, of ugly lives and ugly souls and bodies growing
out of them, of children who should never have been born.

"What a mess!" was Kit's feeling about it.

Sometimes pity moved him, sometimes nausea.

He began to have a profound respect for Mr. Kennard,
the particular assistant surgeon to whom he was attached
as dresser, and in a little while Kennard returned that
respect. Sorrell had a reputation in the hospital. He was
keen, deliberate, ready to accept small responsibilities.
Most young men funk their responsibilities, but Kit did not.

Keenness saved him from being fooled by his self-consciousness.

Kennard impressed upon Kit an example of impartial thoroughness. Soon there was a tie of sympathy between them, and Kit, staying to the very last, and after the senior students had drifted away, would sit on the chair next to the surgeon and be allowed to enter into a more intimate fellowship.

They talked.

One particular talk they had stuck in Kit's memory. Kennard had been examining a pretty French girl who had come with a certain hideous condition, and the blemishes had shocked Kit.

"It's rather damnable, sir."

"It's life, a side of life. There's something to avoid, Sorrell."

Kit was frowning.

"It's a question of stopping it, sir."

"Exactly."

"The Socialists——"

Kennard gave him a quick shrewd smile.

"Environment,—O—yes! And education! But turning life into an orderly cabbage patch won't cure appetites. It might make it worse. Life drives us——."

"Well,—what would you do, sir?"

"Try to see that half the babies are not born. You don't let a garden get overcrowded with a lot of weedy rubbish."

"But the Socialist cabbage-patch?"

"We are not—all—cabbages, Sorrell. The world wants cleaning and replanting,—but the drive of life is different in different plants. You have to allow for that. I would halve the population, and try to see that the half that remained had a better chance."

"But what about industry,—labour?"

"Ah,—industry! It may be a question of choosing between trade—and health—the higher health. Waste products. We manage to use them—sometimes,—but the waste is always ahead of the use. Your feet clogged with the mud of the world's haste and greed and foolishness. Stick to the job."

But his contact with the sick and the diseased and the polluted bred in Kit a seriousness that took unto itself a desire to understand. The scope of the healing craft enlarged itself, and it seemed to him that there could be no finer and more satisfying work than the surgeon's. It was not a mere question of skill with the knife and the knowledge of how and when to use it, but a sympathetic searching out of causes that cut deeper than the knife. He felt himself up against the bigness of life and its human distortions. His attitude towards it was far more subtle and mature than the attitude of the ordinary student who was facetiously interested in disease as a something out of which he would make money. Kit saw much of the humour and the pathos, but he did not see them as his fellows saw them. He saw much deeper. He was the son of his father, that father who had struggled with men and things in order that he— the son—might follow the craft that called him.

Kit had one quarrel at St. Martha's. It came upon him in the person of a fellow named Syme, a fat, sallow, and unclean hulk that rolled about the place emitting gulps of obscene and husky humour. And one day Kit fell foul of it.

"Shut up,—you low beast."

Syme was a powerful brute, and demanding honour, was taken on with gloves in the common-room of the college. Kit smote him with exultation and hatred. He floored the great, sodden fleshly thing, and was liked the better for it. Syme stayed away from the hospital for three days.

A man who could hit as Kit could hit, had every right to be keen, and to carry off the Caley Medal, and the Jonathan Taylor Prize. No one quarrelled with his seriousness, especially when it was a smiling seriousness. Sorrell, coming up to the Opening of the Session, and sitting on a fauteuil and listening to a learned address, saw red gowns and black gowns upon the platform. The prizes were presented by a famous legal luminary, and Kit had to cross the platform twice, collecting his triumphs.

He was cheered and cheered loudly, and Sorrell felt an inward glow, a mother and father pride mingled. The job had been worth it.

They dined at Thomas Roland's, with Cherry at the head of the table, and when they had had music, Cherry told Sorrell's hand. She looked very wise over it, with a wisdom that brought little humorous crinkles round Roland's happy eyes.

"You and your son's hands are curiously alike. But he will do more—with his."

"I hope so," said Sorrell, while Kit, who was standing behind his father's chair, laid a hand on Sorrell's shoulder.

"If so—it's because of his hands. He has given me the chance."

Christopher went often to the house in Chelsea, for it offered him the contrasts that he craved, music, colour, understanding, a glimpse of a beautiful feminine thing, and talks with a man who had outgrown his crudities. You hadn't to explain yourself to Thomas Roland, and Kit was finding that it was possible to spend half your life trying to explain things to people who seemed to have gramophone records inside them instead of souls.

Roland lent him books and gave him an occasional theatre ticket. Also Kit met people in the Chelsea house, people who mattered, who had done things. He was not a great talker; in fact he listened better than he talked, but Thomas Roland's friendship gave him an entry into another world, the world of art and music, and of affairs.

He was asked to other houses and to dances, and he came to know Norah East and her circle, and Viner the essayist, and Phyllis Compton the actress. He fell in love with Phyllis Compton, and fell out of it when he came to realize the extent of her vanity. Women were troubling him not a little, but he kept his troubles to himself. Only once did he speak of them to his father.

"I can't help it, pater, but women are the very devil. It didn't worry me much up at Cambridge,—but London——!"

"Yes," said Sorrell, "I know. It's like going about hungry, and seeing a basket of fruit at every corner."

"You don't think me a beast?"

"I have been through it, old chap. Besides—it isn't beastly. It's the meanness and the concealment and the treacheries that make it beastly."

They were out walking and had paused at the end of a woodland path where bracken grew, and the ground fell away into a deep green valley. Sorrell paused to light a pipe, while Kit's glances seemed to sink into the landscape.

"I see the beauty in woman, pater. It can't be wrong—
somehow, and yet one is so tied up."

"It's just—woman," said his father; "and it is natural.
I can't advise you. But half the women one wants aren't
the women one could live with. Sex is an incident. It has
gained an artificial importance from the fact that we have
to suppress it."

"You did?"

"Mostly. Not always. One can't always. But I don't
think that I ever hurt anybody. Mutual agreement. And
then—of course——"

His face looked deeply lined.

"I went and married the wrong woman. And yet she
gave me you. The whole thing is such a muddle. We
get hustled through life almost before we realize it. If I
had it again I should always say to myself—'Don't hurry.'
It's the hurry that lands one, our hungry haste. Besides—
there must always be the one—right woman."

"I suppose so," said Kit thoughtfully, "and I have a
sort of feeling, pater, that one owes something to her."

2

Kit had one of Thomas Roland's songs running in his
head.

"I bought my love roses, red roses in June."

It was the month of June, and seven o'clock in the evening, and in Tottenham Court Road Kit had bought three
red roses from a flower seller. He saw the sunlight upon
the trees and shrubs of the square, and it seemed to him
that they were very green for London trees. The sky looked
more blue. Four girls were playing tennis in the garden,
and one of the girls wore a yellow silk jumper, and had
black hair. The girl in Roland's song had black hair, and
so had the imagined girl who haunted Christopher's heart.

Kit slipped his latchkey into the door. It seemed a pity
to go in and shut the door, and he knew that if he sat
at the window and tried to read he would find himself watching those girls.

"Oh, it's you, Mr. Sorrell."

Mrs. Gibbins, grown grey, and standing in her doorway

like a grenadier in a sentry box, brought Kit to a pause. Kit had come to respect Mrs. Gibbins as a plain and capable woman who did her job, and who had not turned a sour face upon him when he had been laid up for a fortnight with an acute attack of "flu."

"I'm glad you have come in. A gentleman has been waiting to see you,—since four."

"O," said Kit, appreciating the solemnity of Mrs. Gibbins's face.

"Behaving most queerly too,—banging things about. Ada went up and found him sobbing."

"Who is it?"

"He wouldn't give a name, said you'd know."

"What age?"

"Oh,—about your age, Mr. Sorrell."

Kit sprinted upstairs, to find the blinds of his room drawn, and Pentreath extended in the big arm-chair, a long, stiff, desolate figure, all eyes and ruffled hair. He did not move, but lay looking at Kit with a curious and aggressive shame-facedness. And Kit, in the out-patient department, had seen women with that look upon their faces.

He closed the door.

"Hallo,—old chap."

He had not seen Pentreath for three months, but the Pentreath whom he saw in his chair had a slovenly, un-shaven, frightened air.

"What's wrong, old chap?"

Kit had the three roses in his hand, and as he came round the table he noticed that Pentreath's eyes fixed themselves upon the roses. They were dilated eyes, full of an inward horror.

"Don't—Sorrell——"

He made a movement with one hand, an hysterical and jerky movement.

"Don't bring those flowers near me. I can't bear it. They are so clean."

"My dear old chap,—what's the matter?"

He turned to place the flowers behind a pile of books on a side-table, and he heard the creaking of Pentreath's chair.

"I'm married."

"Married!"

Kit turned and faced his friend.

"I have been married six months."

"Who to?"

"Oh, a girl I met down there where I keep. I felt—I
had to get married——"

He was sitting up now, his long arms rigidly extended,
and his hands clasped between his knees. He looked about
the most broken thing that Kit had ever seen, and yet Kit
was wondering——. Marriage, at twenty-three! The sensitive Pentreath,—shivering at the shadow of his own sex!
But why——?

"You have something to tell me——"

"Good God," said the man in the chair, bending forward
as in agony; "something to show you,—Sorrell. What will
I do?"

The irony of it, that his friend should be his first patient,
polluted in body, and shamed in soul! Kit stood by him,
gripping Pentreath's shoulder, shocked and angry, feeling
himself rather helpless in the face of this sordid horror.

"Steady—old chap. Keep a grip on things. Of course
—you have left her?"

Pentreath made a movement.

"What a scene,—Sorrell,—what a scene! I thought I
was saving myself,—and she has pushed me into a filthy
hell. And she had such innocent eyes——. I thought——"

"Do your people know?"

"Sorrell!"

"About the marriage,—I mean?"

"I kept it secret. And then—when the smash came—
how could I——?"

"Smash! What smash?"

"My father's business. You must have heard. It was
in the papers. The bankruptcy proceedings."

"I'm not much of a paper man, old fellow. I'm sorry,
most damnably sorry. What happened? But don't talk
about it—unless——"

Pentreath wanted to talk. The secret soul of him,
cracked and overstrained, seemed to break in Christopher's
room. He became pathetically garrulous, letting his emotional state expand itself in excited declamation. Kit could
see the retinal redness of Pentreath's dark and sensitive
eyes.

"Of course—the mater has a little money. The old place is sold. They have taken a cottage in the wilds of Sussex. Elsie is married—you know. Freda is at home, no servant, so she does things. They are trying to keep Molly on at school; she's sixteen now——. And of course—my allowance——. And I'm in debt; she left me debts——. O, my God—Sorrell, what am I to do?"

Kit pondered a moment. Then he opened the door, and going to the head of the stairs, called down them to some-one below.

"Ada. Oh, are you there? My friend is going to have supper with me. Can you manage something? Yes. Splendid. Very good of you."

He returned to Pentreath,—and pulling up the blinds, let in the slanting sunlight.

"No need to keep the blinds down, old chap. Face the light; light's good. I'll look after you."

Pentreath burst into tears.

"You are the only friend, Sorrell——"

"That's all right. We have got to fix things up. I can treat you. No need for anybody to know. As a matter of fact, too, I don't spend all that my pater allows me, so I can manage to let you have a little."

3

Kit took Pentreath back to that back street in Clapham and stood in Pentreath's poor little room where the gas spluttered through a worn-out gas mantle, and the atmos-phere of a woman still lingered.

Pentreath had flared into a sudden, futile rage.

"The scent she used. Beastly! I've had the windows open. Of course—I know now——"

"What was she, old chap?"

"In a shop. I thought——. She had such a baby face. Damn it,—I can't know anything of women!"

Christopher turned away. He saw that all the Pentreath photographs had been arranged upon the mantelpiece,—they were great people for photographs—the Pentreaths, and Maurice began to tell him that after the last vile denouement with his wife, he had got out all his photos.

"She wouldn't have them about. Said they looked like

a whole row of snobs, and of course—after the smash and
we began to quarrel——. I put them away. Yes, it happened yesterday; I don't know where she has gone. I
wished her dead. And then—I got out those photos, Sorrell; I wanted to feel that I had decent people——. The
poor old mater——."

He crumpled down in a chair, and Kit pretended to look
at the faces of the Pentreaths, Sir George with that air of
tired and disillusioned dignity, Maurice's mother smiling as
at an audience of working mothers, Elsie sentimental and
pensive, Freda rather like a sandy kitten.—And Molly! Kit
found himself looking more attentively at Molly Pentreath.
Hers was a recent photo, and it seemed to him that she
looked older than her sisters. He was interested. He saw
the broad yet shapely face, two little half-moons of black
hair showing under the brim of the hat, the dark yet fiery
eyes, that wavy and mischievous mouth. Attractive, yes,
a problematical little devil of a girl, with something of the
gloss of browned steel in her eyes.

"Molly's at school," he found himself saying.

"If Molly knew!" said the voice from the chair.

"She needn't know."

And yet Kit had a feeling that he had such a sorry story
to tell he would rather have told it to Molly than to any
other of the Pentreaths. She was alive. She might flay
you, but it was better to be flayed with understanding than
to feel that you had wounded people who would refuse to
understand.

"Look here,—old chap, you will have to stay in for a week
or two. I'll come along each day."

"But the hospital! I'm one of Sir John Durrant's
dressers."

Kit's answer was grave, and unanswerable.

"Write to your house-surgeon and say—O,—say your
people wanted you down with them. And what about
money?"

Pentreath would not reply.

"You must have some sort of allowance."

"A pound a week,—from the mater. And an aunt is
going to help."

"All right,—I think I shall be able to let you have a
pound a week."

"I'll pay you back."

"When you like. It is between friends."

On the following evening Christopher took a late train to Winstonbury. He had wired to his father, and Sorrell met him at the station, a rather anxious Sorrell.

"All right, old chap?"

"Quite," and Kit's hand-grip was steady and reassuring.

They sat up till late, talking over Pentreath's tragedy, though Kit's opening words had disturbed his father.

"I wonder if I might have a little more money, pater. You know,—you let me——"

"Of course——. How much?"

"It's not for myself. Pentreath has got himself into a mess."

Christopher thought that he had never seen his father looking so happy and so well. A great man, his pater! There were times when you felt a kind of inward glow spreading from him and warming you. He had no fussiness. Kit looked across at him sitting so much at his ease in the big chair, one leg crooked over the other, a hand clasping the bowl of his pipe, so ready to listen, so understanding in his judgments.

"We can manage it, Kit. You are absolutely right about wanting to help Pentreath. I can do it without docking you of your money."

"But that's too generous. You see,—I'm not spending much."

"Quite so. I'm banking it for you. You can open an account of your own—if you like."

"No. I would rather you sent me so much extra, and I can pass it on to Maurice. He wants looking after. Not quite enough sand."

Sorrell smiled. He was thanking the unknown God for the blessing of ballast, and for this sturdy structure that was his son. It was good to be able to feel as he was feeling.

Manage it? Of course he could. The Roland Hotels were paying thirty per cent., and the profits made by "Williams of Winstonbury" had risen by some hundreds of pounds above the Grapp level.

Sorrell curled himself up comfortably in bed.

"Life's good. Thank God it was the other man's boy. How damned selfish we are."

XXVII

I

THE night porter knocked at Christopher's door.
"Hallo!"
"Case, sir."

Kit yawned, and sat up. He had been called out once before during the night, and his body resented the second disturbance. He felt full of an abominable and delightful desire to sleep.

"Gates."
"Sir?"
"Is it far?"
"Great Plumpton Street, sir, or just off it."
"Foreign or English?"
"English, sir. I'm keeping the messenger."
"Good."

Kit arose, switched on the light and dressed. He collected the black midwifery bag and descended the stairs to the dim vestibule where the night-porter and a vague feminine figure waited. Gates, holding an illustrated magazine, and keeping the place marked with a fat finger tucked between the pages, opened the street door. Kit marched out, with the vague feminine shape following. The closing door shut out the band of light, and Sorrell and the messenger were alone in the darkness of the silent street, and in the midst of London's most strange silence.

Kit walked briskly. He knew his direction, and he seemed hardly aware of the figure at his side, for it was no more than a shadow, one of London's shadows. The woman walked beside him consentingly, glancing occasionally at his silent and preoccupied profile. They reached Oxford Street without having exchanged a word.

Halfway across the empty street the girl paused under an electric standard.

"Queer, isn't it?"

Kit, coming out of his three o'clock in the morning torpor, became conscious of her as something more than a shadow, a young woman, slim, pale, with dark hair and a wavy and expressive mouth. Her voice had sounded strange and musical in the hush of the great silence. She was looking along the street in the direction of Oxford Circus.

"You don't often see it like this."

"No," said Kit.

"Just as though the whole world was dead, except us two."

She smiled a sudden upward smile at him before walking on,—but she had ceased to be a shadow, and in the dimness of one of the many streets running southwards into Soho, the very dimness of her emphasized her coming to life. Her voice had sounded gentle and sensitive, and his glimpse of her face, pale under the shadowy hair, had left him very much awake. Tom Roland had written a song upon "The pale flowers of London drifting on the flowing streets," and the girl's face was flower-like and pale.

"Off Plumpton Street, isn't it?" said Kit, just for something to say.

"Orange Court."

"I know it. Those workmen's flats?"

"Yes. We share one."

"O," said Kit, and was wonderingly silent.

The girl took a look at him as they passed under a lamp.

"Rather young—aren't you?"

He smiled, unprovoked by a challenge that is annoying to most young men.

"Old enough. Don't worry."

"Oh,—I'm not worrying. What's the use of worrying? Though it is her first."

Her eyes grew curious, vaguely intimate.

"Rather bad—sometimes—the first, isn't it?"

"Not always."

"She's frightened. Don't catch me having children, not in these days."

Kit stared straight ahead.

"Your sister—is it?"

"No. We live together; makes it easier, sharing one of those pigeon-holes."

"Of course," said Kit in a voice that committed him to nothing.

They turned into Orange Court, a mere tube of blackness, and the girl seemed to vanish suddenly into a cleft in the wall.

"Third floor. I'll go first. Not much money wasted on light."

Kit groped his way up the stairs after her, and in the darkness ahead of him she was no more than a movement. He heard a key slipped into a door, and saw a finger of light, and with it came a sudden moaning.

"All right, Gwen; here's the doctor."

Christopher stood in the middle of a minute parlour kitchen. A white china teapot and a couple of unwashed cups stood on the table, and a tin kettle purred on a gasring. Two rooms opened from the kitchen. One door was closed. Through the other doorway Kit had a glimpse of a bed and a girl's fair head, and the tumbled curves of a light blue woollen jacket.

He put the bag on the table.

"I'll take your hat."

She was standing close to him, looking up, her two hands extended, and Kit was conscious of the sudden shock of her appeal. She had very liquid brown eyes, such very innocent eyes they seemed to him. Her long mouth was half plaintive and half humorous. She had a little dark mole just under the right lower eyelid, and very white teeth.

"Thanks."

He picked up the bag and entered the bedroom.

2

Kit's voice called for hot water, and the brown-eyed girl brought it. She moved very quietly, and with a suggestion of conscious shyness.

"Thanks."

She poured water from the kettle into the basin, and tried its temperature with the tip of a slim finger.

Kit appeared grave and absorbed. The brown-eyed girl left the room. He was aware of her standing in the little kitchen, with a hand laid along one cheek. Then, he forgot her for the moment in the business that had brought him there, and his hands and his natural kindness were at the mother's service.

"That's all right. Nothing to worry about."

He washed his hands again, and put on his coat, and stood for a moment by the bed.

"Some time yet, you know."

He was going, and the fair-haired girl, with a frightened whimper, turned in the bed.

"O, please,—stay."

Kit looked at her kindly.

"It may be three or four hours yet, and this is my second to-night."

"O, please don't go. I'm so frightened. Mary, tell him not to go."

Kit found himself in the doorway looking into the eyes of the messenger.

"Do stay. If you want to sleep—there's the sofa. I'll keep very quiet. And if you would like some tea——"

Kit hesitated, his glance moving from her eyes to her mouth, and from her mouth to the little brown mole under her right eyelid.

"All right. I oughtn't to.—There might be another case."

"They can send for you. And aren't there other doctors?"

"Yes."

Her brown eyes seemed to swim with a light that puzzled him.

"Besides, if you went, they might send another doctor, and we'd rather have you."

3

There was a quietness in the bedroom, one of those pauses when nature rests from her labour; the mother-to-be had fallen asleep.

Kit sat on the sofa, Mary in an old armchair. A cup of tea stood on the table within reach of his hand.

"Why don't you go and lie down?"

She gave a little twist of the shoulders.

"Don't want to. Let's talk. We can talk softly."

Kit sipped his tea. This little flat in Orange Court and

its two occupants intrigued him, for he had adventured into
all sorts of holes and corners during the last three weeks,
basements, attics, grimy rooms in old Georgian houses that
had once known patched and powdered gentlewomen.

He had seen woman in her squalor and her anguish,
pathetic, horrible, clean and unclean. He had been shocked,
and he had been touched. He had carried food into one or
two dens, and brought pity and disgust away with him.

As for this workman's flat it was both unusual and yet
sufficiently usual. These two girls! They did not belong
to the particular profession, of that he was sure. He understood that the mother was not married.

"Like to smoke?" asked the soft voice from beside the
gas range.

"No,—thanks."

He observed the interior of his tea-cup.

"Aren't you tired?"

"Oh,—a bit. I'm going to see this through. Expect I
shall be a little sleepy over the programmes and the teas
to-morrow."

Kit glanced across at her.

"Your job?"

"Yes,—at the 'Pelargonium.' "

"There! Why that's Roland's place."

"You mean—the—Roland."

"Yes,—I know him."

"Do you," said she, with an intent look, "and Miss Gent
perhaps?"

"Yes. Cherry."

"Wish I was her. Lovely voice she has. I sell programmes, and do half the stalls. Gwen's in a shop; quite
a good job. Rather bad luck for her, this."

Kit had a feeling that they were slipping into a swift and
extraordinary intimacy. He both fought it, and did not
fight it.

"I suppose it is," he said.

"Yes, he can't marry her, if he wanted to. Men don't,
do they,—when this happens?"

"I don't know."

"She doesn't want it either, not really. Being married!
No thanks. Not good enough."

She sat with folded arms, and seemed to reflect upon life,

her pretty head drooping slightly under the curve of her white neck. Kit replaced his cup on the table, and seized the chance of a steady look at her, and while he was looking her eyes swept swiftly to his. She smiled. He answered her smile.

"Go to the theatre often?"

"No, not very often. Can't afford the time or the money."

"Oh, you are one of the keen ones," she said wisely, as though she already knew a great deal about him, and meant to know more; "one sees a lot of life at the theatre, on the stage—I mean. Makes you think. And then—when you begin thinking——"

Her intelligent smile gave a lustre to her sensuous, flower-like face.

"You get out of your depth," said Kit.

She considered his assertion.

"That depends. Seems to me—when we get to the bottom of things—we all do what we want to do if we can. And where's the harm? And especially—if you don't wallow. It's the people who wallow, and those who are all tied up. Seems—we are more natural since the war. We —are."

"Whom do you mean by we?"

"We younger ones. We are ready to question things, to go on our own,—women especially. Some of you men are such dear old sentimentalists."

She laughed.

"That's that.—Where do you live—in digs?"

"Yes."

"Bit lonely—sometimes?"

He avoided her eyes,—but presently he had to look at her.

"O, yes, damnably so. But I work hard. And then— the glitter gets you, and you want to go mad. Silly, isn't it?"

"Not a bit."

Her glance was soft.

"Why shouldn't you? It's natural. It's the old stuffy people who were always crying stale fish!—I say,—what's your name?"

"Sorrell."

"That's pretty. But the other one."

"Christopher—or Kit."

"Mine's Mary,—you know,—Mary Jewett. Mary,—Mary, quite contrary. O,—there's Gwen!"

A little moaning came from the bedroom, and Mary went quickly and softly into the other woman, a tenderness in her eyes, leaving Kit looking very grave. He heard the two girls' voices, the one soothing, the other the voice of a woman in pain. He glanced over his shoulder. A hand closed the door, and more than a minute passed before it was reopened. The moanings grew louder.

"I think she wants you, Dr. Sorrell."

"Coming," said Kit.

4

The baby was born about eight o'clock, a boy. It lay whimpering and kicking on an old jacket at the foot of the bed, and when Kit had a moment to spare he carried the child to the bedroom door.

"Mary."

She was there, looking very tired and sleepy, with shadows under her eyes.

"What do I do with it?"

"Wash it. I suppose you have some clothes."

"O,—yes."

"And I want a big jug of hot water."

She took the baby and Kit's brusqueness into her arms, seeming to understand the man if she failed in her instincts towards the child. Sorrell was tired. There had been more in the experience of the night than the bringing of a child into the world, and he wanted fresh air, a bath, and his breakfast. He had been close up against life, contending with it in himself as well as in the woman.

"Try to get some sleep. Yes, everything is quite all right."

"You've been so kind, doctor."

He carried the bag and his coat into the kitchen where Mary was sitting by the stove with the baby on her knees. She had washed and dressed it, and was looking at its red and ugly face with an air of puzzlement and of hostility.

Kit put on his coat.

"I suppose you will be here."

"I've a matinée this afternoon. There is a woman downstairs who will come in."

She looked up at him with eyes of weariness.

"And you?"

"I'll come round later in the day."

"I may be out."

She stood up, holding the baby.

"And to-morrow——? Where's my hat?"

She found him his hat.

"I shall be in most of to-morrow."

He was aware of the fact that her steady gaze had a meaning for him, and that her brown eyes were softly blurred. She was very tired.

"Right. Get someone in and go to bed. You want sleep."

"I do."

He turned for a moment at the top of the stairs to see her standing in the open doorway, vaguely smiling, her head surrounded by a haze of light, and ten seconds later he was in Orange Court, gripping the handle of the bag very hard, and walking fast. The liveness of London astonished him. He was thinking of the emptiness and the silence, and of Mary standing in the middle of Oxford Street with that flower-like floating face of hers.

A hot bath was welcome. He splashed about in it,—and emerging, towelled himself vigorously.

"Suppose she lives on buns and tea."

Well,—what was it to do with him?

At breakfast, in the college dining-room he was absorbed and surly, eating fiercely, and in no mood for small talk. Potter, a confrère, was devouring buttered toast and marmalade on the other side of the table.

"Been out all night?"

"Pretty well."

"Thought you looked a bit cheap."

It occurred to Kit that he might ask Potter to take over the case, but the idea roused in him a fierce surge of hostility. He did not like Potter; Potter was considered to be a very debonair and dangerous lad, a fellow who smirked and looked at himself in shop windows. Was he going to send Potter to Mary Jewett?

"No,—I'm damned if I will!"

5

Christopher went to his room and slept till one o'clock. He had other cases to visit during the afternoon, and it was four o'clock when he entered Orange Court and climbed the stairs to the little flat occupied by Gwen and Mary. A strange woman with a red face let him in.

"Yes, she's doin' lovely, doctor, 'ad a nice sleep."

The door of Mary's bedroom was open, and he had a glimpse of a rose-coloured woollen coat hanging from a hook on the door. The coat and its colour were Mary. It sent an instinctive thrill through him, a pang of desire, and even when he was standing by the bed and talking to Mary's friend, his consciousness was busy with Mary, and Mary's bedroom and her clothes, and her mouth, and the way she smiled. The baby was asleep beside its mother, and Kit remembered the awkward way in which Mary Jewett had held the baby, as though she disliked it. Her dislike had surprised him. He had imagined that all women were sentimental about babies,—mother love, and all that sort of thing, and for some reason—which he could not explain, he preferred Mary's hostility. Kit had no illusions about babies. He had seen so many of them of late; red, raw, wrinkled, absurd creatures, he had found them rather repulsive.

But his senses were more alert. He noticed that the pillow was white, and that the bed had a pretty coverlet; the kitchen was clean, the brass taps of the range polished, the table covered with a blue and white cloth. There was self-respect here, the self-respect of women who worked.

"You will be coming to-morrow, doctor?"

"Yes,—to-morrow morning."

Before going to bed that night Christopher took half an hour's walk, and he was surprised to find that the quality of his restlessness had changed. It was happy and pleasant, and he felt a peculiar good will towards all the other strollers, as though he had drunk good wine, and the streets were the paths of a pleasure garden. He found himself outside the Pelargonium, where boards announced that the house was full. He looked through the glass door into the foyer.

"She's in there," he thought; "doing her job. We are workers, both of us."

Kit was not called out of bed that night, and he went with a feeling of freshness and of adventure into Orange Court; and up the dark stairs. Mary opened the door to him, a different Mary and yet the same; she looked prettier; she had more colour, natural colour. She stood there, looking at him and smiling, and yet there was much more behind her smile. It made him feel that he belonged.

"Well,—how's the patient?"

He was shy, and a little formal, but his eyes belied his formality.

"Doing so well. She's asleep."

"I'm afraid I shall have to wake her."

She brushed close to him as he entered, a nearness that was quite unstudied and instinctive. There was a vase full of flowers on the table, rose-red and white asters. The door of Mary's bedroom was open, and her red rose coat was hanging there.

She had observed that quick glance of his.

"I love that colour."

"It ought to suit you—rather well," he said.

6

During the last week of his month's clerkship Christopher saw Mary Jewett seven times, four times at Orange Court, once outside the Pelargonium, and on the two other occasions he took her out to tea at a little place in the Charing Cross Road. On the last evening they had wandered,—it was a Sunday—and they had stood by the parapet in Trafalgar Square, and watched the lights. Thence they had idled down to the river, saying little, but feeling the fierce dear pressure of the young life behind their words. Sometimes their arms touched as they walked.

Kit learnt that she was three years older than he was.

"That means a lot,—Mr. Christopher."

"Does it?"

"Makes me feel motherly. You're such a boy."

"I'm more of a man than you think," he said.

He remembered the time and his duties.

"It is my last night on to-night. I ought to be back at the hospital."

"Glad it's over?"

"Very. The most beastly month——. But—to-morrow——"

"Free. So am I. It is my free evening."

"I say,—I'd like to——. But would you,—come to a theatre or something?"

"I get enough theatre."

"Of course. Well,—a little dinner somewhere?"

"I'd love to."

Once before Kit had visited that little French restaurant in Soho where both the perfumes and the waitresses were foreign, and some of the chairs were none too steady on the legs. Christopher became the occupant of such a chair. The lovers laughed over it, leaning their elbows upon the table and looking into each other's eyes over a vase of fading flowers. Mary's hat threw a faint shadow, so that her forehead and eyes seemed more dim and elusive than her mouth.

"Monsieur?"

Kit ordered dinner, while the painted lady at his elbow jotted down his choice.

"I want some wine."

"Louis. Le carte des vins."

A swarthy little wine-waiter tried to persuade Kit to buy bad champagne, but being the son of an hotel-keeper he had some knowledge of wine.

"Red or white?"

He looked at Mary, and her eyes seemed half closed.

"Red."

"A bottle of Chateau Ducru."

"Bien, monsieur."

They clinked glasses, and Kit's fingers touched the girl's. No words were spoken. It was the sacramental wine of lovers.

Afterwards, they wandered as though London was a dream city, brilliant and strange. They went arm in arm, drifting, pausing inconsequently to look in a lighted window—and so to look at each other. Their eyes were full of the varying lights of the night. In the dim and shadowy places a little intimate sense of being nearer to each other thrilled in each body. Once, in a dark entry between two houses, they stood and kissed, a long kiss, clinging, Mary's hands upon Kit's shoulders. He felt and heard the sigh of the deep breath she drew at the end of that embrace.

"Dear boy——."

"Mary."

They wandered, Kit's arm tucked under hers, and his hand holding her fingers. For whole minutes they did not speak. The houses seemed to grow higher, the streets narrower and more dark. They passed the flaring window of a shop at a corner, and Kit—like a man at sea—picked up the lights of that shop. He knew it. They were within a hundred yards of Orange Court.

"Dear boy,—why are you trembling?"

He was inarticulate. He felt her cheek pressing against his shoulder.

"I know. I'm like that too."

XXVIII

I

SORRELL knew.

He did not know how he knew, but know he did, intuitively, and with a quickness that was feminine.

For the thing was never talked of; it lived there in silence, known and avoided, and yet understood.

A difficult period,—yes, but like all difficult periods not lacking in its human compensations, for in spite of this silence, father and son seemed to draw closer to each other. What was most valuable was Sorrell's victory over himself, that old man self, querulous and interfering, angry and possessive, the eternal Puritan, the foolish parent. Troubled, he exercised a sensitive restraint. He met the old man's preachings and answered them, placing himself in the spirit beside his son, and not opposite him.

What right had he to interfere or to ask questions? Was the son responsible to the father? Was there not a secret corner in every life into which no friend can penetrate, though he may stand on the threshold and listen.

"It is not shame, but decent reticence. Surely—one can respect it."

His attitude towards his son had a wise gentleness. It was as though he wished Kit to feel a fellowship in the midst of this silence, and that Kit did feel it was Sorrell's reward. There were the same week-ends, the same country rambles, the same talks, with a sense of deepening affection in the realization of their common humanity. In Kit's heart there was the same refrain—"Dear old pater," and the boyishness of it merged into the fiercer faith of the man. That he was both happy and unhappy was one of Kit's discoveries, the patchwork of life's emotions, the ranging interplay, the completeness and in the incompleteness of passion. The day's work follows an exultantly tender night. Kit felt that somehow his father knew all this, that he had borne with it, and was bearing with it in his son. His silence was the silence of sympathy.

Kit pondered it all out.

Why did he not tell his father? He knew that it was possible to tell him. He did not want to tell him, and he had a feeling that his father did not want to be told. It was as though there existed between them tacit agreement to keep the thing like a shaded lamp, and to refuse its ray's penetration into the comradeship they shared as men.

Sorrell had his moments of curiosity. He would wonder about this woman, who she was and what she was, and how much ultimate significance she had for Kit, yet she remained a shadow, a creature divined but unseen, a human planet making itself felt in the emotional firmament. And Mary Jewett had the same feelings about Christopher's father, that equally shadowy figure. Kit was very silent about his father, but he let her know that it was not the silence of fear.

"We have always trusted each other, the pater and I."

"And does he know?"

"I think so."

"You haven't told him?"

"No."

For a day or two after those words of Kit's she was more gentle and tender to him, she who was always gentle, smiling out of the deeps of a passionate sadness, for she had a nature that clung. She had the clearness of vision of a woman who is fay. Her love was without hard outlines, though the mouth of it might smile a wounded and foreseeing smile. She gave. She took life as it was, and held it passionately, while looking towards the ultimate shadows. There was something French in the logic of her emotions. This summer by the sea! She asked to forget the mists of November, though she knew that they would come.

Sorrell called her "The Shadow Woman."

It became evident to him that whatever her heritage might be she had no clogging effect on Kit's career or upon his keenness. Samson's hair was uncut, though his eyes were kinder. There was no faltering in his son's stride. He was working for his final, and he went through it with the same long lope, and came down to the Pelican for Christmas, and was glad to be with his father.

He had questions to discuss.

"When I have written and read my thesis, pater,—I can stand on my own feet."

Sorrell was poking the winter fire.

"Earn money?"

"Yes,—after all these years."

Kit was aware of his father's face and head lit by the glow of the flames. Sorrell was growing grey.

"That's not my view, old chap. You have been very good about money. It isn't our idea—is it—that you should become a G.P.?"

Kit remained silent.

"Hospital appointments?"

"Yes."

"And after that——?"

"It may take a long time, pater, and all the while I shall be——."

"Should you mind? Don't take my job away, my son, until I have seen it finished. The most damnable part of life for most of us is that we have to plunge into the muddy stream in order to make money. Before we are ready. Before we have had our opportunity. Money means growth, time to draw one's breath."

Kit had another fit of silence.

"Am I—your job, pater?"

"I think so!"

"You have been so jolly good to me."

"Kit!" said his father, and smiled.

Christopher's hand went out.

"I know. It means such a lot to me. Kennard is to become one of the seniors next month; old Goddard is retiring. Kennard wants me to be his house-surgeon. That will mean six months. And then—six months as house-physician. After that—a surgical registrarship—I'm pretty sure to get one; that might mean another year or two. After that—of course—I should try for an assistant-surgeonship; it might necessitate some waiting; but if I once get on the staff——."

"Say—five years," said Sorrell. "There will be the Fellowship too."

"Yes."

"You will be getting your keep most of the time. And

when you arrive on the staff—that will be the time when you will need capital. I'm saving money, quite a lot of money."

Christopher, with his two fists under his chin, stared at the fire.

"How is it, pater, that you never bargain?"

"Why—bargain——?"

"You never exact—terms. You have given me everything, my chance,—and freedom. You have never tried to tie me down."

"Isn't it obvious——?"

"Very—in some ways."

"One gives to get—the thing that is worth getting."

"You are a great man, pater," said his son.

2

Plucking the red fruit from time to time Christopher found the juice of it sadder and less sweet; sad because of its lessened sweetness, and his sense of being responsible for its lessened sweetness. And why? Because he had tired,—because embraces became more tranquil and comradely, and because that more tranquil comradeship that is marriage at its best had in this case no future?

He owned to moods, moods of tenderness and of pity and of impatience, moods when he accused himself of taking and losing, of thinking less of the woman, and more of his work. He was Kennard's house-surgeon; he was a resident at St. Martha's; the Brunswick Square days were over. And he was reading hard for the final of his Fellowship.

For months he had had a sense of drifting, and his character was not that of a drifter. The romance had begun to worry him; for it had become too real, nor was he one of those cheery egoists who can satisfy himself that an incident is just an incident and nothing more. For the man it is so— in the majority of cases, and also for a certain type of woman, but Mary was not that sort of woman.

He realized her generosity. She had never asked him to "put her right with the world" as the phrase goes, nor had she even hinted at it, for Mary Jewett had felt right with herself. She was a giver, she had had times of very great happiness; something in her had been satisfied.

Yet, Kit was not satisfied. There were certain little
things that he confessed to with shame, broodings, forgetfulness, the taking of love for granted, a vague sense of
limitation, a feeling of giving less and less than his share.

Once, he had spoken of marriage, and she had laughed
and then burst into tears.

"That's almost an insult, dear boy."

"Mary!"

"I went into this with my eyes open. We didn't bargain,
did we? We just wanted each other."

He did not understand her tears, nor those days when she
showed a quiet aloofness, choosing to be a little apart from
him, yet with no insinuation of pique or of suspicion. He
remembered one particular Sunday on the Thames when she
had sat at the other end of the punt, using a desultory
paddle, her eyes looking into the distance beyond him. He
had fallen asleep on the cushions. He had heard a voice
calling—"Kit—Kit!" and had opened his eyes upon a
strangely tragic face. "The weir, I didn't see it." He had
scrambled up with a "Good lord," and had snatched up the
pole and managed to work the punt clear of that sliding
crest of water.

"What on earth were you doing, dear?"

"O,—just dreaming."

A time was to come which would make him wonder
whether she had been dreaming a dream for both of them,
and whether that warning cry had not been torn from her
by an awakened selflessness.

3

Christopher was going round one of his surgical wards
about six o'clock, examining two or three of the more
serious cases, when the hospital porter came in search of
him.

"Where's Mr. Sorrell?"

"In Battersby Ward."

Kit, bending over a man who had been operated upon
for duodenal ulcer, heard the porter's voice behind him.

"Letter for you, sir."

"O," said Kit.

"Messenger brought it from the Charing Cross, sir."

Christopher opened the note. A few words had been written in haste on the back of a case-sheet, and the sheet folded upon itself.

"We have a patient here,—bad street accident, asking for you. The name is Jewett.

"J. T. HOLMES, House Surgeon."

Christopher slipped the sheet into his pocket, made some excuse to the Sister, and hurried out of the ward.

"Get me a taxi, Carter."

"Right, sir."

"Quick as you can."

He felt cold with the shock of the news, and as the taxi carried him down those streets that were so familiar he sat looking out of the window at the meaningless movement without. What had happened to her? Was she disfigured, crushed, broken, this pretty thing who had held him in her arms? And suddenly his passionate need of her returned, but in the guise of an intolerable tenderness. He, who had seen so many red, torn bodies carried into St. Martha's, shrank from the imaginings of the moment, a vision of a dear thing crushed.

At Charing Cross he asked for the house-surgeon who had scribbled that note, and they met in a corridor outside one of the wards.

"I'm Sorrell of St. Martha's. You sent me that note. What's happened?"

The house-surgeon was a brisk little man with quivering pince-nez.

"Motor bus ran over her. Abdominal,—bleeding, pretty hopeless. Winter has seen her,—but thought she wouldn't stand an op. She asked me——"

Kit was very white.

"Conscious?"

"Yes."

"Can I see her?"

"Of course. Relation of yours?"

"Yes. I'm much obliged to you."

The house-surgeon took Kit into one of the surgical wards, spoke to the nurse on duty, and left Kit outside the screens that had been put up round Mary's bed. Those

tragic screens! Christopher knew them so well, and all
that they signified, a frail barrier erected about a little flame
that was flickering towards its end.

He turned back one of the flaps, replaced it,—and was
with her.

"Mary——"

She was white as the pillow, her eyes and hair looking
strangely dark; he had never thought that eyes and hair
could look so dark. Her lips were bloodless. And from
the moment he appeared, her eyes fixed themselves upon
him and never wavered, tragic eyes, possessive, caressing,
poignant. She smiled very faintly, and her smile made
Kit think of the wind stirring the pale face of a flower.

He went on one knee beside the bed, fearing to touch her.

"Mary."

Her right hand moved jerkily and touched his cheek.

"Dear boy——"

"O,—my dear,—how——?"

"Don't—don't let us talk of that. It's—all over, Kit,
dear, all over. Put your arm—under—my head."

He did it—very gently, his eyes hot, his mouth quivering. She sighed; she lay and looked at him.

"It's better—dear—like this. I'm—I'm not frightened.
You see—I knew——"

"What did you know——?"

"That things couldn't go on—always. But, Kit,—say I
made you—happy, just a little——"

He lost himself.

"Nobody else will be——. O, my God, my dear, I have
loved you so much,—and now——"

"Dear boy, don't cry. Oh——"

She caught a little breath of anguish.

"I'm all—crushed——"

"Dear,—have they given you anything, morphia——?"

"I wouldn't have it; I—I was afraid of going to sleep
—before——"

He kissed her very gently, got up, and came out from
behind the screen. The house-surgeon and the nurse were
talking by the ward door. Kit went towards them; he did
not see any of the other patients; the world was blurred.

"She wants morphia,—she said she wouldn't——"

The house-surgeon looked at the floor.

"Quite so. Nurse——"

"Do you mind if I give it to her, if you fill the syringe? I'd like to."

"Quite so," said the little man.

Kit ran the needle into the whiteness of Mary Jewett's arm.

"No more pain, dear. I'm staying."

Presently, her dark eyes grew more blurred.

"Kit,—Kit, are you there——?"

"Yes."

"Do you love me? Did I——?"

"Mary,—my darling——."

"I'm so—so happy."

4

Sorrell was troubled by Christopher's letter.

"Kennard has let me off for a week, and a friend is doing my work. I am coming down to-morrow."

It was a very short letter, and it said less than any letter of Kit's had ever said, yet Sorrell felt convinced that something had happened or was going to happen, and that the happenings concerned the Shadow Woman. He was troubled. He spent one of the most wakeful nights of his life, wondering whether Kit had fallen into the male madness. He thought of Pentreath's son freed from a miserable relationship after months of spying and lawyering and humiliation. If the thing had happened to Kit he was ready to swear that it had happened very differently.

Sorrell did not go to Winstonbury Station. Whatever the crisis might be, he felt that he would let it come to him and not go to meet it. He had taken up gardening, and had developed the little piece surrounding the cottage, and had filled it with roses, and Kit found his father syringing the aphides on his hybrid teas. Kit had walked from the station, carrying his suitcase; he was wearing a black tie.

"Hallo,—pater."

Sorrell's eyes had touched his son with one devoted and careful look, a doctor's glance. He replaced the syringe in the bucket, wiped his hands on his handkerchief, and was conscious of an intense and intuitive relief.

"Had tea, old chap?"

"Yes, pater, thanks."

Kit had lowered his suitcase to the grass path. He was
looking at the roses, but not as though he saw them, but
as though he was looking at something else, something
within himself. His mouth and eyes had an extraordinary
gentleness, the softened fineness that comes with suffering.

"Pater,—I want to tell you straight away——."

"Right, old chap."

Sorrell felt for his pipe.

"I've had—a love affair. It has been going on for quite
a long while. We weren't married."

"Yes, old chap."

"She's dead. She was knocked down four days ago by
a bus. She—she was awfully good—to me, pater. I—I've
been sorry for things,—sorry——."

Sorrell was holding a match to the bowl of an empty pipe.

"I—I understand—old chap. These things——. Well,
you know,—when we look back——. I'm rather glad you
have come down here."

"Thank you, pater. I——"

"Your room's all ready. I'll have our meals sent over.
I shan't worry you. You see, old boy,—I knew——."

"Knew?"

"Well,—something; felt it. In your life, you know. I'm
rather——. Yes, it must have been good. She didn't——.
Poor little—girl——."

"Don't, pater," said Kit suddenly; "things hurt so damnably, especially—your—your goodness."

He picked up his suitcase and went in.

5

Before the end of Kit's week Sorrell had been able to
paint a very passable portrait of Mary Jewett.

He was grateful to her, grateful for her having met Kit
in the wild garden of their common youth, and for having
taken him by the hand and shared the fruit with him, the
wild fruit which grows as it pleases. She had done Kit
no harm; on the contrary she had done him much good;
she had taught him things; she had been one of those sacri-
ficial women who give to men more than men give to them.

Kit talked a good deal.

"The thought that sticks in my throat, pater, is that she wanted to die."

"Perhaps dying is not so difficult, old man."

"Yes,—but——. It's as though she had begun to realize that too much love-making bores a man. I was bored. Horrible, isn't it? But not with her, the real Mary, the pal. One seems to get bored with the woman in a woman. And I suppose a woman, a woman like Mary——. She shouldn't have cared so much. I did not think people cared so much."

"O,—some of them," said Sorrell, "a few. And yet— she didn't interfere with your work."

"Not a bit. She helped. I think she cured my restlessness, pater. Did you ever feel it?"

"Did I not!"

"I was luckier than poor old Pentreath."

He told his father how he had gone to Mary Jewett's funeral, and met an old mother, one of those women with tired and puzzled eyes, and how he had lied to her mother.

"I had to, pater. I said that we were to have been married. We weren't."

"Why not?"

"O, we began it—on the understanding——. She had an idea that marriage spoiled things. I told her to that I could not marry—for years."

"Did you want to marry?"

"No."

"And she accepted it. I think she treated you rather well, Kit."

"So damned well,—pater,—that I don't feel that I shall find anybody else like her.—Do you know, she would never take a penny from me. Just a few little presents, and things like that. And in London—now! Where the place is packed with hard young wenches who look as though they had been cut out of cardboard. I hate their rouged mouths, and their damned—artificial—up-to-date faces. They are hard, pater, hard."

"Perhaps."

"Mary was gentle. She understood."

"Yes," said Sorrell; "that's the thing that matters, understanding."

Each morning before breakfast Kit and his father rode out into Stoneberry Forest, Sorrell having arranged for a

couple of horses to be sent out from a Winstonbury livery
stable, and these early morning rides and his talks with
his father helped Christopher to a new appreciation of life.
He seemed to realize that a phase of it had passed, and
that a particular experience can never be repeated. In the
forest "rides" and upon the heathy uplands of Stoneberry
he was very far from the turmoil of life, and from the
sinister and increasing bitterness of civilization. Organized
life was growing more tyrannical, and the industrial crowd—
in blind strivings to escape—was attempting to impose a
yet more senseless tryanny.

Yet Kit remembered that Mary—the seller of programmes in a theatre—had shown no bitterness. She had
asked to be loved, but she had not asked to be given
children. She had had a peculiar dread of children, and
had shrunk away from the thought of motherhood.

"Give the world another clerk or factory hand? Would
you?"

He remembered her putting that question to him, and
when he had tried to answer it, she had given him an
astonishing revelation of her insight into the soul of "Peter
Pan."

"That's what we want, Kit, thousands of little playful
rebels like that boy. If only a lot of us would refuse to
grow up."

He realized that Mary had been one of the rebels.

Sorrell, sharing in one of these heart-to-heart talks under
the Stoneberry beeches, confessed that his sympathies were
with the rebel.

"Not the mulish mob, old chap, but the free-lance, the
lone fighter."

"Isn't he becoming rather rare?"

"His day will come again. He is the one inevitable
figure. Besides—he is the only really happy soul. A bad
citizen—as organized slaving understands citizenship.
What may good citizenship mean in the future,—being swallowed alive by the Labour Dragon, a clumsy beast crushing
life under its crawling belly. Ha,—the sword of St.
George."

Kit's face was very grave.

"You have had to fight, pater. What did you fight for?"

"For myself,—you."

XXIX

I

SORRELL was fifty years old when he became a gardener, and began to think less of pound notes and more of flowers. The material struggle had passed, and in passing had left him standing like a man made aware of an English Spring after the chill and the greyness of a Channel crossing, those greenly cushioned hills, the woods purple and gold with the swelling of the buds, the innocent faces of the primroses looking up. "Why fret?" And when a thrush sang to him—"Why worry, why worry?" his heart answered,—"Ah,—why?"

The phase came suddenly, and yet no phase is sudden, for a man is what he has been, and there is no growth without roots. To Sorrell it came like the opening of a door in a high, old wall, and within he beheld the ultimate inwardness of his very self, a self that had been growing through all the years.

He had been sitting at his desk in the cottage window with his private ledger open before him, the practical part of his consciousness reflecting the figures on the ruled page. His income! Nine hundred pounds from the Pelican. Two hundred pounds from his shares in the Roland Hotels. Seven hundred and sixty pounds from "William of Winstonbury." He had sat reflecting upon the material foundations of his life, the money that Roland had lent him refunded; the antique business his; a solid share in the four hotels just as surely his; money waiting to be invested.

Suddenly, he had smiled. He was thinking of Christopher, now Surgical Registrar at St. Martha's, a Fellow of the Royal College of Surgeons, a young man well thought of by his elders and instinctively liked by them, which is the most potent form of liking. Kit was well on his way up the ladder, and below the ladder Kit's father had laid those careful foundations.

Sorrell closed the ledger, put it away in a drawer and locked it. He pocketed the key. His fingers played with a pen, a favourite pen that he had used for the last nine years. It was almost a part of his hand, a graving tool with which he had scored in the lines of an indelible success. But his eyes were looking through the window between the folds of the green and white curtains, and in those eyes of his shone an inward vision, something personal that was suddenly awake to a world that was intensely and poignantly impersonal.

He found himself in the garden, standing under the very old pear tree that grew close to the thorn hedge, its grey and twisted trunk rising in a spiral to the spreading of the boughs. The fruit buds were swelling, and their colour was a wonderful pale gold. A blue tit, hunting for insects, flew away towards the orchard, and Sorrell heard its quaint creaking note contrasting with the flute song of a blackbird.

Spring! The silver-gold buds of the pear tree entranced him. How delicate and beautiful they were, almost more beautiful than the flowers that would open from them! Buds of promise ending in the fruit of fulfilment, but not every bud would mature into a fruit. His eyes wandered towards other trees, and to the eyes of his new awareness the whole world was a lacework of buds; lilacs and chestnuts tinted green, but the lilacs more green than the chestnuts; the elm boughs purple against the April blue; beeches bronze to gold; the oaks still dim and unburnished. A thrush was singing on the top of a beech tree.

What a world of buds and of song!

He looked over the hedge into the inn garden, and saw golden daffodils and white crocus in bloom together in a wild patch of grass under the old trees. Never had he felt so conscious of colour, of all that mystery of life which man the money-maker has no time to see. Nor had he realized, somehow, that the song of a thrush can be translated into so many human variants. "Why worry,—why worry? Will you do it, will you do it? Joy,—joy! I'm a spirit; I'm a spirit." Sorrell felt awed.

"How one forgets to look at things! Scuffling in the mud—most of us. Makes one marvel."

Reborn in him was the dim appreciation of the fact that it is good for man that he should marvel, yes, and marvel more at the flowers and the trees and the grasses of the field, and less at his own cleverness. To let himself go out among the golden buds shaken by the wind, into the pine pollen, into the white clouds or the cups of the daffodils. Better than the marvels of science, than "wireless" or the latest aeroplane, or the bending of light, or the quantum theory. Flowers came to your feet. You could take the little quaint face of a pansy between your two fingers, and see the soul of it, the soul of all gentle, living things.

Thomas Roland, coming down about this time to spend a week-end at the old Pelican, and bringing Cherry with him in a blue car, found Sorrell at the beginnings of this most final phase.

"Come and see the violas. We have massed Royal Scott and Bullion together, with a few Bronze Purples here and there."

The crowsfeet about Tom Roland's eyes became more marked as he looked at Sorrell. Little crinkles of affection. So, Stephen had taken to gardening,—and when an Englishman of fifty develops a passion for flowers, one may infer that the leaves of the other passions have fallen.

Roland stood at gaze.

"Paradise regained, old man."

"Like it?"

"You pretty creatures! That's how I feel to pretty flappers—now—Stephen. We are growing old."

"If this is growing old——"

"You don't mind?"

"Why should one?"

"Oh,—I don't know. To go under the grass when you are still full of music,—and the woman you love has no need to dye her hair. I'm always telling Cherry it is time that she began to find grey hairs."

"Is there any need?"

"Seems not. Why,—I don't know. Fellows, young fellows, round her like flies, damn them! Yet, she's one of those absurd creatures who seem to prefer the permanent adventure. We got married last month."

Sorrell was looking at his garden with the eyes of a lover.

"I'm glad. You two have had time to find out. Besides,—there's your music—and her voice."

"Yes—her voice," said Roland musingly.

But Sorrell's garden was there to be enjoyed, wide-eyed and ready to smile, a mute-lipped garden, fortuitously beautiful, unselfconscious, and not crying—"Come and look at me." Nor did Sorrell's self stand in the middle of it, smirking, "Ha, ha, my dear chap, see what—I—have done." The happy amateur in him had not done too much. He had taken the vegetable garden and the little orchard behind the cottage, and leaving many of the old fruit trees standing, he had run a broad turf path down the centre to meet the orchard grass. He had curbed Bowden's inclination to cut down and to tidy up, and to make flower beds of geometrical exactness and to edge them with blue tiles. "Them trees be'nt no use. Better have 'em down." Certainly many of the trees were old, and poor bearers, but Sorrell had left them there, and planted clematis and honeysuckle against the trunks of some of them. His flower beds looked like coloured tapestries flung down casually upon the grass. He had not meddled too much, and the result had come to him as a piece of irresponsible and blessed magic, a cottage garden idealized, with flowers and trees and roses, and bits of yew hedge, and fruit and lilies, and here and there a flowering shrub in disorderly and delightful freedom, so that there seemed no end to it and no beginning, and no fixed boundaries.

Roland, after wandering over this quarter of an acre of charming confusion, and losing himself among violas and pæonies and sweet-smelling stocks, came to rest against the trunk of an apple tree with the air of a man to whom life never ceased to be surprising.

"What incalculable creatures we are, Stephen. And this is your idea of a garden?"

"It grew like this. Either it had to,—or I have a muddled mind."

"And you—an expert hotelier, the man of detail who must organize the very stair-rods and the bath taps——! You are a grandfather, old chap,—and this garden is your grandchild. One is supposed to be more easy with one's grandchildren."

"Things that grow are different—somehow. You have to let them have their way, unless—of course—you are out for profits."

"Ah, profits!" said Roland, and catching sight of his wife by the sundial set on the square of old brick paving close to the cottage, he hailed her. "Come and see Stephen's secret dissipations. Instead of taking to the bottle—in his old age——"

She came down the grass path with that air of eternal youthfulness that was so untheatrical. Once or twice she paused to touch or to smell something, and her face had the softness of secret satisfactions.

"My dear," said her man; "you'll never grow old. What a problem for a man whose tailor tells him——"

"Don't listen to your tailor. But Stephen, you are a genius——"

"I'm nothing. I just muddle about, and the flowers do the rest——"

"Arcadian anarchy! Cherry, do you think that if I had a dish of rose petals for breakfast each morning, or nibbled a blue delphinium, I should discover the secret of eternal youth?"

"Why worry?" she said, shyly and clearly smiling, her voice making Sorrell think of the voice of a thrush, "you will never grow old. People who make music and pictures and gardens——"

"Blessed philosophy," said her husband. "Now, if I manufactured tooth-brushes or printed hymn books——"

Sorrell had taken out a penknife and was cutting an early rose. He held it to his nostrils for a moment before offering it to Roland's wife.

"Just look at the curves of that bud! Wonderful! Makes you feel——"

She inhaled the scent of it and looked with wide eyes at the two men as though both of them were lovable children, but far more lovable than any child.

2

While Sorrell paused upon his autumnal hilltop to sit in the sun of a reminiscent maturity, Christopher had developed the restlessness of a young soldier spoiling for war, and finding no use for his weapons.

Once a month he came down for the week-end, and oc-

cupied his old room in the cottage, meeting many friendly
faces, but none so wise in its friendliness as his father's.
Kit witnessed his father's excursions into the world of
flowers, and wondered at it. Sorrell seemed rooted in his
garden. He no longer seemed to care for long country
walks or early morning rides. Flowers fascinated him.
He had taken to experimenting in hybridism, and under his
gauze cages delphiniums and sweet peas and pansies lived
like sacred virgins waiting upon their annunciation.

Christopher was a little troubled. He was alive to a
subtle change in his father. Sorrell was gentler, slower in
his movements, more bent, yet obviously happy. Kit's eyes
were young. He observed the externals, the objective phe-
nomena, for he had been trained to observe signs, and to
attach more importance to them than to symptoms. He
appraised life with his eyes and hands.

Sorrell was growing very grey. His temporal arteries
stood out on little tortuous curves, and the son, watching
the father stooping over some plant and growing flushed
in the face, would remind himself that Sorrell had never
spared himself. He had taken hard knocks; and he had
never whimpered.

In the evenings Kit noticed that his father appeared
very tired,—but he was far less tired than Kit imagined,
for the pleasant, meditative languor of the older man was
not quite understood by the younger one. In a certain
way their positions became reversed. Kit did not advise
his father upon his ties and trousers, or try to renovate
the old boy, but he did feel responsible for Sorrell's health.

"Why don't you slack off a bit, pater?"

He was sitting askew on the window-sill, watching a sunset, while Sorrell lay in a long chair, puffing at a pipe.

"I am slacking," said his father.

Kit's silence was argumentative.

"You haven't had a decent holiday——"

"I could have had——"

"Well,—why not? The fact is—you have been carrying
me on your back."

Sorrell, lying with half-closed eyes, let the sweet humour
of his affection gleam under lowered eyelids.

"Life gets more automatic. The Pelican is a very obliging bird——"

"How?"

"People are rather good to me; Fanny and Mrs. Marks, and Hulks. The machinery runs as though it were in an oil bath. Sometimes I feel an absolute slacker."

Christopher was silent for a while, lips compressed, eyes at gaze.

"If I became a G.P.," he said, "would you mind?"

"Immensely."

"Pater——!"

He got off the window-sill and stood by Sorrell's chair, eagerly inarticulate.

"I'm twenty-seven. You have been responsible—I'm getting rather sick of hanging about, waiting. It may mean another two or three years, and when the chance comes it will only be a chance. Messing about with records and things—when I want to get at the real thing—and can't."

Sorrell watched the smoke from his pipe.

"It will come. The big chances are worth waiting for. I'm not worrying."

"Pater!" said the son, and stood mute.

His father held out a hand.

"You know me better than that. Things are pretty easy here now. As for the money, it has begun to roll in of itself. A trick money has—sometimes. If you have to wait five years for your chance it is all the same to me."

Kit stood silent in the dusk.

"Sometimes—I feel—like sucking your blood."

"My dear old chap, call it commercial transfusion. Do you think I regret it? I have never found life so good."

But Christopher was worried. It was a difficult period for a young man who had to stand by and watch other and older men doing the things he longed to do, and feeling the urge of those nine years of steady effort clamorous behind him. It was not that he lusted to use the knife. He wanted to try his skill and prove it, and yet he was no mere tool-man, a mender of watches. Always he remained aware of the mystery of the living tissues, of that marvellous and intricate nexus of arteries, nerves and muscles, that wonderful garment in which God has draped man's consciousness. Kit had a reverence for the human body, and when he saw it warped or diseased the soul of his nascent skill yearned to lay hands upon it.

And these months of waiting, of trailing about wards and corridors, this pen and paper game, the clerkliness, while the real work went on about him, and he envied the men who did it, and sometimes came near hating them. He felt like a dog waiting for a bone, some little job to be thrown at him by a man who had more jobs than he needed. He looked back with regret to his house-surgeon days when he had dabbled his hands in the live blood of surgery, and had even been allowed to carry through occasional minor operations.

Meanwhile, his father wrote monthly cheques, and Kit had come both to love and to hate those cheques. He had fancied that he had seen a significant frailness in his father, a wilting of that thin figure.

At Chelsea, after one of those Sunday suppers, he walked up and down the red and black music-room like a young lion in a cage. He had Tom Roland to himself for half an hour while Cherry played music to her marvellous new baby.

"Haven't you noticed——? You must have noticed."

It behoved Thomas Roland to say that Kit's father was not so young as he used to be. But did that matter? Age has a phase of its own, compensations, happinesses. You slackened your stroke, or you took to a punt instead of an eight-oar.

"But it matters to me," said Kit.

"It would—my lad. I'm not quarrelling with you minding,—but it is not easy for us to see the insides of our elders. Oh,—I'm not preaching. Look on it as physiological."

"You mean—he is growing old?"

"About as pleasantly as a man could."

Kit stood by the piano, staring at the keyboard where Cherry's hands used to flutter. He looked extraordinarily grave. The realization of the fact that his father was growing old had produced in him a feeling of shock.

"Of course," he said.

And then he resumed his walking up and down.

"Here am I tied up like a dog, waiting for somebody to let me off the chain. I want results."

"They'll come."

"Nine years, Roland, and he is still keeping me."

"Do you think he minds?"

"I know he doesn't. But it gets me. It's like a flame inside me. I want to give him something back, pride for pride. I want—to—to justify him."

"Well,—you will."

"Oh,—it's nice of you to say that."

"It's not nice; it's backing a big probability. You couldn't have done more, my lad, than you have done. Hang on."

"I'm hanging,—but I'd like to bite the rope through."

"The young man in a hurry! Forgive me. Softlee walkee catchee monkey. Your chance will come."

"Think so?"

"Sure of it."

Before switching off the light that night Roland told Cherry of Kit's impatience.

"Worrying about his chance. Why,—the young beggar, it's there in his face. One of the gods is bound to fall to him."

"Ah," she said, "you always will let yourself be caught by appearances. Mere looks."

"Now that's not fair. I could reduce it to a personal question. Looks do matter. 'I do not like you, Dr. Fell——!' Kit's likeable, tremendously likeable. Those eyes and mouth,—and the smile. Character. Now,—I'll bet you——"

"Do be quiet. I think I hear baby——"

"Explicit," said Roland, hunching up his pillow.

3

There were times when Christopher felt so restless about the future that he became a tramper of streets, one of those unsatisfied young Titans to whom London at night is like every other man's wife. His youth was strong in him, urgent, ambitious, and when doors are locked youth's inclination flies to a crowbar rather than to a key. Moreover, London is provocative to the fiercely obscure, like some splendid courtezan laughing derisively in their pinched and hungry faces, giving herself to the old men and to the rich. To have no flower of fame to offer is to be infamous, and worse than infamous—unknown. Kit was less greedy than most young men, and his vision of fame was both human and fine, but he felt the hustling and contemptuous shoulders of the great city, saw its placards and its sky-signs, read its names, heard its trumpet cries. There were nights when he felt fierce.

There were other nights when he knew melancholy. He would wander round Brunswick Square and recall those seemingly more romantic days. He thought of Pentreath, Dr. Pentreath, solidly established at Milchester as third partner in an old practice. Pentreath—the sensitive Pentreath—was earning his own living. He thought of Mary Jewett; he felt her, and there were nights when he yearned—— Poor, sensuous, dark-eyed Mary! He would go wandering over the ground, gathering memories, memories of arms and lips, and clouding hair in the midst of the warm darkness.

"If she were here," he thought, "I might feel less restless."

Sometimes he faced the thought of failure, comparative failure. He saw himself hanging on and at St. Martha's watching other men snapping up the hospital appointments, while he would end by drifting into some provincial sideshow where as a junior partner his adventurous excursions into surgery would be carefully curtailed. Competition was so fierce.

There were other eager young men shrewdly watching for future niches at St. Martha's, men who went purring softly about the place and rubbing themselves ingratiatingly against the legs of their seniors.

Roland had advised him to hang on, and Christopher,— being older than his years, supposed that his seniors had a wisdom of their own, and a way of looking at things that might differ from the young man's view. Older men were less in a hurry; they had not the same need to hurry; they could afford to be deliberate.

One morning Sorrell was walking along the main corridor with one of his registrar's books under his arm when he saw Simon Orange come limping out of the board-room and stand there looking to and fro like a saturnine ape. Orange was an oddity. Irreverently known as the "Orang" and "Septic Simon," he held the appointment of surgeon to the out-patient department of the hospital. He was swarthy and misshapen and laconic; he had a cleft palate, and his thick yet squeaky voice emitted occasional, bitter sarcasms. His sunken head bulged a big forehead over black and bushy eyebrows, and the eyes beneath them seemed enigmatic to the ordinary male.

For years this man had been the butt of the irresponsibly callow. All sorts of tales were told of him. It was said that as a student he had lived in a slum attic and had helped himself to exist by twanging a banjo and singing comic songs in various pubs. His very swarthiness had made him look unclean, and there had been an occasion when certain bright lads had set out to wash him, but had been surprised and discouraged by the creature's fierceness and its extraordinary simian strength. Persecuted, ridiculed, cold-shouldered, this misshapen little man had pushed on indomitably, showing to the sick and the broken a peculiar, abrupt tenderness, and to the rest of the world a sardonic disdain. The students feared and disliked him. He could bite and did so. To the incompetent and to the cheerfully casual he showed no mercy.

Christopher saw Mr. Orange's deep eyes fixed upon him. The little, thick, simian figure waited, its black coat wrinkled between the shoulders, its big head hanging forward. Its trousers bulged at the knees.

"Sorrell——"

The squeaky gruffness of Mr. Orange brought the eyes of the younger man to attention. Kit waited.

"I have one of my headaches coming on."

Kit did not say that he was sorry. He wasn't sorry, nor did Orange expect him to feel so. Orange's headaches were well known, and they had earned him a queer and additional dislike. Everything about the grotesque little surgeon was transmitted into hostility. Even these attacks of migraine were an offence, for they served to bring out the man's venomous tenacity. He would go aside and vomit, and lie down for half an hour, and take powders of aspirin, phenacetin, and caffeine. He would get up looking ghastly, and go on with his work—if work there was. He clung with both hands, and with feet and teeth, causing the younger men who hungered to get their hands into the blood of precious practical experience to grumble savagely:

"Why doesn't the little beast let us in?"

Or

"Garret,—you remember Garret,—he was a good chap. Used to let each Surgical Registrar have half a day with him."

Christopher was conscious of a sharp and expectant thrill. He said nothing, but just stood still, feeling a little puzzled by the way the shrewd brown eyes of Orange were looking up at him.

"Do you think you could carry on for me?"

Kit took a moment to answer.

"I should love to, sir. It depends——"

He noticed a queer twitching of Mr. Orange's eyelids. Love to, would he? Of course. But the word love was not a mere conventional exaggeration.

"What's worrying you, Sorrell?"

"I think I am up to tackling any ordinary job,—but supposing——"

"Don't funk it. No,—you won't."

"You mean to allow me to be responsible, sir?"

"Of course. Going to lie down. Send for me if you are not sure about anything."

He scrutinized Kit's suddenly flushed face.

"You'll do."

"It's very good of you, sir."

Orange nodded at him, gave him something like a grim smile, and took his misshapen body back into the board-room.

4

Kit passed a dramatic and an historic day. He performed three minor operations, with the hard-bitten, kinky-haired casualty-sister assisting him with critical and voiceless composure. About three o'clock he had to tackle a rather bad casualty, a compound fracture of the thigh with a pumping artery and a mass of lacerated tissue.

"Better let Mr. Orange know," said the nurse.

Kit was frowning.

"Don't want to worry him; unless it's necessary."

He was too supremely interested to be nervous, too full of a quiet exultation in the presence of the live crisis and his contact with it. He had taken one look at the muddied and clay-coloured face of the man, felt his pulse, and sent for one of the house-physicians to give him an anæsthetic. Then, with the patient safely under the anæsthetic Kit seemed conscious of nothing but that smashed and torn limb waiting for his purposeful and methodical hands.

He had ligatured the artery and was cleaning up the pulped muscles when he was aware of a quick turn of the sister's head. She seemed about to speak, but something or someone restrained her. And Kit was taking dressings from the sterilized boxes before he discovered Mr. Orange standing there, his face like a ghastly, pallid mask.

Kit's eyes asked a question.

"No,—carry on."

"I did not want to worry you, sir."

"No need—at all."

At the end of it all there came a sort of pregnant silence. Kit was peeling off his rubber gloves; the anæsthetist was feeling the patient's pulse, and watching Mr. Orange's face as though he expected a sardonic explosion. Rather cheeky of Sorrell tackling a case like this without a word to the "Orang."

Mr. Orange was looking thoughtfully at the splinted limb, his big head tilted forward. He said nothing, did not make a sound until Christopher was getting out of his white smock.

"All right. Nothing else, is there?"

"No, sir."

He turned abruptly and walked to the door, and Christopher did not see him for the next two days.

5

Three nights later Kit was called up on the telephone and was sent for to the porter's room.

"What is it, Hodges?"

"Mr. Orange, sir."

Kit put the receiver to his ear.

"Hallo."

He heard a rumbling and a squeakiness that was Simon Orange's voice.

"That you, Sorrell? Yes. Come round to my place, will you, if you can spare an hour? No. 11, St. Mary's Street. Coming? Good."

That was all.

Yet, when seated in one of Simon Orange's shabby arm-chairs in a room that suggested that each article of furniture had been acquired separately at various second-hand shops, it came upon Christopher Sorrell that this Quasimodo of a man liked him, and with a liking that was eager and inexplicable. He was aware of a bright and awkward shyness in the other man's eyes. Orange brought out a box of cigars, and was gruff yet apologetic in offering them to Sorrell.

"Try one. Not bad."

"Thanks very much, sir."

Orange placed the box very carefully upon the table, selected a cigar, and stripped off the band.

"No need to 'sir' me."

He searched the mantelpiece for matches.

"Got a light? Fact is—it has occurred to me that you might be willing to give me a hand sometimes. I am getting a good deal to do, consultant work, and a certain amount of outside surgery. If you could take over the out-patient work for me—now and again. Care to?"

He did not look at Christopher, but appeared busy with the lighting of his cigar, and yet Kit had the impression that Orange was asking a favour instead of conferring one. This shabby room somehow suggested loneliness, the uncouth and rather pathetic loneliness of a man who had no friends. And Orange was trying to be friendly, like a man-ape who had been made to suffer many indignities, and behind whose scornful ferocity shone two lonely, ape-like eyes.

"You must know what you are offering me, Mr. Orange."

"Know? What?"

"The chance to use my hands.—I have felt——"

The ape-like eyes were on him for a moment, questioning, human, eagerly intelligent.

"Starving?"

"Yes."

"I know what starving means. Several varieties of starvation, Sorrell. Soul and body. You'll take it on?"

"Only too gladly,—if you think——"

"Fit,—quite. I'm not a fool. I'll mention it at the next board-meeting."

With the cigar between his lips, and with knees slightly bent he stood square to the fire, staring into it with a queer and half-malicious smile on his face.

"Don't sublet any of the work."

"You mean——?"

"Those other fellows, Messrs. Starkey, and Blane, and Templeman. Do you think I don't know——?"

He twisted slightly on his curved thighs and looked fixedly down over his shoulder at Christopher.

"You—know, Sorrell."

Kit did know, and he stared at the fender. He knew what his brother surgical-registrars said of Simon Orange.

"That's it. Fawning young Agags. Think me a pretty fool. I have had to learn to hate,—sometimes. Sneer at and use. No,—that's not my motto. Power's good, Sorrell. Don't forget it."

Christopher felt curiously humbled, for he—in his time had laughed thoughtlessly at Simon Orange.

"Loyalty," he said; "there is one man who has taught me loyalty."

"Pretty rare."

"It was my father."

XXX

I

THOUGH Cherry might mock a little at Thomas Roland's whimsies, and at his cult of "A Smooth Surface" as she called it, Roland's christening of Kit as "The Fortunate Youth" betrayed that half laughing insight that comes with maturity. Man has collected an immense store of theory which is useful to him as the small change of existence, but when a big issue gallops up like a March wind, man is apt to forget his little theories. He is inclined to act upon impulse, to let the wind blow through the rags of his social reason. "You do the thing you want to do, Cherry, and afterwards you invent all sorts of nice excuses to prove that you acted like a lawyer, and not like a fool. The lawyer in us is always an afterthought. I fell in love with your face and your voice, not with a category of virtues and vices." When he heard about Mr. Simon Orange, he smiled. "Told you so. Contrasts. Beauty and the Beast. I knew that someone would open Kit's door for him."

Simon Orange opened it very successfully. Call a man an individualist, which means that he objects to being jostled either by mobs or an oligarchy, and you had Orange outlined as a lone, grim, anthropoid creature, hairily grotesque, smashing his way through the jungle. Sometimes, life had caused him to utter cries of rage and of pain, but life, the little oppositions, the class prejudices, had not stopped him. He had been very poor. There had been days when he had had but two shirts to cover his hairy chest, and the tails of these shirts would have fluttered like torn clouds. Even that room of his in St. Mary's Street pictured the long struggle; possessions, books, chairs, a table, a sideboard, an old Turkey carpet snatched up by simian hands and carried off on various occasions. An indefatigable, fierce, laborious creature, with something very human and pleading in the hidden deeps of its brown eyes.

Orange had a consulting-room on the ground floor, and a waiting-room that he shared with three other doctors. They also shared the services of the very plain and capable woman in black who received their patients. And Orange had a growing practice. The grotesque exterior could not mask a skill, a thoroughness, a courage that were unusual. Most of his work took him to the suburbs among people of the lower middle class. His practice as a consultant had come to him very gradually, gathered by those grim hands. He was a man who had come to be believed in by a number of general practitioners. He gave you results; he was reliable, he did not demand his pound of flesh; he never let you down. He had a personality, queer and uncouth no doubt, but it was a personality.

And this was the man who first opened the door to Christopher Sorrell, and did it with an abrupt and awkward shyness, and a look half of appeal. Human intuition. An almost womanish impulse towards that which was good to look at and to wonder at. The straight, well-built body, and the comely, virile head. And more than that. Character, clear eyes, a young dignity, a fineness of emotional outline. Attractions may seem incalculable, but they are more real than the wisdom of the text-books.

The friendship grew. Certain envious young men might gibe, and complain that "Sorrell had buttered the Orang's fingers," but what did that matter. Hostility is homage; envy tribute. Kit had the blood of life on his hands, and of that precious experience which alone can justify a young man's self-confidence. It became his custom to go to Simon Orange's room two or three evenings a week, and he remembered the night when Orange first called him "old man."

It came out gruffly with the tentative shyness of a man afraid of caring too much, or afraid that his caring might not matter.

"Had a good day, old man."

He did not ask a question; he stated a fact. For Kit had one of those unexpected days when unexpected things happen. He had experienced one of those almost dramatic, human clashes that cannot be planned for or foreseen.

"A pretty nasty case."

"Old Ormsby told me about it."

There was a smile on Orange's face as he opened the cigar-

box, and held a cigar to his nostrils. It is good to give of
one's best to a friend, and his best had been such a sorry
thing,—and Sorrell was his first friend.

"If I had known," said Kit, "that Sir Ormsby was standing there watching me,—I should have fumbled it."

"No you wouldn't. A cut throat is a cut throat."

"It—was—a throat. Nicked one carotid, and gone clean
through the larynx. It took me the best part of two hours."

"Ormsby watched you for half an hour."

"As long as that!"

"And then he asked you to do an emergency job for him
in the theatre."

"Just a simple appendix."

Orange held his big and clever hands to the fire.

"Glad—old man. We'll be on the staff together—some
day."

"I hope so. And but for you——"

"I've done nothing."

Orange did not tell Kit that Sir Ormsby Gaunt, that father
of surgery and master of craft, had discussed Sorrell with
him, and spoken significant words. "Good fellow that.
Have you ever seen him blush, Orange?" Orange had seen
Christopher blush, and it had sent a thrill of curious affection
through him. Tenderness—almost. There were people who
thought the "Orang" a jealous and a grudging beast, one of
those fellows who grabbed and held on and showed his teeth
if any other man came too near him, but Orange was happy in
Christopher's success. He could give of his best to Sorrell
because he wanted to give to him.

Nor was the work at St. Martha's the only avenue of experience that he opened to his friend. In his private work he
sometimes needed assistance, and on Sundays Sorrell would
go with Orange to some nursing-home, and add Orange's self-
confidence to his own.

"Doing things, difficult things, day in and day out, and
doing them better and better."

It was through Orange that Christopher obtained his first
appointment, the post of junior surgeon to a hospital in the
north of London.

"There is a vacancy at the Northern Free, a junior sur-
geonship. Sir Ormsby told me about it to-day in the staff-
room. He mentioned you."

Kit's face lit up.

"But, Simon,—why not you?"

"Oh,—I don't want it; too much to do already. Rather a sinecure,—but useful to a man who wants to keep his hands in."

"Do you think I should have a chance?"

"Sir Ormsby mentioned you. I said that I would sound you on the subject. If you are keen——"

"What do you think?"

"Well, go and see Sir Ormsby. He is the senior honorary at the Northern Free."

In this way it came about that Christopher was appointed to his first public post, and was able to go down to Winstonbury with the secret up his sleeve. And in the letting loose of such secrets there is much simple human joy.

Christopher never forgot the quick lift of his father's head when he heard the news.

"Great! I'm glad. You have worked for it."

And as they sat by the fire Kit thought of Simon Orange sitting in front of that other fire in St. Mary's Street, a vivid and gnarled figure bulging out an old black velvet coat, its feet thrust into red leather slippers, and a cerise-coloured tie flapping under a heavy and thoughtful chin. That was Orange, good friend, God bless him!

2

Later that winter Simon Orange became a member of the In-patient Staff, and Kit was given Orange's vacant post.

It was an event. Sorrell came up to town, and Roland and Cherry gave a dinner at Chelsea, and while Sorrell Senior was in London he called upon a very notable firm of house and estate agents and made it known to them that he was ready to purchase a house in one of those decorous streets where the consulting world functions. He was told that there was no such house purchasable at the moment, but that the firm would make inquiries and keep the matter in evidence, and they would hope to communicate with Mr. Sorrell in due course.

Meanwhile, Christopher joined Simon Orange at No. 11, St. Mary's Street, taking over two rooms on the third floor, and arranging to use the waiting-room and one of the consulting-rooms when providence should send him any patients. Sorrell furnished the two rooms for his son, and never had the spending of money given him more pleasure. The rising sun seemed to shine on that little brass plate attached to the green front door.

"Mr. Christopher Sorrell."

Standing one May morning at the open window of Kit's sitting-room, and caressing a grey moustache with a meditative fore-finger, Sorrell looked down into St. Mary's Street and felt that life was good. Kit was arriving. He had his niche in the sacred enclosure; the son of the hotel-porter was one of the elect. The street below him, half in the sunlight and half in the shadow, was as full of the panoply of triumph as any *Via Sacra*. An itinerant flower-seller was trundling a barrow full of flowers, and Sorrell, the flower lover, felt that his happy mood had a posy. Here and there a car was drawn up outside a house; solid, shimmering cars, blue and black and claret and grey. There was one car that suggested to Sorrell a glass of good red wine. Some day before long Kit would have his car.

The flower-seller's voice was to be heard. He had two or three crimson and white azaleas in pots, also a few polyantha roses. Sorrell leaned out with his hands on the window-sill, caught the flower-seller's eye, and pointed to the door of No. 11.

Christopher was arranging some of his books.

"What are you up to, pater?"

"O,—nothing," said Sorrell. "There's a chap down there with some flowers."

A maid came to say that a man with flowers had come to the front door.

"Tell him I want two of his azaleas, one crimson and one white, and two pots of the carmine roses."

"Yes, sir."

"Ask him what he wants for them, and you can take the money down."

When Sorrell had posed the plants to his liking, and touched them with his fingers, he sat sideways on the window-sill, and watched the street, and Kit, and felt that life was still more good.

"Well,—here you are," he said suddenly.

Kit, with a volume of "Operative Surgery" in his hand, smiled gravely at the figure by the window.

"And you, pater."

"And I. We haven't done so badly, old chap. Comes of concentrating on the job. It gives one to think."

"And feel," said Kit.

Presently Sorrell mentioned Pentreath, for he had been able to enjoy a pleasant pity where Pentreath was concerned.

"How's he doing?"

"Settled at Millchester; good old practice. Married again,—you know."

"Who to?"

"A canon's daughter. Haven't seen him for a year. He writes fairly regularly."

"Some men do. Nice mellow, ecclesiastical atmosphere. I suppose it is just the thing——!"

"I suppose so. Arthurian, pater. Millchester, in the West, not much harried yet by the barbarians."

"Ah,—the barbarians," said Sorrell. "Poor, greedy children. Pentreath would be no good with greedy children. Nice fellow."

"He is earning his living," said Kit.

"One can do more than that," was Sorrell's reply.

3

Less than a month from the day of Kit's establishing himself at No. 11 St. Mary's Street, Pentreath reappeared with personal vividness upon his immediate horizon.

Christopher was rung up at St. Martha's. They were calling him from No. 11, and he heard the voice of Page, the woman in the black dress.

"There's a Dr. Pentreath here, sir. Wants to see you very particularly."

"Dr. Pentreath of Millchester?"

"Yes, sir."

"I'll be round in half an hour."

Christopher found Pentreath in the waiting-room, a Pentreath who reminded him of the friend who had come to him that day in Brunswick Square.

"Hallo,—old chap."

He saw at once that Pentreath was fidgety and worried. He shook hands rather too eagerly, and his grip was uncertain and clammy. He stood in the middle of the room, looking with inattentive attention at the pictures and the furniture. His movements were jerky.

"Nice place you have here."

"I have been in hardly a month. How's Millchester?"

Pentreath sat down abruptly in a chair and after some desultory confidences he blurted out the very words that expressed all that Kit had seen in his eyes.

"Private practice is horribly worrying."

Kit had taken a chair by the table where the periodicals and magazines were arranged for waiting patients. He sat with his hands in his pockets.

"So is London. But I suppose one gets hard."

Pentreath winced.

"I can't get hard,—Sorrell. Sometimes I think I'm too soft. There are some cases;—I have one now."

"Let's hear about it."

The face of his old friend hurt him, for in Pentreath's eyes he found a suggestion of horrible cringing.

"A damnable case. I ought to have—had one of the other fellows in, but it was one of my chauffeur's children, and my wife——"

For the moment Kit could not see how Mrs. Pentreath —the canon's daughter—came to intrude upon a problem in surgery, but later he was made to understand that Maurice's wife was a lady of many intrusions. Jerked out by Pentreath's sensitive and rather high-pitched voice, the description of the case appeared very simple. The chauffeur's eldest girl had fallen downstairs and hurt her wrist; Pentreath had been out at the time, and his wife had initiated one of her intrusions. She had applied a cold bandage and sympathy. "When Dr. Pentreath comes back he will see to it."

Pentreath had examined the girl's wrist in the presence of his wife, another superfluous and indiscreet intrusion.

"Obviously, Sorrell, there seemed to be a fracture, a Colles. I suppose I ought to have had another opinion."

Listening in between the lines Kit seemed to catch a whisper of Pentreath's inveterate fearfulness. He suspected that Maurice was a little afraid of his wife. She happened to be one of those very self-sure young women who despise procrastination, and for very shame Pentreath had bluffed before her and proceeded to deal with that hypothetical fracture, when he had known in his heart that old Tombs the senior partner would have been much more competent to deal with it. For with his hands Pentreath had always been a nervous fumbler.

"I put the thing in plaster, Sorrell, and of course I made the girl move her fingers. But when I took the fracture down—a week ago; it looked all wrong."

"They do, sometimes," said Kit.

"And then—you know—one of those silly panics got me, —just as they used to during exams. I bluffed. And now—I simply can't make up my mind——"

"Whether there was a fracture?"

"O,—yes, there was a fracture. I had it X-rayed. But whether I——"

"Didn't you have it rayed again?"

"No."

"My dear old chap, why not?"

"Simply—because I was afraid,—afraid of what I might see."

He gave Christopher a mute and deprecating look.

"Sounds too futile, doesn't it? But the case has begun to worry me to death. Of course I ought to have gone to one of my partners,—but it seemed such a confession of helplessness. I suppose it is difficult for you to under-stand——"

"You can't make up your mind—whether the girl's wrist is right or wrong?"

"Exactly. It must sound absurd to you."

"Not a bit."

He was aware of Pentreath's clasped hands with their fingers interlocked twisted between his knees.

"I suppose you could not spare the time——?"

"I'll come down to-morrow, if you like."

Pentreath's eyes loved him.

"Great man! You see, the girl's father is a rather sus-picious sort of chap, interfering, funny. He had the cheek to take the splints off the other evening. Tackled me about the girl's wrist—next morning. You know how those people like to hint——"

Kit nodded.

"Look here. I had better arrive informally. To-morrow is Saturday. Suppose that I am spending the week-end with you. I can have a look at the girl's wrist—just out of curiosity—so to speak."

4

Mr. Christopher Sorrell travelled down to Millchester by an afternoon train, and found Pentreath's car waiting for him at the station. Pentreath's suspiciously minded chauffeur met Sorrell without troubling to salute him in any way, and allowed the porter to dispose of Kit's suitcase.

Kit had given the chauffeur a smile, and one quick, discriminating glance. He had learnt to place men and women with a shrewdness shorn of all sentimental illusions. He had observed and handled and smelt them for years in the out-patient departments of St. Martha's. He had seen them cringe and swagger and pretend, and try to hide what it was madness to hide; and he had learnt to tell false faces from true ones, and to know almost by instinct when someone was lying. He had his gallery of "types," and the fellow at the wheel in front of him was a rodent, a nasty, acute little man of the Nosey Parker genus, very self-pleased, with one of those long, intrusive noses, a patch of raddled red on each cheek bone, and bright, insolent, treacherous little eyes.

"All right, my friend," thought Kit.

Pentreath had an old red house with a walled garden behind it in Bishop's Way leading from the Close. A maid opened the white door with its lion-headed brass knocker and took Sorrell's suitcase, the chauffeur not troubling to move from his seat. The maid had had her orders; Dr. Pentreath was out, but would be back for tea, and Mrs. Pentreath was expecting Mr. Sorrell. They crossed the pleasant and softly lit square hall of the house, with a Jacobean oak cupboard very black against one wall, and a gate-legged table with a bowl of roses in the centre of it. The maid opened the door, and at the farther end of a long and beautifully proportioned room Christopher saw a tall girl rising from a chintz-covered sofa ranged sideways to a very graceful long window. The end of the room looked all window, and filled with the pleasant smoothness of an old lawn and the further gloom of a cedar.

"Mr. Sorrell."

Christopher looked at Pentreath's wife. She was a fair young woman, tall, with dark eyes, a little Roman nose and a decisive mouth, a beauty, an immediate beauty, but less subtly so when you inhaled the faint, cold perfume of her perfection. She smiled faintly at Kit; it was like turning on a pale light and turning it off again. She did not say that she was pleased to see him. Why should she be pleased?

Such was Perdita Pentreath.

"Maurice has been called out. I don't think he will be very long."

She resumed her place on the sofa. She enthroned herself against the greens of grass and cedar, while Kit sat down very carefully on a chair, and felt that a certain brightness was necessary.

"What a very charming window," he said.

She surveyed him with veiled attention, as though he had surprised her, and she did not permit people to surprise her. She had a beautifully cold presence, the perfect composure of some white flower, manners that were serenely detached. A most exquisite egoist.

"Yes, it is particularly right. The house was my father's wedding present."

"A very delightful one."

He felt himself completely in the circle of her cold consciousness, a figure out of the past, her husband's past, to be observed and considered with courteous hostility. And Kit was thinking— "So this is Maurice's wife! Arthur's Guinevere. What a reaction from the other. She looks as though she had buried something and had planted herself like a lily over the grave. I wonder——." But he kept on talking with a genial glibness, feeling that she regarded him as part of Pentreath's past, and that she utterly disapproved of it, and would hold it crystallized in ice.

And then Pentreath came in with an uneasy brightness, and shook hands with Kit, and looked anxiously at his wife. It became obvious to Christopher that Pentreath was very much in love with his wife, and afraid of her.

"Well,—I have often wanted you two to meet."

She said something about it's being a *fait accompli,* and asked Pentreath to ring the bell. They had tea and Pentreath tried to talk of the old Trinity days, and became self-consciously inept, while Perdita held to her young episcopal throne. Afterwards there was the garden, and golf croquet.

"You still play golf croquet?"

"We do. My wife says that it economizes small talk."

"Remember Molly? By the way,—what is Molly——?"

Pentreath had the toe of his boot on the red ball.

He appeared to look anxiously over his shoulder to assure himself that Perdita was still upon her throne.

"My surgery hours—half-past six. Girl coming in then. You might——"

"I'll stroll in casually—if you show me——. Shall I begin——? Right. And what about Molly?"

Pentreath crooked his long finger over his mallet, and played his ball on to the wrong side of the first hoop.

"O—Molly Haven't you heard? Selling Paris models, and writing novels. Haven't you read 'Broken Pottery'?"

"Novels are not much in my line."

" 'Broken Pottery' sold thirteen thousand. Horribly clever.—Perdita."

He glanced again towards the window.

"Your shot. Perdita refuses to have Molly's books in the house. Don't gee. Perdita's rather old-fashioned."

"Molly used to be rather a fierce young person."

"O, too much so, too much so. Is still. She has been here just once. A pity——"

He potted at a hoop and missed it.

"Dear me! Having things on your mind——"

He looked at his watch.

5

When Mr. Christopher Sorrell strolled into Pentreath's surgery, smoking a pipe and appearing as the most casual of intruders, he surprised the group by the window, Pentreath, Maggs the chauffeur, and Maggs's girl. Pentreath was seated, unrolling a light bandage, the girl standing in front of him, a pale and strumous child with a bulging forehead and weak blue eyes. The chauffeur stood by the window, head cocked with an air of critical and impertinent attention.

"Sorry," said Christopher; "I was wondering whether you had last week's *Lancet* in here."

Pentreath appeared intent upon the splinted wrist.

"On my desk—I think, old chap."

Christopher sought for the *Lancet* and found it, and then dallied smiling at the child.

"Anything interesting?"

Pentreath glanced up as though he had been hardly aware of Kit's presence.

"A Colles. Care to have a look. We are rather proud of our own pet fracture, aren't we, Gladys?"

The girl simpered, and her father made a scraping sound with his feet, a sound of potential protest.

Pentreath removed the splints, and Kit stood looking at the girl's wrist, thinking that a man like Maggs would call a child Gladys; and also wondering how he could manipulate an awkward situation. If Pentreath really had——? The truth was the truth. And he stood and looked, noting a bumpy prominence on the back of the wrist, and a very slight deflection of the hand.

Then he took the girl's wrist and fingers in his deliberate hands, and Pentreath, who was watching his friend's face, saw an incipient and pleasant smile there.

"Move your hand, old lady. That's it. Now, the fingers."

Kit could have laughed, for the result was fairly satisfactory and the slight apparent deformation more or less normal. Pentreath had worried so furiously that he had become incapable of recording a perfectly scrupulous opinion.

Kit patted the girl's wrist.

"Very nice,—very nice."

Instinct warned him that the father was about to say something. And he did say something, in a little, acid, threatening voice.

"What's that lump there?"

"That? Bone—my friend."

"There wasn't no lump like that before."

"Exactly," said Kit; "and now you are wiser."

"I don't know what you gentlemen think, but it looks all wrong to me."

And Kit laughed, but so very quietly. He still held the girl's arm, but he looked at the father.

"Now, Mr. Wiseacre, have you ever seen a plumber's joint?"

"Maybe I have."

"And how does a broken bone unite?"

The man was sullenly silent.

"Not quite like a piece of welding; more like a joint on a lead pipe. Put your finger on the thing you call a lump. Hard—isn't it?"

"I've felt it," said the man.

Kit smiled at him.

"Live and learn. Gladys can watch that lump disappearing slowly. Like to have a bet with your father on it, old lady?"

Kit stayed with the Pentreaths till late on the Sunday afternoon. On parting, Perdita gave him a correct and cold hand, and Pentreath accompanied him to the station. They walked up and down the Millchester platform.

"I'm awfully grateful to you, old chap. Weight off my mind."

"That's all right."

"Nothing more to suggest about that case?"

Christopher stood watching the engine of the incoming train.

"No," he said slowly; "nothing. But—at the first convenient opportunity I should sack your chauffeur."

XXXI

I

HAPPENING to pass a bookshop in Oxford Street on the Monday after his return from Millchester, Kit was reminded of Molly Pentreath and her excursions into literature. That little devil of a Molly taking up a pen and prodding with mischievous fierceness at all the Pentreath traditions! Kit, with his memories of her and her croquet mallet, could well imagine Molly doing it. Moreover, Mrs. Perdita's disapproval of her sister-in-law's books had put an edge to Christopher's curiosity, and he entered the bookshop and asked if they had a copy of Molly Pentreath's "Broken Pottery."

They had. The book was enclosed in a vivid wrapper, showing a green pot lying shattered upon a background of scarlet. Christopher bought a copy, and on opening the book under the very nose of Simon Orange, he happened to discover the dedication.

"To All Those Who Dare."

Characteristically combative! And then, Orange, with red slippers dangling, and his tie adrift above his waistcoat, showed an interest in Sorrell's purchase.

"What's that?"

"A book by a girl I used to know when she was a kid. Molly Pentreath."

"Broken Pottery?"

"Yes."

"I've read it. Damnably clever."

Kit, sitting down in one of Orange's ancient chairs, and turning over the pages of Molly's book, remarked that he did not know that Orange cared for novels.

"Do you good to read a few, Sorrell."

"Think I need it?"

"Well, a good novel is real, far more significant than

311

most of the highbrow stuff—so called. It's like good surgery. Besides——."

Kit looked at him with those clear and direct eyes of his.
"What?"

"You get at tendencies, social atmospheres, even hints
of the latest social perversion or disease. What's brewing
in the wild young blood. It's interesting."

"This book interested you?"

"It did. Shockingly honest—you know. Like a preco-
cious child asking awkward questions."

Christopher was rather shocked by "Broken Pottery,"
and it is probable that the book would have shocked him
even more forcibly had he been capable of reacting to its
more esoteric meaning. He read about that absurd and
somewhat repulsive person "Mr. Gulliver," who concealed
a bullying uxoriousness beneath inches of sentimental fat,
and whose one and only answer to the rebel woman's outcry
was "O, put her to bed and give her plenty of children."
The book was beyond Kit. He ploughed through it like the
direct and rather simple creature that he was, a frontiers-
man blazing a trail, hacking his way, aware only of the
very obvious trees and the general lie of the landscape.
Molly was too subtle for him. He missed her park-like
pieces, the little bosky thickets where the modern nymph
twisted the tail of the unfortunate and bewildered faun.
He was blind to her social vignettes, her little cameos of
sophisticated colour, her raillery, her devilish mischievous-
ness——

"Well, I'm dashed!"

It seemed to him beside the mark, and he was inclined
to sympathize with Mrs. Perdita, but when he came to
discuss the book with Orange he was surprised to find that
his friend did not agree with him.

"She thinks that she has written the epitaph on marriage.
Supposed to be rather out of date, you know, the reaction
against marriage."

"You mean that she is mocking at a thing—that is dead."

"In a way."

"But, good Lord, my dear man, what—is—the alterna-
tive?"

Orange, with his pale face bending down and brooding
with its sombre irony, took a little time to answer.

"So much a question of temperament. Marriage is or was or should be a mere social arrangement for the begetting and rearing of children. That the luxury of sex should have got mixed up with it was all wrong. No desire for children, no marriage. If you want to cultivate the fine flower of sex——? You see, Gulliver was a chap who wanted sex —like a cabbage rose, but he pretended to the woman that he wanted children."

"But—comradeship, Orange, the finer comradeship—and all that?"

"Sexual comradeship? Is there——? Besides,—the new woman is quite logical. If sex is a mere incident and is to be treated as such by sophisticated people, marriage is superfluous."

"I can't follow that."

And Orange understood that Kit could not follow it. He was romantic. He had idealistic youth's vision of the one rose on the tree. He had not realized the other sex's errant and adventurous inclinations. He was not subtle. His very simplicity might some day compel some woman to love him very dearly, and perhaps to hide and imprison a part of herself that he would never divine or see.

"It's so much a question of temperament," said Orange.

"And character, surely?"

"The chemistry of character is organic."

Kit looked very serious.

"But that girl's temperament! I think I should be pretty well scared by it."

"O, like breaking the ice on the Serpentine on a frosty morning. The first plunge, a shock. After that, you might find it invigorating."

"I think I should prefer something gentler."

2

Christopher had maintained his friendship with John Kennard, now one of the senior surgeons, and when Kennard asked Kit to dinner, the younger man found himself one of a party of three. Sir Ormsby Gaunt was standing on Kennard's hearthrug, just as Kit had seen him facing a lecture room with a white-headed, easy dignity that no student

had ever dared to challenge. He had eyes, deep under
bushy eyebrows, that gave the world quick, acute and sidelong glances. When watching him Kit had always been
struck by the perfect stillness of the great man's hands.

To Christopher old Gaunt was a great man. Sorrell's
son had not that pettifogging type of mind, the mind of
little facetious envies that must tie a sneer to the tails of
a man's coat. Kit was sanguine and creative. He knew
how hard it was to do the great things well, and that old
Gaunt had done them well. The little people who tickled
life with straws were not to his liking.

Old Gaunt held out a wholesome, fresh-coloured hand to
Kit.

"Well, Sorrell,—here we are."

And Christopher blushed. He had a feeling that there
was something in the air, a "Tinker Bell" of a nice conspiracy to set some disgraceful but pleasant piece of favouritism floating in through the windows of St. Martha's.
But unlike Peter Pan Kit did not set great store by his
own shadow. Other people saw to the length and the substance of Kit's shadow. Had not Thomas Roland said they
would?

At dinner Sir Ormsby and Kennard talked about needlework pictures and Japanese ivories, and since Sorrell senior
knew a good deal about needlework pictures, Kit was less
voiceless than he might have been. He called Sir Ormsby
"sir," with perfect naturalness, for to Kit the great man
was eminently "sir." Later, they became less archaic, and
talked "shop." Kennard was one of the pioneers of the
new thoracic surgery, and while Sir Ormsby probed his
methods and his results, Christopher sat and listened with
the air of a young man who enjoyed every word of it; which
he did. Later still, they arrived at hospital gossip, and it
seemed to Kit that their gossiping concealed personal tendencies. Lawson was going to retire. Sandys would move
up and become a senior. There would be a vacancy for an
assistant surgeon.

Sir Ormsby, giving Kit one of his sidelong and shrewdly
beneficent glances, supposed that Sorrell would apply for
the post.

"A St. Martha's man. One or two outsiders may be putting up."

It should have been obvious to Christopher that old Gaunt was completely ready to extrude the outsiders. Mr. Christopher Sorrell blushed, and felt a spasm of exultation.

"Of course.—If you think, sir."

"Quite inevitable, Sorrell, that you should apply. Don't you agree, Kennard?"

Kennard agreed. It was a base, male conspiracy, conceived not to keep out any particular man, but to introduce a particular one, for all-the-world-over favours, feminine and otherwise, are apt to go by liking. To be told by Sir Ormsby Gaunt that a certain line of conduct was inevitable was worth to Christopher more than any gold medal that he had won. Old men do not say such things to young ones without good reason. And as Kit sat there with that wise and serious face of his, he saw much of his own past pass rapidly before him, till it entered the doorway of this serene and stately room, and ended as a luminous halo that was the whiteness of old Gaunt's hair.

"It is very good of you, sir."

A vivid shyness attacked him. He wanted to be alone, to walk the empty streets almost like a lover to whom has come the amazing blessedness of a sacred smile. Also, he understood that these two Captains of Accomplishment were to be left together, and he suspected that when he had gone they would have things to say of him. And so, he left early, going out with such a shining of his young good will towards them that they were silent for a little while after he had gone.

"A good lad—that. Wise."

"Yes, very wise," said Kennard, "as some young things are; but also quite simple."

"The wise simplicity that gets there. I think nearly all the big men, Kennard, have had a vein of simplicity. Fatal to be too subtle."

"You think so?"

"Yes, for the doers. Subtlety belongs to the people who pull the wings off things. I suppose they are necessary. It is possible to drown in your own subtlety. Rather miserable people—too."

Carefully he removed the ash from his cigar.

"We will have that lad on the staff. You agree?"

"Oh, absolutely. I think he has some fine surgery in him."

"Character. Even—we—are a little short of it these days, Kennard. Some of our bright young men are just a little—dubious."

"I know."

Before six months had passed Mr. Christopher Sorrell was appointed to be one of the assistant surgeons at St. Martha's Hospital. Orange brought him the news, hot from that formal gathering where Sir Ormsby had taken shrewd care to make sure that it was his own pet cake that was put into the oven. Orange found Kit sitting by the window, looking abnormally serious.

"It is all right. You have it."

Kit remained very still in his chair. His seriousness seemed to increase.

"I hope I shan't let you down, Orange."

"My dear man!"

"All you good people. One never knows—quite—how one is going to react."

Orange looked at him with affectionate attention. Kit was finely strung, and no man who is capable of the big things faces the doing of them with complete complacency. Tremor, a dryness of the mouth, a sensitive agitation before the great speech or the picking up of the pen.

"I suppose I shall have to lecture."

"You'll do it very well."

Kit stared at his hands.

"I wonder what my first big op. will be like?"

Orange's face lit up with one of its deep and sombre smiles.

"The first hurdle is always the worst——. I remember——" He passed a hand over his forehead.

"I did not sleep much. I was to do a nephrotomy. But —then—you see—I had hatred and prejudice against me. I knew that the theatre would be packed with a lot of fellows who would be eager to see me fail. I think that is what gave me my nerve, the knowledge that I had to take the smirk off all those hostile faces. I hadn't one friend."

Kit looked at him suddenly.

"I should have liked to have been there. Yes, that is

where guts come in, old chap. The first time that you are the central figure, wholly responsible."

"If it would not worry you I would like to see your first."

"Will you?"

"Yes. Because I know, Sorrell, that you won't funk it."

3

In the winter and the spring Stephen Sorrell slept with the blind up and the curtains undrawn, and when he woke to see blue smoke drifting through and over the flower buds of the old pear tree, he knew that the under-porter had lit the sitting-room fire, and that the wind was in the north. Therefore, he began the day feeling combative. His mellowness was not proof against a raw north-easter in the late days of March or the first week in April, and however seasonable this wind might be he resented its ugly interference. It was a bitter wind, the enemy of his flowers, making the grass look a starved yellow, and the soil like grey ash, a wind that combed unsuspected rubbish out of hedge bottoms and corners and distributed it over the lawns and the flower beds. So, Sorrell would feel combative, and as likely as not cut himself when he was shaving, for a bleak north wind blowing when his hyacinths and hepaticas and polyanthus were in bloom, and his wallflowers were showing red and gold, reminded him that man is born to suffer interference. This north wind said "Yah, I'll show you! Talk of teleology! What about me?" And even though there were soft things to be said of this north wind, how it pulverized and prepared the heavy soil ridged up in the vegetable garden, and helped towards granulation, Sorrell scowled at it as at an enemy over whom he had no control.

He would go out to see that the protecting bracken had not been blown away from sheltering some delicate child, or that the osier hurdles were standing up to that blustering beast of a wind. He would find Bowden looking black as thunder, glowering like some old English archer lusting to plant an arrow in the deeps of the north-wind's midriff.

"Pretty beastly, Bowden. Good for the soil."

"My soil's all right. That b—y wind ain't no use to me."

"Keeping the fruit buds back."

"O,—that may be. Don't owe it no thanks for that. B—y lot it cares about fruit buds."

Effort,—always effort, a man's little contrivings flouted by forces that blow through all his neat, teleological schemings. The managing of an hotel was a far simpler affair than managing a garden, provided you got the human element well trained; and in these days the Pelican ticked like a good chronometer. No trouble at all, thanks to Fanny Garland, and Mrs. Marks, and Hulks, and the rest of them. But a north-east wind! Wow! And the wallflowers looking miserable, and the little daisies braving it with pinched, red noses. It was his garden that kept alive in Sorrell the combative spirit. You might tame men and money and machines, and terrorize marauding children, but Nature—she fought you with teeth and finger-nails. Well, —well——!

About eleven o'clock, when Sorrell was checking the store of wine in the Pelican cellars Hulks brought in a telegram. It was from Christopher.

"Expect me this afternoon."

Sorrell stood holding the telegram in his two hands. The paper trembled very slightly. The north-east wind had planted in him one of those restless and vaguely expectant moods when the heart of man is ready to be troubled. Why was his son coming down so suddenly? For all that he knew God was in Kit's heaven and all was well with his world. Assistant-surgeon at St. Martha's! An appointment gloriously celebrated and just ten days old, and the firm of house-agents offering Sorrell the opportunity of purchasing a house in Welbeck Street.

Even in the warm deeps of the cellar Sorrell seemed to feel the bitter interference of that north-east wind.

"All right. You might tell Mrs. Marks to send one of the girls over to have Mr. Christopher's room prepared."

"Yes, sir."

And Sorrell stuffed the piece of paper into his pocket.

Mr. Christopher Sorrell arrived about tea time. The Pelican motor-bus had been dispatched to Winstonbury station to meet him and Hulks carried Mr. Christopher's suitcase to the cottage. Father and son met there, in the garden, under the old pear tree where pale gold buds flickered in a moment of transient and windy sunlight. Kit looked cold, far colder than his father who was muffled up in an old ulster.

"All right, old chap?"

Sorrell's eyes were affectionately observant. He thought Kit had less than his usual colour, that he looked rather like a man just recovered from an attack of 'flu. But of course it was a beast of a day, ugly. Even the garden looked ugly.

Kit smiled, but it was a self-conscious smile.

"It's jolly cold."

"Tea's ready."

"Good."

Sorrell felt that somehow or somewhere all was not well. He knew his Christopher even better than he knew his garden, and therefore said the less, and became busy with the fire and the dish of buttered toast on the trivet, and the brass kettle on the hob. Kit drew up his chair and spread his hands to the fire, and his face seemed to relax a little. Something had stiffened it; worry or that infernal wind.

They had tea. Their pipes came out, and while Kit filled his and paused to stare at the fire, his father put a match to the bowl of his long "briar," and with an air of attentive unconcern.

"Ever had 'wind up,' pater?"

Sorrell remained very still, restraining an impulse that would have made him look at his son.

"Often. One does. Inevitable—you know."

Kit lit his pipe, and the hand that held the match was very steady. Sorrell noticed that.

"How did it take you?"

"O, various ways. Quite silly—at times. Like going on parade the first time you have to handle a company. Sort of speechlessness, feeling sure you are going to give a wrong order,—make a fool of yourself. But—one doesn't."

"You didn't."

"Just missed it—somehow. And then again,—like your first day in the trenches, in a devil of a funk and afraid of

it; feel you must do some silly thing just to show the men—
quite unnecessary, but quite natural. Always—before some
new big or strange occasion. Especially if you happen to
be sensitive——"

He ceased, and puffed steadily at his pipe, while Kit,
drawing forward on his chair, with his elbows on his knees,
seemed to absorb the warmth of the fire and another warmth
that was his father's understanding sympathy.

"I had it badly last night."

"O," said Sorrell, "how's that?"

"Good for my conceit,—I suppose. Simply took me
like an attack of gastric 'flu. It is my first big 'op.' to-
morrow."

Sorrell nodded a slow, wise head.

"Yes,—Kennard is laid up,—and I have to do the thing
for him. A pretty tricky case, a papilloma of the bladder,—
apparently. Depends a bit on what you find,—and on your
fingers. The idea did not worry me at first—and then—
suddenly——"

He bit hard on the stem of his pipe.

"Realized I should be the centre of everything, responsible, in the big theatre, full of students, critical, with
that hard-eyed old tough of an instrument sister—Nurse
Biggar—squinting at my hands. It came on me suddenly,
—supposing I make a fumbling mess of it, get stage
fright——. Men do,—you know."

Again Sorrell nodded.

"Some. I suppose there is always this first test; elimi-
nation. The climber has to face his first nasty bit of fly-
crawling. But—you—will be all right."

He looked at his son.

"How do I know? Because I feel sure of it,—somehow.
After all these years—it wouldn't be possible. Not for
me——"

"Pater!" said Kit suddenly,—and held a sidelong hand
towards his father.

"Not for me—old chap. Impossible——"

"To let you down."

"O,—not that—only."

He sat and stared at the fire, and his face seemed to
grow luminous.

"I should like to be there."

"Pater,—would you?"
"I should."

4

The wind changed in the night, and when Sorrell looked
through his window and saw that no smoke was drifting over
the branches of the pear tree he claimed the omen to be
good. Yes, there was a soft moist breathing from the
south-west, a movement with balm and beauty in it, and
as he stood at his window he saw that the face of the earth
had relaxed. No longer was it grey and embittered, but
dewy and gentle; the birds were singing, and as he stood
there Sorrell's heart uttered an inarticulate prayer. "O,
blind and incalculable malice, and all cold, interfering circumstance, go where the north wind has gone—this day."

Descending early to breakfast he heard Kit splashing
in his bath. A cheerful sound—that, not suggestive of
nerves and morbid self-consciousness, and while waiting
for his son, Sorrell strolled out into the garden and exchanged a few words with his flowers. They were looking
happy, and the hyacinths were scenting the air. He bent
down and propped with twigs two or three brilliant heads
that had had to bow before the wind.

He heard his son's voice.

"Shall I make the tea, pater?"

"I'm ready. What have they sent us over?"

"Porridge, and kidneys and bacon. I'm hungry."

Sorrell turned to go in, smiling back at his garden. A
bath and a good hunger, and the sun shining upon the grass,
and the birds singing! Well,—well. He had a feeling that
he need not be afraid.

5

Sorrell walked with his son up the long, white-tiled corridor out of which other brilliantly white spaces opened.
They came to a brown stairway going up in the whiteness
of the wall, and here Kit paused.

"Up there, pater."

He smiled.

"One of the middle rows. Suppose you will be all
right?"

Sorrell smiled back into his son's eyes.

"I think so, old chap."

Leaning upon the metal rail half-way up the tier of
polished wooden steps Sorrell became all eyes and ears,
and expectant consciousness. He was aware of the extraordinary stillness of the theatre, a warm and polished
stillness. Something was making a queer, humming sound,
like a kettle purring on a hob, and the sound was pleasant.
Young men slipped into the places about him and remained
silent or spoke to each other in undertones. How impartial
they all seemed! He watched Nurse Biggar of the in-
struments, a tall, lean woman, with a buttoned-up mouth
and eyes like black currants, whose every movement seemed
automatically precise. The other nurses were mere shadows
beside her. She was the genius of the place, mistress of
those glass cabinets with all their surgical glitter. He was
conscious of the soft, moist heat. The arteries at his
temples throbbed slightly. His mouth felt dry, and under
his ribs a knot of twisted suspense made him keep biting
at his moustache or stroking it with a thin first finger.

A voice whispered near him.

"A tricky bit of work for one's first. Shouldn't like it."

Someone whispered back.

"O, Sorrell's all right,—a man who has boxed for the
'Varsity. Stout stuff."

And Sorrell reached out a glowing invisible hand towards
the whisperer.

Then he saw his son in that space below, swathed in
white, masked, talking to a grotesque figure with an immense head that looked too heavy even for his thick body.
It was Orange. Sorrell had met Orange. Those intelligent
brown eyes looked up at him for a moment and filled with a
flicker of light. Kit's eyes glanced upwards in the same
direction, and smiled. Sorrell nodded, and wondered what
his own smile was like.

A reclining figure was wheeled in, with the anæsthetist
holding a mask over its face. A quiet and orderly activity
commenced. House-surgeons and nurses got busy; the two
surgical dressers waited; someone had brought the anæsthetist his stool and table. Sorrell saw all this but
vaguely, for his eyes were on his son who was standing with
his two gloved hands together like the effigy of a devout

knight in a church. He was talking quietly to Simon Orange.

Other things were happening; figures were busy about the figure on the table. Its legs were being trussed up, an irrigator prepared. Kit and Orange stood by and observed all that the lesser people were doing. Biggar, the instrument-sister, came and fitted a little electric lamp to Kit's forehead, and to Sorrell it seemed to glow like a jewel above that intent and quiet face. Kit was pale, but not so pale as his father felt.

Sorrell gripped the rail and prayed, not consciously, but with a kind of yearning, an outpouring of his will-force, his pride and love.

It began. A white blade drew a steady line that grew red upon the pale abdomen. Sorrell watched. The incision deepened; swabs were at work, retractors; forceps were clipped on; the unconscious and gently palpitating figure seemed surrounded by grave and interested faces, and calm, purposeful hands. To Sorrell Kit's hands seemed to move slowly, with a blessed deliberation. Never had his father seen so intent and absorbed a face. He thanked God for it! He kept very still.

The work went on. Kit's right hand was in that red and white cleft; he was feeling something, his eyes at gaze over the curly black head of the house-surgeon who stood opposite him. He smiled faintly, and said a few words to Orange who was behind him. Orange nodded.

"Difficult!" thought Sorrell, "O, Lord!"

Christopher introduced a speculum. He had to enlarge the wound, and cut one of the rectus muscles. Everyone was very still, critically and interestedly still. Orange's big head seemed to hang forward as though the whole force of him was concentrated upon something. Sorrell never saw his lips move. Difficult! And to Kit's father it seemed that his son was bending for hours over a hole in a body, groping, niggling with a knife, peering, a man absorbed. And Sorrell wanted the end, the result. His arteries were buzzing. He felt that he had no legs. He leaned heavily upon the rail.

Presently there was a species of stir, a sort of rustling amid those intent figures. Something had happened; something critical, and for a moment Sorrell closed his eyes.

When he opened them again Orange was smiling, luminous and sombre, and a substance was lying on a dish. And Kit was peering into that dim, warm interior.

Suddenly he straightened, as though to stretch his muscles and to ease his back. He turned, and his eyes sought a face. He smiled at his father.

Sorrell stumbled up the steps and along a gallery, and down another flight of steps into the white corridor. A sudden blindness came upon him. He fainted.

But Kit never knew of that fainting fit.

XXXII

I

SORRELL, having purchased No. 107 Welbeck Street, had put in a firm of painters and decorators, and when these had departed, a vanload of furniture arrived by road from Winstonbury. A waiting patient looking idly out of a window of No. 106 saw "William of Winstonbury" painted in white upon the green van. For two years or more Sorrell had been collecting the furniture for that portion of Kit's house which would matter, and it had been stored in the Winstonbury warehouse, beautiful eighteenth century pieces, much of it Queen Anne. China too, and prints, and needlework pictures, and old Sheffield plate and silver. Williams, now a partner in that very stirring business, had added to it a large shop in the High Street where the more modern minded could be supplied with everything from a mock-antique four post bedstead to a soap dish. The Young William and the Old William both flourished exceedingly.

The furnishing of this house was to Sorrell like the putting of a last and delicate polish upon the casket of his son's career. It was done lovingly, and with the sensitive satisfaction of a man who had come to realize that beauty in line and in texture has a mysterious and sweet permanence. The mellow sheen of the wood, and the gentle richness of the old colours were a perpetual delight, and in wandering over Kit's house Sorrell knew that most secret joy, the perfume rising from the full flower of accomplishment.

"I can do no more," he thought.

And so thought his son, touched and a little troubled, and perhaps in his heart of hearts vaguely self-critical. If ever a man had had the path of his career blazed for him and made easy——! Yet, he understood his father's reasons, the shrewd and steady purpose of the old gladiator who had fought in the commercial arena, and who knew that the money struggle is not the truest test.

"You are doing too much for me, pater."

Handling lovingly a Famille-Rose bowl Sorrell defended his plan.

"Am I? Well,—I have just about finished. And if you had not backed me what would have been the use? I have had to use an axe, because I wanted you to have your chance to handle a much more delicate and valuable weapon. I wanted to save you the baser scuffle."

"It might have made me soft."

"It might. But it is plain to me that you have had your struggles, your effort; different from mine. And here you are."

One autumn evening Kit stood in front of his glass pulling at the bows of a black dress tie. His dinner-jacket and waistcoat had been laid out on the bed. A pleasant silence reigned in the house, his house, though he had sub-let certain rooms and facilities to Miss Rebecca Morrison, a lady gynæcologist, and Dr. Eustace Weymouth, a specialist in diseases of the skin. There were the three brass plates upon the apple green door. Moreover, a few patients came daily to consult Mr. Christopher Sorrell, unexpected people sent to him out of the seemingly unknown. Their coming still continued to surprise him a little. One young surgeon in the centre of all this complex crowding! He had heard of men waiting for years for work that never came, and making successful marriages in order to be able to wait still longer, or drifting in the end to some more obscure but equally useful field. Some of these patients he could trace to the influence of old Gaunt, others to Orange, but a number came from old St. Martha's men in country practices. Sir Ormsby had retired, but people continued to ask him questions, if they could not command his skill. "Recommend me someone. Not one of your smart fellows. A straight man who won't slash me just for the kudos or the guineas." They did not put it quite so crudely, but Sir Ormsby understood them very well. "Go and see Mr. Christopher Sorrell, 107, Welbeck Street. Young, but absolutely straight. Most able chap. You can trust him."

Christopher was dining at Chelsea. Driving in a taxi through the ordered confusion with its ever increasing glare, he thought of his father before his cottage fire, probably reading some bulb catalogue or a book on soils. Sorrell had ceased to care for London; in fact he actively disliked it, and Kit could fancy him thinking the words—even if he did not utter them—"Different in my day." When Sorrell thought of London he thought of it as the London of hansom cabs, and when it was possible to walk along Oxford Street without becoming involved in "that crowd of idle and superfluous women." His mind had become reminiscent. All that appeared ordinary to Kit, the absurd crowding, the noise, the thundering herds of motor buses, seemed strange and alien to the father.

The Rolands were people who contrived to look ahead, ironically, perhaps, but their irony was pleasant. Kit enjoyed these evenings at Chelsea. He had to be very much on the alert there, with a live twinkle in his eyes, his serious workaday tail left behind him. It was a house of laughter, mellow and mischievous and kind, the *Punch* attitude to life; mature, invaluable. It corrected Kit's too much seriousness. It gave him that very necessary glass of champagne.

Kit sat on Cherry's left. A very pale young man posted somewhere across the table and wearing enormous spectacles and speaking with a slight lisp, said that some book or other was like an aeroplane dropping bombs. Kit was watching the young man's pink, crimped mouth. And Cherry, fingering the stem of a wine glass, glanced at Kit remindingly out of her rogue's eyes.

"Read it,—I suppose?"

"What?" asked Kit.

" 'The Amazon.' "

"The river?"

"No,—my child, Molly Pentreath's latest."

Kit had not heard of the book.

"I read her 'Broken Pottery.' "

"Like it?"

"I thought it a beast of a book."

He saw that he had amused her.

"Well,—I can't help it, Cherry. I used to know Molly Pentreath as a kid. She raised a bump on my head with a croquet mallet."

"She raises bumps now, my dear."

"I dare say she does. Same sort of croquet mallet. And she used to cheat like blazes."

"Be careful. I know her."

"Do you?" said Kit, and he felt a desire to be told what Miss Pentreath had grown into, but Cherry did not tell him. She had duties to a rather dull little man on her right who wrote very serious books on ethnology, and brought his own bread with him when he went out to dine. Kit had heard him saying "No sugar, please, no sugar," and Kit thought that he looked like it. To Cherry he was something of a saccharine responsibility.

Some two weeks later Mrs. Roland met Molly Pentreath at the Minerva Club. It was the occasion of one of the Minerva guest nights when the members collected a selection of male celebrities and poked fun at them. Molly and Cherry Roland happened on each other in the smoking-room. The speeches had been very boring; the fish had shown themselves shy.

"Hallo. I had someone dining with me the other night who used to know you."

"Who's that?"

"Christopher Sorrell."

Molly looked straight and hard into Cherry's eyes.

"Oh, old Kit-bag! I hear about him occasionally from my brother. An appendix-snatcher, isn't he?"

"We are rather fond of Kit. He told me that he had read your 'Broken Pottery.'"

"Poor lad!"

"Yes. He said that he thought that it was a beastly book."

Miss Molly Pentreath laughed.

2

Kit, being of a wholesomeness that needs exercise and cannot live to the top of its bent without it, took to fencing, and became a member of the Foil Club. Also he walked, varying his objectives or terminal pylons, and the chief of them were Kensington Palace, the Roman Catholic cathedral at Westminster and the northern boundary of Regent's Park. He had walked through this park on one of those bland March days when the virago month becomes treacherously gentle, and had sat down on a seat in one of the side-walks. The sun shone; there was not a cloud in the sky; he saw daffodils nodding heads of sensuous gold, and beyond a grove of budding lilacs a row of old houses spread a glimmering whiteness.

Kit heard shouts, a scuffling of young feet. Half a dozen urchins, having with a lucky stone shot broken the wing of a sparrow, had captured the creature, tied a thread to one of its legs and attached a white paper bag to the other end of the thread. Then, they had let the bird go, and were following up its desperate and broken little flutterings, shying their caps at it, and shouting.

Kit got up to intervene, but someone else was before him, a tall girl in soft apple green who rose with swiftness from a seat farther along the path. Her intervention was fierce and sudden, selecting the biggest of the children, and taking him by the coat collar. She cuffed him with vigour, and the boy, responding like the little savage animal, kicked at her ankles. Kit took two strides forward, and then turned and resumed his seat. His interference would have been superfluous, for the Green Lady went on with her cuffing until the boy had ceased to respond with kicks. She held him by the collar, and talked him into tears.

"Now—how do—you—like it? How do you think the sparrow liked it? You little beast."

Releasing him she went to catch the bird, and having freed its leg from the trailing thread and paper, she held it in her hollowed hands with that small group of depressed children staring at her.

"Who threw the stone?"

She got no answer, and stroking the bird's head with a finger, she turned fierce eyes upon the sportsmen.

"Just think—now. Supposing one of you were left out here with a broken leg, and with a lot of tigers about? It is so easy to throw stones,—but you can't mend a broken wing. No one can."

She left them dawdling and depressed, and with the bird in her hand went past Christopher's seat, walking with a fierce, swift litheness. Her green costume was touched at the throat and wrists with threads of gold. She wore a little black hat that came down low over her broad straight forehead, and from under the brim two jet black curls painted

half moons upon the white skin. She had one of those milky
skins, and a very red, wavy and expressive mouth, sinuous,
mischievous, fearless. Her dark eyes were equally fearless,
and they were bright and fierce when she passed the seat
upon which Christopher Sorrell sat.

His body swung forward at the hips.

"Surely—it is——"

He had not spoken, and she had not looked at him, but
he rose and followed her, wondering where she was going,
and what she would do with that bird. Molly Pentreath!
The same as of old and yet different, a brilliant, gleaming
figure sweeping with swiftness through the March sunshine.
She walked fast. Those long legs, the legs of the irrepres-
sible, tree-climbing Molly! And something in Kit thrilled as
he followed her. How she walked, skimming, a beautiful,
live, fierce, compassionate thing. He drifted after her,
wondering, like a drawn shadow. He felt that he had no
desire to overtake her, at least not yet. He simply followed
after her as though she were the figure of Spring, and he
a mere mortal man instinctively pursuing all that Spring
cried for.

She led him out of the park, and down Portland Place,
and turning to the right, struck out a course that passed
within a hundred yards of Mr. Christopher Sorrell's house.
She was quite unconscious of being followed. They crossed
Oxford Street somewhere near Selfridge's. Three minutes
later they were in Taunton Street. She entered a shop just
where a primrose-coloured delivery van was drawn up at the
curb.

· Christopher drew level with the shop. Costumes, a hat
or two, a pair of shoes, a girdle! He glanced up at the
fascia board and read the name "Salome."

"Of course!" he exclaimed to himself; "didn't Maurice
tell me?"

So this was Molly's shop where she sold Paris models
to the understanding few and the imitative many. He
strolled past, glancing at the window, and catching a sheen
of green. Proceeding a little way, he faced about and returned, and crossing the narrow road, pretended to be interested in an "antique" shop. A minute later he was
gazing across the road and through the glass door. Kit's
eyesight was very good.

Molly Pentreath had her back to him. A man was stand-

ing opposite her and very close. The first thing that Kit
noticed about the man was that he was wearing no hat.
His slightly bent and attentive head showed a large sleek
blackness above a large white face, one of those formless
faces, as though someone had flung a mass of dough against
a wall, moulded it casually, and stuck in two big coffee-
berries for eyes. The two figures pivoted slightly. Molly
had the sparrow in the closed hollow of her hand, and the
man was stroking the sparrow's head.

Kit rubbed his chin.

What the devil was the fellow doing there without his
hat? Looking very much at home too, and peculiarly
friendly. Intimate, almost.

Kit walked thoughtfully away.

3

Mr. Christopher Sorrell turned up at Chelsea some three
evenings later. Roland was out, and Kit had no quarrel
with Thomas Roland's absence, for Cherry was the person
whom he wanted to see and to whom he wished to talk.
Quite casually of course. His curiosity, a surprisingly aggressive curiosity had been pricking him. Very absurd, but
he would not allow that there was anything more in it than
curiosity.

Cherry was at the piano in the red and black room, enjoying one of those idle and solitary hours when music comes
and sits at your elbow. She smiled at Kit, but did not leave
the piano, and he sat down behind her, and at a distance, in
one of the black and gold chairs.

"Want to talk or listen?"

"O, go on, please," and she knew at once that he wanted
to talk.

But dallying with the notes for a minute or more before
turning on the square stool, she was more attentive to him
and the feel of him than Kit imagined, for when a potent
and purposeful young man like Kit arrived in the room
and set it vibrating Cherry caught the tremor of his un-
realized mystery and turned it into music.

"Tom is dining at the 'Savage.' "

"Is he? I have never been there."

"Get him to take you some night."

"I will. What's that you were strumming? Some new thing of his?"

"No. A piece of Ravel's. How are all the domestic arrangements at No. 107? Has the doctor woman——?"

Her rogue's look puzzled Kit.

"We made an arrangement. My two maids are splendid women,—but somehow they and Miss Morrison could not hit it. I don't know why; so I had to suggest to the lady——."

"That your two servants were of more importance——."

"Well, so they are. Rather awkward telling the good woman that her own sex wanted to call a lock-out. Now—there is peace. Wynter, a throat-man, has come in instead."

He nursed a knee, and looked at Mrs. Cherry's shoes, and seemed to meditate. And then he said quite suddenly, and with an air of bright innocence—"Who do you think I saw the other day? Or—I'm sure it must have been her." Mrs. Cherry became smooth as a cat.

"Dear lad, how can I guess—if you are not sure of the identity of the person you thought you saw? Rather involved——."

"Oh,—it was Molly Pentreath. She went into a shop, a dress shop; I believe she runs a shop as well as writing novels. 'Salome' was the name over the shop."

"Then it must have been Molly."

"I thought so.—By the way—who is the man?"

"What man?"

"In the shop—with his hat off—as though he belonged there?"

"My dear lad,—how should I know. Unless it was Oscar Wolffe—her partner."

"She has a partner?"

"I believe so. That is to say—the man Wolffe financed the enterprise."

"Who is he?"

"Something in the City; an insurance broker—I think."

"Not married—are they?"

"Have you forgotten 'Broken Pottery'? That's Molly Pentreath's attitude to marriage."

Christopher made some rather foolish remark about such an attitude being a pose, and Cherry, with an "O—no, my dear," turned again to the keyboard and began to play fragments from her husband's operas. And now and again she threw a few words at Kit, almost as though she was singing them. "One's view point changes. Old wine and new wine,—you know. Hasn't it ever occurred to you, Christopher, how marriage limits a woman?" He sat, attentive and silent. "Molly is one of those women who have no intention of being limited. There are women who are keen on their jobs—their careers,—just as you are."

She glanced over a shoulder at his grave face.

"I suppose so," he said.

"And suppose—for a moment—dear lad—that some tumultuous woman came and married you and shut you up in a house—and you had to look after the children—and the servants,—and the work of your life had ceased, and you were expected to be glad about it. How does that sound to you?"

"Oh,—I quite agree," he said, "that if a woman has a career——."

"Well,—Molly Pentreath has. And I imagine she believes with many of us that bringing children into the world —and all that—is for the specialists—the women who want children. All women don't—you know."

Christopher examined his finger-nails.

"Don't think me rude, Cherry, but I wish you would tell me——"

She swung round and faced him.

"Now—I know what you are going to ask me.—I had to,—and when we had to—we wanted to. Marriage seems to happen sometimes without your being able to help it. Besides——."

She sat poised with that thrush-like tilt of the head.

"Some men understand things,—and when they do——. Well, a woman's fine resolutions may blow inside out like a sunshade. But—the Mr. Gullivers——. How would you like to be tied to a Mrs. Gulliver?"

4

A week or two later Christopher received a note from Cherry Roland.

"Come and dine with us on Saturday. No formalities We shall expect you at 7.30."

Kit went. He had had a strenuous day, and feeling
pleasurably tired, he followed the maid up the stairs of
Roland's house with a quiet appreciation of its coloured
stateliness. The Chinese carpet under his feet, the soft
prints upon the gold brown walls, the play of the light upon
oak and walnut and lacquer impressed upon him their
soothing sensuousness. He heard a piano being played by
a woman's hands, and it seemed right to him that such a
house should be lived in by a woman.

Cherry rose to meet him. She was alone, and in her eyes
there was a mischievous gaiety.

"Hope I'm not too early?"

"No. The others are in the garden. Tom has just
bought an Italian well-head."

She moved towards the spacious west window with its
central arch and white flanking pillars. The panes were
full of the sunset and the dark branches of a budding plane
tree. Kit moved with her, aware of the smile on her face,
a glimmer as of sly dew in her eyes.

She stood looking down into the garden which was a
creation of Roland's, he having rescued it from a bare,
sour smuttiness, and converted it into a pleasant, stone-
paved court set with statues and clipped trees in blue tubs
and grey vases. Treillage painted a dark green screened
the walls. In the centre of the court stood Roland's Italian
well-head, and he and a girl were looking at it. She turned
her head as she spoke to Roland, and Christopher saw her
profile.

For a moment he stood looking at her while Cherry played
with her finger-tips upon one of the window-panes.

"You wicked woman!"

"How wicked, my dear?"

The gong thundered, and the two up above went down
to meet the two below in the hall with its eastern rugs and
old English furniture.

"See what I have produced for you, Molly."

Her surprised eyes looked straight at Christopher.
Cherry had planned a mutual ambuscade.

"Surely—old Kit-bag!"

He held out a hand, his eyes as steady as hers.

"My Lady of the Mallet."

She gave him a sudden smile.

"That's hitting low——. We used to quarrel——"

"Shall we resume it?"

Her open eyes, shrewdly and widely alive to him, turned a sudden slanting glance on Cherry.

"And he has read one of my books. A rather beastly book——!"

"O, come now, you two," and Roland's hand was on Kit's arm, "don't resume it here—please. And I'm hungry."

Sitting opposite to Molly Pentreath and looking at her across the clothless, polished table, Christopher felt a curious confusion in the midst of which his consciousness of her strove like a blurred light. It was she who confused him. He could not say quite why or how, save that there seemed to be something peculiar and unique about her, a sureness that was challenging. He remembered that she was a celebrity, and yet she struck him as being supremely natural and fiercely unaffected, Molly of the mallet, and yet a far more mysterious Molly. That was it; she had mystery, at least for him. She was unexpected. He felt that he had no more understanding of the woman behind those fearless and level brown eyes than he had of the mystery of life. The whole of her was disturbing, her glances, her movements, the unforeseen and unforeseeable flashes of her temperament. He was aware of a personal crudeness in the setting up his consciousness against hers. He felt that if he spoke he would say things that would sound platitudinous and Gulliverish, and that she would look right through them and him. Yes, she was brilliant, and her brilliance troubled him. It hurt.

They had arrived at the fish before Kit uttered a sound, and that was in answer to a question of hers.

"I hear you spent a week-end with Maurice."

"Yes."

Nothing came but that single, silly word, and he pushed himself to amplify it.

"I liked his house——. We played golf croquet."

"And Perdita——?"

"No. Only old Maurice and I."

"I suppose you beat him."

"I think I did."

She turned to say something to Roland, and while her
eyes were elsewhere Kit looked at her deliberately and
with a combative curiosity. He could not help wondering
why she made him feel combative, confusedly quarrelsome.
She was wearing black; and a green jade necklace hung
about her throat. He watched the moving curves of her
expressive mouth, and thought how black her hair was.

And suddenly she looked at him, and seemed to draw
the veil of her self about her with the haughtiness of a
proud thing taken unawares. He realized that he had been
staring and there was a quality in her quick glance that
reminded him of foil play, as though her glance were pressing against his and turning it aside. Something in her
resented the way of his studying her. Her face seemed to
grow thin. It was as though he had touched her and she
had cried out fiercely—"Don't touch me."

He reddened and looked at his plate, while the Rolands
exchanged a glimmer of the eyes.

"Have some more Burgundy, Kit?"

"Thanks."

"Had a heavy day?"

"Fairly so. In the theatre for three hours; rather difficult cases."

He had become suddenly possessed by a fierce desire to
swagger, to ruffle his plumage under the eyes of the challenging presence on the other side of the table. Why should
she resent his looking at her admiringly? For he had been
admiring her.

He began to talk, and the more forcibly he talked, the
more silent grew that other presence. She was watching
him, appraising him just as he had done while she had been
chatting to Roland. He felt it, and he resented it. He began to think of her as a clever, satirical, enigmatic young
woman.

5

Cherry was singing, and a full moon had risen and was
shining upon Thomas Roland's garden. He had opened the
window before his wife's hands had touched the piano, and
standing there and looking down into the garden, with the
smoke from his cigar spreading out into faint, horizontal

films, he appeared to be listening. The April night had a
soft warm breath.

Cherry's voice ceased, and with her hands still resting
on the keyboard she sat and waited.

"Lovely night," said the man at the window; "come along
you two and see my garden by moonlight."

He paused by the piano.

"Sing, Cherry, sing. You should hear her voice dropping down into the garden, with my Narcissus listening——"

Molly Pentreath was given a cloak, and refused it, and
had it placed upon her shoulders by Roland's insisting
hands. He led them out to look at the white figures of his
statues, and the shadows cast by them upon the moonlit
stones, and at the well-head with its circle of blackness.
Christopher stood beside the figure of the Dancing Faun,
and opposite to him Narcissus,—one finger raised—seemed
to be listening to Cherry's voice. She had chosen "Samson
and Delilah." She sang it with passion and with a tenderness that made Kit bow his head as though he were
sinking into the deep water of her lovely voice.

A silence came. Molly Pentreath was leaning against the
well-head, while Roland looked up at the window of the
music-room.

"What a voice she has!"

In an underchant he sang a few notes of some song, and
then made suddenly towards the house.

"Wait a moment,—I'll get her to sing out of 'Cherry
of Chelsea.' You have got my garden, you may as well
have my music."

And he did not return. They stood there in the moonlight and waited, Kit by his statue, Molly by the well-head,
listening to some amiable, domestic argument that appeared
to be taking place in the music-room. They heard Cherry
laughing, and striking an occasional and casual note upon
the piano, and Roland's voice, big and deep and amused.

Silence. Two people rigid as Roland's statues. Kit
looked at the girl,—and the girl surveyed the moon. She
was a figure of irresponsive blackness, calmly poised, waiting
not upon him, but upon the music that was to be. And he
felt a sense of conflict within him, as though he were silently
wrestling with her silence.

"What did you do with that sparrow?"

She did not move. It was as if he had thrown an urchin's
stone at her, and her very silence—like a magic shield—
had turned it aside.

His sense of conflict increased, urging him on against
her silence.

"Did you wring its neck?"

Her voice came low and casual.

"No—I bought a cage for it. Either it was that, or a
twisted neck. Cherry is a dear, but she talks too much."

"Wrong," he said; "Cherry did not talk. I was there."

He realized that she was looking at him.

"The long arm of coincidence! Were you the man on the
seat?"

"I suppose so."

"Just a man on a seat."

He felt a trembling, a quivering of all his senses, and
this was new to him. Just a man on a seat! Well—very
likely.

"I wasn't sure."

"No."

"I wondered what you would do—with the bird. So you
have got it in a cage at Taunton Street."

She made a movement as of drawing the folds of the
cloak more closely about her.

"It comes out and sits on the table. Full of cheek, quite
a cockney of a cock-sparrow. They are arguing about something up there. Good-night, Narcissus."

Kit followed her in, feeling flushed about the ears and
heart, and as she ascended the stairs she began to talk to
him dispassionately about poor old Maurice. "Safely
canonized," as she expressed it; "with a stained-glass wife,
and a holy bambino expected." Kit felt her level voice
trampling upon him. She carried the conversation into the
music-room and trailed it serenely under the eyes of the
two by the piano.

"It is just the atmosphere for Maurice. He always
looked at life as though it was just a nice church window,
all Burne-Jonesy—you know. No; I don't see very much
of them——"

Kit felt that if she had been ten years younger he would
have pulled her hair.

XXXIII

I

KIT'S passionate progress was a very rapid one.
Ingeniously learning, no matter how, that Molly
Pentreath went daily to her club and drank China
tea, and that the path she chose lay through Hyde Park, he
became a loiterer when his work allowed him to loiter.

But not as a suppliant. How the fierceness came upon
him was beyond his comprehension, nor did he attempt to
comprehend it when the leaves were showing, and the gilli-
flowers were smelling, and even those London trees splintered the sun's lances on shields of green. If Sorrell had
shown a fierceness in his struggles with the luggage, his son
showed an equal fierceness in this love affair.

As Molly wrote of him in her diary—"No 'if you please'
at all. Came striding down on me like a young Berserker;
eyes all blue north wind and sea scud. All that he needed
was redressing, a winged helmet, a hauberk, a shield, and
a sword. Anyway—you know where you are with him."

She did, and she did not—but that was to be a subsequent discovery. For to feel convinced that you are ten
years ahead of the most advanced of your contemporaries,
and not to allow that you are also the child of your hot-
blooded and ancestral past is to challenge complexities—the
most modern of problems, how to eat your cake and have
it. Kit disturbed her. She was supremely frank with herself over the sex-reaction as she called it.

She met him too with a level-eyed fearlessness. No
feminine tricks. He wanted her and she knew it; the
apple was nothing but an apple. He was waylaying her
almost daily, and she took no trouble to avoid him; she
sailed her ship on the same course, and when his Viking
galley came surging down on her she gave him battle. For
it was a battle, Norseman and Southern woman, as far
apart as their seas, looking at life with different eyes, and

339

asking quite different things of it. Even the language each
spoke had a strangeness for the other. Kit's directness was
a hurtling spear; she, with an almost equal directness, put
up an implacable bright shield, and thrust from behind it
with a sword. She was infinitely more clever than he was,
swifter, more temperamental, more subtle. He made her
think of a big, strong, blundering, generous thing, poignantly male, capable of supreme tendernesses and of exasperating exactions. It was not that he was obvious, or
that there were whole spaces of life that he did not understand, mere lacunæ in the male brain. He understood a
part of her only too well. The trouble was that he did not
or would not understand the part of her that mattered to
herself.

"What do you want with that shop?"

She told him.

"Independence."

"But with your books. You are much better off than I
am. A flat in town—and a bungalow at Marley."

"You interfering devil."

Interference may be flattering, but there were times when
she lost her temper with him, or pretended to lose it, and
said things to him that she thought were unforgivable. And
he had a way of turning rather white, and of smiling at
her, and of betraying to her another side of himself. If she
hurt him he would not show it.

"Well—if I do interfere, it's because I care rather damnably—and you know it."

"Does caring give you the right to talk like a bishop?"

"Your view of life and mine don't tally."

"Well—well! You missionary! Take Bibles to the
Chinese. Do you think I am to correct my way of life?"

"Molly!"

"Be quiet. The old bird in the cage idea. What an
obsolete creature you are—my dear."

"I'm old fashioned."

"Don't say that. It's such humbug."

"I can't help it. Besides, it isn't humbug. Nobody in
these days says 'I love you.' Why is it? Are we too
squeamish, and self conscious and self critical? Or is it because we don't believe?"

"I don't believe."

"No?"

"Exaggerating an incident. O, you know what wicked rot the whole thing is. And do you think I am not keen on myself? I adore myself and my work and my ambition, and success and the money I make. It is the breath in my nostrils. And you want me to fold my wings——"

"I don't."

"Demure wings—and think about dear little children. Little beasts! Can't you understand that I won't give up my liberty; I wouldn't, even if I cared."

"You don't care?"

"No."

There were pauses in the struggle, when both of them drew apart, a little out of breath, and she would not see him for a week, and when she had not seen him for seven days she would want to see him. Molly liked combat, the adventure of the thing, this passionate game with a man who was so very much in earnest. She had not said "Come hither"—and it was he who attacked, and so the responsibility of it was more his than hers. She had no thought of surrendering as Kit understood surrender, for the whole urge of her strong young nature was against the old time ties. She both loathed and despised them. Antiquated tyrannies and limitations!

She was free, and freedom is the most precious possession, the very crown of living, and Molly Pentreath had crowned herself. Moreover, she loved her work, her own particular job as much as Kit loved his. She expressed herself in it, just as the duller sort of woman expresses herself in her children. She had an audacity, an independence of mind that demanded a relationship that should leave her free, should she ever consent to give that part of herself to a man. It was not that she was cold. She had ardour, and also a fierce fastidiousness, but she refused to see in sex anything but an incident, and woman's fate had been to have this incident imposed upon her in the form of a permanent bondage. To Molly the idea of marriage as a career was so obsolete that Kit's wilful blindness to what was so obvious tended to make her impatient.

But his persistence and his staying power were equally obvious. He appeared to her as the born husband, a man capable of giving great happiness to a gentler type of woman. His duty was to fall in love with a dormouse, or some easy, clinging creature to whom his square virility would always seem splendid and final. Her own cleverness would always be knocking against the corners of his robust and rather simple stability. He was like a fine piece of furniture, good oak, lasting; and her mobile temperament revolted from the idea of being shut up in an oak cupboard. She preferred lacquer, something lighter and less solemn.

Their affair grew almost grim. He walked into her shop one afternoon at the very moment when she and Mr. Oscar Wolffe were making merry over some new Paris frocks. In fact she was trying them on, disappearing into the ivory-painted fitting-room, and emerging with mischievous frivolity. Wolffe sat on a stool with a sleek smirk on his formless face, and his clever little coffee-berry eyes glimmering. There was very little that Wolffe did not know. His broad and pulpy nose was a very organ of sophistication. His ugliness and his air of pallid sagacity were attractive; he understood the finer, decadent shades; he knew at once what was wrong with a dress. Nothing shocked him. He had the whole Monte Carlo culture vibrant in the tips of his thick but sensitive fingers. He made you laugh, and he made a lot of money.

One moment they were alone, delicately fooling,—and then Kit was there with a face like a white squall. Always this Mr. Oscar Wolffe had been stormily sinister in the back of Kit's mind, but he had never spoken of him to Molly. His interference had not gone quite so far.

Molly introduced them. They nodded at each other, Wolffe slyly secure on his stool and looking upwards with whimsical solemnity at Kit's stiff face.

"Interested in frocks?"

Kit was not interested in frocks. He was chiefly conscious of that solemn, pudgy countenance, so sagacious, so enigmatic. He divined the smile at the back of it, the ironical attention of the worldling who was pleasantly amused.

"I have tickets for the Haymarket to-night. Can you come?"

He turned squarely to Molly, interposing himself between her and the man on the stool.

"Afraid not."

"Oh, all right. Thought you might be able to. Just turned in to see."

He went out abruptly with the same fierce white face, ignoring Mr. Oscar and leaving that Paris atmosphere disturbed as by a rush of north-east wind. Wolffe glanced quizzically at the door.

"What a draughty fellow! Wanted to blow me out into the street."

Molly was looking at herself in a long mirror, not because she was interested in her reflection, but because she had realized the hidden violence of Kit's coming and going. Also, Wolffe's flat and watchful face was an embarrassment, like a full moon shining suddenly upon unsuspected emotions. She had not wanted these two men to meet. Each of them symbolized a part of her incompatible impulses and cynicisms. With little body movements she appraised the hang of the dress.

"A little too—rigid."

"Not enough flow for you. That young man ought to wear cast-iron trousers."

"Oh, he has his virtues."

"Not very flexible—I think. Reinforced concrete."

"No, not rubber."

She looked into the mirror with hard eyes. She was thinking that in half an hour she would be walking to her club, and that if she went through the park—and alone——. Yes, probably. One of those Norse onslaughts. She might take Oscar with her and interpose him like a big white pillow. But—then—did she want him interposed? So flabby and flexible and so sophisticated! A man who understood everything, and condoned everything. No passionate rage. All very well as a judge of frocks and as a playfully cynical sleeping-partner. But on the North Sea, with ice about, and a wind blowing, and a man on the prow of a ship with a live sword in his eyes.

No; she would go alone.

And so she went.

He was waiting for her inside the Grosvenor Gate, on the other side of the road, sitting on a green chair, leaning forward with a stick between his knees. Yes, like a man with his hands on the pommel of a sword. He came across to her, passing almost directly in front of the nose of a big car.

He looked extraordinarily serious, not angry now—but serious.

"What—exactly—is that fellow's business?"

Interference with a vengeance!

"Oscar? Oh, Oscar is an insurance broker."

"You know what I mean. What is his position with regard to—your business?"

Each spoke with nice precision and restrained distinctness, faces turned full south.

"He financed it. He is half 'Salome';—whichever half you please."

"I see. He found the money?"

"Exactly."

"And—what—precisely—does he——?"

He had gone too far, and she answered him with sudden, extraordinary fierceness.

"How dare you? Caddishness——. Have I to explain my interior motives—because—you——"

"Sorry," he said, with eyes of frank distress. "You are right. That was caddish of me. I'm sorry. But I do hate——; I think I'm a little mad——"

She seemed relentless.

"Indeed! That a man—you—should ask me such a question! If I choose to have an affair—what business is it——?"

"Molly!"

"Well——?"

"Don't mock me. Don't pretend. You—you couldn't make such——"

"Is it any business of yours?"

"My dear, it is——. I can't help it. I love you."

She walked on for some way in a still white silence. "Those old words! And the same old-man-of-the-sea meaning! You Gulliver, you Gulliver!"

2

There followed an interlude, marked in Kit by an impulse towards humility. He wrote and apologized. "I'm sorry

I behaved like a cad, and I have no excuses to offer. When may I see you again?" His letter came to her at a moment when she was standing between yesterday and to-morrow, at the summit of a little hill of restlessness towards which she had long been climbing. Decisions sometimes seem to happen of themselves, or a mood puts on the clothes of a considered purpose, only to find that it was nothing but the shadow of that very purpose.

The shop in Taunton Street had begun to bore her; it had become superfluous, for the success of her books had made her independent of it; also it absorbed too much time. She was finding herself a very busy young woman, in the public eye. Editors approached her, asking for articles and stories; her views upon the topics of the day had social value; her agents were suggesting that she should lecture, and the more provocatively—the better. She had found her career; her work fascinated her. As for "Salome's," it had been a piece of mischief, an adventure, a testing of her wits, and now she was ready to be rid of it.

And Mr. Oscar Wolffe? On the peak of her little hill she discovered with a self-questioning surprise that she no longer needed Mr. Wolffe. It was not that he bored her; rather was it that he had lost his significance. He had become frog-like, cold, and his humorous croakings vaguely irritated her. He suggested a white fog through which an urgent sun was beginning to shine. Clammy. Yes, he was clever and clammy. Their relationship had been a mere flirtatious, financial jest. He had expected more of it, as a discreet and sagacious worldling, always appearing perfectly dressed in an easy understanding, in no hurry to grab at his bone.

She decided to sell her share of the business. It was a paying concern and Mr. Wolffe could dispose of his portion of "Salome," head or bust or legs, whatever he chose to call it. As usual he would have made money. There would be no obligation, and over that she smiled a little cynical smile. Bad luck for Mr. Wolffe! She had been tactlessly successful. There should have been little difficulties, calls for additional cash, and therefore additional but unpressed calls upon her complicity. She had entered the affair with her eyes wide open, and she would leave it with them still more widely open, and wholly unabashed.

Incidentally she wrote to Kit, a letter that in the old
days might have been described as sisterly. She said nothing' of the change in her plans.

"It seems difficult for you to realize that a domestic partnership
does not enter into my scheme of things. That's to say—if I ever
cared. I am just as keen on my work as you are. I suppose it
is not easy for a man to get past his ancestral prejudices and to
understand that there are women nowadays who wish to be themselves. I mean to be myself, always and everywhere. I wish to
remain free. Cannot you understand that? And my love of my
job, and my revolt against interference, especially against that
particular form of interference that has made individual creative
work impossible for women? The sexual servitude, for it is a
servitude, argue as you please.

"Therefore, dear man, I advise you to eliminate me. I am a
Vestal. I suppose that I ought to feel flattered. But why should
I feel flattered because certain physical trixies of mine happen to
pique you?

"I am not your kind of woman. I am not the sort of woman
who could make you happy, for—in spite of the philosophers—we do
live for happiness, though its forms differ. You need someone gentler
than I am, someone more easily pleased. I get so fiercely bored,
and so quickly. I must be moving, chasing moods, and putting them
on paper.

"Take off your hat nicely and say good-bye, and in twelve months
you will be wondering what on earth you saw in me."

Yet, her curiosity remained alive after the ending of that
letter. She had made it sound so final, and yet she knew
that there is no finality in anything, but merely repetition.
She was centuries older than Christopher, who was in the
stage of seeing finality everywhere, in love and marriage
and work, and in those solid results that we call progress.
How would he react? Would he accept her decision as
Mr. Oscar Wolffe had accepted the decease of "Salome"?
With a sort of humorous shrug of the shoulders? She
thought not.

She did not see Christopher or hear from him for a
fortnight. She should have guessed that her lover had been
to Chelsea, and that women—mothering women—pass on
good news to their adopted children.

"Molly has decided to sell that business. You see, her
books matter. She is the rage."

And Kit had walked back from Chelsea with a glow of
homage towards his lady. Magnanimous of her—that!
After the way he had spoken! It must mean—it could

only mean——! No, damn it, he was no prig to feel sleek and self important about it, but the event had a significance. Yes, she was big.

He wrote his letter, and when Molly read it she felt an immense desire to slap him.

"DEAR MOLLY,—I'm sorry, but I remain in chains. Won't you leave me the possible chance of a compromise? Let these twelve months elapse, and let us see what sort of prophetess you are.

"I hear that 'Salome' is dead, or transferring herself to other owners. I can't help feeling glad, because you are so much finer than you will allow——."

She dashed off a hot reply.

"DEAR KIT,—Go and be damned. Salome has gone because she bored me. And because my real work is the one and only thing. Man has no spoon in my porridge plate.—Yours—with utter sincerity,
                                        "MOLLY PENTREATH."

XXXIV

I

FROM that moment Molly Pentreath disappeared. She had let the flat in the Taunton Street house, and inquiries at her club produced no profitable information. Miss Pentreath had not been at her club for a week, nor had she notified the club-porter of any change in her London address. At Chelsea Cherry Roland had no news for Kit. She could only point out to him that Molly had a temperament, and that people who write books have a way of disappearing while they were "with book." But then, of course, there was the bungalow at Marley.

Kit had not forgotten the bungalow on the river, Molly's "Self's Paradise" as she called it. It stood on a small island, away from the shouts of little common children, and on a part of the river where humanity drifted but seldom. "No boatloads of cheap voices, no breezy young men, and jumperish young women. The skylarks over the water meadows,—and in the evening a green twilight."

It was a Saturday in June when Kit took a train to Marley where a blue grey and overcast sky overhung the green valley and the breathless calm of the river. No sunlight in June, but nature went her way, just as Kit went his. Molly's island had a name of its own, and having no notion of its whereabouts, he asked a porter at the station. The Pollards lay a mile or more up the river. You took the lane past Marley Church, and it brought you out on the towing-path within a hundred yards of the island. Or Kit could hire a boat at one of the Marley boat-houses and scull up stream. There was no lock till you reached Hambdon.

Christopher's mood was for walking. He left Marley red and old among its elms and poplars and went westwards into a world of willows and of fields green and secret under a heavy sky. The day had a melancholy, sweet stillness,

348

and on the hills flanking the valley great beech woods
gloomed. Silent, empty country dreaming dreams, and
English in its sadness under that moody sky. Kit did not
hurry, for there was no haste in the landscape, nor in the
glassy glide of the river, nor in the droop of the willows.
He was conscious of a curious reluctance, of a slow desire moving in a world of foreboding. Blind love wandering between the hedgerows, with a little flame in its
heart, and a vague foretaste of the eternal bitterness under
its tongue.

And why? Ah, why? This one particular woman, this
bitter sweet creature, whose own mouth had warned him
that she could bring him no happiness! What a fool's
passion! And yet he was conscious of the inevitableness of
it, and that it had the same quality as this English sky.
Tantalizing, grey, elusive, tricking the eyes with a promise
of pale sunlight.

But he went on. He came out upon the towing-path and
upon a deserted stretch of gleaming water, with the interminable willows feathering the banks, and the green fields
heavy and sweet. Not a boat, not a voice; rain in the west,
stillness. He felt a kind of shivering excitement, a hard
anguish. He turned to the right and walked on towards a
whiteness upon an outjutting boss of green, the bungalow
and the island. She might be there, and she might not.
An uncertain anger at the very uncertainty of it stirred
in him.

The bungalow enlarged itself. The island lay towards
the south bank, and was separated from it by a backwater
overhung and clogged with trees. The island stood feath-
ered with willows. It had a rough lawn and some roses,
and he saw the droop of a hammock between two old apple
trees. A deep loggia with its posts painted white ran along
the front of the bungalow, and Kit's eyes told him that the
loggia was not empty. He saw two figures in deck chairs,
the figures of a girl and a man. A green punt, and a
white dinghy were moored at the wooden landing stage.

Sorrell's son stood quite still upon the towing-path,
directly opposite the landing stage, and looked across the
river. He did not call or wave; he waited, and with a kind
of inexorable and angry obstinacy. All that was sensitive
and soft in him became ice.

The man in the chair sat up. Kit imagined an ironical wave of the hand.

He saw Molly coming down to the landing stage. She was in green picked out with cerise. She unfastened the dinghy, and sculled across, turning the boat under the northern bank so that she was facing Christopher.

"Do you want to come across?"

"I do."

"Get in."

Her face seemed to him absolutely expressionless, and during the crossing to the island they neither looked at each other nor exchanged a word. Mr. Wolffe was waiting on the landing stage. With intimate and helpful serenity he caught hold of the painter and fastened it to the iron ring.

"You are just about in time. It is going to rain."

Kit landed and watched Molly shipping her sculls.

"Usual June weather," he said.

She emerged lightly, and going straight to the loggia, reseated herself in the same chair. Oscar Wolffe was equally practical. Kit, seeing a third chair leaning folded against the wall, opened it, placed it on Molly's unoccupied flank and sat down.

No one said anything. They sat and stared at the water and the willows, until the one flexible temperament bent under the tension of the silence, and producing a cigar case, opened it.

"Try one."

He leaned across Molly with arm extended.

"Quite mild."

"Thanks."

Kit accepted a cigar neither as a peace offering nor as a challenge. He realized Wolffe's position, and understood it in finding himself one of the three. The fellow had sense, and the easy balance of the worldling, and Kit was aware of the need for balance. The two of them poised with that incorrigible slip of wildness between them! And Christopher was thinking—"Did she come down here to write—or because——? And how long has that fellow been here? And did she ask him to come? Anyhow—I'm staying."

He began to talk, and not to the reclining and enigmatic woman in the middle chair, but across her at the sallow and sagacious face, and the little brown chocolate coloured eyes of Oscar Wolffe. A sudden sense of power had come to him, of staying power, callous and untiring. He felt himself like a block of conscious stone bedded down in the green cushion of the landscape. Unshiftable.

He talked the most platitudinous stuff.

"Quite out of the world here. Where have all the motor boats gone to?"

"Good weather forecast in the paper. People go by opposites. That's the significance of a daily press."

"Low pressure system approaching over the Atlantic."

"Even the office boy is given a chance to talk about isobars."

Kit smiled at Wolffe's formless face. The fellow understood the game; he was something of a sportsman; Kit hit the ball over the net to him and he returned it, and they maintained these interminable rallies. Molly, silent and sunk in a kind of staring, cat-like malevolence, neither moved her head, nor raised an eyelid. She was the net, the inevitable net. An immense weariness seemed to possess her, an apathetic cynicism. The water glided past; so did life; so did men.

About five o'clock Wolffe pulled out a gold watch, and appeared to be making silent calculations. Was there to be any tea? With dry matter-of-factness he informed Christopher that he had to catch the 6.15 train at Marley. "Dining in town, you know. Not much margin." Kit looked at the willows across the river, and felt the mutterings of a coming storm, for Molly had risen and was stretching herself like some feline thing.

"You greedy things shall have tea. It is ready. I have only to boil water."

She paused in the doorway, looking back at them with eyes that seemed preternaturally dark.

"What time is it, Oscar?"

"Two minutes past five."

"If you two leave here at ten minutes to six."

Kit got up, with his hands in his pockets.

"I am staying the night at Marley."

She said nothing; but went into the bungalow, and Christopher strolled down to the water's edge and stood staring at the dark sloth of it, and Oscar Wolffe watched him. "That young man will get a scratching." He was quite sure that he knew more about women than Kit did; he had every right to think so.

2

Molly stepped down into the green punt, for it was more roomy than the dinghy, and the challenge to Kit was as obvious as she could make it. He bent down and unfastened the painter, and held the punt against the stage while Wolffe was getting on board, and Molly was slipping the punt pole from its straps. She stood up with the pole trailing, her eyes on Kit's.

But he, without a word, and with a tranquil and fateful face, thrust the punt away from the stage, and stood up and nodded at Oscar Wolffe. There was complete silence. The situation was accepted and laid aside for its ultimate solution. Molly began to pole the punt across the river, and Mr. Wolffe's formless and pallid face receded like a whimsical mask in which the eyes became two little expressionless dots.

Kit, with his hands in his pockets, watched the swirl die out of the sleek brown water. The punt swung sideways into the opposite bank, there was a mooring post by the steps, and Kit heard Molly's level voice, and saw Wolffe's response to it. He climbed out with the painter and fastened the punt to the post. The green figure joined him on the towing path.

Wolffe waved an ironic hand, but Molly Pentreath's head remained in profile. They moved away together towards the end of the lane.

Kit felt for his pipe and pouch, and filling his pipe, with conclusive deliberation, lit it, threw the match into the river, and considered the significance of the manœuvre. Obviously, she was walking with Wolffe to Marley station, hatless and in that green and cerise knitted frock. Would she come back? Her temperament was capable of taking her up to town just as she was, in mood and dress. If she did not come back there was the dinghy, but he realized that if he were left to ferry himself across in the dinghy it would be a passage of humiliation, self-tempted. Wolffe would go to that dinner with a pleasant smirk upon his face. And what a piquant little tale it would make when the first glass of champagne had begun to simmer warmly! The buccaneering lover left to soliloquize upon an island.

But Christopher was not coquetting with his sense of humour. He looked at the still water and the heavy hills, and that sky of amethyst threatening rain, and at the sadness of the willows and the fields. Yes, it was the very setting for his mood, sombre and inevitable, deep with a soft green northern intensity. He was in the very midst of it. There was no break in his purpose just as there was no break in the sky. That sophisticated farceur was out of the picture. Two figures were left in the green gloom, his own and Molly's.

He glanced at his wrist-watch and found that the time was six o'clock. If she waited to see Wolffe's train steam out of Marley station, and walked back at once, she should be on the river bank soon after half past six. He had half an hour's idleness before the battle, if battle there was to be, and he wandered about, smoking his pipe and exploring the island, her island. It was less than fifty yards long, and about half as wide, in shape like a green turtle floating upon the water. The backwater, overhung by willows and alders, had a mysterious blackness, and the murk of the water hid rotting wood and sodden leaves. And he thought—"What a place for a lone woman. All right in the sunlight, perhaps. But on a grey day or a wet one." Yet, he had to suppose that Molly liked it, and her liking of such green isolation led him towards the unknown in Molly. How little he knew of her, the real Molly; and leaning against one of the old apple trees supporting the hammock he fell into a contemplation of her hidden self. There was so much of her that seemed to him unknowable, elusive, secret. Clever—yes! Confound that subtlety of hers. There were times when he felt that he was being left to stare at her like an uncomprehending boy. To love did not mean to understand. Perhaps it made for misunderstanding, a blurring of the personality, conflict, repression? And then a rain drop splashed upon the hand that was resting on the hammock rope. He glanced at the sky, and then across the water. No Molly. The hands of his watch stood at half past six.

The raindrops increased. They were beginning to blur the surface of the water, making little, widening, vanishing circles that met and disappeared and were followed by other circles. The hammock was getting wet. He unhooked it, gathered it over one arm, and carrying into the loggia, hung it on the back of the chair that Wolffe had occupied.

That fellow! Was he chuckling in a railway carriage over a disconsolate fool, and catching Molly's satirical eyes?

He faced about, and then stood very still. Molly was unfastening the punt's painter. Her white face looked like a distant flower against the dim, wet greenness. She stepped into the punt, picked up the pole, and came gliding across with smooth fatefulness.

Kit went down to the landing stage.

"You must be wet?"

"O, nothing."

"I have brought the hammock in."

He bent down and held the punt against the stage. She stepped out, and leaving the pole lying in the punt, fastened the painter.

"Oscar caught the train—and the psychological moment. Let's go in."

3

There was a deep sofa under the window, and she let herself sink into it, with her head upon a black velvet cushion. Her neck, from chin to the low collar of her dress, showed as a white curve. Kit stood by the window. The room seemed dim and shadowy, with the overcast evening sky, and the rain steaming down upon the river and the trees. An early and green twilight covered the earth.

"How it pours," she said.

One arm, bare to the elbow, lay along the top of the sofa, and Kit could see the movements of her dress as she breathed. Her eyes were half closed. There was something in her languor which gave him a feeling of breathlessness and wonder, for her very languor seemed to embody a secret expectancy. The dim light or some emotion had softened her face; her young fierceness lay relaxed.

"I could not help coming here," he said.

His eyes were fixed upon the hand and arm that rested on the top of the sofa.

"Obstinate old Kit."

Her voice made him tremble.

"I asked Oscar to see me here on business. We have dissolved partnership, and there were some figures to be looked into, and one or two papers to sign. How did you know I was here?"

"I did not know."

"Guessed?"

"Partly. Came to see."

"And you brought a suitcase with you?"

"No."

"No."

"But you said——."

"I was bluffing."

"Then you are not staying at Marley?"

"No."

There was a pause, and the hiss of the rain filled it.

"What time is the last train?"

"O, somewhere about ten, I think."

He moved to the other end of the sofa, and sitting slantwise on the back of it, half facing her as she lay, he looked out of the window. The landscape was sheeted in rain. It dropped from the roof of the loggia; the feathery green of the willows seemed to droop under it. The hills were blotted out. And he thought how secret and strange this place seemed on its island in the midst of the river and the rain, and that he and Molly were alone together as they had never been before. Her relaxation, her sudden acceptance of their aloneness, had confused him. He could look at her hand and her arm, but somehow he could not bring himself to look at her face, as though he were leaning over the brink of a crisis and felt giddy and bewildered, and her face—shining dimly out of the deeps of the crisis—might make him throw himself over.

He was aware of a little, restless movement below him.

"Still raining?"

"It looks like keeping on."

"Lucky for you that I did some shopping this morning, or Man Friday would have found himself empty."

"I'm Man Saturday. And I can fast."

"Six eggs, six raspberry tarts, some Stilton. And I can raise a bottle of Pommard."

"Your rations for the week-end. But six eggs for supper! Is that necessary? We must leave something for your breakfast."

He looked at the hand. It was lying palm upwards now, and hollowed like a cup, and he felt an impulse upon him urging him to stoop and press his lips into the hollow of that hand. He resisted the impulse, and sat rigid, and tried to think of the rain, and the ten o'clock train at Marley station.

She turned her head on the cushion.

"It is not going to stop."

"No; it does not look like clearing."

"How final," she said, and stirred gently, and looked at nothing through half-closed eyelids.

Final! The word seemed to echo in him; it was like the crying of some bird in the grey of the dawn.

"O, nothing's final, unless——"

He lost himself for a moment in looking down at her dim face.

"Not even the weather? Our temperamental weather! It seems to have made up its mind——"

She held up a hand, not the hand on the sofa.

"Listen. On the water, on the leaves, on the grass. Drip, drip. And we two—on an island—with the grey green twilight——"

"It's—it's beautiful," he said with a voice of a passionate awe.

He saw her eyes looking up, and suddenly he seemed to fall forward, and his mouth was pressed into the hollow of her hand. He trembled. Something touched his hair; he felt the pressure of her hand upon his head.

4

At six o'clock in the morning Kit bathed. The sky had cleared, but a mistiness lay upon the water and the fields, and a hugely yellow sun shot arrows of gold at him as he swam up the stream. That cold plunge and the glow that had followed it were a part of the mystery of the moment, and when he climbed back into the punt and stood and towelled himself he was yet more conscious of the morning's mystery. What a night and what a dawn! The confused emotions of yesterday had come forth clearly into this world of green and of gold, with the deep eyes of the river shining, and the willows a shimmering grey green mist, and the beechwoods splendid against the rain-washed blue of the sky. He understood to the full the exultation of a man's tenderness.

He dressed, thinking of many things, swift, incongruous, chasing thoughts. He had a twenty-four hour's beard upon his chin and no razor,—but if he caught an early train that detail could be remedied. Yes, it was his duty to catch an early train. He was responsible now, sacredly responsible. Amazing! The suddenness, the exquisite poignancy of it! He bent his head between his knees and remained thus for a moment like a man faint. He remembered his father. Dear old pater! He would write and tell him at once that he and Molly Pentreath were to be married.

And suddenly he heard her voice, and raised his head and sat still. She was singing—or rather murmuring some song. He heard a clatter of china, and the song changed to a soft whistling. Absurd, dear, intimate clatter of plates and tea-cups! They were to breakfast together.

"Kit."

"Hallo!"

"Did you say two eggs?"

"How many are there left?"

"Three."

"Boil one hard and we'll halve it. Or I can do with one."

He heard her soft laughter.

"If an egg and a half——? I have a pot of marmalade. What are you doing?"

"Dressing.—I say,—Molly,—dear,—you will have to over-look a beard."

"I will. You may be able to persuade a barber man in Marley to break the Sabbath. Anyway—why worry?"

"I'm not worrying.—I feel that that old yellow sun had just been hoisted for the first time into the sky——"

"The Creation of the World."

"That's it."

"But we—arrived—together. No old rib business. Say, do you like China tea?"

"Not much."

"Well,—Indian. My coffee is like someone's sad past."

"Right."

"Hallo! Is there much water in the punt?"

"A little. Shall I mop it up?"

"Presently. I'm just about to time the eggs."

Kit ran his hands through his hair, and made some show of smoothing its wetness. He extracted a collar and tie and a stud from his coat pocket, and put them on, standing up in the punt and facing the sun.

"Ready."

She was standing in the doorway, and with a suggestion of swiftness he went to her, and grew suddenly and bigly shy, and touched her gently.

"It is all so very wonderful."

They sat down at the oak table, opposite each other, and while Molly was handling the old flowery Amhurst Japan teapot, Kit cut the bread.

"Suppose there is a train somewhere about nine."

He did not see the look she gave him.

"I dare say. Is there any hurry?"

His serious and happy face struck her as being poignantly innocent. Didn't he understand?

"O, no great hurry. But I'm feeling responsible. Rather a precious responsibility,—dear heart."

She handed him his teacup, and he sat stirring it, and smiling over some secret and sacred thought.

"Dear," he said; "if I seem a rather practical idiot—you'll know why——. Because I'm so profoundly yours—in all my thinking."

"I know."

She seemed to stiffen, to be ready to resist something.

"When are we going to be married?"

"We are not going to be married. Dear lad, don't you understand?"

5

For most of that day Christopher strove with her passionate ruthlessness. She had shocked him, and at first he had been unable to believe in her seriousness, but when he had realized it he knew the depth and the breadth of her. And she was unshakable. She lay in the hammock, looking at the sky, while he sat beside her with all his tense, old-fashioned chivalrous temperament contending with her newness, and finding itself baffled. For she had a rightness of view. He could put up against her the figures of sentiment and convention, and she put out a hand and sent them flying.

Never had he suspected such frankness or such intelligent honesty. Yes, she supposed that she loved him. Had she not given him proof of that? She had given herself. And did he expect her to give him everything that she cherished, to strip herself of her career, the work that she loved, all her passionate prejudices and propensities? Was that love? Man's love? While he and his work went on unchanged! And pots and pans, and domestics, and children! She made him realize that she disliked children and childishness, that she was not temperamentally made to be a mother. Noise, and napkins, and little raw egotisms, and disorder, and the eternal struggle of the mature mind with the little savage selfishnesses. "A woman who loves her craft has to choose, Kit. I have chosen. Intelligent egotism makes life intelligible. Children would drive me mad."

His stricken face hurt her, and she tried to soothe him. "Don't you understand compromise? I have compromised in order to love you. I give all that I can honestly give, and you cry out for more. Do you wish to drag every shred of me through the mangle of marriage? Is not there something better for two workers such as we are?"

"But I cannot take it," was his refrain; "not in that way. It's impossible."

"An intrigue?"

"Yes."

She broke out scornfully.

"Ah, you are afraid of the good women, the good married women who are more cruel than any beasts shut up in cages. They have no mercy on the animal outside the cage, the animal who refuses to come in."

"Isn't there some reason for it?" he argued.

"How?"

"The man—to—has to be——"

"Shame on you. Do you think I ask for a caged mate, a thing that slinks and fawns, and snuffles through the hypocritical bars? Why,—I'm working for your freedom, the worker's freedom, as well as my own."

Plead as he would Kit could not move her.

"There is something in a man you don't understand, dear."

"Ah,—the idea of permanence, of possession——"

"Something more than that. It is unexplainable—somehow—sacred. Everything or nothing."

She looked at him steadily.

"You mean—that you won't go on?"

"I can't go on," he said. "For your sake,—I can't go on."

He was as sincere as she was, and as obstinate as she was ruthless, nor would either of them give way, and in the cool of the evening they faced the river and the parting of the ways. She stood in the punt with the pole in her hands, waiting to ferry him across. She had borne the struggle better than he had. His blue eyes looked tired in an unshaved and haggard face.

"Poor old Kit."

He stood in the punt and stared at the water as she poled across, all the greenness of the world withered, and the setting sun red with defeat.

"I'm sorry, Molly, more sorry than I can say. If I had known——"

The punt touched the bank, and he stepped out.

"Never regret things that you cannot help, dear lad."

"It's not for myself——"

"Give and take, give and take."

Leaning upon the pole she watched him walk away. At the end of the lane he paused and looked back as though he were taking leave of something, but he did not wave to her.

"No, my dear," she thought, "you shall not kill all that is best in us."

XXXV

I

IN July Sorrell came to spend a few days with Christopher at No. 107 Welbeck Street.

Sorrell still retained that peculiar sensitiveness towards his son, and on the very first night Kit gave his father an impression of restlessness, of some inward hunger that was unappeased. For, indeed, Kit was restless, chafing under the hair shirt of his obstinate scrupulousness, feeling both a fool and a hero, and looking like neither. He had erected a prodigious and chivalrous fence around the memory of that June night upon the island; he had written one solitary letter to Molly and had received nothing from her but silence. He had not seen her.

But the erecting of fences is very well, provided that you cease to be curious about what is happening on the other side of the fence, and Christopher was curious, most savagely curious. Obviously, a very attractive young woman need not remain alone, shut up in a garden. There are other adventurous males in the world. And that some other man should seek to possess himself of what might have been his brought Kit such mad restlessness that the cark of it could not be hidden.

His impatience would not let him be. It gathered like blood on the knives he used, and in the wounds he made, a film of blurring restlessness; it seemed to weave itself into his diagnoses; it quivered in his fingers; it kept him awake at night. It would whisper in his ear "You fool, you noble fellow, you scrupulous ass. It is quite true what she said. You are afraid of the old women." Another thing that exasperated him was the fact that he did not know Molly's London address. He had not written to Molly. There was nothing to prevent him going to her club and trying to find out, but he did not go. He was a mass of warring impulses and inhibitions. And there were those tempestuous mo-

ments when he felt that he must leave everything; crush on
his hat, and rush out to find her, somehow and somewhere.
He had nothing to say. It was just a torrential and inevitable impulse, a crave, both physical and spiritual. He
wanted to see her, to be sure that she existed, to inhale the
perfume of her existence, to feed his heart upon it.

On the second night he talked to his father, like the boy-
man that he was. They sat near an open window, with
the dusk gathering, and a few stars pointing the sky above
the horizontal darkness of the roofs opposite. Sorrell sat
very still, in contrast to the quick and changing movements
of his son.

"Well, what was I to do? The big thing, you know,
at last, pater. I couldn't play with it. I could not let myself go."

Sorrell had grown impartial, but he had learnt to value
security. A nice and elvish cunning tempers a man's
maturity, and now that he had made that little green and
secret sanctuary for himself and filled it with flowers, life
seemed less disturbing. He did not feel things so acutely;
he was growing old.

"She won't marry you—because she is keen on her job?"

Kit nodded.

"Says that we are both workers."

"Well, is not that true? Why should a woman marry—
when marriage may mean the end of everything—so far as
her inspiration is concerned?"

"Pater, do you really believe——"

"Marriage as a career? O, for some women, of course.
But not for the Molly Pentreaths; not ordinary marriage."

Kit looked infinitely disturbed.

"You agree with her, pater?"

"Oh,—I don't know. Partly. She was willing to give
you a good deal, much more than most women are capable
of giving. Then, of course, there is Mrs. Grundy, very
much alive still, always will be, though she wears a hat
instead of a bonnet. Dangerous old lady."

"The problem seems as old as the hills."

"And young as youth. Each generation, and the same
old problems dressed up a little differently. What about
your own job?"

"It would not suffer."

"Through marriage? I dare say not. But any other sort of relationship, awkward, delicate——"

"Don't, pater," said the son. "I have made up my mind as to that."

The making up of Christopher's mind was more full of the subconscious process than he knew. We may design our ethical clothes to disguise our desires, the passion for complete and individual possession, the lust of the hunter to kill, all the old moral rages of the "jealous God," but the sublimated elements are there. Molly was wiser than the man.

Pursued, she knew that complete capture cannot be tolerated by a woman who has her life to live. Even as the Amazons burned off their right breasts in order to use bow and sword the better, so Molly knew that a woman with a creative urge other than the urge towards motherhood, may be happier with no breasts at all.

As she said to Cherry—"Kit thinks he is being the noble fellow, when he is nothing but a romantic male tyrant."

"I don't suppose he thinks about it—at all," said Cherry; "we go the way we are pushed."

"Every man is at least a lawyer. He wants the human document signed and sealed."

Incidentally, she met Sorrell. They were brought together by chance in Cherry's music-room, and the old gladiator and the Amazon sat down together and crossed glances. She had smiled straight into his eyes with a gleam of humorous defiance. She assumed that he knew everything, which he did. Their mutual introduction would have astonished Christopher. They seemed to understand each other from the very first, responding to a temperamental sympathy, those flashes—half intuitive—half inspired. Sorrell had given himself to his garden, but he was somewhat wise as to women. And as he looked at this frank, fearless, fastidious creature with her deep eyes and her expressive mouth, he thought of Kit's boyishness.

"Is it war or peace?" she asked him.

She understood his smile. Here was a man who knew something of life as it was lived.

"I am Kit's father."

"And his mother."

Sorrell nodded.

"A mother sends out spies to survey Canaan."

"Oh,—I am not a woman of Canaan. Why should I let your son hurt himself in hurting me? The problem is so simple if you remove it from social interference."

"Can one?"

"All social affairs imply compromise? Yes, and in the end a sense of humour."

Sorrell looked at her kindly.

"Kit is too much in love to have a sense of humour."

She suffered him to see her passionate seriousness.

"And I—cared sufficiently—to suffer from a sense of responsibility. He is rather a dear boy. He knows so little of the real me,—thinks I should be so easy. I shouldn't. I'm a temperamental devil."

"And you—know so much more of him."

"Perhaps. And you,—after all these years, mother and father in one? Yes, he has talked a good deal. You have always been splendid to him. He is so young still, so lovably young, always will be—perhaps. And I was born old, like one of Shaw's young women out of an egg. I am keen on my work——."

She saw consent in Sorrell's eyes.

"One's job. I know. And your job is not a childish one. Neither is Kit's. But in his affections—he is thorough——."

"I could be thorough. Loving one's job need not mean——. If Kit understood——. I can't lie to him, pretend that marriage should be a complete surrender. It might take him years to learn that,—and meanwhile—wreckage——."

"How did you learn it?"

"Oh, I don't know. Born with it. Ask the theosophists! But there it is. What is your feeling?"

Sorrell sat and stared at his hands.

"Feelings are complicated things. Kit has been my job—so to speak—all these years, and the completion of a job——. Rather precious. I allow—that a woman is bound to have a hand in it."

"You are not jealous?"

"That's the unpardonable sin—in parents. I only ask for the right woman."

"And I——."

"I think you would be," he said, "if he understood you as you understand him."

2

Tom Roland, leaning over his Italian well-head, and looking at Narcissus, while he smoked an after-dinner cigar, gave Sorrell the product of his reflections.

"Both right. But Molly is right for ten years, Kit for ten minutes."

"Is that quite fair? Some of us have an extraordinary capacity for caring."

"I know. Kit has. But then—it always seems to me that when a young man storms a tower with the idea of keeping it—and not just sacking it and treating it as a sexual orgy, he doesn't quite foresee the funny ways of the civil population. A tyrant is all very well. Your civilians have to be humoured. And Molly understands that. A dual throne, you know, and a happy handling of the fool mob. Kit might storm his town, but Molly is thinking of the fool mob that might be asking for free wireless sets ten years hence. Molly has vision."

"I know what you mean. If Kit——"

Roland caressed the carved stone.

"Stephen, old chap, hasn't it struck you that woman's cleverness is a different sort of cleverness from ours? In some ways I feel myself a sort of child with Cherry. And there you are! A clever woman may love the simpler sort of man,—and never let him suspect her cleverness. Contrasts. She spins a conspiring web about him. Something maternal, too. And provided that the man is a happy lad, and not an inflated—listen-to-me—my dear—sort of ass——"

"And not a bore."

"Oh, a woman will stand a lot of boring from her particular man."

"Aren't you rather flattering the women?"

"Some of 'em. As for Molly and Kit, these sort of problems seem to solve themselves. Things happen—if both parties really want them to happen."

Unknown to Christopher his father became the friend of

Molly Pentreath. She had taken a minute flat at the top of
a high building not half a mile from Westminster Abbey,
and Sorrell went to tea with her. Behind his son's broad
back—too! And Sorrell saw her writing-table, and her
books and papers spread about, and felt himself in the midst
of her young, individual, creative keenness. A thinker and
a worker, and full of adroit mischief. She had caught Sorrell's old time cry of "No secrets." She confessed to her
hatreds. "I don't pretend to like what I don't like. I'm a
bad citizen. I mind my own business and write about
other people's business. The only children in this block are
three flights down, otherwise I should not be here. Noise;
it is like a slap, and I want to slap back. Bad for one's work
—that. And I don't love humanity, and I'm not an im-
prover. God knows—there is enough work in your own job
without our making jobs for each other like the Socialists.
Nasty people. Want me to pretend with them that I am
thinking more of seeing that my neighbours are getting their
dinner before I get my own. I'm not. I'm cheerfully and
intelligently selfish."

She made Sorrell laugh.

"Does Kit read *Punch?*"

Sorrell thought not. Kit was busy with his job.

"Well, you can tell him that when he is caught chuckling
over *Punch*—I'll marry him—with reservations."

3

Sorrell went back to the Pelican, and his beloved garden,
but not before his gardener's soul had discovered in Molly
Pentreath characteristics that were worth perpetuating. If
Kit needed a woman in his life, well—Sorrell thought that
Molly might be that woman. She would bring to the comradeship the security of a subtle understanding. Her very
insistence upon individual freedom would make for freshness; and the fruit would retain its flavour and its tang.
Those flat, pulpy marriages whose only permanence de-
pended upon a commercial slavery that rendered escape too
costly! How insecure they were, for to be stuck in the
mud of a mutual boredom could not be called security.
Sorrell valued security, as men with gardens do. It is a high

wall built about the pleasance of a man's independence.

But on the night before he left for Winstonbury he told his son that he had met Molly at the Rolands.

"So—she is in town."

"And I have been to tea with her. I have seen the room where she works."

Kit had the air of wishing to ask his father all sorts of questions, but was baulked by his own passionate obstinacy.

"She once told me my infatuation would not last a year. —I should like to disprove that. But—then—you know, one is always wondering——."

"Whether some other fellow——?"

"Yes, just that."

Sorrell smiled at his son's broad and bothered back.

"That young woman has her career. If you realized her keenness,—dear lad——."

"Yes,—that is the whole trouble."

"You are jealous of it."

"I suppose I am."

"Because she refuses to jump over the precipice——?" Kit brooded.

"Pater—if she dared the precipice—I feel that there is nothing that I would not give up to her. Yes, all sorts of things. I'm not a fool. I understand—I think I understand—better than she realizes. But I can't help the way I feel about it."

Sorrell's eyes were intent, interested.

"Your feeling is——."

"There ought to be complete surrender. Not this bargaining, this hanging back. Life takes its leap. If she would take it with me she would find that she had taken it with a comrade, not a little petty domestic bore."

XXXVI

I

SOME days seem made for tragedy, and on that bleak January morning when Hulks brought a telegram to Sorrell's office, and Sorrell read it and then sat looking at the rocking and complaining trees, he was conscious of fear. The telegram had been sent by Simon Orange from a post office in Berner's Street at half-past nine that morning.

"Your son ill. Come at once."

Sorrell caught the twelve o'clock train from Winston-bury, and with his eyes watching the grey country cowering under the bluster of the wind, he too felt his spirit cowering under the menace of fortuitous happenings. From the very first his intuition had reached out towards something that was to be feared. He had felt it in his soul's marrow, nor was there any comfort in the thought that Orange was no alarmist.

His taxi broke down in the Marylebone Road, and he left it, and carrying the suitcase into which he had tumbled a few things, he walked the rest of the way. And what a pinched world it was, blue of nose, and hurrying and fretful. The faces that passed him seemed to suggest that nothing good could happen. Fear and insecurity, and a helpless muffling of body and spirit against wind and circumstance. Sorrell hurried, but when he came to the door of No. 107 he found that he was afraid of that door. He looked at the brass plate with his son's name upon it, and was absurdly reminded of a name as a coffin. He pushed the bell, and rallied himself against panic. What was the use of panic? A man could receive a telegram and not tumble into emotional forebodings.

When the door was opened he entered with an air of confident briskness.

"What's this,—'flu or something?"

The woman in black looked cold and worried.

"Mr. Sorrell is not here, sir."

"O, but I had a wire."

"He is at the hospital."

"Then he can't be——"

"In a private ward, sir."

She saw the rimmed whiteness of Sorrell's eyes. For the moment he was unable to speak.

"At St. Martha's?"

"Yes, sir."

She was astonished by his sudden fierceness.

"What is it,—what's all the fuss about?"

"Mr. Sorrell cut himself at an operation, sir. I don't understand—quite. Only two or three days ago——"

She stood watching his vanishing back, for he had turned and walked out of the house with that same strange suggestion of rage, lips pale, nose sharp and pinched, eyes brittle. She had seen fear before, but not that sort of fear, and she did not recognize it. She realized that he had gone off, lugging the suitcase along with him.

"Poor gentleman. One of the worrying sort."

As though a man was not justified in worrying when the labour of half a lifetime was in danger of slipping into the sea! For Sorrell had begun to feel so secure; he had founded his edifice so carefully, and watched it grow while he himself had grown old in contemplating its completion. So Kit had cut himself at an operation? A mere nick of the knife. But what—exactly—did it mean? Why all this panic, and a private ward, and the queer look in that woman's eyes? The mere nick of a knife! But Orange had wired——

At the hospital the porter said to him with that bland, English gentleness—"Hadn't you better leave that suitcase with me, sir?"

Suitcase! He had been quite unconscious of the fact that his concentrated grip had made the thing a part of himself,—and let the porter take it from him.

"Yes,—I suppose so. Mr. Orange wired to me——"

"I know all about it, sir."

"My son——"

"Yes, sir. Mr. Orange left instructions; he is upstairs, sir. If you will come with me."

From the warmth of a corridor they passed into the

bleakness of the hospital garden where the plane trees
complained above the dingy asphalted paths. A grim and
sooty rockery built of old bricks and clinker seemed to
contain the corpses of a few miserable ferns. The porter,
pushing open the swing-door of a red brick building, and
catching sight of a nurse, called to her. "Mr. Sorrell's here.
Tell Mr. Orange." But Orange was waiting. He appeared at the doorway of the sister's room halfway down
the corridor, and beckoned, and to Sorrell he had the look
of a man who had been fighting with his back to the wall.

"Come in here."

He closed the door, and stood with his big head hanging
forward.

"Sorry; it is rather bad."

He did not look at Sorrell, who stood with a rather vacant
and helpless air in the middle of the little room.

"Quick as you can. I may as well know."

"One of these septic cases. Kit was operating, and cut
his left hand through the glove; scarcely noticed it—I dare
say. A virulent bug. Cellulitis, left hand and arm. We
have operated twice. Kennard and Sir Ormsby want the
arm off at the shoulder."

Sorrell rocked slightly on his heels. He made a little
sibilant sound as though he had drawn his breath in sharply.

"Left arm?"

"Yes. Seems to be the one chance of saving him, if it's
done at once. What is called blood poisoning—colloquially
—you know. Kit won't have it."

"No."

"Says he would rather go under than be a one-armed
cripple,—career gone."

He looked up at Sorrell questioningly from under the
dark briskness of his eyebrows.

"What do you think?"

Sorrell was the colour of linen, his face old and plaintive
and grim.

"You mean—it is the only chance?"

"Afraid so."   .

"It might not be certain—even if——?"

"No."

"Can I see him?"

"He wants to see you."

"Good," said Sorrell, looking as he had looked sometimes during the war, and not knowing that he faced a forlorn hope with the eyes of death.

It was the simplest of meetings, so quiet and in its way so brave. Kit's face was both earthy and flushed. His left arm was a mass of dressings. Sorrell sat by the bed with a face that twitched very slightly, and eyes that hid their fear.

"My own fault, pater."

"O, no one's fault——."

"But—I want you to say——. Don't you agree? I'd rather go under fighting—than come out crippled."

Sorrell sat for a moment with his head in his hands.

"Life's good," he said.

"But one's job? Half a life."

"Let's take it fighting," said his father; "all or nothing."

He sat and held Kit's hand. He felt bewildered, and yet holding to some grim ideal, scared and sick and cold but obdurate. Almost he could remember the cold and clammy feel of a trench wall, with the sandbags close to his face. And death going over, and his feet numb, and his belly full of emptiness.

Then he understood that Kit wanted to say something.

"Pater, dear old pater——."

Sorrell's head jerked stiffly.

"I should like to see her. Would you——?"

"I'll go and find her."

2

"O, my dear, haven't you heard?"

Molly had come into Cherry's red and black room, as though life can be triumphant even when your enemy is only the weather. That rich, white skin of hers defied the cold, and her eyes glimmered with the wind. She wore black, a long coat with a collar of some mouse coloured fur. She had stood by the fire, throwing back the cloak like a sheath, hair and eyes gleaming.

"What? Not measles in the nursery?"

"No, Kit; he is dying. O, the poor father!"

There was a stillness. Molly had a hand on the black oak

mantelshelf and a foot on the brass curb. Her eyes turned
suddenly upon Cherry.

"What do you mean? I have been out of town. I only
came back this morning."

"Kit cut himself operating on some wretched case. It
is his arm,—blood poisoning. They still have hopes if his
arm could be amputated, but Kit won't have it——"

She got up and walked quickly to the bay window.

"The father has been here. Oh,—if you had seen his
poor face! He has been trying to find you."

Still that white silence upon the face of Molly Pentreath.

"All frozen, and a kind of burning fire behind it. O,
my dear, isn't life cruel! After all these years of devotion.
I don't believe a man ever loved his son as Sorrell——.
And then—just when success had come, and pride in
it——"

Molly's lips moved.

"He wants me,—to see me?"

"Yes."

Her whole body seemed to become swift and purposeful.
She refastened her coat as she went towards the door.

"Where is he?"

"At St. Martha's. His father was here an hour ago.
He has gone to your flat. Tom went to the 'club.' Wait,
—there's the bell."

Molly had opened the door. She stood there waiting,
listening to two voices. She turned her head and spoke to
Cherry.

"It is—the father. He is coming up. Do you
mind——?"

Cherry slipped past her and up the stairs, and Molly
went back to the fireplace. She was drawing on a pair
of fur-lined gloves when Kit's father came into the
room.

It was she who spoke first.

"Have you a taxi?"

He nodded, and sat down suddenly in a chair near the
door. He looked ghastly, and his distress was a wind that
went to the core of her. She saw his head go down into
his hands; he was faint.

She went quickly towards him, and standing by the
chair, let her hand rest on his shoulder.

"Keep still a moment,—and your head down. I heard only five minutes ago."

She felt him trembling, and her eyelids and lips quivered, but when she spoke her voice was very steady.

"I'm different—now. We will go to him as soon as you feel ready. There must be some hope."

Sorrell's figure straightened. There was an almost childish pleading in his eyes.

"He won't give up his arm."

"And you——?"

"I?—— Oh,—I said the same. I don't think I knew——. But if there is a chance——."

She stood there, with deep eyes looking down into the heart of life, her hand still upon his shoulder.

"Does Kit want to live? But—of course. And the arm——. We want him to live. If it matters so much to you—and to me——."

Sorrell looked upwards at her white and urgent face.

"To you——?"

"Yes. If I can help, O—yes—everything. I'll give everything. Let's go. Do you feel able?"

He rose; she slipped her hand under his arm, and her strong young body made his stooping figure look very old. But her strength was gentle. If she bent towards him compassionately it was towards a splendid veteran.

3

What two people say or do not say at such a moment in their lives is written in the sealed books of the gods. A few disjointed words, a meeting of the hands, a stripping off of all pretence, a throwing of every little personal bauble into the great furnace. So, Molly Pentreath came out from Christopher Sorrell's room with a shine upon her face, the woman eternally surrendering, and becoming sacred by reason of her surrender.

She met the group of men, Sorrell, old Gaunt, Kennard, Orange, and one or two more. Their eyes waited upon her. She had gone in to persuade a man to lose his arm and live, or take his last chance of living. She came out to them with wet and shining eyes that smiled.

"He wishes to keep his arm. I think he is right."

No one said a word, but old Gaunt seemed to toss his
head like a restive war-horse, and Orange stared at the
wall as though he were looking through it into some other
world. Only—Sorrell the father made a sound, a sort of
sound as of something breaking in him. And instantly she
was with him, slipping her arm through his, and pressing
it firmly.

In the taxi she sat very erect, holding his hand, and looking out of the window.

"I think he was right. To you it must seem such wanton
and cruel waste. But—I still hope."

Sorrell had passed beyond hope. He was feeling as old
as sorrow, a fatalist, and her hope seemed to him a mere
flutter of helpless wings.

"They—don't hold out any hope."

"Those wise men! But Kit wants to live."

She smiled at the passing show in the fretful streets,
and if there was any radiance left in life she had brought
it with her from that bedside. Sorrell's lamp was out. He
sat in that inward darkness, thinking of yesterday as some
impossibly serene and very distant past.

It was she who paid for the taxi, and in Kit's empty
dining-room she took off her hat and laid it on the sideboard.

"I am staying here. I can sleep on a sofa."

"No need for that," he said dully; "they can fix you up
a bed. I'm glad you are staying."

He wandered about the room, looking at the furniture
and the china and the pictures, and her next glimpse of his
face warned her that a mood of mockery had been forced
upon him.

"All this——! I collected every piece. Like the war,
being blown to bits—for next to nothing."

"O, no," she said; "things do matter."

His wide eyes remained fixed upon hers. She puzzled
him, the change in her, this flippant and brilliant thing
grown suddenly deep and compassionate. The whole quality of her was different. Before she had made him think of
a clean, cold, audacious dawn, with a little frost in the air.
But now——! Even her voice had a new meaning.

"I suppose you have had nothing to eat?"

"I'd forgotten——"

She rang the bell. The whole house seemed to be in her hands.

"O, can you manage some lunch? Mr. Sorrell has had nothing."

The woman in black disappeared, and lunch was forthcoming. She ate in order to make him eat, and at the end of the meal she continued her persuasion.

"Go and lie down,—or read. I am going round again to the hospital. No need for you to have to face that door."

His eyes lit up for a moment.

"How you understand! I'm getting a bit old. I haven't the nerve I used to have."

"That's not quite true," she said gently; "you had the courage to go out for all or nothing. I'm going now."

She bent down and kissed his forehead.

"I'm willing—hard, willing—and feeling. I am one of those who believes that it helps."

4

Molly returned after dark. It was raining now, and she had walked in the wind and the rain, and her face was wet with a little glistening moisture. Yes, a face of the trenches, of war, of a set and bitter courage, so Sorrell thought, but there was a gleam too of something else.

She found him hunched over the fire as though the very marrow of him was cold. Yes, she had been with Kit, not talking, but sitting with him and holding his hand.

"The temperature is down a little."

"What do they say?"

"Not much. But Kit is fighting, and fighting hard. Have you had any tea?"

No, Sorrell had not had tea. He got up mechanically and rang the bell, and when the woman in black answered it he appeared to have forgotten what he had rung for. He was staring at the fire.

The two women exchanged looks.

"Can you manage some tea?"

"Of course, Miss."

The woman in black had placed Molly by a photograph

that stood on Mr. Christopher Sorrell's desk. A stolen photograph—too.

"Mr. Sorrell is just a little better."

"I'm very glad to hear it, Miss."

When the door had closed she found Stephen Sorrell's eyes fixed upon her.

"Did you mean that,—what you said?"

She gave him a grave movement of the head.

"Two of us pulling,—you and I. He understands."

And then she went close to him with the air of invoking a comrade.

"You don't grudge me that, do you? I ·should never take him away from you."

"My dear," he said, putting out his hand; "if he lives, I want his job to live. That—and a comrade—make a man's happiness."

5

She came to the door of No. 107 in the grey of a winter dawn. The very pallor of her tired face seemed to be triumphing over the mere weariness of the flesh. She had a latchkey with her, and with steady and untrembling hand she slipped it into the keyhole. Someone was scrubbing the floor. She went past the inquisitive yet crouching figure into the dining-room where Sorrell was sitting in front of the fire. He was asleep, his head sagging forward, his hands on the arms of the chair.

She stood near and looked down at him with a little smile of compassion, and with some of her old mischief trembling in the corners of her mouth. The old gladiator, white headed, overcome by sleep and by the suspense of waiting! She could picture his head rising with a jerk, and his eyes challenging hers. *Ave, Cæsar——!*

She touched his shoulder.

He came to life, just as she had pictured it, with a jerk of the head, and a deep, harsh drawn breath. His eyes were both hard and eager.

"Well——?"

"Six hours' sleep."

"I?"

"No,—Kit. The temperature normal; the arm half its size."

Sorrell staggered up out of the chair.

"My God!" he said; "then, the arm and everything?"

She nodded.

"I left that Orange man with an awful beard on, grinning like an ecstatic ape. O,—my dear——!"

She had to catch him, and help him back into the chair.

"I'm getting old," he said; "my God,—I'm getting old."

XXXVII

I

KIT descended the steps into the Green Park, and after looking at his wrist-watch, strolled on down Queen's Walk. It was the first Spring day when the world had ceased suddenly from looking shabby, and the grass—sleeked by the sun—caught the suggestion of a young greenness. The hard eyes of the sky had softened for a moment, and even the faces of men—city men—looked softer and less brutish.

A seat offered itself and Kit sat down under the bare branches of a plane tree. At the other end of the seat two Germans—a man and a girl—kept up a guttural babbling over a Baedeker's guide. The pleasant and diverse façades of the houses warmed themselves in the afternoon sunlight, so individual and so English after the fashion of an England that was dead. Kit found himself gazing at one particular house built of mellow-gold brown brick, with faded blue blind-cases and a dark old balcony. A chestnut tree was opening its green buds against this background of warm brickwork flecked with blue, and Kit was touched by the beauty of it.

Yes, life was good. And he glanced again at his wrist-watch, and between his baskings threw an occasional quick and expectant look in the direction of Piccadilly. An old park loafer, seedy and shiny, had joined him on the seat, and producing a pipe, applied a match to the foul dottle remaining at the bottom of the bowl. Sot though he was he examined Kit with appreciative interest, and a shrewdness that was alive to the meaning of those expectant and quick turns of the head. Here was a young toff, waiting for a girl. Good business on such an April afternoon. And the little blue eyes in the inflamed face examined Kit's shoes and trousers and his clear brown profile, and then went on to discover the emptiness of a matchbox.

"Haven't a match, sir, have you?"

There—spoke the voice of a man who had known other days, and Kit produced a matchbox, and observed the patched boots, and the frayed trousers, and the greasy cuffs, and collar of the old black tail coat. The man was sucking hard at the pipe. His chin was all grey stubble, his nose and cheeks a network of little blood vessels.

"Much obliged, sir."

He handed back the matches, and smiled a yellow, broken-toothed smile at the fortunate one.

"Worth being alive—a day like this."

"It is."

"Even me. Dry feet,—and no draught under what you might call by courtesy a shirt. Nice bit of colour that, ain't it?"

He indicated the brown and blue house with the stem of his pipe.

"Used to do a little with the brushes—myself—once, till I started paintin' my nose. Hee, hee!"

He chuckled, and Kit felt the sunlight, and a happy man's human compassion. His hand disappeared into a trouser pocket at the very moment that he saw a particular figure floating on April feet down the Walk of the Queen. A surreptitious hand passed two half-crowns to a consenting and ready paw.

Kit stood up. So did the greasy one.

"Much obliged. Don't you mind me. The lady can have my seat."

He gave Kit a friendly, human leer, and with a considering and appreciative glance at Kit's lady, he raised his ancient bowler hat and mooched off with a contemptuous stare at the two Germans. Honeymooners! Boch honeymooners! Their lingo still smelt of that old and almost forgotten war. What the hell were they doing in England anyway? Made him think of the prison camp he had inhabited, and the German women who used to stand and mock at him through the wire fencing. He turned about for a moment to observe the coming together of the other two. English people, his people! By Jove, some girl too; moved as though corsets—and all tight constraints—were things of the past! The willowy, audacious, quick-eyed type, black and white. Damn it, he had always admired that sort of woman! A fine pair, and good luck to them.

Kit took the place that the derelict had vacated, and gave Molly his. The two Germans, suddenly and internationally sympathetic, arose and strolled away.

"You brown man," she said.

He sat sideways on the seat, smiling and looking into her eyes.

"I couldn't say what I wanted to say—yesterday—at Chelsea. The time and the place——."

"It is very good here. The young green——."

He bent towards her.

"Molly,—why did you make no terms?"

She glanced at his eyes and then at his tie.

"Does one,—when life rushes on one—like that? I surrendered."

"You gave—with open hands. And so—will I——."

She put up a hand and began to speak, but he took her hand and laid it gently on the seat.

"No,—my turn. I understand things better now. I have been thinking a lot—while I was away. It began during those days. Listen——."

His eyes had that happy inward look.

"Your job—as well as mine. We are workers both of us. I'm thinking that work is the worker's child. Half a house each, or a whole house each. Your—atmosphere—as well as mine. No cramping sentimentalities. We go and come as we please."

He covered her hand for a moment with his.

"That last book of yours. Great. I'm proud,—but I am going to be much prouder,—because I'm learning. I'm an awful kid, dear, in some ways."

Her hand turned over on the seat and clasped his.

"Some things are greater than books. Be patient with me, Kit, sometimes."

2

Sorrell had finished tea. He filled and lit a pipe, and after standing at the open window for a minute with a thoughtful face from which came rhythmic puffs of smoke, he went out into his garden. He had grown very grey these days, much greyer since the crisis in Kit's life, and but for the flowers at his feet his figure might have seemed lonely. For a while he just wandered up and down and to and fro, under the fruit blossom and between the beds of spring flowers. There was a wonderful show this year, the best show that he had ever had, and he enjoyed one of those rare half-hours on a perfect evening when the eyes see deeper, and perfumes are more poignant. He sat down on a rough seat under one of the fruit trees over against a half wild patch of purple and rose aubretia, red daisies, blue myosotis, purple and gold tulips, and burning orange Siberian wallflowers. His eyes remained fixed upon this richness; he puffed at his pipe; he reflected. It occurred to him that a man's last and best friends might be his flowers. They grudged nothing; they gave you results.

Yes, and how little in the way of results could most poor, flustered conventional lives show. Just pathetic rushings to and fro after the passing of that state of semi-savagery and vague rebelliousness which is childhood. Getting up in the morning and going to bed, catching trains, eating indifferent food, responding rather blindly to the sex urge, squabbling with other individual men or groups of men over twopence on the wage-sheet, going with crowds of other human cattle to some cheap holiday resort and finding the same stale crowds there. Never to be alone, or to produce anything of significance, save perhaps a few children who would repeat the same obscure slave's march.

The social system! Citizenship! Boodle!

And it seemed to Sorrell as he sat there in the green corner of his own contriving that the intelligent rebel, the grim lone fighter, was the man to be envied. Not all men could be rebels, ploughers of lonely furrows. Nor had he any quarrel with the inevitableness of the crowd; it was just frog's spawn glued together. And becoming more and more so.

Poor people! Townsmen.

Bending to touch a flower he thought of death. He thought of death quite often now, much as he might think of the fall of the leaf, and with surprising serenity. He could remember the days when he had known blind fear. He had feared his son's death with the same terror, but that was because he had felt the urgent and vital youth in

Kit. Christopher's death would have been a tragedy. But
dying was not tragic, when one had obtained one's results.
Just sleep, the rounding off of the life's effort.

He relit his pipe and thought of Kit's coming marriage
early in June. He was glad of it. Five years ago he might
have grudged him to Molly, but now he had come to look
on life as a flowering and a setting of the fruit, a beautiful
mystery to be shared in and not hindered. Let them be
happy. Let Kit cleave to his wife. Some things are un-
forgettable and perhaps Sorrell understood almost without
realizing it, that as his son came nearer to the final maturity,
the memory of his father would grow more vivid and more
significant, an ever present nearness. To be felt and remembered—in that way—years hence—would matter. It
would be shining out of a life's afterglow.

The happiest hour of Sorrell's day was before him. He
left the seat under the tree, and going to the red brick
out-house where he kept his tools, he took a Dutch hoe
from the wall, and a trug and a weeding fork from the
potting table. The soil in the rose beds needed stirring,—
and there were young weeds among the violas. The hoeing
he did first, taking his coat off and hanging it over the bough
of a fruit tree. With the soil of the rose beds broken up
into a brown and powdery mulch, he set to work among
the violas. The viola beds had been dressed the previous
autumn with heavy loam, and the weeds of the old turf that
had not rotted were thrusting up, docks, bulbous rooted
buttercups, and here and there a blade of couch. It was a
job that needed thoroughness and patience, and Sorrell
crouching and working away with the weeding fork, forgot
everything but the intruding weeds and the blue and yellow
and purple faces of the flowers.

Suddenly, he sat back upon his heels and remained quite
still for some seconds with a look of attention that also
expressed anxiety. Not fear, but disquietude. It was not
the first time that this twinge of pain had gripped him, like
a hand twisting something at the pit of his stomach. Queer,
disturbing, a nuisance. He had noticed that stooping seemed
to bring it on. But hang it all, half gardening is stooping!

In a minute or so the pain had passed, and Sorrell resumed
his weeding. He had cleared half the bed, and he was in
the act of changing his position when the pain caught him

with an abruptness that made him hold his breath. He dropped the trug, and stood up, pressing his hand to his body, conscious of this pain as of something menacing and strange. It brought on a feeling of faintness and of slight nausea.

He went to the seat and sat down. He was conscious of a sense of stillness, not of fear, but of disturbing curiosity. Instinctively his hand explored that part of his abdominal wall under which the pain knotted itself. It was rather high up, in the V-shaped space between the ribs. He could feel nothing but a tenseness of the muscles.

"Indigestion," he thought; "stooping after a meal,"—but at the back of his mind more than a suspicion had crystallised itself that this pain betokened something very different. He had suffered from indigestion in the old days, but this thing was not the same. It stabbed you suddenly, and remained as a knot of gnawing anguish, just as though a claw were digging into your vitals.

He sat attentive and wondering, drawing his breath very lightly. The pain was passing, leaving him conscious of physical relief, but the sense of mental tension remained. He was aware of a vague menace.

A voice came from close beside him.

"What's the matter, Stephen?"

He found himself looking up into Fanny Garland's clear but anxious face. Maturity had come upon her with kindness; a pleasant and mellow shrewdness lived in the blue eyes.

"O, nothing,—indigestion. Stooping about too soon after a meal. Getting old."

He gave her a whimsical little smile.

"I had better try China tea."

She looked at him gravely.

"You had better see someone,—Kit——"

"O, it's nothing. If I get much more of it,—perhaps. I have some weeding to finish."

3

Two weeks before Christopher's wedding the pain under Sorrell's ribs grew more persistent. It had been intermittent

and elusive; there had been one whole week when it seemed
to have disappeared. He had called in one of the Winstonbury men who had happened to be attending a visitor at the
Pelican.

"I am getting some indigestion. I dare say you will be
able to give me something to stop it."

The doctor had looked at Sorrell's tongue, asked him a
few questions, advised him what not to eat, and had pre-
scribed a simple mixture.

"If that does not put you right—let me know."

A week or two of amelioration had been followed by a
disturbing recrudescence. Not only was the pain more persistent and more frequent, but Sorrell had a queer feeling
that something had arrived there under his ribs, an alien
thing, obscure yet growing more definite. Lying in bed at
night, and pressing his hand gently against his body he
fancied that he could feel a resistance that was almost but
not quite a new substance. He was not afraid, but he would
lie awake feeling chilled and troubled, conscious of a sudden
sense of insecurity, and the nearness of the unknown.

Well,—what of it? His mind was full of Christopher's
wedding, that new and adventurous phase. He was going
up to Welbeck Street a few days before the affair, and it
was no wish of his to carry a sick face to his son's wedding.
The future was full of their mutual plans. They were
keeping on the bungalow at Marley, and the top floor at
No. 107 was to be Molly's. They had faced the problem of
two workers in one house. At Marley Kit's wife could
take her temperament into retreat. Kit would go down for
week-ends, and bathe, and sun himself on a punt, while
she—full of her creating—would draw the curtain aside and
come to him out of the midst of it. "Let's play—now. It's
down on paper, and I'm happy."

Sorrell lay awake with a tense forehead, and that alien
thing gnawing its greedy way under his ribs. He faced the
potential reality. Two or three weeks of stoicism, and a
mood of soldierly resignation! He was not going to whimper, and if the thing was what he thought it was, well—he
would have to face the finality of it. He did not want to be
fussed or messed about. As for the Winstonbury doctor-
man Sorrell decided to leave him to think that that bottle
of physic had done the trick.

He knitted himself together, and put a clear face upon it. He would carry on through that last tour of duty in the trenches, and come out to billets with a stiff smile. After all, there was nothing like sticking it.

He was growing thinner; he observed this,—though his appetite remained fairly good.

On the morning before going up to town, he noticed, while he was shaving himself, that his skin had a faint yellowish tinge.

4

On the night before the wedding Kit looked suddenly and attentively at his father. He had been absorbed—yes —happily absorbed in that mysterious new future, and now that it was so near he seemed to come back to his normal self for a moment, much like a man who has been packing before a journey and who realizes when he has finished it that a whole night lies between him and the morrow.

They were standing at a window—talking.

"You don't look very fit, pater."

Sorrell smiled a queer, elusive little smile.

"I have been a bit liverish. Smoking too much—perhaps I am cutting off some of it."

"No pain?"

"O,—nothing."

"Quite sure?"

"Quite."

"No secrets, you know."

"Yes, no secrets, old chap," said Sorrell, somehow feeling that doomed lie sweet under his tongue.

5

At the reception after the wedding a few of those who best knew Stephen Sorrell noticed a peculiar change in him after the first flush of the crowd's congratulations. He drew a little apart beside an unoccupied sofa, and stood there behind it with an indescribable and vacant look in his eyes. He was very pale. And some of those who loved him well thought that he had drawn apart to bear within himself the stress of some lonely emotion. They left him there, to come

back to the smiling occasion when he could bear to smile
with the crowd.

It was Tom Roland who saw Sorrell make that surreptitious yet hurried move towards a table where a waiter was
filling champagne glasses. Sorrell almost snatched at a glass
and drank it, one hand bearing heavily upon the table. He
reached for a second glass and drank that also with little
painful gulps.

Roland went quietly up to him.

"Feeling a bit—faint, old man?"

Sorrell's jaw was set hard. His hand reached for Roland's
shoulder.

"Let me hold on a moment. Shall be all right in a moment. Don't want to be a ghost at the feast."

"What's wrong?"

"Nothing. A bit faint. Regular old woman, Tom. I'm
all right now."

The wine had worked, and the spasm of unbearable pain
was dwindling; some of the colour came back to his face.
He looked flushed and smiling when Kit's voice was heard
in the crowd.

"I'm looking for my father. He seems to have got
lost——"

Roland put up a hand.

"Here, drinking healths——"

Kit came pushing through. He looked happy, so very
happy, and Sorrell's heart yearned fatally towards him.

"Pater,—I have been looking for you everywhere."

Smiling, Sorrell led his forlorn hope forward.

"Tom and I, a couple of bibulous old fogies——"

"Molly is going to cut the cake,—and she wants you——"

"Right, old chap," and Sorrell took his son's arm.

Half an hour later he saw them make their escape through
a crowd of excited women and showers of rose petals. He
stood on the lowest step under the red and white awning.
Rose petals showered on him. Kit paused with a very
flushed face, and eyes that had a slight dimness.

"Good-bye, dear old pater——"

"Good-bye, old chap, good luck and God bless you."

He gripped Kit's hand. He felt the soft warmth of his
son's wife's lips as she kissed him. Then, they were gone.

XXXVIII

I

SORRELL wrote two or three very cheerful letters to the two in Switzerland, and since the increasing pain had begun to sap the strength of his charmed silence, he called in the man from Winstonbury. On this occasion there was no reticence and no reference to the bottle of physic. Sorrell, with that deepening tinge of yellow in his skin, advanced a frank fatalism.

"You might examine me. I think I have a lump here."

He became aware of the little doctor looking very grave and rather grieved. He had been observing, palpating and percussing, and asking pertinent questions.

"How long is it since I last saw you?"

"Five or six weeks."

"But—why—on—earth——?"

Sorrell was lying on his bed; he raised his head from the pillow and smiled.

"I had reasons. I have a pretty shrewd notion that my number is up. If you can help me with the pain."

"My dear sir, it is not a certainty. I should like you to see someone in town. Meanwhile, I'll have you X-rayed. I am inclined to think that the mischief lies round your gall-bladder."

Sorrell was X-rayed, and the photo proved inexorably cheerless, for it did not contain the details that the little doctor had hoped to find. He closed a prim and grave mouth over the inevitable conclusion.

"I should like you to see somebody——"

Sorrell had not expected to escape his doom.

"I am waiting till my son returns. He is away in Switzerland——"

"But, my dear sir, if the thing is operable——"

"No, thank you. Besides, it is only a question of a few days. If you can help me to fight the pain."

On that day Sorrell began to take morphia.

He had received two letters from Thomas Roland and had evaded the direct answer to his old friend's question, and a week before the homecoming of Kit and Molly, Roland and Cherry came down by car. They arrived unheralded, and Roland saw Fanny Garland and Mrs. Marks before Sorrell knew of their arrival. The women had sad eyes.

Roland found Sorrell lying in a long cane chair in his garden, close to his roses. He had that peculiarly serene look of a man whose body is under the influence of morphia, and whose brain is calm and lucid. His eyes seemed to have grown bigger, perhaps because his face had begun to thin. They were extraordinarily intelligent eyes, keen, with a queer glassiness, eagerly interested, missing no detail.

Roland sat on the grass beside him, and looked at Sorrell's roses. He had been shocked by the change in Sorrell, by that sharpening profile and that yellowing skin. Even in the passing of two or three weeks those fatal signals had developed a striking emphasis.

"Heard from Kit—I suppose?"

"Yes, they will be back next week."

Roland seemed on the point of asking a question, and while he was .hesitating over the asking of it, Sorrell told him the truth.

"I've got cancer, old man."

His voice was quite unemotional, and Roland saw his eyes fixed upon the flowers with a soft and melancholy tenderness.

"Glad I saw the roses out. And Kit—married. I think it is going to be a happy marriage——"

But there was emotion in Roland's voice when he answered him.

"But—my dear old man—how long——?"

"Some months—now—I suppose. Suspected it quite a long while. My doctor man pretended to hope that it might be gallstones or something,—but I felt pretty sure."

"Does Kit know?"

"He doesn't. I thought it would be time enough when he came back to work."

"But—surely—something can be done? Why didn't you tell people, take some steps——?"

Those large and human eyes smiled at him.

"Oh,—I don't know. My job is done, old man. And somehow—I did not feel like being messed about. I have been very lucky. Life is a fairly rotten business for most people. A good thing they don't realize how rotten it is,— what flies we are—buzzing against a window pane."

Roland sat all hunched up, looking grim.

"If I believed——" he said.

Sorrell went on speaking, and in a way that left Roland imprisoned in silence.

"I don't believe in anything. I have just done a particular sort of job—and loved it. The whole business is beyond me. Sometimes I have felt that there is a plan, but then—there is so much against the idea of a plan. Just a warring of blind forces—pushing—like a lot of beasts. And yet—there is much that is wonderful, the struggle that plants—live things—have made against the devil of impersonal cussedness. Yes, and not even cussedness. That is the thing that has always got me, Roland, the fact that there is nothing that cares, the utter-impersonal callousness of the scheme, the soullessness of it. We don't matter. Man matters only to himself. He is fighting a lone fight against a vast indifference. A gardener learns that. His flowers are fighting the same sort of lone fight, and perhaps that is why he loves them and pities them. Man invents religion to hide the full horror of the universe's complete indifference, for it is horrible. He tries spiritism. Oh,—anything to escape, to colour the spectacles. I have always felt myself up against—not only the human scuffle—but against the crushing—impersonal foot of the heedless universal. It just treads on you, or it does not. They called Ajax mad for defying the lightning; he wasn't mad; there was something in Ajax that knew. So—I—have gone about with a savage grin on my face—— And now—I'm tired. I feel I have fooled the great indifference—just a little, got my job through in spite of it. I don't care much now that it has put its foot on me—at last. I have kept my pygmy back stiff; I have managed to buzz a bit before it pulped me on the window pane."

For a while Roland said nothing; he just stared. For the truthfulness of a doomed man can be rather terrible.

2

Mr. Christopher Sorrell was writing letters on the morning after the return to Welbeck Street when the door bell
rang, and the woman in black came to announce Mr. Thomas
Roland.

"O, show him in."

Kit swung round in his chair. He had had a busy two
hours picking up the threads of his work from Simon Orange
who had been carrying on for him during the holiday, and
to Tom Roland he showed a brown and happy face. Kit
was a more expressive and a more sociable soul than his
father; he met—even casual people—with a pleasant smile,
perhaps because he had not had to scuffle with them. But
Roland was not a casual person.

"Hallo, sir. How is everybody?"

Roland's smile puzzled Kit. It was affectionate yet
enigmatic, coming from behind a cloud.

"My family has started an orchestra in the nursery. In
self-defence I had to join it. Had a good time? I can see
you have."

"Splendid."

And Kit waited. He was asking himself why Roland
had come to see him at this hour, and with a smile that
was like a kind and warning touch of the hand. Not for
personal or professional reasons—surely? Roland had the
face of a brown, whole-meal loaf.

"Cherry and I have been down at Winstonbury."

The manner of his saying it was to Kit like the opening
words of a story. Once upon a time——

"How did you find things? I had two or three cheery
letters from the pater. We thought of going down next
Sunday."

Roland looked at the floor.

"Your father thinks that he has cancer."

Kit travelled to Winstonbury that afternoon, and his
wife went with him. They had a first-class compartment
to themselves, and Kit sat and stared out of the window.
Molly, who lived in two worlds, that of her creative spirit,
and that of her senses, found herself in an attitude of
speculation. Kit had come to her with a shocked face. He
had said very little. "I want you to come with me. Will

you?" There had been a hurried packing and a hurried
lunch, and in the taxi he had given her a few broken
glimpses of a part of himself that was suffering. Sorrell was
ill. And it seemed to Molly that her husband had some
quarrel with himself and that she was involved in it.
Curious how baffling a mood could be, and the disturbed vi-
brations of a loved comrade. She was made to reflect upon
life as she felt and saw it, and life as it welled up out of her
subconsciousness. It was easier to write than to read. She
knew all about the people in her books; in fact she felt that
they were more intimately hers than the man who sat in
the corner opposite her. She was aware of a passionate
urge towards him. He was one of her problems, perhaps
her most dear problem; she had to understand; this understanding was a precious and poignant compulsion laid upon
her; eluded, unsolved, it would spell failure, the worst sort
of failure.

She kept very still. There was a part of her that seemed
to be groping towards the hidden silences of her mate.
And suddenly she felt that she had got it, touched the knot
of soul pain in him, and that she could unravel it.

His eyes met hers with a sudden questioning uneasiness.
He was conscious of that other intelligence.

"Sorry to drag you off like this."

"Do you think I mind?—It was I who dragged you
away."

His eyes seemed to give a little start of surprise.

"What's that,—Molly? How——?"

"He has been hiding something from us both."

Kit got up and came and sat beside her.

"Roland says—that he has cancer."

Her right hand found one of his.

"O,—my dear!"

His face was all puckered.

"What a blind brute! I thought he looked rather seedy.
I asked him——. Of course—now—I see it all. He put
me off. But—I—I ought to have known. A man whose
whole business——! And I didn't see it in him—the one
man who has given me—everything. I was too darned
happy, too horribly happy——."

He felt the pressure of her fingers.

"My sin—too—dear heart."

"O, no."

"Yes."

"But think of it. Think of the sort of man he is—to hide that thing—and let us be married and go away. And I was fooled. What must he have thought?"

She drew him to her.

"It is what he wanted. O,—but how splendid! It is just the big thing in life, Kit, the only thing that matters. To him it mattered so much—that it made him happy——."

"Happy!"

"Yes. You'll understand that. You do understand it. What a memory to carry about—in the future——."

"What a wound!" he said.

She sighed.

"A memory may be a wound, but what is life without wounds? They are sacred."

3

Christopher found his father where Thomas Roland had found him a week or so ago, lying in a long chair in his garden, in the midst of his flowers. It was a serene and windless evening, and the face and the eyes of the doomed man shared in this serenity. He held out a thin hand to his son.

"Well, old chap——."

And then he saw that Kit knew, for his son's face was unsteady with distress.

"Father, why didn't you tell me?"

Sorrell smiled and was silent, but Kit turned aside, with a hand pressing against the trunk of one of the old fruit trees. He spoke with difficulty.

"I ought to have seen. You gave me everything to fit me for my job,—and yet—when—you wanted me—the very soul's craft of me——."

"But I told you a lie. I think it was one of the very few lies——."

"But I ought to have seen. You let it all happen and you let us go away—like a couple of blind and selfish fools."

"It was my pleasure, old chap," said his father.

Something happened to Kit, but he seemed to shake his shoulders and to put his head back. He came and stood by Sorrell's chair, and his eyes and his voice were gentle.

"I want to look at you."

"Need you?"

"Father,—I must."

Sorrell moved in his chair, and Kit bent down and helped him up. They entered the cottage together and passed into the sitting-room.

"Will the sofa do?"

"Yes. The light is pretty good. I want your things undone. Let me——."

Sorrell lay with closed eyes and a cushion under his head while his son's hands touched him. They were cool and deliberate, but back of them he seemed to feel a quivering of Kit's courage. So, it mattered to Kit. He thanked life for it, and for the infinite solace of his son's caring.

"Hurt at all?"

"Just a little."

"Let yourself go slack, pater, and breathe deeply."

Sorrell opened his eyes for a moment on his son's face, and in Kit's eyes he saw death realized. There was a silence. Kit pulled down his father's shirt as though he were drawing a curtain, turned aside, and stood looking out of the window.

"I should like Orange to see you."

"All right."

"I'll wire for him. One—one can't judge quite accurately, pater, when one's——."

Sorrell was fastening his braces, and with a little effort he sat up.

"I know. But I am afraid there is not much doubt about it, old chap. My *finis*. I'm not afraid."

Kit moistened his lips.

"It's damnable," he said, "utterly damnable. The thing might have left you——. You might have had years——"

Sorrell gave a little wincing smile.

"But it hasn't. Besides—my job is through. I'm a little proud of it, old chap."

His hands hooked themselves under the wooden frame of the sofa.

"Could you give me a hypodermic? I have to have it now. Pain;—coming on again."

"My God!" said Kit to his own silent soul.

4

Simon Orange and Christopher went out into the garden, and when Kit had glanced back at his father's window, he drew his friend through the gate in the hedge to one of the Pelican lawns.

"Well——?"

Orange's heavy head hung forward.

"Afraid so. Not much doubt. He must have had it for months."

He did not look at Kit.

"Can anything be done——?"

"Old man,—would you?"

"Oh,—I know. Hopeless,—even a palliatory operation. The liver is down to his umbilicus; a cancerous mass."

Orange nodded.

"Nothing but morphia. Will you tell him, or shall I?" Kit's eyes had a strange blueness.

"I will. I think he knows. He is an extraordinary chap, my father. Never anybody like him, never will be."

5

That night, for the first time in her life, Christopher Sorrell's wife saw a man's tears.

XXXIX

I

DURING the whole of that July and the first week of August Stephen Sorrell passed the greater part of the day in his garden. So long as his own legs would carry him into it he used them, and when his strength failed towards the end, big Hulks would carry him out in his arms and lay him on a long chair. Sorrell had refused a trained nurse, and as it happened a nurse would have been superfluous, for all those good friends with whom he had worked gathered round him with so practical a devotion that he lacked for nothing. Moreover, he had not to buy the softness and sympathy of ministering and tender hands.

Molly had taken her husband's sorrow as her own. She was living in the cottage, occupying Kit's old room, and it was she who realized—even more than Kit did—the extraordinary nature of this man's fortitude. He was never out of pain, for the morphia had ceased to quell completely the gnawings of that greedy and alien thing. The very business of living had become full of physical distresses, pathetic struggles, yet never did she hear Sorrell complain. She knew how he suffered; she heard it, felt it, yet when Kit appeared—he was travelling to and fro from town every other night,—Sorrell would greet him with a smile. "Oh, it is not so bad, old chap." But Molly knew how bad it was. That pinched, yellow, hawk-like profile endured against a background of pain, patiently and proudly. His poor neck was a starved yet magnificent stalk upon which his courage refused to wilt. His patience amazed her.

She called him "The Old Roman."

For the crumbling of a diseased body can be a sordid and repulsive process, yet Molly's fastidiousness was never shocked. Sorrell—somehow or other—refused to be overwhelmed by the squalor of his own poor body, illuminating

its starved yellowness with the glow of his unconquered self,
investing its grotesqueness with an uncomplaining dignity.
At night, sometimes, she would hear a little groaning, and
she would get up if Kit was away, slip on her dressing-
gown and go in to him.

"You want morphia."

With that emaciated head propped high, he would climb
to the height of a wry smile.

"No. I have managed it. Don't bother, dear. I rather
prefer to get my dog-fight through in my own corner."

It seemed so heartless to leave him alone, and yet she
felt that he preferred it. He hated fuss.

"I'm not lonely——. I can feel you all—near."

Other sides of life were revealed to Molly during those
weeks of Sorrell's passing. He wrung from her a compassion, a tenderness, and an admiration that taught her to
approach her own creative world with a new humility and
a more poignant understanding. The merely clever became contemptible under the eyes of this dying man. He
liked her to sit and talk to him. He grew reminiscent,
and his wanderings into the past had a peculiarly vital
interest, for these were not the meanderings of an old man,
but rather the pregnant sayings of a very live one, the sap
of a tree that was to fall in autumn and not in winter. He
talked a great deal about Kit. It was as if he were living
life over again, or re-reading a beloved book and making
little wise, tender comments upon it, and his acceptance
of her as part of the great plan touched her very deeply.
When he was dead she would carry on. Kit would need
her.

"And I," she said, "shall need him."

But she helped Sorrell to play his part, and to keep
that old Roman head of his erect. The compact was a silent
one, but realized by both of them. She worked; she had
never worked better or with a more human insight; she
shared with Fanny Garland the picking and arranging of
his flowers, for the room was kept full of them. Sometimes
she read some of her work to him,—and they discussed it.

"Yes,—you are much cleverer than Kit," he said to her
one afternoon; "but I don't think you will let him find that
out. It won't matter. I don't think he will bore you."

She asked him what he meant by cleverness, and he was unable to explain his meaning.

"I don't know. Just seeing an inch or two farther—and more quickly than the others. It is not the sort of cleverness that hurts people—provided that it does not want to show off."

She looked at his thin hands lying on the rug.

"You have got me——. I did want to show off. You have stopped that. It would have been bad for my work."

"And Kit."

"Who never shows off. Never seems to occur to him. He is right in and part of the heart of his work. I am learning."

He smiled that little wincing smile of his.

"You will do big things. Life should be a good business for both of you."

2

Days came when Stephen Sorrell went no longer into his garden, but looked at the trees and the sky from the little platform of his bed. He would never leave it again as a live man. He was an earthy coloured, emaciated creature whose very knees seemed to be thrusting through the bedclothes. He was dying of pain and of starvation and of sleeplessness, but on that poor stalk of a neck a head, that looked enlarged, continued to endure. Looking at him Molly would wonder how he kept his soul erect, for he had no definite faith in a life beyond. It was just the quiet, indomitable nature of the man refusing to complain, to appeal, or to cry out.

But, during that last week, it was she who realized how near Sorrell was to breaking-point. She understood it better than did his son, though Kit was with them now till the end should come. Sorrell's son looked tired, gently and desolately tired, a little dazed too and dumb, with helpless, waiting eyes. He would sit and look at his father as though it hurt him to look, and yet as though there was nothing else to do. He gave him morphia, but the pain had become a flame of anguish that would not be quenched.

Kit seemed benumbed. He suffered with his father, but more like a child than a man. He watched and waited with an inarticulate, dry helplessness. It was Molly who rebelled, understanding the dumb appeal of that other rebel, the old gladiator who asked of death nothing but that last and merciful stab of the sword.

They were lying awake, and she drew Kit's head to her shoulder.

"Oh, my dear, why don't you do it?"

"What?"

His voice expressed the anguish of a tragic weariness.

"Put an end to it. Or—if you wish it—I will."

He drew away from her and sat up in bed. A moon was shining upon the window.

"He is in torment," she said.

She felt Kit trembling. Then he slipped out of bed and she saw him dimly, putting on his clothes. His silence was almost furtive. He left her; she heard him go into his father's room.

Sorrell was awake, with the blind up, and the moonlight shining upon the bed. He was in great pain.

"That you—old chap?"

Kit's voice was half broken.

"Anything I can do?"

"I'm thirsty—I could eat—one of those peaches——"

"Yes, father."

Christopher switched on a shaded light. A dish of peaches lay on the table beside the bed, and the bloom of the fruit contrasted with his father's tortured and ruined face.

"I'll peel one for you."

A dessert knife and fork were there, and as Kit stripped the soft skin from the juicy pulp of the fruit he felt his throat full of a dry anguish.

"Thanks, old chap."

Sorrell ate eagerly, and with a pathetic and starved relish, his eyes large and glassy under his lined forehead.

"If you will give me a dose——"

"Yes, father——"

"A little sleep. O, my God; it's bad—you know, Kit——. I——"

Something broke in Kit. He felt that it was another man

and not himself who went to the table where the hypodermic
case lay on a clean towel. His fingers fumbled. He had
his back to his father, and his wet eyes could hardly see
the syringe.

"Make it a strong one, old chap," said the voice from
the bed.

"I will."

Kit was rather a long while filling the syringe, for he
was smothering tears. Yet, that last act was done quickly,
with an almost fierce and eager gladness. Kit rubbed
gently with a finger on the loose skin of his father's wasted
arm.

"That will put you to sleep, pater. I will come in again
soon."

"Thanks, old chap."

"Shall I turn out the light?"

"Please."

Kit bent down and kissed his father on the forehead,
turned out the light and went softly out of the room.

But in that other room he broke down.

"I—I've done it,—an overdose."

She took him into her arms, and he lay with his face on
her bosom, weeping.

3

Kit lay and listened, and his wife listened with him,
for from that other room came the sound of faint stertorous
breathing.

She had felt Kit trembling.

"I gave him a big one. He—he mustn't wake again.
He must not wake."

She knew what was passing in her husband's mind, for
she too was listening to that heavy breathing, praying for
it to cease, willing it to cease. Hours seemed to pass, with
the moonlight dwindling, and the room growing dark, and
still that rhythmic breathing continued.

She felt Kit stirring beside her.

"Not enough——"

He sat on the edge of the bed, holding her hand, and
she, feeling his anguish and his weariness, willed with all

her strength for that sound to cease. It made her think
of the playing of interminable and gentle waves upon a shore
where night lay dying. She felt that she must speak to
Kit.

"He had you to do it for him."

His hand pressed hers.

"What a last service! And yet—I'm glad."

Presently, she became aware of a changed tension in
his listening suspense. There was a pause, a break in the
rhythm of that heavy breathing, and when it recommenced
it had a fluttering and hesitant shallowness.

She felt the sudden grip of her husband's fingers. He
got up and left her with silent abruptness, and went into
the other room. The uncurtained window showed as a
square of greyness; the breathing figure in the bed was
dimly visible.

Kit went to the window, and while he was standing there
a long pause came in the flow of his father's breathing.
Kit's own breathing seemed to pause with it. Again, it was
resumed, but very gently, and with a rustling and pathetic
serenity. Life was passing, and all the pain and the stress
were passing with it.

The window grew more grey. Kit could distinguish the
branches and the foliage of the old pear tree black against
the gradual dawn. And suddenly, he turned quickly and
looked towards the bed. His father's breathing had ceased;
he saw the dim face on the pillow. The stillness held.

Kit turned again to the window where the grey world
was coming to life before eyes that were wet and blurred.